Peng Shepherd

THE
BOOK
OF

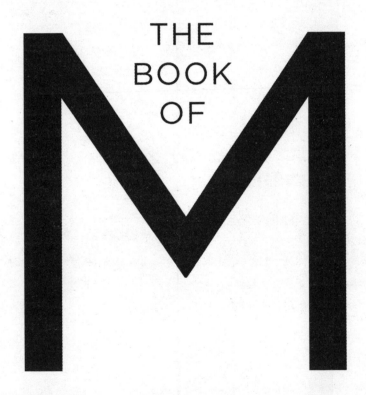

Peng Shepherd

# THE
# BOOK
# OF

HARPER
Voyager

Harper*Voyager*
An imprint of HarperCollins*Publishers* Ltd
1 London Bridge Street
London SE1 9GF

www.harpercollins.co.uk

First published by HarperCollins*Publishers* 2018
1

A catalogue record for this book is available from the British Library

ISBN: 978-0-00-822560-5 (HB)
ISBN: 978-0-00-822561-2 (TPB)

Printed and bound in the UK by CPI Group (UK) Ltd, Croydon CR0 4YY

MIX
Paper from
responsible sources
FSC™ C007454

FSC
www.fsc.org

# PART I

# ORLANDO ZHANG

THE END OF ORY'S WORLD BEGAN WITH A DEER.

He went outside at dawn to where the trees began, to check the game trap. Followed the trip wire, pushed away the leaves, uncovered the hidden metal cage. Empty.

The air had already turned his hands red with cold before he'd scattered the dried twigs back into place with the nose of his shotgun. The last time there had been anything snared inside had been two weeks ago, at least. Pale orange bruised into gray around the edges of the horizon, a gangrenous dawn. He and his wife, Max, were down to just one meal now that it was too cold to catch anything—a jar of spaghetti sauce he'd found the last time he broke into an abandoned house in western Arlington. There was no delaying it any longer. Ory would have to go into the city again to scavenge for food. Go or starve.

On the way back in, he saw it, frozen midstep in the weeds a few feet from the tree line. A deer. Its huge, dark pupils gleamed as they stared warily back, calculating. It should have dropped its antlers for the coming winter already, but they were still there, perched between its pricked ears. *We're saved,* Ory thought. He raised the double-barrel Remington in silence and aimed. Then he saw.

White steam billowed around its muzzle. The obsidian eyes blinked. It had seemed like a deer, but now he could see that it was not. Almost, but not quite. Where its bony, branchlike antlers should have been, instead a pair of small brown wings sprouted from its forehead, mottled feathers spread in the same way horns might curve.

*Max.*

Ory made for the shelter at a sprint. Inside, he scrambled to lock all the locks and re-prop the wood plank at an angle under the doorknob as fast as he could. Max was still asleep when he had left her, snoring lightly on her stomach, hair in her face. Ory went straight to the bedroom, straight to her.

"Blue," he said as soon as her drowsy, dream-heavy eyes fluttered open and met his own. He waited, breathless, for her to speak. It was their test, their way of telling whether or not she still knew who he was.

"Fifty-two," she whispered back.

They met at a football game.

# ORLANDO ZHANG

LATER, HE STOOD IN THE BATHROOM, SHARPENING HIS KNIFE. It made more sense not to shave—cover against the cold, camouflage for how thin he'd become, thus how little of a threat his starved body might be—but the act was hard to give up. There were so few things left he could still do that reminded him of the rest. Electricity. Cell phones. A desk job. Ory watched his arm glide past his face in the mirror. At how it blocked the light and cast the dark shape of itself back against his cheekbones, his chest. "Still there," he said to himself. He closed his eyes for a moment and waited for the hammering of his heart to slow. *Still there.*

Two years ago, when the Forgetting first reached the United States, he and Max saw its effects. They had watched a shadowless man speaking perfect English walk straight into a fire, not remembering what it was. Heard children with no silhouettes ask flowers where the nearest water flowed as if the flowers could understand, but then inexplicably were able to head directly to it. Once a woman missing her dark twin named all the coins of their currency, but when she opened her hands, the metal pieces were in shapes they had never seen, engraved with designs of no country.

Why had it turned out to be that shadows were the parts of bodies where memories were stored? Why did it happen to some and not others? Once it finally did happen, why did some people forget things after two weeks and some hang on much longer? And when they finally did forget, why did the earth itself seem to forget, too? The image of the strange creature in the woods outside came to him again. Why when a shadowless forgot that deer didn't have wings on their heads, did it become true?

Those kinds of thoughts he didn't talk about with Max. Not anymore. Not since she had lost her own shadow seven days ago.

"Mr. Clean-cut," Max said when she poked her head into the bathroom. Her loose bronze afro floated in the air above her head, living a life of its own. He loved that hair. It was as soft and untamable as she was. It was one of his favorite things about her.

"You mean Mr. Sexy," Ory replied. She winked. He watched her in the mirror as she leaned against the doorframe, warm brown skin bathed gray in the dim light. At the empty space on the floor beneath her feet. At how nothing skipped darkly across the ground after her when she moved.

The amnesia happened at a different speed for each person, but by any measure, Max was doing very well, even after a week. Addresses, phone numbers, how Ory had proposed to her, what they'd done for their last anniversary, she could still recite it all. *Blue, fifty-two.* In his most hopeful moments, he tried to convince himself that because she hadn't forgotten anything important yet, maybe, just maybe, she might not ever—even though he knew that was impossible. There had been small things. Tiny. So tiny, they had been easier to ignore than accept. Ory turned the blade over and inspected it when he finished shaving. The handle had been black when he'd found it obscured by a fallen cash register in a shuttered sporting goods shop. It was green now, he realized with a sinking dread. Max's favorite color.

And now the deer.

"I don't want to go," Ory said. It would be the first time he'd left her to scavenge Arlington for food since she lost her shadow. "Let's just starve instead."

"Okay," Max smiled. Her untethered feet moved away. "I'll get your canteen."

*One more day,* Ory wanted to beg. But she was right. What were the odds that while he wasn't home to protect her, she would forget something devastatingly huge? There was only one answer, each of the seven days he had delayed going out—worse tomorrow. According to the news, back when there had been electricity to watch it, today was the day that over 70 percent of victims forgot their first-degree relatives. Tomorrow would be the day that mothers did not remember their children. Yesterday would have been better than today, the day before that better than yesterday. But it was too late now. All he could do was go today instead of tomorrow, before she forgot something else. Before it was more than a knife handle that was changed, or a forest deer.

ORY COULD HEAR HER GOING THROUGH THINGS IN THE MAIN room as he checked his backpack. He'd changed to his heavier coat, both for warmth and for the small amount of protection its padded layer gave. He hoped she wouldn't notice.

In the beginning, after the stores closed, Ory and Max had turned to looting. Broke glass windows and climbed inside darkened shops, and took what they needed. So had everyone else left that still had a shadow. They all understood that it was their last chance. Shelves were picked clean within a matter of days, and people had 250 bottles of shampoo in their apartments, or 40 pounds of bagged beef jerky in their attics.

Then it spread further. The ones left all started forgetting too, and disappeared. Wandered right out of their houses and couldn't remember how to get back, or died of starvation in one room, unable to figure out how to unlock a door or that there was an upstairs, until the doors themselves vanished from the walls and the stairs flattened to hallways, trapping them forever. How to get back to a shelter, how to use a can opener, that rain existed. Who would have thought that you'd need a shadow to work a key or recall your mother's name? Ory once saw a place outside downtown where a collection of nearly identical houses all crowded desperately onto a small stretch of grass, metastasizing on one another. Some with no windows, some with a hundred doorbells, some with the roof on the floor and the floor on the roof. In the middle, an emaciated skeleton was curled. Two streets over, he found a house that looked like it might have been the original, the one the dead man had been desperate to return to, but couldn't remember where it was. Inside, there had been enough food for him and Max to survive a month.

Ory had combed Arlington that way as it was destroyed, looking for the houses where the last things had been hidden and not re-found. But by now, the world had long been picked clean. There was only one place left to go where there might be anything left.

"Your hands are shaky," Max said as he walked into the main room.

"They're not shaky."

"They are," she repeated, and continued searching for the canteen. Ory took a deep breath and balled his fists, then relaxed. It didn't help.

Everything would be fine. He'd done it a hundred times by now. Walk, look, take, walk home. It didn't matter that this time Max didn't have a shadow, or that he was going to Broad Street. He'd be back just before sunset, like always.

"I'm fine," he finally said.

"I know," Max said. She turned back to the table—she'd found the canteen. "I won't forget until you get home. Promise."

It meant nothing. It wasn't in her power to promise it anymore. They both smiled anyway. The old stainless steel container clinked as Max filled it up from the bucket of boiled water they kept for drinking. She screwed the lid on and handed it to Ory.

He took it slowly from her. "Okay, they're a little shaky," he confessed.

Max laughed as he stuffed it into his pack. Her head was tossed back, lips grinning. For an instant she was frozen in profile, as if painted into the moment. There, standing in front of the table—but nothing draped against the wall, nothing spread across the floor.

He wouldn't have thought it would make a difference, but to watch a person move around and cast no shadow anywhere became terrifying after a while. There was a strange weightlessness to it. As if they weren't actually there.

"Blue," Ory finally said.

"Fifty-two," Max replied.

He looked back down at his pack before she could see the relief on his face. Did it hurt or warm her that he checked so often? Did she think it was because he loved her or because he didn't trust her any longer? There was no way to believe either answer. Ory reached into his pack, fingers searching until he felt it. "There's something I want to talk about, before I go."

She turned to face him, eyes focusing on what rested in his grip. An old-school tape recorder.

"Ory," Max started tiredly. "Not again."

"Please, Max," he begged. He pushed the recorder into her hands. She held it stiffly in her long, dark fingers, as if it were a dead bird.

"We already talked about this," she replied at last. "I thought we'd agreed."

"Let's just try it. We have to *try*." They looked at each other. "The deer," Ory said. Meaning, *it was getting worse.* That now they knew she would start to forget bigger things.

The corner of the tape recorder glinted dully in her palm. Ory could just barely see the red REC button on the side. He had thought, before it finally drove them apart, that her forgetting might bring them closer together. But every day was more and more strange. Every argument had become a horrible calculation: Was it worth it? How many hours would they lose to awkward silence in the aftermath?

"Okay," Max finally said. "Yeah. Who knows. Maybe it'll work."

They both looked at the little machine in silence. At last, she awkwardly tried to jam it into the too-small pocket of her coat.

"Oh, one more thing," Ory added. He dug around in the front zipper of his bag until he found the long, thin coil. It was a loop of stainless steel cable, from god knows what dilapidated graveyard of a hardware store. There was a sturdy notch on one side of the recorder's plastic body to connect a safety loop—he threaded the cord through there and secured the clip. When he finished, the little machine hung like a necklace just below the swell of her chest, at a perfect length to lift up and record and to be tucked safely away underneath a shirt.

Max wrapped her arms around Ory and buried her forehead in his shoulder. They swayed.

"Wait, let me turn it on . . ." She was smiling. Her thumb pressed the stiff REC button, and she held the machine up to his mouth. "Okay, say it now," she whispered.

"Blue," Ory said awkwardly, shy at being recorded, but with feeling.

"Fifty-two," Max replied when she'd pulled it close to her lips. She clicked it off and let it drop back down on the cord, still holding him. Ory held her back.

He thought at first she was cold and was using his body heat to warm herself up like she always did in the mornings, but that wasn't what she wanted.

"I won't be able to explore very far if I don't—" he started.

"Who cares," she cut him off as she pried open his belt. There was a new desperation to her movements. Before she'd finished stripping it off him, Ory knew he didn't care anymore either.

*The deer.* Would the recorder actually make a difference? *The color of the knife handle.* Had he given it to Max because he still had hope, or because he had none?

He felt something rip as she pulled: a hem, a belt loop. The sound burned into his brain, and he played it again in his head, to remember the popping tear of the thread, what it sounded like when she knew it was him, and he was the one she wanted. "Blue," he whispered again.

"Fuck me already," Max hissed. She pulled the tape recorder over her head and tossed it onto the pile of discarded clothes.

It was all right. They could have secrets from each other, for the short time they had left to have secrets. She had agreed to try the tape recorder. Ory didn't have to admit to her that his determination to keep her whole was more for himself than for her, that he was afraid she would be no different from the rest of the shadowless—that she would also love the strange magic of her amnesia more than him, and stop fighting to remember. She didn't have to tell him if she believed it, too.

# ORLANDO ZHANG

THEIR HOTEL, WHICH THEY DIDN'T CALL A HOTEL ANYMORE, because it wasn't really so much a hotel as it was a "shelter," was built on a high peak in the center of Great Falls National Park, overlooking Arlington and the other suburbs of northern Virginia. It meant Ory had to hike down every time he went to the city. But it also meant anyone from the city would have to hike *up* to it. He passed the wooden post where he'd long ago removed the sign that used to point the way. ELK CLIFFS RESORT—300 M, it once had read.

When the last radio signals went quiet, Ory had made some renovations to the shelter, so it wasn't obvious from the outside that anyone lived there. He taped up all but one of the windows with cardboard to hide his and Max's movements, and then did the same to some of the other deserted guest rooms in the building, so their own would not stand out to anyone from the outside, if anyone ever came so close. He dragged broken furniture into the front yard, bent fence posts, burned fire marks into the exterior walls. Any food they did find, he kept on the ground floor, in the abandoned ballroom where they'd once watched the sparkling color and whirl of Paul and Imanuel's wedding, eternal years ago. They would lose it all if someone found them, but maybe that would be all they would lose, he reasoned. He killed a rat he caught in the basement, smeared its blood over the wood floor in the entryway, and let it stain—one word from the oldest language that was always understood.

It worked, for a time. For two years, they survived that way. Some days Ory even felt safe. But that all had ended last week, when Max lost her shadow.

When they'd finally stopped crying, they made one last change. They came up with a set of rules about things that could be dangerous for Max to do, once she forgot more. "*If,*" Ory had insisted, not *once,* but Max just shook her head. "*Once,*" she repeated. She'd gone to get the last of their scrap paper because Ory had refused to move.

Max didn't need them yet, but it was better to begin practicing earlier rather than later, she'd said. So they'd already know what to do once—*if*—the time came. After they'd finished writing, she carefully folded and tore the paper into strips and had Ory tape each rule near the place where she'd need it—the front door, the guest kitchenette, and so on. That way, in case she forgot that they had made rules in the first place, she'd still see them before doing something she didn't want to do.

They knew it wasn't perfect, but it was the best they could come up with. They didn't know what else to do.

### MAX AND ORY'S RULES
1—Max doesn't leave the shelter without Ory.
2—Max can use the small knives to prepare food unsupervised, but not the fire.
3—Max can never answer the door.

Max still knew him, knew his voice, but Ory always carried a key when he left, and had hidden another in the courtyard, inside a false rock he'd scavenged from a deserted housing goods store. He didn't want to ever get into the habit of knocking and asking her to let him in, no matter how tired or injured he was or how much he was carrying. Because even though it was fine now, later it wouldn't be. Because later, she might remember that he lived with her, but not that no one else did. That everyone else had left the mountain and the hotel a long time ago. Later, if he was out looking for food and Max was alone, it would be too dangerous to ask her to remember that she let one person in every evening when he came home—Ory—but not another.

4—Max can't touch the gun.

Just in case.

That one made him sick to think about. He didn't want to write it down. It felt like betraying her somehow—as if his believing that she'd forget who he was would somehow cause it to happen.

Max made him write it anyway. Just in case.

ALL OF THAT MATTERED LESS NOW. THE WINDOWS, THE blood, Ory never asking her to let him inside instead of using a key. But in the early days, it might have saved their lives. The streets were in constant flux then, changed one way from a bad memory and then changed again from another. Ory'd had to check every direction through a pair of binoculars before he could move a step, for fear of being ambushed by shadowed men or mauled by terrified shadowless. But now there were no shadowed ones left, because they'd turned into shadowless, and almost no shadowless either, because they couldn't remember that they should stay. Now everything was always still. Nothing moved, nothing made noise, nothing changed. There was no one left to change it. Shops became lonely graveyards, houses became monuments.

There were very few places he was ever worried about running into another living soul anymore. But Broad Street, where he was heading, was one of them.

When Ory reached the Falls Church neighborhood, he began to jog. He did not follow the roads. Instead, he cut through abandoned backyards in a straight line between the shelter and Broad Street, to make up for the late start. Most of the houses had no fences, and when they did, the wood was long since rotted. Even though he'd stayed in bed with Max for another half hour after they'd finished making love, there would still be enough time to search, Ory reasoned. He pried apart a pair of sagging planks and slipped through into a ruin of tall grass. There was still plenty of time. And even if there wasn't, it had still been worth it. *I need to make Max more presents,* he thought. Or—maybe it was just that he was in such a good mood after the sex that the joke struck him as funny instead of horrible—he could just keep giving her the same present over and over, and she'd love it every time.

*Don't laugh at that,* Ory scolded himself. *That's terrible. You're a terrible person.* But he did anyway. Quietly.

Twenty minutes later, he was a cul-de-sac away from Broad Street.

MAX HAD BANNED EITHER OF THEM FROM GOING BACK TO Broad Street again after the last time they'd searched there, more than a year past. It also had been the last time they'd run into another person.

Ory stayed crouched in the undergrowth and watched the weathered row of apartments that lined the infamous road. Beyond the empty stretch of grass and across the asphalt, nothing gave itself away.

The person they'd met that day had been a shadowless, only a few weeks gone. The man had remembered just enough to know it was bad not to have a shadow, but didn't remember how it worked. He tried to take Ory's.

Ory shuddered at the sudden memory of sharp, dirty carbon steel against his skin. The shadowless had been a firefighter before the world ended, still in his giant flame-retardant coat when they had seen him wandering around. His coat, his helmet, his boots—and his metal fireman's axe, gripped tightly in his right hand.

Neither Ory nor Max were doctors, back when there were jobs. It was pure luck that he hadn't lost the arm or died.

They'd argued about it a few times before, but Max won after that.

Abundant as Broad Street was, Ory promised her that he wouldn't go again. No matter how desperate, how starving.

They'd said nothing about what would happen if she forgot the promise, though.

Ory put his hand on the butt of his knife in its holster, and crept across the street toward the entrance of the apartment complex. The wind picked up and a gust of dead leaves swept past, hissing. He cleared the communal front lawn as fast as he could, aiming straight for the first door. He didn't stop until he was crouched against the front wall, shoulder scraping the brick facade. He pressed his ear to the wood and listened: for footsteps on rotting floorboards, whispered instructions between family members or reluctant allies, the zip of a travel pack, light snoring. Nothing.

Ory took out the knife and tried to steady his grip. He hated this part the most.

"Do it, Ory," he murmured, for courage. He always tried to imagine Max's voice was saying those things. "There's no one in there. There hasn't been for a long time." He heaved himself against the door.

The rotted wood gave way, and he slipped into the lobby of the building, knife pointed.

The room was empty.

Ory closed what was left of the door behind himself so he couldn't be seen from the street. Waited for his eyes to adjust to the dim glow of weak sun on glittering dust, and for the pounding in his rib cage to ease. The knife slid slowly back into its leather sheath.

There were scuff marks on the wood floor. Deep grooves that had been there long enough to have healed over from the odd rain through the shattered windows. He cleared the lobby and leasing office and began his search, but all the units on the ground floor were bare. Someone had made good use of whatever furniture had been there. The kitchens were similarly picked over; the doors of the cupboards were gone, drawers missing. Ory stared at the empty open shelves in one apartment, trying to imagine what they used to look like full of boxed food. The silver faucet fixtures on the sink had vanished, too.

The next floor was just as empty, and the one after. On the fifth floor, he couldn't go past the doorway of most units, because the stench was too strong. The remains of whoever had lived in those were still inside. Ory cleared the first tower block and moved to the second. Fire, then flood damage. A gym where all the exercise machines resembled gleaming metal horses, posed mid-gallop. The vending machines played music, even though there had been no electricity for years. Elevator shafts gaped, doors jammed open.

The third block still had a front door. Ory went much more slowly, encouraged. All the furniture, but no food, no clothes. One of the units reminded him a little of their own apartment, back in D.C.—if it was even still there. It had the same sort of classic modern style of Max's that had impressed his parents when they'd come to visit. He checked the walls for hollow places, where something might have been hidden inside. In the bedrooms, he saw the names.

In the early days, when there were more wedding guests still hiding with Ory and Max at Elk Cliffs Resort and they took more group trips down the mountain to brave Arlington, seeking supplies or information, he had seen them. Written on shelves in stores where the aisles had been picked clean, spray-painted onto the backs of buildings. People who still trusted others enough to talk whispered from the narrow mouths of alleys. *Have you heard about the Stillmind? The One Who Gathers?* They traded food for information, rallied curious crowds to make mass pilgrimages into the strange lands to see if they could find out more. Someone in this apartment had scrawled *The One with a Middle but No Beginning* in charcoal over where the bed should have been. Ory touched the tail of one smudged letter softly, powdering his fingertip in dark gray. Those few left with shadows were just the opposite, he thought. All beginning, no middle. Middle had become an ever-shifting, never-ending apocalypse.

A soft crack broke the silent complex. Ory flinched, ducked instinctively to the floor before he'd breathed. His knife was out again.

He counted to five. The sound had been dull, as if it had come from outside, some ways off. He peeked over the edge of an overturned dresser, toward the open wall that should have been a glass sliding door to a small back deck. There was some struggling grass, and another looming dead apartment tower beyond the sagging wooden fence.

"Trees," he said to himself. "Just trees." The area was wildly overgrown. It reeked of rotting mulberries. When he looked closer at the ground, he could see the white ones that had dropped from overhead before they were ripe, like little pale maggots. "Keep going, Ory. Do the upstairs bedrooms," he ordered himself. He pried his hand away from the hunting knife and crept down the hall toward the steps.

He stayed away from the windows, half kneeling on the floor. His heart jumped as he peeled back the dirty carpet in the closet and found a section of wood floor had been cut into a tiny trapdoor—but someone else had already discovered it. Whatever had been in there, it was empty now. Ory left the carpet rolled and didn't bother putting the door to the little hiding spot back. Save someone else the same letdown. If there was anyone left in the city. It had been so long, Ory had started to think he and Max might be the only two left in Arlington, maybe farther.

He might be the only one, soon.

The soft crack sounded again, and he threw himself to the floor. The animal part of the brain that built blueprints was racing, searching for an escape: there was a bed frame, but no mattress to hide under. A closet with no door. Window too high. To be upstairs was bad. Too far from a way out.

Then a pealing scream, high-pitched, hysterical. Ory froze.

He knew that sound.

He was down the stairs, out the back door of the unit, into the grass, dashing toward the shriek in an instant.

It was a rabbit, and that was its unmistakable dying cry.

A fox or coyote would bolt, maybe drop its prey if he could get close enough. There had been no food in the apartments, but damn it if he was going to go home with nothing at all. He and Max would eat rabbit tonight, fresh, succulent meat that hadn't been dried and salted and sitting in their cupboard for three months. If he could give Max the memory of a delicious, freshly cooked meal for as long as she had left, maybe that was worth more than five cans of tasteless, cold non-perishables, now or ever.

Ory sprinted past the second row of apartment buildings to the back courtyard where the community pool was, hands already outstretched to spook an animal. But as soon as he rounded the corner, he stopped dead.

"Oh, shit," he finally managed. It came out like a squeak.

Thirty feet ahead of him, gathered in a casual circle on the empty pool's cool deck, was an entire crowd of people watching the one in the center take a rabbit out of a makeshift trap. They turned to him one by one, eyes calmly sliding from their prey to Ory cowering in the middle of the grass.

"Oh, shit," he repeated, dumbstruck.

There were so many of them. He hadn't seen so many people at once for so long. He hadn't even seen a single other person but Max for at least a year.

And they were all armed.

*Do something,* he thought wildly. Some looked surprised, others amused. They were all healthy, all clean. Their hair looked washed, their clothes mended. There were no hollow cheeks, no bones jutting out. The men's arms were nourished enough to have muscle. More muscle than his own. *Run, Ory. Fucking run.* But he couldn't move. He just stood there staring at them all.

The one in the center finally stood up. It was an older woman, with a worn face and graying hair shaved close to her skull. Ory watched, petrified, as she gently let go of the rabbit wriggling in her iron grip, as if it was nothing, as if there were still three grocery stores at every intersection, and didn't even cast a glance after it as the terrified creature shot off into the weeds to safety. Silently, she stepped through the group to the front. Her eyes were hard-lined, mouth frowning. And now in her hands was a bolt-action hunting rifle, already cocked. Slowly she lifted the long dark barrel and pointed it at him.

"You're too late," she said.

# ORLANDO ZHANG

ORY STARED AT THE WOMAN IN SHOCK. AT THE WEATHERED hunting rifle swaying gently in her easy, sure grip. The muzzle hovered just south of his sternum.

"You're too late," she repeated.

Too late? Too late for what?

"He's gone," another of them said, and spat.

"He's not gone, he's got a shadow. Look." The woman pointed at the ground behind Ory with the neck of her gun, like it had always been part of her arm. His shadow was huddled on the grass, a withered shape of terror.

"Too late for what?" Ory finally managed. It had been so long since he'd talked to another person besides Max that it felt strange to speak to them, as if he'd forgotten what language was and accidentally made sounds that weren't words. His hunting knife felt pitifully light on his belt now as he cowered.

They all looked at one another, as if trying to decide what he'd meant by that.

"To join us," the man next to the woman with the gun said. The smoke from his homemade cigarette was bitter. "No seats left. The group's already long been set."

"I—" Ory glanced nervously between them, trying to glean the man's meaning from their faces.

"Twelve is the most," he continued. "Only have room for twelve."

Ory didn't know what to do. He edged his hands up even higher over his head, trying to show he wasn't a threat.

The woman in front finally lowered the barrel of her rifle slightly. "You haven't been out much, have you?" she asked.

Ory shook his head.

They all looked from one to another silently again. Ory snuck a glance at the cracked, weathered cool deck where they were gathered. Twelve bodies, four shadows. *Four* shadows. He stared. *Four. Shadows.*

Finally they all looked back to the woman at the front, one by one, waiting for her verdict.

"You have anyone?" the woman asked. She was one of the four.

"Yes," Ory said. "She, uh . . ." He gestured lamely to his own silhouette.

That seemed to soften them. The wrinkles in the woman's face deepened, and she scratched the short velvet buzz on her head with the back of her hand. "How long?"

"Seven days." He tried not to think of how many were left. How many more days that she'd still talk in funny voices when he was upset until he laughed. How many more days that she'd bravely attempt to make meals out of their scant ingredients, even though she was the worst cook they'd both ever met. How many more days that she'd sit in silence with him in the mornings and watch the sun come up through their tiny kitchenette window. He loved those sunrises with her.

"I'm sorry."

Ory shook his head, refusing to accept the sympathy. Sympathy made things real. "She's very strong. She's only really just started forgetting," he said. He tried not to stare at the group of shadowless at their center. He wanted to ask them what to do. How far gone were they? Did they have rules? How were they making it work? Most of all, how were the ones with shadows not afraid of the ones without? At what they might do at any moment—like the deer, or maybe worse—if they forgot something?

"That's pretty impressive for seven days," one of the shadowless ones whistled. His blue eyes were unnaturally clear.

"He doesn't even remember which one of us he's related to," a woman next to him joked, and a couple of them laughed. The shadowless man grinned sheepishly. After they quieted, two women with jet-black skin muttered, "Tell him already," to the one with the gun.

"You ought to head south, to New Orleans," she said at last. "Something's happening there."

"What's happening?"

"We don't know," she confessed. "But something. Everyone's heading for it. Arlington's almost emptied out; we're the last group that we know of. We were waiting for—" She cut off abruptly, but Ory knew the tone. He'd heard it often in the beginning. It was the tone of someone who'd refused to give up a hope she shouldn't have anymore. "We've heard a lot of stories," she finally continued. "A lot of names."

Ory thought of the ones he knew. *The One with a Middle But No Beginning. The One with No Eyes. The Stillmind.* "They're rumors," he said. "Just a bunch of rumors."

"But they're all about the same *place*," the woman replied. "Whatever the names mean, they're all about someone or something in New Orleans. That can't mean nothing."

That much was true. Whenever one of the names came up, almost always so too did the city. But *what* it meant, if anything at all—that was the part that mattered to Ory.

The woman cleared her throat. "Besides, we've heard rumors about D.C., too. Bad things are happening there. And it's spreading. We waited as long as we could."

"Bad things?"

"I don't know what they are," she said. "But the few people that have come through here, before they stopped coming altogether, they said it's bad. And they were saying the same names, and all heading for New Orleans. So that's what we're doing, too."

Ory looked from person to person in the group. He was suddenly keenly aware of how many of them were studying him—his watch, his knife, his pack. Or perhaps they were just looking at his shadow. "You trust what they say?" He asked.

"I've been in this complex a long time," she said. "You learn to watch, not to listen. I've ignored what they said and watched what they did. And it's what I told you—people are leaving. They're coming from Arlington and they're coming from D.C., and they're all going south, to Louisiana. Something's happening out there."

"If the names are all real, I'm not sure I'd want to go."

The woman shrugged. "Then don't. But I'd rather be running toward than away from something." The others behind her nodded.

Ory tried to read her face for some kind of tell, but the woman looked earnest. She was tired, and too wise to hope for too much, but there was no lie there. Whatever the rumors were, that they existed and that people were heading for New Orleans, at least, was true.

"Then why are you still here?" he asked.

"We aren't," she said. She rested the butt of the rifle gently on the ground. "We leave today. As soon as this one finishes his goddamn cigarette."

The smoke trailed out between the tiny gaps in his teeth as the man beside her grinned. "Helps me remember," he said.

They all waited in the silence as the man exhaled and put the roll of embers to his lips again. Against the cool deck, its tiny shadow floated in midair, attached to nothing. After a last long drag, he pushed the remains into the ground and then placed his shoe slowly over it, snuffing the life out. It was time to go.

"How are you getting there?" Ory asked when they all looked at him again.

"We can't—" she started.

"No, I know. I didn't mean . . . I just meant, how are you getting there?"

The woman crossed her arms. "We've been saving. There are still cars that run if you look for them. Victor here was an engineer before everything went to shit. He calculated it for us. How much food, water, gas. We want to survive, but we want to travel light. We've been building our group for a year, and have just enough to get the twelve of us there, no more. That's why I said you were too late," she said, an explanation as an apology.

"There are only two of you," the shadowless man with the blue eyes said. The wind pushed his pale yellow hair in front of his cold stare for a moment. "You'll travel fast as such a small unit." His face was grimly determined. "Find a car. You'll make it."

"I just . . ." Ory shook his head. He looked at the ground-floor unit closest to the pool that had obviously been theirs. There were bicycles propped up against the railings in the back, a grill chained to the wall, clothes hanging to dry. Here they were, sitting around the empty pool in the last warmish sun of the season, smoking cigarettes they had made themselves. It was almost a normal life. "You're leaving all this—you're going to go *out there*—for a rumor?"

"We have to," the woman said. She looked at the shadowless man, and they watched each other for a long moment. "Or there won't be anything left anyway."

IT WAS A LONG WAY BACK, BUT AS SOON AS ORY GOT AWAY from Broad Street and was cutting through backyards again, it was quiet once more.

The older woman's name was Ursula, she'd said. Ursula. The first shadowed person Ory had met since the Forgetting took Arlington. And probably the last.

Ursula told him he was welcome to everything they'd left in their unit—which wasn't much, but it was still better than what he'd hoped to find at all. They had finished packing a few days ago, and were leaving what was there behind. "We'd rather you have it than anyone else, I guess," she'd said. Ory scrounged around every corner and crack. There was no food, but in the end, he was dragging back to their shelter two of the bikes, four small knives that were still fairly sharp, a bottle of vinegar, three glass jars, and the curtains from every window. He knew the bikes were too cumbersome, but he took them anyway—one looked just like Max's old roadster, and he wanted to see her face light up when she saw it. Maybe they could ride them around the grass outside the shelter once or twice, like the old days. By the time he finished packing and went back outside, the pool area was empty. They were already gone.

The return took longer, with such a heavy bag and guiding two bikes with a hand on each of their handlebars. It was later than usual—the sun had already almost disappeared beneath the horizon, and the last dying rays backlit everything into a dark shade of greenish-blue. Ory had to make good time to get home to Max by when he said he'd be there. He looked down between his boots as he stepped. His shadow lurched with him, slithering jaggedly over the overgrown lawns, fragmenting around tangled weeds. Still there.

*They were crazy to leave Arlington,* he thought. Just when things had finally started to get quiet. Just when it was finally starting to get safe enough that he could walk around to the back of their shelter to check the game trap without fear, no longer needing to jump at every single little snap of a twig or rustle of leaves in the overgrowth. They'd finally gotten to a place where they were almost safe.

And honestly, now that he knew almost everyone with or without a shadow had emptied out of Arlington, and the only things left he'd have to contend with were the last straggling shadowless and the odd wild animal that had moved in from the lurching woods, it made Ory want to hole up in their shelter and stay even more. Maybe society had been nice before, but he wasn't sure it would be great again. Maybe after everything was settled there in New Orleans, after they'd figured out some way to control the place. Maybe years from now, he'd consider it. But with what was coming for Max, they couldn't move now. They needed to stay, and be safe, when the time came. Max would agree with him.

Ory had just about convinced himself that the last thought was true when a strange ripple in his shadow caught his gaze. But it wasn't his shadow, he realized—just as something heavy and metallic smashed into the back of his head.

fell, everywhere, golden. Candles, sunset. Overhead, a wrought-iron elk, leaping over a wrought-iron cliff. The guests raised their party noisemakers to their lips again and blew.

"Champagne?" Max slipped her arm into Ory's. She shouted over the squealing chorus. The soft, brown coils of her hair spilled across the sleeve of his suit as she leaned to him. Lavender, warmed by the summer air. Bubbles popped against the crystal.

"Here they come!" someone cried. The band roared. Felix Mendelssohn's "Wedding March." Another hand clapped his shoulder. "Best man! You're up!" Streamers exploded above.

"Ory?" Max asked. He turned to look at her—and everything froze. Things suddenly moved as if underwater. The piano echoed, time-stretched. Twirling slivers of gold imprisoned, floating in midair. He loved her so much. "Ory?"

Ory's eyes opened. Everything was gone. The music, the sound. The world was black. He was blind.

He felt the cool, wet grass beneath him then. No. He wasn't blind. It was just night. Then he knew his pack was gone.

Of course. That and the supplies were what he'd been attacked for. He shivered at the absence of it against his back. Naked, as if the clothes were stripped off him. The blackness blurred, and he realized he was crying. All gone. His knife, his watch, the canteen, his first-aid kit, the flashlight. His pack. His *pack*. Every precious thing it had taken so long to collect. Everything that kept him alive when he scouted. All gone. Ory clutched at the shoulder straps for comfort as he hugged himself, realized they weren't there either anymore, and started to cry harder.

When the strangled sobs finally subsided, he sat up as cautiously as he could. His head was pounding. Everything else was numb. He couldn't tell if he was injured anywhere below his neck yet. His fingers dabbed at the back of his skull and came away warm and wet. He couldn't see it in the darkness, but it felt like blood. *That's not good,* he thought vaguely. Then he pitched over and vomited onto the grass.

MINUTES OR HOURS LATER, ORY WAS SHAKILY ON HIS FEET. There was no way to tell what time it was. It was just dark. So dark he could barely see his hand in front of his face, even with the moon out. Night now was not like night before, navigable in the vague, faint haze of streetlights. Night now was oblivion.

Was it a shadowless that had knocked him out, ripped his pack off his back, and sprinted away? he wondered. Or a shadowed survivor like himself, who had been stalking him since he entered Broad Street? A chill shuddered through his clammy body. Was it the group he'd just met? They were about to set off on a dangerous journey. They'd seen his hunting knife, his backpack. They had plenty of supplies, but why not have a few more? He tried to picture Ursula circling back, her buzzed hair, her solemn face, creeping calmly up behind him, the butt of her gun raised with grim determination. Would she have done it, knowing he had a shadowless of his own to take care of?

*Max,* Ory thought then. He took a few faltering steps. There was no point in wondering who'd gotten the drop on him. It didn't matter now. His pack was gone, and the bicycle he wanted to give her, but he was alive. And so was Max. And she'd be panicked out of her mind by now. Ory had never been this late before, ever. Not even the first time he went out and almost got killed, and then got lost trying to get home. He wanted to sit down and close his eyes again. Instead, he kept walking.

HOW HE MADE IT TO THE SHELTER WAS HAZY. HE MUST HAVE retraced his steps from memory, able to navigate the demolished neighborhoods even in darkness. Once or twice he thought he heard something rustling in the bushes nearby, but he was too dizzy to spot it, and in no shape to fight it anyway. It was almost as bad as death to lose that pack, everything he'd had in it, but he might not have made it back at all in his condition if he'd been carrying all that extra weight.

Suddenly he was on the ground floor of the shelter. He'd made it. He leaned over and vomited again, and then almost fell into it.

Just two floors to go, and he'd be home. *Please let her still remember how to clean a wound,* Ory thought. *Please let her still remember everything right now.* Tomorrow he could face it, but not now. If he opened the door and it was the moment that Max had forgotten who he was, in his current state Ory doubted he could string together a coherent sentence at all, much less convince her they'd been married for the past five years, and he went out and got himself almost killed like this every week. At least she wouldn't remember that he'd had a pack to lose.

Ory climbed the stairs slowly, leaning against the wall as he ascended to stop the world from spinning. The back of his head felt freshly wet. He'd need Max to check it to make sure it didn't need stitches. He grimaced as he imagined the possibility. Her having to shave a patch in the back with their last dull disposable razor, the piercing pop of one of her sewing needles through the skin, over and over, a sensation he knew far too well by now. The back of his scalp tingled in reluctant anticipation. *Just don't fall asleep,* Ory thought dimly when he reached their door. He'd read that somewhere once—if you had a concussion, you shouldn't go to sleep. Otherwise you might never wake up. That was all he wanted now, though. To curl up with Max and close his eyes until everything didn't blur and tilt.

But as soon as he put his key into the tumbler and started to turn it, everything snapped into humming, crystallized focus.

The door was unlocked.

*No.*

*No, no, no.*

Ory shoved the door open and ran inside before he could think about it for another second. Before the terror of all the horrible things that could have happened to her—bandits, robbers, wild animals, her memory—could overwhelm him. *Please don't let something have happened to her in the hours I was gone,* he prayed. Please don't let it be that if he hadn't gone to Broad Street, if he'd only been home on time, he could have caught her before she forgot. "Max!" he screamed, and tore across the living room to the kitchenette, then the bedroom, then the bathroom, and then farther out, down other halls, into other rooms, searching every inch of the shelter. "Max! *Max! MAX!*"

She was gone.

WAIT, LET ME TURN IT ON . . . OKAY, SAY IT NOW.

*"BLUE."*

FIFTY-TWO.

# PART II

# MAHNAZ AHMADI

NAZ DREAMED OFTEN ABOUT THE NIGHT IT ALL BEGAN. THERE was just so much joy, so much wonder. No one knew then what the shadowlessness would lead to. Even when she dreamed about it now, now that she'd seen what it all became, the dream still never turned into a nightmare. She didn't know what that meant. Maybe it didn't mean anything at all.

Naz, her coach, and her teammates were celebrating the approval of her green card that evening. They'd just found out the paperwork had gone through, and she was officially allowed to stay in the United States forever, to keep training. It sounded silly, because tryouts weren't even for another three years, but somehow the green card made it all real for her. She might someday become the first Iranian to medal in archery at the Olympics. She might even have a shot at *gold*.

They were all gathered around the couch in her apartment's living room in Boston, her coach leaning over the coffee table to uncork a bottle of wine. Two of her teammates had gotten a banner printed that read, *Congrats, Naz! Olympics, watch out!* and another that said, *Bull's-eye!* and hung them on the wall right above the case where she stored her competition bow.

She'd mostly tuned out the vague blinks of color coming from the TV as they laughed, drinking and snacking on a cheese plate and a cake she had baked, but something caught her eye. A red news ticker at the top of the screen flashed: BREAKING NEWS. That's when she first heard the name Hemu Joshi.

There was an annual festival that day in India, so the local news crews were already out in the bigger cities, including Pune; they'd been on Hemu for all of seven minutes before someone working for an international station caught sight of their live feeds. Everything exploded.

Within six hours, it was on every channel and website in the United States, and crews from every country were touching down in Mumbai and frantically renting cars by the dozen to drive three hours away to the outdoor spice market in Pune—Mandai, the locals called it—in a span of time that seemed impossibly short for a transatlantic flight. Naz, her coach, and her teammates all stared transfixed at the screen, unable to look away.

At the time, none of them knew that they actually should have been terrified. Instead, they were fascinated. Obsessed. And Hemu obliged them. He stood gamely in the street of Mandai's largest aisle for those first three days, giving demonstrations for curious passersby. No matter how many times he did it, it never got old. Naz could watch him for twelve hours straight, with breaks only to microwave food and bring it back to the couch or go to the bathroom.

First he would smile and say something, to prove he was real and that it was live, not a tape being looped. Then he'd hold out his hand, or stand on one foot and dangle the other one in the air. The street children who had been haunting Hemu like little ghosts since the first moment would giggle and run circles around him. Photojournalists had a heyday with those shots. News sites were filled with vibrant images of the kids playing with him, laughing, dust swirling around them, the oranges and purples of the open-air spice stalls throbbing with such rich color that it made Naz squint.

Fortune-tellers made their way in rickshaws and on bicycles from every corner of the city to look upon this new wonder. Cripples were carried to Hemu by their relatives as if he could somehow cure them. Fathers were in the street, shouting at him and waving pictures of their daughters. By the end of the first day, Hemu had sixty-two marriage proposals, all from extremely wealthy families. There was a picture of Hemu's mother, a sturdy old woman with hair still as ink black as his own, trying to hold all of the photos of prospective brides being pressed upon them. She'd pulled down the shoulder sash of her sari to use it like a makeshift basket, but there were so many pictures that they overflowed, the tiny faces of so many beautiful young women escaping her arms like dragonflies, flitting away down the crowded street.

The day before, Hemu had been a junior customer service representative at a call center for a U.S. cell phone company, and a second-string amateur cricket player for the Maharashtra team. A glorified benchwarmer. He'd batted once in the last fifty games, if that. Now he was almost godlike, something out of a fairy tale or a science fiction film. The world was captivated.

Hemu Joshi was the first person to lose his shadow.

WHEN NAZ AND HER LITTLE SISTER, ROJAN, WERE KIDS IN Tehran, the year before their father died, he bought them a little telescope for one of their birthdays, to take up to the roof of their apartment building to try to spot constellations. The girls both went every night, but for different reasons. In truth, Naz could have cared less about it. She was already old enough to be allowed into the specialized sports section of the gymnasium after school, where the bows were kept. She helped drag the heavy metal instrument up the stairs as soon as darkness fell because Rojan cared. Because she had never seen her little sister so spellbound. Astronomy had become Rojan's version of Naz's archery. So every night Naz grabbed one end of the telescope and helped Rojan edge up the dark stairwell.

The rest of the family used to joke that those two things never really seemed to go together, archery and astronomy. To Naz there seemed to be a connection, though. The dark sky, the stars. The white gold of the sun. Her arrow arcing through the air beneath them. She wanted to watch Rojan watch the stars forever. But when Naz won nationals at the age of twenty-one, and the man who would become her coach called from faraway Boston, his English fast and whining and almost impossible for them to understand,

and she heard his offer—athlete visa, sponsorship, the Olympics in a few years . . .

After Naz moved to Boston, she went back home only once. That was the last time she saw her sister. She hadn't meant to mention her first American boyfriend to her mother, or dating at all. It had just slipped out. But then in the heat of the ensuing argument, she spitefully told the old woman everything about him—and the ones after.

She wasn't welcome in the house anymore after that. Her mother swore she'd never speak to Naz again. Naz swore the same. She left that night and went to visit Rojan at her university, where she was studying—Naz's heart swelled for her—astronomy. She'd managed to win a full scholarship. The next evening, they sneaked into Rojan's lab to see her research. By then Rojan knew far more than Naz did about the sky, but Naz followed as best she could. She'd remember forever the stolen looks through the telescopes she shared with her— the glow of distant planets, the streaks as comets shot by.

Naz often wondered now what happened to all of them. The telescopes. It would be strange to find them again someday, if any of them were still standing in this new world changed. Survivors would come upon them in their silent domed houses and look through their tiny glass eyepieces and think they were magic. Sometimes science seemed like magic. To watch Hemu Joshi live and breathe without his shadow was like watching magic.

There were attempts to turn his mystery into science, of course. And actually, there *was* some science to it. It was an obscure astronomy fact, but Naz had learned it from her sister. It turned out that actually, in a few countries, shadows disappearing happened every single year on a specific date.

It sounded impossible, but it was just physics. It had to do with the angle of the sun and the seasons—the lands between the Tropics of Cancer and Capricorn, and sometime in late spring to early summer, to be exact. "No matter where you live, you always think of the sun as directly above you at noon each day, but that isn't actually true," Rojan had explained to her once, when she still lived in Tehran. Naz had tried to explain it to her coach and teammates as they watched Hemu on TV—the looks on their faces had made her laugh. But it was true. The earth was too big and too curved. Even though it looked like it, the sun was actually never *exactly* overhead. Except in India, on a certain day in mid-May.

Or as the locals called it, Zero Shadow Day.

The most insane, unbelievable thing, and it happened every year. Rojan had always wanted to visit. Zero Shadow Day had become a small festival there over the decades, celebrated on successive days as the earth tilted each dawn to position a different city directly under the sun—complete with basic astronomy lessons, parades, and kite flying. Every year just before noon, huge crowds would flock to open squares in the markets to wait for the moment that the sun was so exactly poised above them that their shadows would disappear for a few stunning seconds. Teachers encouraged kids to place various objects in the street—flashlights, basketballs, cricket bats—to see if they could outsmart the sun. They never could. Under the rolling hum of hand drums and sitars, as the earth and sun became perfectly aligned, all the shadows in the city and beneath the people slowly would shrink to tiny little dark specks on the ground, vanish, and then come back as the earth rotated on and away. Always.

A perfectly scientific explanation.

There just wasn't any scientific explanation as to why after that brief window, everyone else who was outdoors on that day watched the dark shape of themselves flicker back into form from the tips of their heels, while Hemu Joshi stayed shadowless and free. No explanation but magic.

So for three magical days, the entire world watched Hemu Joshi dance around untethered to the earth, captivated by the un-understandable beauty of it. Magic. Flights and hotels were monstrously overbooked, people were sleeping in restaurants and on the streets, television channels played his clips endlessly, poetry was written about him. He even appeared to Naz in her dreams. Scientists went wild, but not a single one could prove exactly what was going on. And the day after Hemu's shadow disappeared, news broke that it had also happened to a group of eightysomething people in Mumbai during the celebration of their own successive Zero Shadow Day festival. The news started calling them the Angels of Mumbai. It didn't sound silly at all. And then a day after that, the third day, it happened to a group of fifteen in Ahmednagar, and a group of twelve in Nashik . . .

The reports kept coming in late into that third evening, as more and more scattered cases across the state of Maharashtra were reported, family after family, village after village. It was like watching a miracle. When she heard about the Angels of Mumbai, Naz actually thought that they were all about to transcend into some kind of higher existence. And as ridiculous as that kind of statement sounded when uttered out loud, the world was so in awe that she didn't feel self-conscious. Not even a little. She was standing wrapped in a towel in her bathroom, dripping everywhere, waving her arms around and declaring it to one of her teammates and the toilet while she brushed her teeth, and she didn't feel silly or dramatic in the slightest. That's how taken the world was with it.

Then on the fourth day, it all started to go horribly wrong.

HEMU JOSHI HAD PROBABLY BEEN FORGETTING THINGS SINCE the first moment of Zero Shadow Day, but it wasn't apparent until the morning of that fourth day.

The morning that the bad news broke, Naz got up early and turned on the TV so she could watch Hemu while she fried some eggs for breakfast. The sizzle from the skillet garbled the reporter's voice-over, but the view was familiar. Since Zero Shadow Day, Hemu had been living exactly where he was first spotted—outdoors in the center of the Mandai market—disappearing only to quickly change clothes or go to the bathroom. There had been such a desperate outcry on that first night when he tried to go home to sleep that his two brothers had given in and dragged some bedding out and down the crowded, winding streets to him. Now the three of them camped in the center of the breezy, fluttering textiles aisle. By the middle of that first night, so many people had brought them blankets and other offerings of fruit and silk that their little patch of dusty concrete looked like some kind of ridiculous sultan's love chamber.

Something was strange, though. Since Naz had turned on the TV, only Hemu's brothers had been on the screen, instead of Hemu. She glanced away to give the eggs a good push with her spatula, and when she turned back, she realized they looked concerned this time, not friendly. One of them was shouting, "No cameras!" The other brother reached toward the cameraman, and the screen went dark as his hand grabbed the lens and yanked it down toward the ground.

"What you just saw was our most recent footage of Vinay and Rahul Joshi, Hemu Joshi's brothers, taken just minutes ago." The screen abruptly cut back to a sharp-shouldered, severe news anchor. "Since five this morning India Standard Time, Joshi's family has refused the media access to Joshi after he was found wandering through the business district of Pune, apparently disoriented and—"

Naz turned off the burner, leaving the eggs half-done and still translucent in the pan, and went to get her laptop. By the time the yolks had hardened into a yellowy mess, she had pieced together what happened. When the news crews woke up and turned the cameras back on at dawn, they realized Hemu wasn't sleeping beside Vinay and Rahul anymore. They woke the brothers, and the two of them went home to see if Hemu was there, but he wasn't. A search was mounted, and that's when they found Hemu stumbling around the opposite end of the market, confused and agitated. He was shouting at the crowd that he didn't want to be followed and he was sick of the news crews, which was understandable. But then his brothers pushed to the front of the mass, and that's when the strangest thing happened: Hemu didn't recognize them at all.

Most of the news crews were still obsessed with getting a shot of Hemu, the man who had captured the attention of billions. But there was a second-rate team from some American gossip channel in Nashik—attempting to drum up interest in a group of twelve children they were trying and failing to dub the Nashik Cherubs, a terrible rip-off of the Angels of Mumbai—who turned this from a curiosity to a tragedy.

Their cameraman and reporter started sending video back to their little news studio in Los Angeles, but within minutes it was all over the international networks: the Nashik Cherubs were also starting to forget things.

# ORLANDO ZHANG

ORY TOOK THE NOTE OFF THE REMINGTON. 4—Max can't touch the gun.

The shells were in a box on the floor of their closet, like a pile of discarded body parts. He loaded the gun, then in pairs he fed the rest into the pockets of his pants until the box was empty. Then he grabbed all three of his moth-eaten sweaters and put them on one over the other, and covered them with the red *Elk Cliffs Resort—STAFF* windbreaker he'd found in the housekeeping office. Max's clothes were still there in neat piles, but it looked as though some were missing. A shirt or two. Maybe she had seen the stack on her way out of the shelter and still been clearheaded enough to take some. Ory hoped that's what had happened. There was no blood anywhere, nor signs of struggle, so he had to believe that she had left by herself and not as someone's hostage. All he had to do then was find her. Find her fast.

Next was supplies. Matches, first-aid kit, flashlight. Again, some of it seemed like it was missing. He was sure they'd collected more boxes of matches than what was in the drawer. Maybe they hadn't. Or maybe Max had forgotten the exact number they owned and thus changed it, the way she had with the color of the knife handle. Ory stood there at the useless sink, cabinet drawer open, staring at a pair of scissors and the blank space beside it where he could have sworn they kept a spare. It was hard to tell.

Last, a photograph of Max.

In the floorboards by his side of the bed, he'd carved a simple trapdoor. He pulled his old wallet out and gently wiped the dust off. One debit card, one credit card, four dollar bills, a gym membership card, and his driver's license.

Ory eased the license out of the plastic window. If the Forgetting ever happened to him, this would be his tape recorder, he thought. Name, date of birth, height, weight, a tiny photograph of his face. It wouldn't tell him anything he really needed to know, like that Max was his wife and he would step in front of a bus for her, that they had no children, that they met at a football game he almost didn't go to and then almost left early from, that he was absurdly good at skiing, or that he was secretly terrified of bees. But it would at least tell him his name. And it also was a shield for the thing that really mattered. A wallet-size photograph of Max.

It was from the night before Paul and Imanuel's wedding—after the shadows had disappeared in India, Brazil, and Panama, but before it had gone much further than that. That evening the guests all had been in the hotel ballroom just downstairs from where he was standing now, eating chocolates and drinking champagne. Paul and Imanuel had opened some of the gifts early, and one of them had been a Polaroid instant camera that produced tiny, refrigerator-magnet-sized instant photos.

The camera was passed around as the party got later, and when Ory got ahold of it, he took a picture of Max. She had been standing right at the open French doors that led out into the courtyard, but the light from inside was bright enough that when she turned to look at him as he said, "Excuse me, ma'am," her face was bathed in a yellow glow that made her eyes shimmer. "Blue," he said. He snapped it just as the smile had started to spread across her lips.

One of the other women pulled her away to gossip about something before it was done developing, so Ory stood there in the night air just outside the doors, shaking the film lightly, peeking every few seconds to see if it had finished. By the time he found her again and she pressed another flute of Dom Pérignon into his hands and whispered in his ear, breath hot, her voice light with a hint of buzz, "You are not going to *believe* what Imanuel just told me about the second groomsman," she'd forgotten he'd taken a picture of her at all.

Ory slid the photo back in and put his driver's license securely on top of it. Even though she was all done up, hair pulled into a messy bun and makeup on, Max still looked almost the same, and it would do for showing people he passed, if he ever passed anyone, to ask if they'd seen a woman who looked like this. Assuming they could remember how to speak, or anything they'd seen at all.

Back in the main room, the paper that had been taped to the inside of their door since the beginning caught his eye again. There was one rule he and Max had made, long before she'd lost her shadow and they had made the rest of them. Rule Zero, they had started calling it after they'd written the list. He pulled it down and crumpled it into a withered ball. There was no way Max could not have seen it when she left. What did that mean? How much had she forgotten?

They'd made Rule Zero when they became the only ones left at the hotel. For months there had been no electricity, no running water, then no radio. Then finally there were no other guests. They couldn't avoid the conversation about it any longer.

"It's not fair," Max had said. "If it was me that went missing, you'd come after me."

"No, I wouldn't," Ory replied. It didn't even sound believable to him.

"Yes, you would," Max argued. "Besides, it's different. You go out all day, and I stay here most of the time. If I disappeared, it would be because I lost my shadow and forgot to stay, so of course you shouldn't follow then!"

"Don't—" He grimaced. It felt like tempting fate to ever mention the possibility it could happen to either of them.

"I only meant, if you were the one who didn't come home, it would probably be because you were injured somewhere and needed my help."

"I'll make sure to get killed, then, so there's nothing to come help."

"Ory," Max said, her voice horribly small.

The silence settled between them, heavy. "Sorry," he finally murmured.

They looked down at dinner—one plastic bag of potato chips. What he'd found the last time he'd gone out.

"I just can't," Max said. "It would be one thing if one of us forgot. But if you go missing while you're out looking for food, I'm going to go to where you said you went and try to find you."

"That's not the deal," Ory said.

"That's as good as you're going to get," she shot back. "I'll give you that if one of us forgets, the other doesn't go after. I can't do any more than that. Okay?"

"Okay," Ory finally said. He used paper from the abandoned guest book—wrote the rule in silence and hung it up. *You never go after the other person if they forget.* They didn't speak for the rest of the evening.

It was the best they could do, but it wasn't enough. Over the next few weeks, Ory stopped telling Max where he went to scavenge for scraps each day, or if she refused to let him out the door without an answer, lied so blatantly she knew it was so. Eventually she stopped asking, because she knew what he was doing.

Later that night, after they'd made Rule Zero, Ory used a tiny bit of the precious soap they had left. The shelter had contained boxes and boxes of surplus inventory, back when it was Elk Cliffs Resort, and in the early days they'd squandered it. Bathing whenever they liked, washing their hair at least once a day. It made things still feel normal. They realized too late that what had looked like an endless supply in the housekeeping closets actually wasn't. They now had two hundred toothbrushes left, but no more toothpaste. Nine hundred towels, but barely any body wash. Now they were trying to stretch what was left, bathing only every few days, and only washing the essential areas. He dipped his finger into the plastic container and tried to scrape every millimeter of excess back in. Only what was needed. He reached down, away from his face and hair, and worked the slippery cleansing film over his testicles. He pulled back the foreskin, trying to spread the soap upward, working painstakingly to scrub away the vague, inescapable musk.

Max was already in bed when he toweled off after his bucket bath and slipped into the darkness of the bedroom. He crawled in next to her, naked, self-conscious. Her breathing echoed softly in the darkness. When soap was infinite before, bathing never used to mean anything. It didn't reveal things one didn't want announced so clearly. But now, with so little left, and bathwater from rain that they were collecting in buckets on the roof, it somehow became shameful. There was no subtlety in a world without soap. No room to pretend what one desperately needed and what one could skip tonight, no big deal, only if you feel like it, too.

Ory touched her back, under the tickling puff of her hair, and his fingers brushed against a T-shirt. Max rolled over, pulling him into a lazy hug, and he felt her realize he was nude and still damp mid-embrace—her arms paused for an instant, legs half-entwined with his own, her body recalibrating with dawning understanding. Ory withered, but he dug around clumsily for the bottom hem of her shirt anyway, trailed his hands upward inside of it until he felt the silken, heavy curve of her breasts.

She drew him closer and took hold of his slackening stiffness with one hand. Her fingers wrapped around firmly, and she pressed her other hand over his own on her breast through the fabric.

He tried to forget. The soap. Being the only ones left. Rule Zero. Everything. Her hands moved, warm, pulling him toward her.

He couldn't.

BEFORE SUNRISE, ORY WAS PACKED AND READY TO HEAD OUT to search for Max. His head had stopped bleeding. He sat on the edge of the bed waiting for first light, too tense to sleep. *If only,* Ory thought to himself. *If only.* If only he'd come home three hours earlier. If only he hadn't chased the rabbit. If only he hadn't gone to Broad Street again. *If only. Max would still be here.*

He picked up the ball of paper with Rule Zero on it from the floor and crumpled it further, crushing it until it had compacted into something the size of a walnut. It had looked the same as all the rest of the rules when he'd written it, hanging mutely around the abandoned hotel in their relevant places. *You never go after the other person if they forget.* But the rule was always meant to apply only to Ory. Never the other way around. This—now—this was not how Rule Zero was supposed to play out, not the way things were supposed to happen. This was not an unfortunate scouting accident. It was his fault. His fault that he didn't return home in time to stop Max from leaving because she had forgotten she was supposed to stay.

Ory surveyed the shelter for the last time. The more he thought about it, the more sure he was that none of it made much sense. Max knew how dangerous it was out there, so the fact that she was gone likely meant that the Forgetting had accelerated, that she was starting to bleed memories like a sieve losing sand. That much was clear. But from the early cases they'd all seen, before the TV networks and the internet went down, it was usually terrifying. Victims were panicked and sometimes violent because they couldn't figure out what was happening or where they were, or even who they were, but still had a grasp on other far-flung parts of their minds.

In Max's case, she'd been calm enough not to scramble through all their belongings, trying to parse back together her history from the clues. She had still shut the door when she left, and had maybe taken some food and supplies with her on her way out. It was eerie.

And she had taken the tape recorder with her. Ory had searched the entire shelter, and was sure of it. It was nowhere there.

# MAHNAZ AHMADI

IN THE SUMMERS, NAZ'S ARCHERY PRACTICE WAS VERY EARLY, before the humidity became too unbearable. From June to August, Boston was like the inside of a clay baking tagine. It was almost worse than Tehran. She had to get up at four A.M., but would still watch the news for updates on Hemu Joshi's condition while she dressed in darkness before pulling herself away to go to practice.

It only got worse. By the third week, Hemu had forgotten almost everything about his life. He couldn't recognize his mother, and when asked if he had any siblings, couldn't name his brothers. He could recite his phone number but not his address. He knew he was born and raised in Pune, but didn't seem to know that Pune was in India or that India was a country. Then he forgot what cricket was.

On the archery range, Naz tried to concentrate, but her mind wasn't there. She wondered if she should go back. India was scarily close to home. Her sister emailed and said to stay, not to give up her training, that there was nothing she could do in Iran to help anyway. Naz hid her phone in her sports bra between shots, then would lean down so her hands were hidden and text someone—her next-door neighbor, her friends back in Tehran—anyone, it didn't matter. They were all talking about the same thing. Did you see the test where HJ could only remember 4 of the days in a week? Or HJ just tried to list all the streets in his neighborhood, did you watch that one?

Yeah. Did you see the clip where they showed him pics of his classmates from high school and he tried to name them? they'd reply. It was constant. After a few days, Naz started to worry she was going to get kicked off the team, but then she peeked down the line of targets and realized the other archers were all doing the exact same thing. Go to CNN live stream, they have an update.

She kept waiting for good news, but there never was any. Only bad and worse. Then the Angels of Mumbai began to follow Hemu's path as well, just like the Nashik Cherubs. All suffering various degrees of amnesia, with no discernible pattern across age, sex, education, or geography. There was one woman from Mumbai who seemed to be decaying the slowest, while one of the teenagers from Nashik had completely forgotten all the facts of his childhood and his ability to speak Marathi, the local dialect, within five days of becoming shadowless.

Scientists from every country took over the television channels, armed with hypotheses and ideas for experiments to explain why the shadows never came back, or why without one, a mind starts to flake away like ash on a cindered log. In India, doctors ran test after test on Hemu, trying to prove it was early-onset Alzheimer's, trauma-induced amnesia from one too many cricket balls to the head, stress from the fame, hippocampal damage due to alcoholism he didn't have, whatever. They took a brain scan from a patient in the United States—a middle-aged man who had suffered total and permanent retrograde amnesia in a car accident just a few weeks before Hemu Joshi's own case appeared—to compare to that of Hemu. Patient RA, he was dubbed by the media, to protect his privacy. Oddly, there was nothing abnormal about Hemu's images. The news reported that the two men even met, the American amnesiac and Hemu Joshi. They flew Patient RA from New Orleans all the way to Pune for a week, to see if talking to another person suffering a similar affliction might knock something loose.

It didn't. Patient RA flew back home with his entourage of doctors, to return to his assisted-living facility. After that, videos of Hemu never appeared on air again. Naz didn't know what that meant.

Reports about the other shadowless from Mumbai and Nashik still filled every broadcast, though. The experiments grew wilder as the scientists grew more desperate. They shocked them, hypnotized them, starved them of sleep and then tried to plant memories in their delirious states, cut into their brains. Nothing worked. It sounded silly, but Naz knew there was no other way to say it. The earth's rotation aside, what happened to them wasn't science. It was magic.

Even so, she couldn't stop staring at the scientists poking at them on the news, whenever they gave interviews. The world kept following. Everyone hoped they would all get better. That they'd remember who they were, that they'd recognize their families again. But they never did.

She probably would've kept watching forever, rooting for them, but eventually she had to stop. There was just nothing left to watch. Stories about the shadowless disappeared from broadcasts, and even the skeleton crews pulled back, until there was no coverage at all. It seemed to be the end.

Until eight days later, a curly-haired kid in Brazil looked down during lunch recess and realized he didn't have a shadow anymore. And then two days after that, he couldn't remember his own name.

THE BRAZILIAN PRESIDENT WAS ON THE AIR ABOUT FIVE hours after the news broke, announcing that he'd closed Brazil's borders to all international travel, to help contain whatever this was. Brazilians abroad weren't allowed to return, and noncitizens could go only as far as their embassies. It was an international outrage, but no other country dared to actually retaliate or rescue their citizens by force—they'd have to send soldiers in for that. Into the place where shadows were disappearing.

The kid's family vanished. There was POLICÍA—NÃO SE CRUZAM tape up around their property on the news, and the Brazilian government released a statement that said they'd been taken into custody in order to provide them "the best treatment possible." The phrase chilled Naz. Their neighbors put themselves into self-imposed quarantine. None of them lost their shadows. Americans camped angrily out in the consular hall of the U.S. embassy in São Paulo. Australians built a giant barbecue on the front lawn of their own. Naz emailed Rojan about going home again, but tickets had jumped to $15,000. Airports everywhere but Brazil were overrun with desperate travelers trying to run to—or run away from—somewhere. So instead, Naz just held her breath, hoping it was some kind of strange fluke.

But it wasn't. Another case showed up on the other side of Brazil, completely unconnected, near the border with Peru. Then a week after that, it seemed like all the shadows in Panama disappeared at the same time.

I DIDN'T LEAVE A NOTE, BECAUSE I THOUGHT THAT MIGHT BE worse. If you just think that I forgot you and wandered away, you could eventually forgive yourself, I hope. You'd still follow our first rule, before we had the other rules. The only rule that matters now. That you won't come after me.

I know, Ory, I know. I know you made that rule to protect me. You never thought that someday, I'd be the one who didn't return. But don't you see? That's why it had to be like this, like I'd already forgotten you, so you wouldn't follow me. I did it to protect you, Ory. Not to hurt you. If you knew not only that I had left, but that I did it on purpose, while I still remember you . . . you wouldn't understand. You still have your shadow—you *can't* understand. No note I could leave could ever convince you not to look for me—convince you that I left because I had to. I *had* to. To save you.

So I left nothing. Just disappeared.

⏸

Everything looks so different, it's hard to tell where I am. I thought I was prepared. I mean, I've seen the back of the shelter where the trap is, and some of the overgrown hills nearby—but the resort was always sort of foresty anyway, all grass and trees. I haven't been outside the grounds probably since everyone else from the wedding was still here. So when I got to the bottom of the mountain and looked left and right, trying to figure out where I was, it looked so unlike Elk Cliffs Road that I never would have recognized it in a million years. I had to close my eyes and figure out what it had looked like before, how to get where I wanted to go, from memory. Which is kind of hilarious, considering. It's fucking hilarious.

Sorry, bad joke. I guess I'm more nervous than I thought I'd be, out on my own like this.

It's been only a few days, but I'm actually not as hungry as I expected. You remember what the scientists said, back when it started—that once a shadowless has forgotten everything, it also forgets it's hungry or thirsty, or even that it needs to breathe. God, I hope I forget to eat or drink before I forget to breathe. I'd rather starve a hundred times than suffocate to death. Can you imagine? All that pain, the fire in your lungs, the slow, darkening stillness, and all you'd have to do is just take a breath, if only you could remember that your body could do it?

I'm sorry, Ory. I'm sure you don't want to hear that. I find myself thinking about stranger and stranger things. Maybe it's one of the effects.

Part of me still can't believe I did it. That I actually left you. It almost seems like someone else's memory when I think back on it now, for as long as I still can—like I'm watching someone who looks like me, but isn't.

The morning of that seventh day, when you finally went to the city to search for food, you gave me one last nervous look before you shut the door behind yourself to head off. The key twisted in the lock. I waited until your footsteps had faded. If there was a window uncovered that faced the direction you were walking, I would've watched you hike through the ever-tangling weeds until you disappeared. Instead, I counted to five hundred.

Then I went into the closet, took down the bag of sweaters from the top shelf, and filled the purse I brought for Paul and Imanuel's wedding with the essentials: underwear, some of our first-aid kit, one flashlight, our spare hunting knife. My tape recorder.

I worked quickly on purpose. So fast I couldn't think about what I was actually doing. If I'd gone any slower, my resolve would have failed. I zipped up the inner pocket of the purse, threw it over my shoulder, marched to the door, turned the lock, stepped out, and then shut it behind me. Click.

That's when I paused.

The finality of it really hit me then. That as soon as I walked away from that door, I'd never be able to find it again. I'd forget it, or the way back to it. This was really, really it.

The only thing that got my feet to move was the idea that came to me at that very moment. Until that point, I'd planned to go east, to try to make it to our home in D.C. Just to see it one last time before I forgot what it looked like. Before I forgot you. That's probably where you would guess I tried to make it to as well—tried, but got lost and then . . . You know.

But then I thought, *Why? Why not do the opposite? Why not see somewhere completely new for my very last days as Max?*

So I went west instead.

# ORLANDO ZHANG

THAT WAS HIS LAST NIGHT IN THE SHELTER, ALTHOUGH HE didn't know it at the time. Ory, sitting alone on a thin mattress, gun over his knee, everything he could carry stuffed into his pockets. So very different from the first night he and Max had spent there.

It was afternoon in the courtyard that day, years ago. Ory was standing on the lawn, holding a champagne flute in one hand. They called that place Elk Cliffs Resort then. The late sun warmed the left side of everything—faces, tables, each blade of grass. Beside him, Paul was practicing his speech, cursing every time he had to look at the thin, sweat-soaked book in his hands.

"Fuck. Fuck!" he growled.

"You know, for a poet, that's kind of an underwhelming opening line," Ory said.

Paul glanced at him. His brow shone in the high-altitude light. "I can't remember the words," he confessed sheepishly. "You'd think—I mean, I wrote the goddamn thing for him." He sighed, meaning the book, all the poems in it. It was his second published collection, dedicated to Imanuel. "You'd think I could memorize the one I want to use for my vows."

"He's a doctor. He'll never notice," Ory said. Paul laughed. Across the grass, Max winked at him from afar, dress billowing in the breeze. The game trap was now there in the place where she was standing. "You'll get it," Ory tried to reassure him. "One more time."

Paul put the book back in his jacket pocket and took a long, deep breath. He squinted into the light. "Seven years, and I'm nervous," he said. "Isn't that funny?"

"Wouldn't be worth it if you weren't." Ory grinned.

That day was ancient history. Only about four weeks after Hemu Joshi first stepped out to the ravenous flash and whir of news cameras, and a few days after the cases in Brazil and Panama appeared. The U.S. had announced it was considering closing its borders, but aside from the cases that had begun appearing in Latin America, that was as near as the Forgetting seemed. It was still a dim, vague thing, a thing that was happening there, not here. Until suddenly it was.

It was almost funny when he thought back on it now. There they all were, tuxedoes and dresses fluttering in the fresh mountain breeze, tables set, candles lit ahead of the warming dusk, preparing to celebrate exactly the opposite of what was about to happen: the joining of memories, the promise that they would last long after the people were all gone. Instead, they witnessed the Forgetting reach the United States just before midnight.

THE CEREMONY WAS BEAUTIFUL. PAUL AND IMANUEL HAD been together longer than Ory and Max, and their love was old news to him—he hadn't expected to cry when they read their vows. And then when he did, he couldn't believe he had ever expected not to.

Ory could see only half of Max's face from where he was standing at the front next to Paul, but he looked at her anyway as Rabbi Levenson pronounced them married and the room erupted in cheers. She leapt to her feet and stuck her fingers in her mouth in a piercing whistle. Paul and Imanuel were lost in a kiss, but Ory jumped at the sound, and then laughed when he realized it had come from her.

Ory helped herd everyone into the ballroom, where dining tables and a dance floor were set up. Someone had passed streamer poppers around the crowd, and when Paul and Imanuel entered last, Imanuel red-faced with joy, Paul doing a comical prance and singing a theme song he'd made up for them both, they all pulled the strings and rained a kaleidoscope of sequins and twirling crepe paper scraps down on them.

"Official co-choreographer," Max said afterward as she and Ory savored their champagne, disbelieving his claim that he'd helped Paul invent his entrance dance. They were outside in the sloping courtyard with a handful of other guests, looking at the stars and vast darkness of the forest beneath. "I'll believe it when I see you perform it."

"Oh, you'll see it," Ory teased. "You'll see it tonight, in our room."

"I look forward to it," she said, clinking the rim of her glass against his.

He could tell that in one more drink or so, she'd be ready to go make a fool of herself on the dance floor with him. She was not a great dancer, all angles and elbows, but he loved the fact that she didn't care at all. He was ready to be a clumsy, gangly embarrassment too, to hold her hands as they spun and to try to dip her, to feel her hair stick to his sweaty cheek as he pulled her back in close. To feel her fingers clutch his shoulders for safety until it pinched when he tried to pick her up into a twirl. He leaned in to smell her perfume, but it was the back of her head facing him suddenly, not the side of her delicate neck. Someone had just pulled her into a hug.

"Here he is." Ory grinned and wrapped his arms around both her and Paul, making them into a gigantic, six-legged monster. One of their champagnes went everywhere, disappearing into the grass.

"My best man," Paul laughed, and mussed Ory's hair as he put a protective arm around Max's shoulder. "Now, you've only known him for a few years, but let me tell you something about kid-Ory," he started, but then Imanuel was there also, holding a glass of bourbon in one hand and his phone in the other.

"Husband!" Paul interrupted himself, and the stern expression on Imanuel's face, whatever had been distracting him moments before, melted away for an instant as they kissed again. "Is that a patient? Is someone in labor? During our *wedding*?" Paul teased as he pulled back.

"No," Imanuel smiled sheepishly, but then the solemn expression returned to line his features. Ory saw he had an internet browser open on the screen of his phone. "I went to get a drink and I heard the caterers talking. It—it happened to Boston."

There was a moment when no one knew what he meant. It was probably the last moment that anyone ever didn't know. Now nothing ever meant anything else.

"The shadows?" Ory finally asked. But it seemed impossible. The rumors had begun that said perhaps it was something contagious, the new century's black plague, or Ebola, but it seemed like hysteria, still easy to dismiss. There was just no real information—no one was sending any signals out of the afflicted countries, by phone or email or post or television or radio—and besides satellite images and high-altitude military flyovers, which showed nothing but stillness and the occasional flicker of a terrified shape wandering through streets or jungle, there was nothing else to go on.

"It happened in Boston?" Max asked.

"Not *in* Boston." Imanuel shook his head. "*To* Boston. Almost everyone there."

BY MIDNIGHT, WORD HAD SPREAD THROUGHOUT THE WED-ding party. The courtyard was deserted, champagne glasses abandoned half-full where they were, and everyone was crowded back into the ballroom. Some were on their cell phones, and the caterers had turned on the TV bolted to the wall in the corner of the room.

"Don't," Max said. She put her hand over Ory's to stop him from opening the browser on his own phone, cradled now in his palm. They'd left their apartment in D.C. late that morning, and hadn't packed a charger in the rush to make it to the wedding on time. "Save the power, just in case." It wouldn't matter—cellular signal would go down in another day or two before they'd run out of battery—but they didn't know that then. Ory nodded gratefully at her good thinking and edged the device back into his pocket.

On television, helicopter footage cut between downtown Boston and one of the larger highways out of the city beneath a reporter's voice-over. The National Guard had circled the metropolis and blocked all routes in and out, putting the entire population under indefinite quarantine. There was a mini screen in the bottom right corner running at the same time as the live feed; it was a rerun of the president's speech that had apparently aired half an hour before, when the news about Boston first broke. He was in the middle of assuring the public that the nation's top scientists were working around the clock to figure out the cause of the epidemic—the world was still calling it "the epidemic" then, as if it was some kind of simple biological quirk, some twisted proteins or mutated virus that could be solved by the right vaccine—and advised everyone not to travel except in emergency circumstances. *"Stay safe, stay inside, limit travel, and limit contact with others whenever possible,"* his grainy image repeated. *"We are doing everything we can to find a way to neutralize the spread. I promise you, as soon as we discover a cure, we'll be sending FEMA and Red Cross agents door to door through every neighborhood to distribute it."* His voice was calm, but the message was clear. Do not go to the hospital. Do not go to the grocery store. Do not leave your house. Wait.

Now, it was clear the Forgetting was not contagious. At least it didn't seem like it was. The number of times that Ory had been curiously examined or attacked by a shadowless while out scavenging, the number of random survivors he'd tried to help in the early days who later succumbed, and he was still here, still whole. If it had been contagious, he'd have lost his shadow years ago. He still had no idea what it actually was. And he'd given up trying to figure it out. But back then, as they all huddled in the ballroom, terrified, watching nervous soldiers try to say—then yell, then desperately mime—instructions to stop and turn back around at the confused, terrified shadowless man approaching them, no one knew if it was or wasn't something that could be passed by breath or touch. Everything else in the world had always worked that way. At the time, there was no reason to think this was any different. They couldn't be blamed for what happened then.

The president's little speech box disappeared, and the split screen suddenly dropped the view of downtown to focus on only the highway feed as the commotion started. A shadowless man had wandered away from the city and was now stumbling toward the line of soldiers, crying, but not saying any words or seeming to hear the ones being shouted at him. He looked to be in his fifties—still strong, but balding, and beginning to grow a middle-aged paunch. He wore brown corduroys, a button-down shirt, and a navy blue sweater over it, pristine in the harsh blaze of the emergency floodlights. *He looks like a university professor,* Ory thought dazedly. A university professor with no shadow.

The soldiers were screaming now, some waving, some holding an open hand straight out in the universal gesture to stop, to *fucking stop,* stop or we have to shoot, we have to shoot to kill. The man didn't seem to recognize or remember any of it at all.

The station tried to cut away, but they weren't fast enough. Several guests in the ballroom screamed as the shadowless man on-screen snapped to a halt, frozen upright for one lingering instant, and then crumpled to the ground.

The news anchor materialized on-screen again, looking disoriented and unprepared, stumbling through a statement that was being fed to him through his earpiece. "We want to apologize for that graphic video clip . . . It was not our intention to air such an upsetting image . . . Unfortunately the nature of live news sometimes . . ."

"Holy shit, Ory," Max murmured, her whole body tense. "Do we know anyone in Boston? Do you have friends or family there?" People had started arguing now, some calling for calm, others shouting across the room to each other for any new information they could dig up on their phones. Someone had a laptop out and was connecting it to Elk Cliffs's Wi-Fi.

"I don't think so," Ory said, but his head was swimming. He felt dizzy.

"This is really bad," Max kept saying. "This is really, really bad."

Ory tried to refute that, to be the strong, steady one who would keep them both anchored, but he couldn't find the words. The TV was back on the helicopter camera hovering over Boston city limits, the body of the fallen shadowless man still in the street, this time pixelated into an indiscernible mass. Ory couldn't tell for sure, but it looked like even in death, his shadow hadn't returned. The thought sent a chill through him.

The National Guard were still shoulder to shoulder, a wall across the road. They looked shaken, as if they were clinging to one another instead of forming a blockade. One was holding a black body bag in his hands, gun strapped back across his shoulders, but he was held by orders in the line, unable to go forward and lay it over the dead man, in case whatever was causing the Forgetting was transmissible through the air. The soldiers suddenly tensed, and guns rose from their downward angle to point straight forward with agonizing dread. More shadowless were approaching. Some running, some screaming, some silent.

This time the station didn't waste any time. The screen cut back to the anchor at the desk, who was scrambling through freshly scribbled papers and a blaring earpiece, trying not to listen for the sound of impending gunfire through the tiny speaker. Mid-speech he stammered. A long, horrible pause. He closed his eyes involuntarily. Then he opened them and kept going.

Ory glanced around the room and swallowed hard, to try to calm himself down, and looked back at the screen. Then he heard the anchor say something about Denver. He pulled Max closer, wrapped his arms around her, and squeezed with everything he had as the news cut to a reporter in Colorado. Someone had begun to sob.

"Hey," he said as he crushed her into the hug. The shocked, rising hum of too many voices at once echoed off the stone walls of the ballroom. Shouts and ring tones blended into an eerie, doomed musical harmony. He wanted to say something comforting, to sound like he was there for her, to make it feel like it was all going to be okay soon, but the fear had numbed his mind. "Blue," he finally managed, no more than a whisper.

"Fifty-two," she whispered back.

I CAN'T REALLY AVOID IT ANY LONGER, I GUESS. NOT TALKING about it isn't going to change that it happened, so I might as well say something before I forget how it went. I don't know if I believe you yet, Ory. If recording things will really make a difference at all. But if it does—well, I don't really know what are the most important things to get down on tape yet, so I figure I should probably just say everything I can think of. Including this.

So. The day I lost my shadow.

It was two weeks ago now. Which is a pretty long time for me to still remember as much as I do, judging by past cases. Everyone's different, though, they say. Hemu Joshi started losing his memories so quickly, just a few days in, but there were reports of some people in Mumbai who took a month to forget anything significant. I think the longest one I ever heard about before the electricity went out was about a month and a half. So hopefully I'm more toward that side of the average. These past two weeks have felt like a year, in some ways. To have a month and a half left before it all goes, it might feel like an eternity.

This is strange, talking to myself and you like this. Especially since I'm not there with you anymore. I have a confession: I actually wasn't going to use the tape recorder, even though I promised you I would. But then I got out here, alone, and I just—it feels good to talk. It makes me feel real still.

I know I'm the one who left and that you'll never hear this, but before I start, I want to say, just in case: Ory, if you're listening to this—somehow, some way—it didn't hurt. So don't worry about that part, at least. I hardly felt it.

[II]

There was nothing about that morning two weeks ago that seemed different. I'm sure you'd say the same. I looked normal, felt normal. We split a can of corn from our dwindling cupboard supply, and then you left to check the trap and then the city. I've racked my brain for anything. A sign, a twinge, a premonition. But there was nothing.

After you left, I went into the kitchenette to do the counting for us. How many matches. How many shotgun shells. How many pills of found Tylenol, amoxicillin, doxycycline. I felt like a squirrel, counting how many nuts we'd managed to store in the hole in our tree to see if it was enough to last through the winter.

You know this already—the kitchenette was my favorite room in the shelter, because the window was so small and our floor was high enough up that a person couldn't see in from the ground, so the glass there could stay uncovered. At first you wanted to block it like the rest of them, just to be safe, but I managed to convince you to leave just that one open. I don't think you have any idea how much time I spent in that room on days you were out scavenging for supplies or skinning a mouse from our trap. Some mornings, I just lay on the floor there, sunbathing.

Sometimes, on particularly bright days when the wind was very still, two little gray sparrows would land on the branches of the tree outside that window. I think they might even have been mates. A few weeks ago, even though it was already getting cold, one of them came back with some sticks, and I was so excited that they might be building their nest there that I forgot to do anything I was supposed to do that day, which was quite a bit: I had at least three of your shirts to sew because you kept ripping the seam where the sleeve joined the shoulder, and I was supposed to repair the cardboard covering on one of the first-floor windows where it had peeled loose and was flapping against the cracked glass in the breeze. You were afraid the movement might attract passersby that otherwise wouldn't have noticed or considered the building. I agreed that this made sense. I just completely forgot, because of the birds. We got in a pretty big fight about that when you got home, I remember. That was before my shadow disappeared and you started handling me with kid gloves. Now, when I forget to do something, you barely say anything at all, or sometimes even tell me it's fine, that you're just happy I'm still doing well and had a good day. But the look on your face now is so much worse. I'd rather have a hundred thousand fights than see that look on your face again. Well, I guess I won't have to anymore.

Okay, stop being grim. I'm off topic.

I remember grabbing a jar of spaghetti sauce mid-count when I first noticed it. The strange stillness in the room. It was always so still when only I was home, but this was stillness of a different quality. It was full of something, rather than absent.

I looked down at my shadow there on the floor, and because of the light from that little window, it was perfectly stretched out in front of me. We were the exact same height and shape. There was no distortion from the angle of the sun or a bump in the floor or a wall that might have cut into the silhouette. We matched exactly. *Perfectly.* Down to the eyelash.

I lifted up the jar, and so did my shadow. We both leaned over and set the sauces on the counters, and returned our hands to rest at our sides. It was like I could feel that something was about to happen. Like I shouldn't look away.

Then something did. This is going to sound absolutely crazy, but I swear it's true.

I was holding perfectly still, under the spell of that feeling, just watching my shadow. It was looking back at me, in the same pose, waiting.

Then I saw it tilt its head ever so slightly to the side, all by itself.

There was a moment of coldness, like the entire room had dropped twenty degrees. I tried to take a breath, but I couldn't move. Then it was gone.

[II]

I didn't cry. Not that whole afternoon. Instead, I kept busy, taking inventory of our first-aid supplies, cleaning, making sure the window coverings were still secure, double-checking that we had sufficient shotgun ammunition, cleaning and resetting the game trap. I felt like there were so many things to make sure of, and so little time. Like it was all going to end that same night, and I'd just vanish too, forever. I kept spinning around to look behind me, to see if maybe I'd been mistaken, that the sun had just disappeared behind some clouds for a second, or I simply had cabin fever. But it didn't matter how many times I looked or how many different directions I shone our spare flashlight on my hand. I couldn't make a silhouette against any surface. In the light on the wall, the plastic cylinder looked like it was floating in midair all by itself, careening wildly about, pointing every which angle. As soon as I noticed, I put it down immediately. I couldn't touch it again.

I forgot to start dinner. Instead, I shook out the winter clothes in the storage trunk so they wouldn't have moth holes in them by the time we needed them. I still didn't cry.

Even when I went back in the kitchen and saw that jar still sitting on the counter, and its own twin still painted darkly on the floor, I *still* didn't cry.

Not until after it had gotten dark, and I heard your key in the door.

# MAHNAZ AHMADI

THAT NIGHT, THE NIGHT THE FORGETTING REACHED BOSTON, Naz had spent the afternoon out on the range with her coach, but every shot was terrible. She bungled them one after another for so many hours that finally he cut the practice short, and told her to head home and go to sleep early. Naz knew something was really off when she didn't argue with him about getting soft on her, for once. Her mind just wasn't there. It was like she knew something was coming. *It's in your DNA,* her mother would have said. *They say that DNA has a memory, too.* That the things that happen to a people are passed down. Naz would have told her that was nonsense. If they hadn't disowned each other so long ago.

When the Forgetting hit, after dark, it surprised Naz that her mother was who she thought of first. Then she thought, *I can't.* She'd kept her promise never to speak to her again—since the last time she'd visited Tehran. Her mother had, too. Outside, on the street below, she could hear people screaming in the night.

Naz picked up her cell phone. She had started seeing someone recently, maybe seriously. She didn't know. She scrolled to his number, but her finger stalled, hovering over the screen. What did two and a half months mean, really? Fourteen dates, five lays, eighteen glasses of wine, one drive to the airport for a weekend trip. He hadn't reached out for Naz. There was no message flashing urgently in the blue glow of her screen. It was all right, though. Naz understood. There were other people who mattered more, to them both.

The call didn't go through the first time. Naz was sure everyone who hadn't lost their shadow was busy calling everyone who had. She hung up and immediately dialed again. She was ready to leave a voice mail. *I just wanted to say I'm okay, that's all.* Something like that. She was surprised when her mother picked up.

"Are you safe?" Her mother was sobbing. It was disorienting—to listen as things that used to matter so much evaporated. What filled their empty places to justify all that lost time? Naz was scrambling for her shoes and wallet. Would a $15,000 charge even go through on her credit card? She couldn't remember how to get to the airport, what freeway.

It didn't matter. They'd closed Boston airport, her mother told her. She'd seen it on the news. Naz couldn't go home. "Are you safe? Tell me you're safe," her mother pleaded.

Naz told her she was okay. Everything was slowly draining out of her. When she'd needed to be brave for someone else a moment ago, it was one thing. But it was hard to be brave for just herself. She backed away from the windows, sank to the carpet. Red and blue alternating flashes passed on the street outside, casting ghostly streaks across the ceiling. *I have to get out of the city,* Naz thought, at the same moment that her mother was telling her they'd quarantined it, that they were shooting people trying to break the line. "Turn on your damn TV, Mahnaz!" she shouted.

The president's face flashed up in front of her, alongside helicopter feeds of various neighborhoods. Naz even saw her own.

"What should I do?" she asked her mother. "Should I go upstairs or go in the basement?"

"No!" her mother cried. "You have to leave the house. Now. Anyone could find you there, because that's where you're supposed to be."

Boston was a place where her mother's paranoid advice had stopped terrifying Naz long ago. It was a place where no one made two extra turns on the way anywhere, to lose a tail. Where no one memorized license plates. Where no one had a secret hiding place in the hall closet. It was a place where Naz had all the answers, and her mother would flounder embarrassingly on the sidewalk, gaping at the things teenagers carelessly shouted, the crop tops, the virtual reality demos at pop-up game booths on Newbury Street. But this wasn't the Boston Naz knew anymore, and her mother had lived this life before. She had learned a world where one had to know what to do if people were being killed, if someone might be coming to find you. Naz felt herself nodding vigorously at her mother's words.

"Where can you go that no one will think to look? Somewhere that wouldn't be worth checking."

That's how Naz ended up living in her perhaps-boyfriend's music studio.

SHE FIGURED, NO SERIOUS STORES OF FOOD, NO WEAPONS, no camping or survival supplies. A vacant, soundproof studio inside of a nondescript commercial warehouse was about as unattractive a target as possible. Why would anyone go there to try to wait out the chaos that was happening outside?

Naz dumped everything in her pantry, everything in the top drawer of her dresser, her toiletries, and her bow and quiver into a duffel bag.

"Do you see anyone? Are you there yet?" her mother asked.

"Please stop talking," Naz begged. She'd put the Bluetooth earpiece in her ear and clipped the phone to her belt holster so her mother could stay with her as she sprinted down every side street she could find to reach the studio. The intersection ahead exploded in a hail of bullets. Naz threw herself to the ground, flat against the sidewalk behind a battered parked car. Ahead, a person fell, and someone whooped, as if it was a game. More bodies came sprinting down the street, just on the other side of the car. They moved too fast for her to see if they had shadows or not.

"Then you talk," she said. "Please!"

"A roadblock or a riot, I think," Naz tried. "Maman, I have to— they'll hear me."

Naz went around. It was the same on the next street. Someone had either shot out the streetlamps or the power grid was starting to fail. All she could see in the glow of the red traffic lights were things running, whipping past each other. Two crashed—a shattering of glass or something. Men screamed.

"Police!" the police shouted. Sirens burst to life, and a white car materialized out of the night. The mob attacked the car. Then another mob attacked the mob attacking the car, swinging metal baseball bats.

"Fuck," Naz gasped.

"Mahnaz? Are you there?" her mother cried.

"Maman, shut up!"

"Okay," she said more quietly. "I have a map, the tourist map you sent me when you first went. The only neighborhood I haven't seen on the internet news yet is Dudley Square. This is on the way to the studio? Can you go through there?"

Naz cinched her bag tighter across her chest. "Okay," she said. "But no more talking."

DUDLEY SQUARE WAS QUIETER, BUT IN A TERRIFYING WAY. THE lights were all out, even in the houses. Naz could see people in their windows by the light reflecting off their eyes from emergency candles. Her legs were so weak the muscles burned cold as she tried to move them, but she kept running. She was too afraid to walk. *Please don't shoot me,* she thought. *Please see there's still a little dark thing on the sidewalk following me.*

When she reached the parking lot of the warehouse, there was a single car there, parked in the exact center of the lot. Naz crouched in the hedges at the edge of the property, staring. Was someone inside? Or were they in the building? Would they kill her? Did they have a shadow? The last question sounded so fantastical, so unnatural and horrifying, that she almost giggled hysterically. Her mother waited, breathless. It took Naz fifteen minutes to work up the courage to approach the car, bow drawn. She couldn't tell until she was right up against the driver's window that it was completely burned out, to cinders, with only a skeleton at the wheel.

She used her copy of her perhaps-boyfriend's key and climbed the stairs to the third floor in pitch-blackness.

"Are you there yet?"

"Yes," Naz panted as she reached the landing. She pushed the door open. Across the gray industrial carpet, she could make out the dim outline of his band's door, their handwritten name still taped to it. She'd made it. She'd survived the trip.

She ducked back into the stairwell and vomited everywhere.

HER MOTHER STAYED ON THE PHONE WITH NAZ UNTIL SHE fell asleep sometime just before dawn. Her mother knew the boy wasn't there, but Naz didn't mention him, and she didn't ask more. Naz was just happy there was someone with her. Well, sort of with her.

When she woke up, the phone was dead. She uncurled from the floor behind the huge speakers and tried to sit up. Everything ached. It felt like she'd pulled every muscle in her body the night before trying to run there. Maybe she had.

She crawled over to the wall and plugged her charger into the outlet. When the phone came back to life a few minutes later, there were forty-two messages.

Are you all right?
Can you see the news from where you are?
Text me back if you're okay.
They're saying on the news that the quarantine is going to continue.
Just let me know you're still okay.
Call me!!!

"I'm okay," Naz said, but gently, when she picked up.

Her mother stayed on the line with Naz again for the rest of the day. And the day after that. She never heard from her perhaps-boyfriend.

Maybe he'd called his mother, too. Maybe he lost his shadow as soon as it hit Boston. It didn't really matter. She never called him either, in the end.

The day after that, her sister, Rojan, was on the line as well, both she and her mother crouched over her mother's mobile phone placed faceup on the kitchen table, shouting slowly and loudly so Naz could understand them. Naz broke down sobbing when she first heard Rojan's voice. She'd left Tehran University as soon as she could put all her research on hold, and took the first bus to their mother's home.

"What about your studies?" Naz had asked her.

"Fuck my studies," Rojan said, to which her mother clucked her tongue, but for once didn't admonish her daughter for cursing. "Just deal with the fact that you need us, for once."

Naz slowly explored the rest of the warehouse to make sure no one else was inside. Her mother ordered her to raid the staff refrigerator on every floor and eat everything in there first, and save her packed nonperishables. For breakfast, Naz had birthday cake, egg salad, and pickles. Rojan told her to turn on the laptop she found on top of the drum case, but its battery was dead and the charger was nowhere to be found, so her mother and sister relayed updates to her from the news on their television set instead. Cases had now been spotted in Wyoming, New Hampshire, California, and the D.C. area. Planes had been grounded, interstates closed. Some cities were practically under martial law. Sometimes the three of them didn't say anything at all. They just stayed on the line together. Every four hours, Naz went back to the wall outlet and lay on the floor while her phone was plugged in, to charge it back up before the call cut out.

"Where exactly is this studio?" Rojan kept asking her. "How do you spell *Dorchester* Street?" She became obsessive about it, about being able to pinpoint Naz's exact location. "What does the building look like? How many stories? What shape? What color is the outside?" She asked so many questions that their mother finally shouted at her to get her maps and pens out of the way or she was going to throw them all in the trash, and started knocking what sounded like stacks of paper off the table as they argued.

"I know what you're doing. Don't try to come here," Naz whispered into the phone to Rojan late that night, after their mother had fallen asleep.

"I won't," Rojan replied.

"I mean it. Don't try to find me. It won't help anything."

"I won't," Rojan repeated, but Naz knew she was lying.

"Tickets are thousands of dollars anyway. The airports—"

"How much?" Rojan interrupted.

"I don't know, like probably twenty or more thousand to fly in now, because no one wants to come near," Naz answered.

"*Fuck.*"

"And Boston airport is closed and under quarantine, I'm sure," she finished. She dropped her voice lower. "I'm serious. I can hear people dying out there. It's not safe. Don't come." She tried to think of something she could say that would force her sister to listen. "Stay with Maman. Don't leave her alone. Don't make it so that she has *two* daughters here instead of just one. Okay?"

Rojan made a small sound, like Naz had physically hurt her. "So what, you're just going to be alone over there, trying to survive without any help?"

"What would you coming do anyway?" Naz asked.

"I don't know, but *something*. Anything," she said. "You're my sister, Mahnaz."

"Don't come, Rojan," Naz warned. "Don't leave Maman."

She could hear Rojan breathing slowly on the other end of the line. It sounded like she was trying not to cry. "Okay, I won't come," she finally said.

"Promise," Naz ordered.

"I promise."

Naz settled back against the wall and cradled the phone between her ear and shoulder. She still didn't know if she fully believed her sister, but she also knew that if Rojan *was* still lying, arguing about it further wouldn't convince her. All it would do was wake their mother up when one of them started shouting.

"Can you see the stars?" Rojan asked in the silence.

"From the roof," Naz said.

"Go up there."

THE DAY AFTER, NAZ WOKE UP TO LIGHT RAIN PATTERING against the windows. *I should try to collect that for drinking,* she thought groggily as she rolled over on the carpet to unplug her phone from the wall. But the charge was barely full.

Naz called, and her mother picked up crying. She and Rojan already knew from the news that the power had gone out in Boston overnight. "How much battery do you have left?" Was all she said.

"Seven percent," Naz answered.

NAZ LEFT THE EARPIECE IN FOR WEEKS, EVEN THOUGH IT WAS useless. She knew even then that it seemed a little crazy, but she kept talking to them as if they were there. She needed to. "Whew, that was heavy!" she'd say when she finished lugging down water from containers she'd found around the building and put open-faced on the roof. Or "Remember when we found out I'd been accepted to train here?" or "Did you hear that?" when an errant sound had terrified her in the middle of the night. It turned out to be a rat in the ventilation system, not a human.

Naz asked Rojan which office she should move to when the music studio grew boring and small, then babbled about the pros and cons. She described what other floors looked like.

She asked her mother if they'd both known what would happen, would she still have cut Naz off to try to stop her from dating? If the shadowlessness had never come, would she have held out until she died, or given up and reached out? She asked if she might try to be better to Rojan than she had been to Naz, if Rojan wanted something else someday, too. Slowly, slowly, Naz stopped talking.

# ORLANDO ZHANG

AS SOON AS IT WAS LIGHT ENOUGH TO SEE, ORY SPRINTED. Out of the shelter, down the mountain, all the way to the first ruin of road. That's where he stopped, jerked to a halt at the edge of that asphalt path.

He had no idea which way Max had gone.

The sun was out, burning so bright everything was white instead of yellow. It made the blow to the back of his head from the night before throb painfully. East, toward downtown Arlington, and then past the river to D.C., was slightly more traversable. West, toward Fairfax County and all the western cities like Falls Church and Oakton and Centreville, was overgrown and wild. Ory gritted through the headache, studying the ground for tracks, but there weren't any. There was too much grass and rock and not enough dust to see any footprints Max might have left.

How much of her memory had she lost, exactly? Even if it had been a devastating amount, there had to be some figment of it left that would have made her choose one path over the other. A spray of birds shot across the sky from one tree to another, screeching, then disappeared into the leaves. But what if whatever remained wasn't a part he knew?

The birds chattered again, and then fell silent. Every second that went by was a day. How far could a person who didn't know where they were going get? No explanation, no clues, no map. She had vanished without a single trace, as silently and mysteriously as had her shadow.

Where *did* the shadows go? Ory wondered. He didn't even care about the why anymore. Only the where. The why was inexplicable. Ory didn't believe in magic, but he knew in his heart that what had happened was nothing that could be understood by humans. It was no natural disaster, no disease, no biological weapon. The best name he'd ever heard for it was *curse*. Because in the end it didn't matter who you were. No one escaped—either because they were someone who lost their shadow, or because they were someone who loved someone who lost their shadow.

Ory gritted his teeth. It was impossible to hope now, but he had to believe that the person he was chasing was still Max. Otherwise what would be the point of trying to find her? And if he was chasing Max, then there was only one direction she would have chosen. She'd try to go home. Not the shelter, but their real home. The apartment where they'd lived in D.C., before the Forgetting. Before they'd gotten in the car that weekend so long ago to drive into Virginia for Paul and Imanuel's wedding. Before everything.

Ory held his breath and ran east, straight into the low-hanging morning light, as if he could outrun his terror. If he could just make it far enough, the rising sun would turn into a bridge, and then he'd be in D.C. And Max would have to be there. She'd have to be.

THAT'S WHAT HE TOLD HIMSELF UNTIL HE COULDN'T RUN anymore.

Odricks Corner had turned into a willow forest, curtains of leaves everywhere. For some reason, the sidewalks had been refashioned into spirals. Ory rested only long enough for the sweat to dry across his forehead. He went on with the gun out then.

Since Paul and Imanuel's wedding, neither he nor Max had returned to their apartment. She had wanted fiercely to go back, but it was too dangerous. Before the news went down, they'd seen the scenes from Boston, San Francisco, D.C.—fires, looting, roving gangs. There was plenty of food at Elk Cliffs Resort from the wedding, and the slope of the mountain provided natural protection.

Over the years, as more and more of the other guests disappeared, or left to try to make it to their own homes, Ory became convinced that only their mountain was safe. Who knew what was lurking there in the east, in the great silent black hole that had been their capital. For a moment, he remembered the strange group he'd met on Broad Street, what their leader, Ursula, had said. *Bad things. Bad things are happening in D.C.*

THERE WAS A RUSTLING IN THE HEDGES ALONGSIDE OLD Cedar Road. Ory didn't like it there, in that part of Arlington. Houses lined both sides of the street, set far back, with low-hanging trees. No one was inside, but the shades behind the windows blinked languidly on their own from time to time, like drowsy eyelids. On the side of one garage, someone had scrawled in charcoal *The Dreamless One* and *The One Who Gathers*.

There was more movement, a nervous shuffling. Ory looked and saw no dark shape there under the trembling leaves. He raised the gun and ran.

HE CROSSED UNDER THE I-495 IN LATE EVENING. WOULD MAX have made it as far east as McLean in one day? Perhaps, but no farther. Ory had scoured the ground for signs of her as he went—a dropped supply he might recognize from their stash, a tear of familiar clothing, even a footprint—but had found nothing. Nothing from anyone at all, even. There was a shoe that had been in the gutter so long it was fossilized in mud. A ways after, there had been a bone, but it was old. So old he did not have to look away as he passed it.

In the night, Ory heard something inhumanly heavy cross the interstate, walking over the top of the overpass instead of below. He huddled closer to the dank concrete wall as it passed. Even with the moon, it was so pitch-black, he could not have seen if there was a shadow or not. He didn't try to look. He held the wall and prayed the sound above would move on.

IN THE MORNING, HE CLIMBED ONTO THE OVERPASS TO SEE what might have been there. But there were only wildflowers and a single car tire.

THE MORNING AFTER THE BOSTON EMERGENCY BROADCAST, I opened my eyes to the worst hangover I've ever had. Dim flashes of the night before returned. Marion, my best friend from high school who'd become almost as close to Imanuel as she and I were to each other, calling for calm. Jay "Rhino" White, someone's plus one—although we never quite figured out whose—declaring himself captain of an investigative scouting team he'd just created. Paul saying, "Fuck this, I'm getting the champagne," and going to get it. All of it. "If this is the last day on earth, we can't waste a drop." Do you remember that? I had to agree with him.

It all became a blur after the eighth glass. At some point during the night, I'd managed to get myself to our guest suite, pull the blankets and pillows off our bed, bring them back downstairs into the ballroom, and pick us out a spot on the east edge, in the corner where the wood wall met the glass one. I woke up with my face buried in your tuxedoed shoulder, which smelled of Bollinger, candle smoke, and cinnamon, somehow. The light through the trees was so clear it was blinding. Sharp, piercing beams cut through the branches and seared white shapes into the dark grass.

The news was still on the TV in the corner, the volume lowered so that only the people clustered beneath it could hear, to allow the rest of us to sleep. I tried to blink the world back into focus. Capitol Hill was on the screen, and then the Golden Gate Bridge replaced it, some kind of ticker running below.

"Ory." I nudged your arm. "Wake up."

You sat up slowly, but by the time you were fully upright, you looked alert. "What happened? Where else?" you asked. We both turned back to the TV.

"You're awake," Rhino said when he saw us sitting. I noticed Paul,

Imanuel, and Marion already standing awkwardly next to him, as if ordered to be there. "Volunteer?" he asked hopefully.

That was how we became the first scouting party for the Elk Cliffs Resort survivors.

"They're for the occasional bear or wolf that wanders too close to the grounds," the resort maître d', Gabe, said as he unlocked the STAFF ONLY closet. He brought out two shotguns and one hunting rifle. "Not even occasional, very rare. *Very* rare," he corrected himself on instinct, still thinking of us as luxury guests. Maybe we all still did as well.

"How many bullets do we have?" Rhino asked.

"Enough for an exploratory trip down the mountain," Gabe replied.

"Enough for hunting when we run out of food?"

"That's getting a little ahead of ourselves," Ory said.

Rhino shrugged. "Is it, though?"

"What will the rest of us use?" I interrupted. There were six of us—you, Rhino, Paul, Imanuel, Marion, and me—and only three guns.

"Well, I can actually shoot," Marion said. The others all looked at her. "I grew up on a ranch in Texas. A little cattle ranch. What?"

"Okay, one for Marion, one for me," Rhino said. "Imanuel?"

"Give it to Ory," Imanuel offered politely.

"Give it to *Max*," Paul overrode him. You rubbed the back of your head, cheeks reddening.

It was not the right time to smile. Paul and I tried not to, without much success.

"This isn't soccer," you protested weakly.

"Exactly," Paul said. "It's worse. Definitely give it to Max."

"What is the matter with you?" Imanuel whispered sharply to Paul. Paul finally choked, and the giggles escaped him in a strangled gasp. You had been the only kid in their high school to ever score a goal for the opposite team—*twice*, I finally explained to the rest of them as Paul collapsed into a fit of laughter.

We climbed down the mountain in silence, walking just next to the paved road that led up to the picturesque resort from Elk Cliffs Road. You, Paul, and Imanuel carried huge backpacks instead of weapons. "Odricks Corner," Rhino said to us as we marched. "That's the first neighborhood we'll hit." The trees opened up ahead.

I braced for the eerie, deserted silence of Boston we'd seen on the news after all the shooting stopped, but Odricks Corner was chaos. Cars blaring at each other, women herding families back and forth across streets, people biking with mountains of belongings strapped to their backs. Men defending laden shopping carts in parking lots with their lives.

"Food," Marion said when she spotted a grocery store. It all dawned on us then. How much food did we have at Elk Cliffs Resort? Imanuel had booked caterers for the ceremony and reception, but how long would those leftovers last? How much was in their deep freezers for regular guests? How long would deep freezers last if the power went out? Would the power go out?

Rhino stayed outside with the guns, asking passersby for information. The rest of us went inside the shop and pulled everything we could find off the shelves. You, Paul, and Imanuel tried to look large and intimidating as Marion and I snatched whatever was left. Single shoppers approached, eyed the five of us, then slunk away for other aisles.

"Grab the rice," Marion hissed at me as we wheeled ourselves into the never-ending line to pay. I grabbed as many as I could. In a strange way, it reminded me almost of something she and I might have done in university with our friends, while too drunk: run to the campus food store just before it closed and play various games— who could fit inside the plastic shopping cart seat like a kid again, who could swipe an entire shelf into the basket at once without dropping a single item, who could finish their list first and race to the checkout line before the other teams. But no one was laughing this time.

"Please—I have children," a woman behind us said. We turned around. Her cart was a third as full as ours, with food half as useful. The shelves were almost bare by then. "I have children," she repeated. I wanted to crumble inside.

"We have children, too," Marion lied before any of us could answer. She knew me too well. She stepped in front of us, between me and the woman, so I had no choice but to set the rice back down into our own cart.

"Please," the woman said again, but weaker this time. "No, it's all right."

"Has it reached Arlington yet?" Paul asked her gently. "We're all—we're on vacation. With our kids. We only just found out."

"I don't know," she said. "But I think Maryland, at least. I saw something like that on the news. That's when I came here. My sons are still at home."

"It's in D.C.," the man in line ahead of us said. He held up his phone. "They caught a guy downtown near the Verizon Center this morning."

The woman moaned. She sank lower over her cart.

"How are we going to pay for this?" I suddenly whispered to you. "I didn't bring my purse." It was probably a month's worth of food, and all I had was a handful of crumpled bills in my jeans pocket from the day before, from when you had to pay a toll fee on the highway into Virginia from D.C., to reach Elk Cliffs.

"Put it on my card," Imanuel said. "Wedding expenses."

"Oh, God," the woman behind us said suddenly. We turned to look at her. She was holding her wallet as if it were white-hot porcelain, searing her fingers, but too precious to drop. "Oh, God." We all looked inside. The dark green ink on the bills had somehow vanished. The papers were completely blank.

"What the fuck," Marion said in horror. "What is that?"

"My children," the woman wailed. "I have to feed my children!"

"I'll pay for it!" I gasped. I was crying, terrified. I tried to shove whatever bills were in my pocket at her, desperately pressing them against her chest. Far at the front of the line, a fight broke out. People began to yell. Then we all realized that my money had become the same impossible blank things as well.

| II |

Three days after that, reports said that almost everyone in D.C. was now shadowless. We sat in circles around the main ballroom TV, cutting marshmallows into tiny pieces and eating them slowly, to make them last. The brand on the front of the bags was a name I couldn't read. The letters looked like they had once spelled something, but didn't quite look like letters anymore. Rhino suggested we start trying to hunt game for food in the forest around the resort with the guns.

| II |

Philadelphia, Baltimore, then Arlington. After that, Elk Cliffs Resort lost power, because we were on the Arlington grid.

| II |

The day after there was no more electricity, Rhino and Marion returned from the far side of the mountain stumbling under the weight of a small elk. The wedding band made a fire in the fancy stone pit in the courtyard using the strange, empty dollar bills as kindling. We burned it all. Not a single person kept even one piece.

We wanted it gone. They roasted the elk while you, me, and a couple of other guests from Paul's side went through what was left in the kitchen and separated it into "eat tonight, before it goes off," "eat within the next few days," and "save as long as we can."

The singer didn't want to sing that night, or anymore. The rest of the band played something instrumental, and we all feasted on elk steak, shrimp, random fillets of fish, and a metric fuckton of ice cream.

Tomorrow was going to be a lot worse than today, I realized dimly as I sat in front of the fire, digging around in my own personal gallon of mint chocolate chip. There was so much that every single guest got their own container. And the day after tomorrow was going to be a lot worse than tomorrow. Today was probably the last good day. After I finished that ice cream and crawled under our blankets with you and fell asleep it was never going to go back up again. Only down.

"Want some rocky road?" you asked, and we swapped. The chocolate fudge was so gooey and sweet that it made the glands at the back of my jaw pinch painfully. That was probably never going to happen again either. A kind of sweetness so artificially strong that it could make my mouth ache.

Suddenly I was crying again, before I even knew what was happening.

"I have to pee," I said hurriedly, and scrambled away from the fire before anyone else realized my eyes were swollen and red. I don't think you saw.

I stopped as soon as I left the manicured part of the hill and hit the trees, and found myself gulping desperately as I pressed the heels of my hands into my eyes. *I should have savored it more,* I thought. *I should have fought violently for my favorite flavor.* Then I realized someone else was already out here, probably doing the same thing in the trees.

"The ice cream?" Marion asked through the darkness.

I nodded. "It just . . ."—I tried to clear my throat—"it was so fucking good."

Marion snorted gently in agreement. I could tell she dug the toe of her shoe into the dirt only by the sound of it grinding.

"It's the phones for me," she murmured.

"Fuck," I said. Her husband and daughter were still in San Diego. He'd had to skip the wedding to take care of their little girl who'd caught the flu. "Fuck, Marion." I felt sick for having forgotten, in all the chaos. "What are you going to—"

"Don't," Marion said. "I can't think of it directly. Not yet."

I wanted to go to her, to hug her like we always did when one of us had just argued with a boyfriend or done poorly on an exam, but I didn't know how to. We stood there for a while, pushing rocks around with our feet instead, not saying anything.

There was no more ice cream. There was no more of a lot of things. But there was still you, Ory, here with me. That was something. That was more than hope.

Marion's outline, barely visible in the night, was leaning against a tree, holding some kind of leaf. It was so dark, I realized I couldn't tell if either of us still had a shadow anymore. I think that was the first time it occurred to me to wonder, and the last time I could ever have that thought without compulsively checking to make sure my own was still there. Of being able to do nothing else, not even breathe, until I saw that it was still a part of me.

"What do you think—" Marion spoke suddenly. "What do you think caused this?"

"I don't know," I said. It was true. I didn't—not for sure.

She laughed. It didn't sound much like a laugh. "Rob and I separated," she finally said. All the air went out of me. "Two weeks ago. Hallie doesn't have the flu. I was going to tell you at the reception, once we were drunk enough. But then Boston happened."

"Marion."

"I know it's not karma," she interrupted, cutting me off. "That would be—stupid. But I just can't help but . . ." She took a shaky breath. "You and Ory, Paul and Imanuel—happy. Here we all are at the end of the world, and you guys are here together. I'm the only one with marriage troubles—and look at where I am, where he is."

"It's not karma," I said, desperately. "Karma doesn't exist."

"I know," Marion replied. "But it sure seems like it, doesn't it?"

I didn't know what to say, but it didn't matter. I knew what she wanted me to know: that if she'd known somehow that it really was going to end now—not in some far future time, but now, right now— she never would have left him. She would have cherished all the moments. We waited in silence for what felt like hours.

"I'm going back now," I finally said. I couldn't think of anything to comfort her. There was nothing to say, without looking at the truth of it head on—no way to offer hope without also reminding her that she might never see them again.

"I'm going to stay," Marion answered.

When I reemerged from the woods and sat down beside you again at the fire, Rhino was standing, stating to the group that he was going to drag his blankets out onto the grass after we put the fire out, because now that there was no electricity and therefore no air conditioning, it was going to be disgustingly hot in the ballroom where we were all camped out.

He wasn't really announcing it, I knew as I watched him. It was more that he was trying to ask the rest of us to join him without begging outright. For comfort in numbers. I realized that none of us had even tried sleeping in our individual guest rooms once. After the wedding reception had been interrupted by the news about Boston, we'd all banded together in the ballroom and never left, save to retrieve our suitcases and bring them back down. The courtyard where Rhino wanted to sleep was a couple hundred feet from where the rest of us were still set up inside. Nine days ago, that wouldn't have been enough distance for me to be from a random stranger. Now it felt terrifyingly far.

"That's a good idea," you said. "Let's all move out here."

Over the top of the flames, Rhino looked at you so gratefully it made my eyes tear again.

# MAHNAZ AHMADI

THE NIGHT NAZ CONSIDERED KILLING HERSELF, SHE SAW HER sister again.

It was a few weeks after she finally took the Bluetooth headset off. She wasn't sure of the exact date, but it was snowing outside, which meant she'd been in the studio for four or five months by then. Hiding, talking to herself, and beginning to starve. She'd rationed well, but there was no food left in the entire building anymore, or in the duffel bag. She'd gone out a few times to the roof, but all she could see beyond the vast, empty parking lot was darkness and the glow of flashing police lights, and all she could hear were the echoing sounds of people crying or being killed. She had her bow, but it was no good in situations like that. In the open or one-on-one, she might win. But against a crowd, in a city, a bow was almost useless. In close quarters, she'd never stop every single one of a gang before one of them reached her and took her down.

She planned to jump. Or at least think about jumping, soon. Before the hunger made her too weak to find a quicker, more dignified death than starvation. Her mother had almost starved once, she'd told her. When the times were very bad. It was a way of leaving life that Naz never wanted to experience.

But that night, there was a small, solitary shape standing uncertainly in the center of the parking lot. A woman.

The sight didn't frighten Naz. She assumed the woman was just a ghost. Naz had seen the apparitions of her sister so many times after the phone cut off—in the hall, across the room, sleeping beside her. Why not also lurking among the empty car spaces, looking up at her? She was about to ask it to point out some constellations, for old times' sake.

But then she saw that the ghost had a shadow.

"Mahnaz?" it called softly.

Naz was down every flight of stairs and out the front door before she even realized it. "Rojan?" she was screaming.

Rojan had run for the entrance too, and had been pulling on the front door before Naz had made it to the ground floor and flipped the lock. They tumbled backward into the dark warehouse in a tangle of limbs, and then clambered to slam the door shut behind them and do up the locks again.

"You promised. You *promised*," Naz kept wailing, over and over. "You promised you wouldn't do this. You promised you wouldn't come."

Rojan was clinging to her so hard she could feel her skin going numb and bloodless on the parts of her arms where Rojan held them. They kissed each other's cheeks until they had smeared the tears all over their faces, until all she could taste or see or breathe was stinging salt. "Thank God you're here." Rojan sniffed, and kissed her again. "I was so scared—I thought I'd finally make it here and you already would have left or something."

"You—you—" Naz could barely speak between the heaving sobs. The miraculousness of it was finally starting to pierce the anger. "You're really here."

"I'm sorry," she said. "I know I said I—" She reached down and pulled a wad of paper out of her pockets—handfuls of notes she'd made, neighborhood maps she'd tried to draw, descriptions of the building she was looking for—everything she'd written down from their phone conversations. "I just couldn't let you be alone."

"But how did you get all the way here from Tehran?" Naz interrupted. "How did you even get out of the house without Maman freaking out?"

"What do you mean, 'Maman freaking out'?" Rojan shook her head. "She's the only reason I *did* make it here. You think I just had thousands and thousands of U.S. dollars lying around in my student dormitory room for a plane ticket?"

Naz stared at her. "But—" She couldn't finish.

"The day after your phone died, she gave me everything she had. Emptied out her accounts. She *told* me to find you."

Naz was shaking. "She . . . she . . . she helped you come here?" She ran her hands up and down Rojan's arms over and over, as if each time she did it she might discover Rojan wasn't real. But she was. And she was in Boston. And now she was going to die, too. "Here? *Here?!*" Naz was screaming again, unable to control herself. "Didn't she hear me? What this place is like? Why would she help you come here? Why would you do it?!"

"There was a case in Tehran," Rojan said softly. Naz fell into a stunned, paralyzed silence as the words sunk in. *There was a case in Tehran. There was a case in Tehran.* The words echoed in her mind, over and over. *There was a case in Tehran. It was everywhere now.* Rojan looked down at her hands as Naz swayed. "Naz, she *made* me come."

Naz heard what more her little sister meant to say. *Because she wanted us to be together at the end.*

They both sat in silence in the darkness. Naz reached out and took Rojan's hand and held it, and they stayed that way for a long time.

"It had only just happened—the shadowlessness. Tehran Airport wasn't a madhouse yet. I got to London fairly easily. But Heathrow was not what I expected. I got stuck there in 'departures' for almost two months. I couldn't find a flight out that was going to the United States. All the airlines had just stopped going there. I ate out of the vending machines—they were having to refill them twice a day, there were so many of us. Finally I overheard someone saying Switzerland might be making U.S. flights, or was making flights to somewhere that was making U.S. flights. I managed to get to Zurich a week or two after that, through Geneva. In Zurich, I found out the closest to Boston anyone was flying was Providence, in Rhode Island," Rojan finally continued. "I mean, the sign said Boston, but they told us they were really flying to Providence—because it was safer, because for some reason that city is almost empty of people now—and we'd have to make our own way from there. They were charging—I don't even know. I just kept throwing money at the counterperson out of Maman's savings until the lady gave me a ticket. Someone tried to rob me after that, but the airport staff beat him off. I went in the bathroom and put everything I had left in my bra and underwear then. Not like it was much."

"What happened in Providence?"

Rojan shrugged. "The guy sitting next to me on the flight said he has a daughter here in Boston somewhere. I gave him the rest of what I had in exchange for a seat in his rental car. Well, the car he found in the rental car parking lot and hot-wired. We split up at the roadblock on the freeway just outside city limits."

"Fuck," Naz said. "He could have killed you or something."

"I—yeah," Rojan admitted. "I kind of—I kind of can't believe I did it now. I just didn't know how else to get here."

They sat close, shoulders touching, as they ate the last of the bags of airplane peanuts the stewardess had generously gifted Rojan on the flight. Naz's stomach ached ravenously. It was more food than she'd had in a long time. "So . . . what now?" she asked.

THEY DECIDED TO HEAD FOR NEW YORK, BECAUSE THAT WAS the only place nearby that Rojan thought she hadn't seen come up on the news by the time she left Tehran. It struck them as a little funny—that of course it would be New York that would survive when the shit hit the fan. "Things weirder than this probably happen in New York every day," Rojan joked as she held open the duffel bag while Naz packed it with what little they could take from the studio.

"That's just movie New York," Naz said, but still, a part of her had hope. If anywhere in the United States was still functional, she couldn't help but believe it would be New York, too. Although even if it wasn't, nothing was going to be worse than Boston. "Take off your necklaces," she added. "They draw too much attention."

"They're Maman's," Rojan protested. "I'm not just going to leave them here."

"Wrap them up and put them in the bag, then. You can't wear them."

Rojan obeyed, reaching for a pillowcase. "How long do you think it'll take on foot?" she asked.

"If we really rush, ten days, maybe?"

Rojan nodded. "Good thing I packed soap."

Naz smiled. She didn't have the heart to tell her sister that they weren't going to stop long enough at any point to allow washed fabric to dry, so there'd be no washing anyway. But they could survive each with a few pairs of underwear and the same bra. The bow was what she really needed to make sure they were safe, once they got out into the open country.

They had to get out first, though. The roadblocks were still in place all over the city, held by police and emergency military personnel, the main streets all locked down. There was only one place left the government couldn't monitor very well.

"The water." Rojan grinned.

It was how she'd avoided the roadblocks and reached Naz in the first place, it turned out. After watching the man she'd shared a ride with turned away by police in riot gear carrying huge machine guns, Rojan had decided she didn't want to press her luck and started hunting for an unguarded street—but she couldn't find one. Sooner or later, she always ran into another roadblock or a roving patrol, blue and red lights dazzling the night. By accident she found herself crouching behind a small overturned boat in a trash heap to hide from a passing cluster of police, and that's when she got the idea.

"I dragged it up onto the bank where I came out and tried to hide it in the bushes," she said. "I can show you where from the roof."

Once they were ready, they went up for the last time. Rojan walked to the far side of the roof and pointed. From Dorchester Street, it was just a few turns from the shore of Old Harbor, where she was sure the boat was hidden. They waited until 1:30 A.M. exactly and then ran down the road as silently as they could in the pitch-blackness. Sure enough, the little metal boat was there, stuffed into the shrubs. As they dragged it the last few yards to the shore, Naz stepped into the icy water by accident with one foot and gasped in agony.

"Naz!" Rojan whispered, panicked.

"Fuck, that's cold!" Naz hissed.

"Don't do that! I thought something was wrong!"

"Something *is* wrong!" she snapped, but she shut up. Her sister was right, she could be freezing later. Rojan climbed into the boat and set her backpack and the duffel bag down, then put out a hand. Naz slipped the bow over her shoulder and grabbed Rojan's palm.

They rolled up their sleeves and paddled with their hands until their fingers were numb, because there were no oars. They drifted south, south, south. At some point in the darkness, they bumped into something floating. Naz's first thought was that it was a body, but thank God it wasn't—it was just a piece of wood.

When they finally found a shore that seemed far enough away, they crawled out of their own dinghy and crept between the carcasses of other half-sunk boats to the asphalt.

"Heritage Drive." Rojan read the street sign overhead softly. She looked at Naz expectantly, waiting to hear if they'd gone far enough, if they were clear of Boston proper and the roadblocks.

"I think we're okay," Naz muttered, dumbfounded. Somehow they'd paddled all the way to Quincy. *How far was that?* She tried to estimate. *Five, six miles?* "Let's go slow." She pulled the bow off her back and kept it ready. The streets were even more unnervingly still than from where they'd come.

On the back wall of the next building, glowing under the flickering light of a roof security lamp, someone had graffitied a phrase in spray-paint.

"The One Who Gathers?" Rojan read softly. The name sent a chill through Naz as her sister said it. Rojan reached out and touched the bottom drip of paint—it was long dry. "What on earth do you think it means?"

Naz shook her head slowly. "I have no idea," she said.

# THE ONE WHO GATHERS

LATER, HE CAME TO HAVE MANY NAMES. THE ONE WITH A Middle but No Beginning. The Stillmind. Patient RA. Last, most important of all—The One Who Gathers. But in the beginning, he had no name at all.

Once he had recovered enough to walk on his own, he was discharged from the hospital and moved to an assisted-living facility, to begin therapy with a specialist named Dr. Zadeh. This was years ago, some three months before that ominous May day when Hemu Joshi became the first man to lose his shadow. It was still early spring where he lived, in New Orleans—the sun rose late and set early in the gently crisp air there. Dr. Zadeh had come to him in the ICU on the first day, once the surgeons told him that his new patient was awake.

Things were a blur then. Emptiness and fear. He couldn't lift his head or speak. The nurses were so harried that none of them realized he might want to know what was going on, let alone stopped to tell him. But then Dr. Zadeh strode in with his starched lab coat, pen in hand, clipboard bursting with papers that must contain answers, and looked directly at him. Not at his vitals monitor, or his Frankenstein's monster scalp incision, but at *him*. The man felt a chill when he did it. Until that moment, the man hadn't been entirely sure he was alive at all.

"I'm Dr. Zadeh," the doctor said. He spoke slowly and clearly. "You are in Ochsner Baptist Medical Center, in New Orleans. You were involved in a car crash and suffered injuries. Some of them were very serious. You were in a coma for a week, but you're out of the woods now. Blink once if you understand."

*Yyyyyh,* he tried. His mind could not will his tongue.

Finally he gave up trying to speak, and blinked once. It felt strange, as if only one eye had done it.

"Good," Dr. Zadeh said, so encouragingly that he felt as if he'd accomplished something superhuman. "I'm going to ask you a few questions to better understand where we are with your recovery, and then I'll be able to give you more information. I want you to blink once to mean yes. Blink twice to mean no. Do you understand?"

The man blinked once.

"All right. First, are you in pain?"

He stared at the ceiling. Slowly things darkened and then brightened again twice in a row, to mean *no*. Blink, blink. The drugs were good. In fact, they were so good that he almost wanted pain—only so he could know that the rest of him was still there, on the bed.

"That's excellent, excellent. If you ever are in pain, I want you to blink very rapidly and continue until I notice. I'll be able to adjust your dosage immediately through your IV and then find the surgeon on duty."

He blinked again once, to indicate he understood. Dr. Zadeh took a slow, thoughtful breath. The man waited, curious. He couldn't imagine a single thing the doctor might want to know. He couldn't move or feel, or really even think. He seemed to just exist—nothing more. "Do you know your name?" Dr. Zadeh asked.

*Oh,* the man thought. *How strange.*

"I need you to blink your answer to me," Dr. Zadeh reminded him gently. "Do you know your name?"

Blink, blink.

"Thank you," Dr. Zadeh said in a practiced, neutral way. "Next question. Do you know to where you were going in your car when you had the accident?"

The man looked at the walls, then the ceiling. His eyelids shuttered twice.

"Thank you. Do you know what city you grew up in?"

Blink, blink.

"Thank you. Do you know where you went to school?"

He hadn't realized that such things as cities and schools existed. Then as soon as Dr. Zadeh said the words, he could name the names of a hundred of them—but not a single thing about himself. Except that he had eyelids. Blink, blink. He waited for the next question. Blink, blink. Then the next. Blink, blink. Gradually the ceiling grew hot, then wetly blurry.

AFTER HE'D HEALED ENOUGH TO BE ABLE TO SPEAK EASILY again, the man was told more of what had happened. In the rain, the car on the other side of the street had hydroplaned. He'd swerved to avoid a head-on collision and rolled his own vehicle down the side of a hill. It had been pouring so hard that night, the other driver didn't realize where the man's car had gone, the police report stated later. That it wasn't still on the dark road, traveling safely away in the other direction. It was another passing driver who noticed the headlights, like two stars in the black, but floating far too low to be in the sky. The man had been wearing a seat belt, but something went wrong. His head still hit the windshield twice, fracturing his skull and one eye socket. Underneath the gauze patch on the left side of his face, there wouldn't be an eye, he was warned ahead of the bandage's removal. There had been nothing left there to save. The man listened to it all, waiting for any fragment of that terrifying crash to hit him again. But there was nothing.

Dr. Zadeh spent a full week on his assessment. Brain scans, endless questions, more brain scans. He came in one day without his clipboard and sat on the edge of the man's white hospital bed. Total retrograde amnesia, from the moment of the accident, Dr. Zadeh told him softly. He was born at forty-two years old. A man with a middle, but no beginning.

THE ASSISTED-LIVING FACILITY WORKED MOSTLY WITH ALZ-heimer's patients, but Dr. Zadeh managed to secure him a room there. He was one of the foremost neurologists in the country, the man learned from a fellow resident during a game of bingo. The hospital funded the facility for Dr. Zadeh in exchange for his research. The man became his star patient.

Every morning Dr. Zadeh gave him another test or watched him practice something he'd learned in afternoon rehab the day before. The man grew skilled at reciting his personal information from the flash cards he'd made, but it was worth nothing. It was like learning the stale, meaningless biography of another person. He didn't want to know that he learned how to sail in high school. He wanted to singe his palms on the rough rope, breathe salty air. He wanted to feel whether he had hated it or loved it.

He should have clung to it, but he began to despise the name that was stated on his driver's license. It was not him. It was someone else, whom he was never allowed to know but also not allowed to forget.

The other patients could feel it. Small parts of them inside understood. They began to call him anything but that name. *The newcomer. The young one. The car-crash lad.* Most often, because it was not Alzheimer's that stole his past but an accident: *the amnesiac.* The man—the amnesiac—loved them for it.

Midway through the first week, Tilly, who at a hundred and three years old had the revered title of oldest person in the facility, grinned at him as she was wheeled past. "You have a visitor today, Henny-kins," she sang.

"That's not your Hennykins," her nurse said gently. Hennykins was what she had called her youngest son, Henry, when he was a baby, when she remembered that she had a son.

"Of course it is," she said. She eyed the nurse. "Who are you, though?"

"You actually do have a visitor," Dr. Zadeh said, coming up behind him.

A visitor? Someone had come to see him? The amnesiac stood speechless for a moment. It was a weightless, dizzy feeling. There was a person in the building who had known him from before.

He didn't know which way to walk, so he started walking in circles until Dr. Zadeh led him hurriedly to one of the community rooms. "Take it easy," he said to the amnesiac kindly. "I'll be right outside if you need anything, all right?"

Inside, a middle-aged woman with shoulder-length blond hair jumped stiffly to her feet as the amnesiac closed the door behind himself. They both stood there, staring at each other. The amnesiac waited to feel the sensation that had been described to him as familiarity—a wave, a warm rush, a tingle, a lightning bolt. Nothing.

"My God," the woman said. She put a hand over her mouth.

*Oh, my eye,* he realized. She must have known him when he'd had two. "Hello," he finally said back.

"How are you feeling?" she asked. She paused before she sat back down on the couch. She was trying to decide whether or not she should hug him, the amnesiac deduced. They knew each other at least somewhat well, then.

"Very well, thank you," he replied. He went to the armchair across from her. The next line came out automatically, more like a long musical phrase rather than distinct words, he had practiced it so many times. "I'm sure Dr. Zadeh told you, but I suffered neuro-logical complications from my accident. Would you kindly tell me your name, and how we know each other?"

"Um. Of course." The woman shifted awkwardly and tucked her hair behind her ear. She was not pretty, the amnesiac decided. That was not the word he'd use. "My name is Charlotte. We went to college together."

"Oh, yes. I have a bachelor's degree in history," he recited. He watched her for another long moment. The way she had answered made it seem like not the full truth. Not a lie; just not everything. The flash cards said he did not have a sister. "Did you also study history?"

"No, anthropology." She smiled. "Very marketable."

"Did you become an anthropologist?"

Charlotte laughed. "I'm in marketing. Data storage company." She uncrossed her legs, crossed them again the other way. "You—you also didn't end up becoming a historian," she offered.

"No." The amnesiac nodded. "I went into law." So were the facts.

"Yes, I know." She smiled.

That excited him. "Did I enjoy law school? How did I seem there?" he asked.

Charlotte pressed her lips together. "Well, probably no one *enjoys* law school—it's a lot of studying, a lot of competition. But I think you enjoyed being a lawyer. You always seemed passionate when you talked about your job."

"I'm glad," he said. That was very nice. He was happy he had liked being a lawyer. Charlotte pushed her hair behind her ear again and clasped her hands. It struck him then. *Fixed.* That was the word he would use. He meant it in the best of ways. He felt as though he was spinning around the world, unanchored, careening all the time. But for Charlotte, the world spun around her. He could feel it. She did not move an inch. She was the most fixed thing he'd found so far.

"I'm sorry I didn't come sooner," she blurted suddenly. "This was as early as—I didn't know you'd been in an accident. Dr. Zadeh only called me last week. I guess it took them some time to work everything out off your driver's license. Who you were, everyone you might have known."

"It's all right," he said. It really was. He hadn't known to miss her at all.

Charlotte tried not to fidget. She was trying to look at him intently without actually looking at him.

"You can ask me anything," the amnesiac said. "I don't mind."

"So you remember nothing? Nothing from before you woke up in the hospital?"

He shook his head. "The first thing I remember is a nurse. She was leaning over me, trying to adjust my IV bag, when my eyes opened."

"But you remembered what an IV bag is."

"Yes."

"And how to talk."

"Yes."

"Could you walk? And dress and eat?"

"Well, at first everything was too broken for me to move. But once I healed, then yes."

Charlotte leaned back on the couch. "Huh," she said to herself, mystified. "Huh." The plate of cookies the facility staff had supplied for the visit sat untouched on the coffee table between them. He thought she might be about to cry.

The amnesiac understood then what she wanted. Why her answers were true but incomplete. The answer was no. No, no matter how long she sat there with him, he would not suddenly remember her on his own.

Dr. Zadeh suddenly appeared in a burst of starched cotton and papers. He was the way he was when on the verge of another idea to test on the amnesiac—excited, moving at double speed. He seemed to have forgotten that they were mid-visit, that Charlotte was even there. "Sorry to interrupt," he managed at last, aiming a remote at the sleeping television in the corner of the room. He looked at the amnesiac as the screen blinked on. It was a festival of some kind, it seemed. At the center of all the colors, there was a man. A man with no shadow beneath him. "You have to see this."

THE AMNESIAC SAT BACK AND SETTLED HIS ELBOWS ON THE armrests. The chair was uncomfortably small. "Have I ever been on a plane before?" he asked.

"Many times, I'm sure," Dr. Zadeh said as he fastened his own seat belt.

The amnesiac nodded, considering. The endless, low droning sound that filled the cabin of the plane made him feel like he was back in the hospital, hooked up to something. He wouldn't notice it after a while, Dr. Zadeh had promised. "Have I ever been to India before?"

"That you have not," Dr. Zadeh replied. "The consulate didn't have any record of previous tourist visa applications under your name when I filed for this one."

The amnesiac nodded. "Good."

"Good?"

"This will be my first experience that hasn't actually already happened before." He smiled. "My first real memory."

THE FLIGHT WAS VERY LONG. BUT NOT AS LONG AS HE HAD laid locked into his broken body in the hospital. The amnesiac sat comfortably. Any amount of time that was shorter than three weeks, he imagined he'd be able to tolerate quite easily. The plane sailed through the sky. He waited.

They brought a meal around. It looked different from the food at the assisted-living facility. He had never seen anything like it. Or perhaps he had. He took note to ask Charlotte about it at her next visit, to see if she knew.

"Lamb vindaloo." Dr. Zadeh pointed with his fork. "It's pretty good."

"It is," the amnesiac agreed. "Is this Indian food?"

"Not even close." Dr. Zadeh grinned. "This is airplane Indian food."

An hour later, he had finished the tea they gave him. It was strange how it worked, retrograde amnesia. He knew what tea was, what India was. He knew the words for everything, and all their meanings. He knew people spoke English in Pune—among other local dialects—as all schooling was taught in English in India. When he heard that Hemu Joshi played cricket, he realized he knew what cricket was, the rough idea of the game, even what the ball itself looked like. But he couldn't say for the life of him if he'd ever seen one with his own eyes—eye.

He wondered if it was like this for Hemu Joshi, too. Inside, he thrilled at the knowledge that he would meet him soon. Someone else who would understand what it was to be like himself—or *not* himself, rather. He hoped it would work. That one of them might somehow teach the other something and unravel this mystery.

He turned to Dr. Zadeh, but the doctor had fallen asleep while looking over the amnesiac's file again, leaving it open on his foldout tray table. The amnesiac slid it to his own.

He read the police account of the car crash again, and the paramedic's report. A collection of colorful ovals filled one page. *My brain,* he thought. They seemed bright enough, he guessed. He didn't know which part meant that his memories had been knocked loose. His visitation log was also there. Charlotte's basic information. Name, phone number, relationship to patient. Ex-wife.

Another fact to add to his collection. He had been married once. For a moment, it didn't mean anything. Then it did.

"Charlotte," he said. He waited for the name to sound different now, but it didn't.

Dr. Zadeh stirred. His eyes opened, beholding the man drowsily. They settled on the file open in front of him. His whole face sharpened, coming to life.

The amnesiac pointed at the paper on top. "My ex-wife," he said again. He swallowed. "That was cruel of you. *Cruel.*"

Dr. Zadeh looked down. "I'm sorry. That wasn't the way I wanted you to find out."

It wasn't good enough. "Wasn't the way you wanted me to find out? How could you do that? How could you keep that from me?"

"I had no idea she wouldn't tell you," he said back. "When she didn't, I—I felt wrong betraying her confidence without speaking to her first."

"Her confidence?" the amnesiac snapped. "What about *my* confidence? I'm your patient. I'm the one you're supposed to help. I'm the one who doesn't know who he is. Even *you* know more than I do!"

"I—"

"Yes, you do. You knew who she was! You want me to get better? Why tell me some things and withhold others? Are you trying to—to *curate* me? What else do you know that I don't?"

"Noth—"

"Shut up! Just shut up!"

"Sir!" the flight attendant cried.

"Please, it's all right," Dr. Zadeh said to her. "Everything's under control. We're the medical case on your passenger register. We've been invited by the prime minister."

The flight attendant narrowed her eyes. Dr. Zadeh was holding his passport out so she could verify his name, but she moved on with no more than a warning nod to him, ignoring the document. She had already known where they were sitting, the amnesiac realized. Everyone in the world knew who he was but him.

He sucked in a breath so he could start shouting at Dr. Zadeh again as soon as the flight attendant was far enough away, but he glimpsed a sliver of the sky through the window as he shifted in his seat.

The pure blue, the white. The clouds were so thick and rippled he couldn't see the ground. Above, empty; beneath, endless silvered fog.

He pressed his forehead to the cool safety glass. "Enough . . . ," he trailed off. The clouds glided by below. They remembered nothing either. They drifted, they rained. How had he forgotten how beautiful they were? Somehow that hurt most of all. How was it possible to forget something like this? "I can't think clearly and look at the clouds at the same time."

"I'm sorry," Dr. Zadeh murmured again. The plane relaxed into a curve of warm wind, a gentle lingering dip, then out. The amnesiac realized that it was true—he barely noticed the drone of the engines anymore.

"Dr. Zadeh," he said softly.

"Yes?"

"Do I have any children?"

"No," Dr. Zadeh said, wounded. The amnesiac looked at him. "No. I promise you. No."

THE DAYS MELTED TOGETHER IN THOSE EARLY MONTHS AT Elk Cliffs Resort. Even in the mountains, the heat was oppressive, humid and heavy, like a forest swamp. Do you remember that, Ory? The nights were only barely better. It was as if the breeze had stopped when all the shadows did, the air still and thick between the trees, the grass beneath us so warm that I could barely stand to touch you as we slept, as much as I wanted to feel the comfort of your arms around me, the solidness of your body. I began to dream about air conditioning, vivid hallucinations that made my skin prickle at the imagined chill.

It almost felt like camping, on the good days. Sleeping in the grass, blankets stretched into tents over our heads. Everyone had agreed it was temporary, just because of the heat, but after a while I couldn't imagine moving back inside to the ballroom, even if there was frost on the ground. I think it was because we were all inside when we found out the shadowlessness had reached us. Being in there at night brought it all back too vividly. It was like the building itself remembered.

After a month, things started to change. People began leaving. First three slipped silently away in the night, too cowardly to say goodbye properly, and a fourth ended up sobbing hysterically by the fire as she tried to explain why she had to go. Libby, from Paul's side of the guest list. They had been on the high school swim team together, you told me later. Paul walked her all the way down the mountain, arm in arm, and came back crying. That night around the fire, I heard more people whispering about when it might be their time to leave, too. When it might be too soon, just right, too late. Whether they lived near enough that it might be worth the risk, or too far. I watched you through the flames as you eavesdropped. Your and Paul's families were still in Portland, where you both had grown up, but all of mine were in Maryland—a survivable distance from Elk Cliffs. We'd seen reports about Baltimore on television before the signal had gone out, but if there was anything left, maybe they were left, too. We could make it if we tried.

But how to convince you? I'd been waiting for the right moment for weeks. You hadn't been ready to hear it. I felt like I had only one chance—and if I blew it, we'd never leave.

"The second scouting party didn't come back," Rabbi Levenson said when Paul and Imanuel brought the idea of going up again. We'd sent the second party out one week after the electricity had gone down at the resort. There had been fierce debate over forming a third one after that—questions about whether we were sending the last survivors on earth to their deaths, or possibly worse, alerting dangerous people, shadowed or shadowless, to our secret haven—but in the end we had to do it. There was nothing—no television, no cell phone network, no internet, no radio—or at least nothing that we could pick up. We had no other way to know what had happened down below. Rhino had led that group too, with one of the shotguns. They never came back.

"What else are we going to do?" someone argued.

Rabbi Levenson persisted. "We don't know what's out there. We can't put any of us in such danger. It isn't fair to ask."

"Then we'll only accept volunteers, like the first time."

"The risk is too great. We're all we have left."

"So we should just stay up here forever?" Paul's voice was loud, on the border of threatening. Just weeks ago, he'd been smiling, tears of joy streaming down his face as he stood trembling with Imanuel before the old man. To watch him face off against the rabbi now, red-eyed, was deeply unsettling. Some of us were trying to calm him down; some of us were already shouting over him, demanding the third scouting party be formed.

"We have to figure out why it's happening!"

"It's too dangerous!"

"We're going to die up here if we just wait, then!"

"What are we even waiting for?"

"The last group didn't come back!"

"I'll go again," Marion said. Everyone fell silent. I looked down before she could make eye contact with me, ashamed that I wasn't brave enough to volunteer once more as well. The fire hissed as it ate a fresher twig of pine, then quieted again.

"Me too," Jae-suk said, and rose from the grass. On the other side of the flames, Lauren and Pierce also stood.

⏸

They returned a week later; all had survived. I almost didn't believe it when I heard until I ran back to the courtyard and saw them cresting the summit, climbing over the low decorative stone wall. You, Paul, and Imanuel were already there, pressing glasses of boiled river water into their hands. Jae-suk's wife was sobbing with joy, clinging to him.

"Did you see any signs of the second group?" I asked after they'd finished hugging everyone.

Jae-suk shook his head. "After the mountain—just, nothing."

"We did bring back a bunch of first-aid kits, though, from some of the abandoned stores," Marion said. "And a jacket. We found one jacket. For later, I guess." She had her right arm tucked tightly against her, as though sprained or fractured somewhere.

I took off your button-down that I had been wearing over my T-shirt for sun cover and wrapped it around her arm protectively, like a sling. "Imanuel needs to look at that," I said to her. Imanuel was an obstetrician, but he was the closest thing we all had to a paramedic.

"It's an arm, not a baby." She smiled. Everyone burst out laughing, it seemed so funny. We were all just so relieved they'd made it back.

There wasn't much more to the third team's report. They'd walked until they reached downtown Arlington and then gone through every home and shop, cautiously at first, then desperately, then hopelessly, searching for survivors. Buildings were burned or emptied out, windows smashed, doors crushed in. If there were any shadowed survivors in hiding, they must have been too afraid to make contact. The group was late back because they got lost a few times, because there inexplicably seemed to be streets through the city that hadn't been there before. At that early time, none of us understood how that could have been possible.

■

The camp began to divide that afternoon, around the embers of the fire that was about to be lit for the evening. Half of us thought it was still too early and too dangerous, and the other half maintained that the worst of it had happened. If there was a time to go, that time was now. Sweat trickled down the small of my back and soaked into the waist of my pants. I watched you watch the rest of them argue, trying to determine which side you were on. And I watched Imanuel. You and Paul's families were too far away to hope to reach, but Imanuel was originally from Philadelphia—and Baltimore was on the way to Philadelphia. The four of us together, at least until Maryland, was the best plan we were ever going to get. I'd seen the way Imanuel had watched the ones who were leaving lately. He was growing more and more ready to leave too, just like I was.

*Maybe I will talk to him and Paul,* I thought. See if together, the three of us could convince you that we should go with them.

That was when we heard the screaming.

■

I sat outside as you, Paul, Imanuel, Rabbi Levenson, and Gabe talked quietly in the ballroom. I'd been invited, but I refused to participate. Instead I watched the darkness, listened to the wood creaking as the trees shifted in the breeze. For once, I couldn't feel the sauna-thick night air. I couldn't feel anything at all.

"What do we do?" I heard you ask faintly through the closed glass doors.

Marion's shadow had disappeared.

⏸

The rest of the search party was all right so far, but the guests were too terrified to take any chances. They had been with Marion. Jae-suk was quarantined in room 382 of the resort—with his wife, Ye-eun, who refused to be separated from him—and Pierce and Lauren in rooms 390 and 392 respectively. They had to be persuaded at gun-point. Marion went willingly into room 300.

"Marion—" I said in the moment before Gabe, a T-shirt wrapped around his face, pulled the door shut on her and locked it. Her eyes jerked up to mine for a single instant. There was something terrifying in them, a desperate ferocity to hang on to that name. "Marion," I said again, leaning against the smooth, silent wood on the outside of the door.

I never told you what I did during those three long days, Ory, while the camp debated what to do. Not because I wanted to hide it from you, but because you would've convinced yourself that I had been "contaminated," but been too afraid to say anything, because you'd never be able to consign me to the same fate. I just didn't want you to worry.

"What's your name?" I asked quietly through the door.

"Marion," Marion replied, slightly muffled. I imagined her sitting in the same position as me.

"Where are you?"

"The honeymoon suite, I think," she said.

I laughed despite the grim situation. It came out like a snort.

"Going okay so far, I guess," she continued after a few minutes. "It's only been a day, though."

"A day and a night," I countered.

"How are the others doing?" she asked hesitantly.

I chewed my lip.

"Max," she said.

"I don't know," I admitted. "I haven't visited. Their rooms are all too close together. Easier to be seen."

"Is there a guard?"

"Sort of. Just Gabe, at the main door. I keep coming in the back, through a door in the lounge. No one else wants to get too close, so no one's really checking the inside of the building."

I imagined her mulling it over on her side of the door. Wondering why I was just inches away from her then. "So you don't know if . . . if any of them have lost their shadows yet." It was both a question and a wish, that they were still all right.

I left and found you after a short while, so you didn't notice I'd been gone, but I was back with her after dinner, saying I was going to help the cooking crew with the washing-up at the river.

Do you know what's a horrible, dehumanizing thing to have to do, Ory? To wait for someone to squish food so flat it can fit through the crack between the bottom of the door and the floor, and then eat it off the carpet like that, licking the dirty, shoe-stained fibers.

"I don't know how to get you water," I said helplessly.

"It's okay," Marion murmured after a long time. "There was—in the bathroom."

I closed my eyes in shame. She was having to drink from the toilet. We sat for what seemed like an hour in silence.

"What's your name?" I asked at last.

"I still remember, Max," she said. She shifted. I heard her try to swallow and barely succeed, the dry sides of her throat sticking together. "Do you think they're hoping to starve or dehydrate us to death? Is that the plan?"

"I don't know," I answered. "I think everyone's just too afraid that if they open the doors, you'll all run out and . . . touch them or something. That you wouldn't cooperate and stay back. We're just trying to figure out what to do."

Marion sighed, long and slow. "Did you see me when we all first realized it had happened?"

"I didn't," I said. "I wasn't there."

I heard her change position again on her side of the carpet. I realized that I couldn't see anything shift through the tiny gap under the door. It was so strange. My senses went numb from the confusion. It was like hearing one person say something while watching someone else move her lips.

"Oh," Marion finally said.

"What?"

"What's this place called?" she asked. "I forgot."

By the end of the next day, Marion wasn't talking much, weak from the dehydration. Whatever was in the porcelain bowl must have been long finished, and it was just so hot, without the air conditioning and being unable to open the safety catches on the windows. The day was bright, but when I crept into the empty hall, I was dripping wet. She was dying of thirst, and it was raining, but only outside her side of the building. I tried to stop thinking about what it might mean. I tried not to think about it at all. And I didn't tell anyone. I couldn't; they'd know I was sneaking in.

I just wanted to fix her arm—that was the only thing about it all that *could* be fixed. I felt like it was my fault for not saving her. I was the reason Marion was here. I had been her friend. I had introduced her to Paul and Imanuel once you and I had gotten serious, trying to combine our social circles. I had begged her to take the flight, to see all of us again after so many years. But I didn't know how to bring her shadow back or stop her from forgetting. The room was starting to smell faintly of shit, from whatever corner she was relieving herself in. When she did speak, it was a strange mix of piercing detail and huge vague swaths. She recalled one of her two names—her first but not her last. She remembered that we were at a wedding but not where it was or who had gotten married, that I was her friend but not what my name was.

"Why am I in here?" she asked again for the third time.

"You're . . . sick," was all I could think of to say.

"Sick," she repeated. I heard her shift again, saw nothing move on the floor. "I don't feel well."

I didn't tell her it was because she was dehydrating to death. "They promised to make a decision by the morning," I offered. "To figure something out by the third day."

"It's been two days?" she asked. I tried to remember how it was reported to have been with Hemu Joshi. She seemed to be forgetting much faster than he had.

The last time I visited her, at dawn on the third day, I was surprised to hear her already awake.

"Do I know you?" she asked as I sat down.

"Yes," I said.

"Okay," she said.

We both waited awhile, until it felt normal for me to be sitting there again. "My name is Max," I finally told her.

"Max . . . ," she said to herself, as if rolling the word around in her mouth. I felt cold as I sat there. She really didn't remember me at all.

"Marion." I scooted closer and dropped my voice.

"What is a Marion?"

We sat in silence for a long time. "What's it like? To forget everything?" I asked softly. "Are you afraid?"

She settled against the door. "Maybe I was," she said. "But now I'm not. Now it just feels . . . simple. It probably seems terrible, but it's not. I just . . . At first I was angry. But every day I forget more. Maybe I'll forget so much I won't remember what I've lost, or that I've lost anything at all. You can't miss what you don't know you had, can you?"

*Do you remember Hallie?* I wanted to ask her. *Do you remember your daughter? Your husband?* "Do you know what karma is?" I finally whispered.

"No," she answered.

When I left her and sneaked back outside through the rear lounge door, the sun was so strong it felt like the grass was curling under my shoes. I came around the corner and tried to look like I'd been strolling through the trees this whole time. When I reached the patchwork lawn of blankets, I saw you walking toward me. Thank God. I started to jog. If you were outside, instead of in the ballroom, that could only mean one thing. You all had figured something out. You were going to do something to help Marion and the rest of the third scouting party. Your shoulders jumped in surprise when you saw me, and I started to smile with relief, but then I saw the look in your eyes.

I argued, but no one listened. Not even you. It had taken your group three days to decide what to do, but actually I think all of you had known what was going to happen from the first moment. It just took you three days to rationalize it into something that would let us face one another every morning thereafter.

# THE ONE WHO GATHERS

THE NURSE LEANED DOWN AGAIN, HOLDING THE COFFEEPOT out to him.

"No, thank you," the amnesiac said.

"I will have more, though," Dr. Zadeh cut in, and raised his mug. He rubbed his face slowly, as if trying to stretch it into a different shape. "Jet lag." He smiled, and she nodded sympathetically as she refilled his drink. Overhead, the central air conditioning clicked on, blasting the waiting room with icy wind. When they'd stepped off the plane, the air in Pune had been as warm and thickly humid as it was at home in New Orleans, but everywhere they'd gone since— the private government car sent to retrieve them, their five-star hotel, the car again to bring them to Maharashtra Regional Hospital, the now-quarantined psychiatric ward—was almost arctic cold. He just wanted to go outside and look. All the colors. The movement. Pune was so much more alive than the antiseptic, manicured courtyard of his assisted-living facility.

"Did I like coffee?" the amnesiac asked when the nurse had moved away.

"I don't know. That wasn't information I could find from your records or emails."

The amnesiac took another testing sip of the steaming dark liquid.

"Maybe Charlotte will be able to tell you?" Dr. Zadeh tried tentatively.

The amnesiac shrugged. He would ask her when they were back, but he didn't know if it mattered. For this new him, the taste made his tongue curl. "I don't like it now," he said. "Would that mean I didn't like it before?"

"Sometimes." Dr. Zadeh nodded. "It can."

He most likely did not like coffee before. He would add this fact to his flash cards.

"Plenty of people don't like it," Dr. Zadeh continued, in case he was feeling excluded from some societal ritual. "They just drink it so as not to feel like a truck ran over them." He took another sip. "Like right now."

"I feel fine," the amnesiac replied.

"Now *that's* weird," he said.

They laughed. The amnesiac couldn't stay angry at him. He had no one else in the whole world.

"Why me?" he finally asked. Dr. Zadeh glanced up. "Why was I chosen to meet Hemu Joshi?"

"Well, it was mostly my doing." Dr. Zadeh grinned sheepishly. "When I saw the first videos of Hemu after he began experiencing memory loss, I called the Indian Psychiatric Society. Explained who I was, emailed copies of my articles, my research on you. They eventually managed to put me all the way through to the team here. I told them about my idea."

"I know that," the amnesiac said. "I meant, there must be hundreds of retrograde amnesia cases in India from which they could have chosen. Why fly us out here?"

"Because you forgot so much," he answered. "Everything, really. Most RA cases aren't as complete as yours. And it happened at almost the same time as Hemu Joshi's incident. You're both still experiencing the effects of your diagnoses on your lives, learning how to cope with the loss. You were the closest match to him that we could find."

"Do you really think I can help him?"

"I think you have a better shot at understanding him than any of us do," he said. After a moment, he put his hand on the amnesiac's shoulder. "Just speak with him. That's all. Don't worry about the results, okay?"

The amnesiac nodded.

"Excuse me—we're ready for you now," a voice called. They turned from their seats to see an older woman in purple scrubs, perhaps sixty or so, her long silver braid shining against the warm brown of her skin.

"David Zadeh," Dr. Zadeh said, extending his hand as he went over to her. "This is . . ." He paused, grasping for a way to explain the amnesiac's aversion to his legal name. ". . . my patient. He prefers to be addressed by description rather than by what he was named prior to the accident. 'The visitor,' in this situation, perhaps. Or any relevant equivalent."

"A method of your rehabilitation?" she asked Dr. Zadeh.

"For him, I suppose yes," he said thoughtfully.

The woman nodded. "Dr. Zadeh, Visitor, I'm Dr. Avanthikar," she said. "Lead researcher for Mr. Joshi's team."

The amnesiac put out his hand to her as well. Her grip was firm—and excited, he thought.

"We've informed him you're coming," she continued as the two of them followed her down the hall. "He remembered twenty minutes ago when I checked." An aide caught the tail end of her sentence as they entered a small control room and shook her head. "Oh." Dr. Avanthikar sighed. "Never mind."

"Thank you again for this invitation," Dr. Zadeh said. "To be able to help with this, even in a small way, it's an honor."

"Well, let's hope it *does* help," Dr. Avanthikar replied. "I don't have to tell you—I mean, I'm sure you've been following the news."

"Nothing's working," the amnesiac finished for her.

"I've just—" She paused, words failing her. "I've just never seen anything like it."

"Okay, we're all set. Patient is inside," another aide interrupted softly.

"Right." Dr. Avanthikar straightened up. "Okay. Let's take you in there and introduce you, and then once you're both comfortable, we'll hook up the sensors so we can get some data. See if you two can maybe inspire each other into . . . anything, really."

The amnesiac didn't know what to expect. He braced as Dr. Avan-thikar went to the side door into the observation room and pulled it open.

"Oh." He blinked, surprised. He walked in. It didn't look like a hospital or a rehabilitation center or a patient observation room at all. It looked just like a living room, or what he imagined a living room in an Indian house might look like. There were couches and a few chairs in vibrant patterns, a rug, potted plants in full bloom. In the corner hung a wide wooden swing. The walls had been painted a warm color and adorned with framed photographs. In the center, sitting cross-legged on one of the couches, was a young man in a simple white tunic. Hemu Joshi.

*This is his living room,* the amnesiac realized. They had re-created it here to try to spark something during his therapy.

"I have a visitor for you," Dr. Avanthikar said from behind the amnesiac. Hemu looked at him blankly, waiting for more information from her. The amnesiac smiled. It was a new, wonderful feeling; to meet someone who didn't already know more about him than he did—in fact, who didn't know anything about him at all. "He's also lost his memory. Everything from the moment he was born until just a few weeks ago."

Hemu's eyes slid to the carpet, to where the amnesiac's shadow stood patiently behind him against the fibers.

"He lost his memory in a car accident," she clarified. The amnesiac felt her hand on his shoulder. "Please make yourself comfortable." She pointed to the only giveaway the room was actually a medical facility, a rectangular two-way mirror hanging in the center of the same wall as the door he'd used to enter. "We'll be just on the other side, if you need anything."

The amnesiac sat down on the plush chair opposite Hemu's couch. "Hi," he said when they were alone.

"Hi," Hemu said. He was studying the amnesiac's face intently. "Do I know you?"

"Not in the slightest," he said. "We've never met before."

Hemu perked up then. Something new. Not a replay. "And you really remember nothing? Even with a shadow?"

"It was due to an injury. My head hit the windshield at a bad angle. So they tell me."

"What's a windshield?"

"The front window of a car."

Hemu squinted for a few moments, trying to make sense of the words.

"Not important," the amnesiac said. "I hit my head very hard, and it damaged my memory."

"Hmm." Hemu studied the smooth scar where the amnesiac's left eye should have been. "And you won't . . . you won't regain your memories someday?"

"My doctor is hopeful. But the chances are very slim."

Hemu looked down at his hands for a few moments. "I hope you do," he said.

"I hope you do, too."

Hemu studied the amnesiac for a while, pondering something. "What was it like when you woke up?" he asked. "Could you even speak?"

"Oh, yes, I could speak," the amnesiac answered. "Uh. It's complicated, retrograde amnesia. That's what they call mine. You often remember the way things work, but not your personal experience of them. I knew what a mother was, but not anything about mine. How to read, but not how I learned it. I remember the rules of football, but I don't know if I've ever played."

"That's interesting," Hemu mused. "I'm forgetting, but not in any order. I don't remember—I don't know what they call it, but I remember primary school before it, and university after. There must have been something in between, but it's blank."

"You still remember more about yourself than me." The amnesiac smiled.

Hemu scrunched his face up, thinking. Suddenly he sat forward, his expression intensely serious. "Do you remember what sex is?"

The amnesiac laughed. He liked this Hemu.

THEY WAITED FOR DR. AVANTHIKAR'S AIDES TO PEEL OFF THE adhesive backings and apply the sensors to their foreheads and temples. It was more normal to do it with someone else, the amnesiac thought as he watched them brush Hemu's hair out of the way and stick a little white circle above his dark eyebrows, then attach a thin cable to it.

"Of course you already know," one of the aides said to them both. "But please refrain from large or sudden movements, so as not to disconnect the wires."

Hemu watched them file out and close the door behind them. "The way your amnesia works, you wouldn't remember your favorite food then, would you?" he asked the amnesiac.

"No, unfortunately."

"That might be for the best," he said. "I still remember mine, and it makes what they feed me here that much worse. So healthy. So tasteless."

"I like your food," the amnesiac said. "Indian food, I mean."

"Not this stuff," he sighed. "It's all just medicinal mush. I want something different—like American food. Yeah, I want American food."

"What American food do you like?"

"All the stuff you can get in the Western restaurants downtown. Pizza, french fries, macaroni and cheese." He paused. "You know, they say that in the latest stages, the shadowless forget to eat. Apparently it's happening with some of the others in Nashik. They're fitting them with stomach tubes now so they don't starve or dehydrate."

"Oh," the amnesiac said, looking down. The thought was horrible.

Hemu glanced around awkwardly. He held his hands in the shape of a small brick. "I, uh, I met an American tourist near the cricket field once," he continued, trying to steer the conversation away from the dark place it had gone. "He told me about a sandwich Americans eat as children. A jelly peanut sandwich?"

"A peanut butter and jelly sandwich." The amnesiac smiled. He pictured it in his mind, and wondered if he'd also never had one.

Hemu nodded. "Yes, that was it. That's what I want. A peanut butter and jelly sandwich."

"I can try and get you one," the amnesiac offered.

"No—I'm sorry," Hemu apologized. "I didn't mean to impose. I was just complaining."

"I think it would be no trouble," the amnesiac said. He considered their hotel. He was sure the lobby restaurant could make one if he asked, or at least tell him and Dr. Zadeh where a Western grocery store might be so they could buy the ingredients themselves.

"I'm grateful," Hemu said. "Only if it's easy. Please don't go out of your way."

"Really, I'm happy to."

Hemu nodded thoughtfully. "I want to share something with you. To repay you, for the sandwich."

"Oh, you don't have to," the amnesic protested, but Hemu waved him off.

"It's not much, really. Given . . ."—he gestured to the room, to mean his enforced stay in the hospital—"I really can only give you memories—that's basically all I've got. Well, I've got them for now."

The amnesiac bowed his head solemnly.

"There's an old story from our mythology—sort of related to all this." Hemu nodded at the amnesiac's shadow. "Have you ever heard the legend of Surya, the Hindu god?"

"Uh," the amnesiac said. "In these first few weeks of my life, probably not."

Hemu sat up straighter, visibly pleased. The amnesiac knew the expression all too intimately—the pride at knowing something the person to whom you were speaking did not. It was the closest simulacrum to personal memory either of them could experience. "Very important. He's chief of the Navagraha and presiding deity of Sunday. Surya rides a chariot drawn by a horse with seven heads, and has four arms in which he holds—" Hemu paused to collect himself, realizing he was getting carried away. "He's one of the oldest gods. From the Rigveda, the oldest book. The oldest memories, in a way—not that any of us were there, but we all know the stories. We all know them in almost the same words. It makes me happy to think about them. To realize I still remember them, too." He put up a finger, to indicate something important was about to follow. "The point, though—Surya is the god of the sun. And his consort was made from a shadow."

Now that seemed like something that might go somewhere. The amnesiac wished they'd given him a notepad, or even just a piece of paper. "Really?" he asked.

Hemu nodded. "In the Rigveda, Surya marries Sanjna, goddess of clouds, mother of the twin Asvins. Those—the Asvins—symbolize the shining of sunrise and sunset. Each one crosses the sky once a day in their chariot, bringing either the light or dark. They—" He paused again, scratching at one of the sensors. "Sorry," he said. "The twins are also beside the point. Sometimes I just . . . It makes me happy to realize how many details about something I still remember, if that makes sense."

The amnesiac shook his head. "I understand," he said. "Honestly, I'm impressed even people with shadows can remember this much. All of you know these stories?"

"It seems to me no different than knowing all the names and statistics of current and past heroes from your favorite American football team, and the moments of their careers," Hemu shrugged.

He had a point. "But you were saying," the amnesiac said, remembering their audience on the other side of the observation panel. He was supposed to keep them on track.

"Yes, yes," Hemu continued, grinning again. "So Surya marries Sanjna with her father's blessing. But when Sanjna comes to Surya's house, because he's the god of the sun, she realizes that she can't bear the brilliant radiance of his light. She's unable to even be in the same room as him, let alone look at him. Sad, no?"

The amnesiac nodded.

"This is the interesting part. To escape the blinding light, Sanjna takes her own shadow and makes it into Chhaya, an identical copy of herself, then transforms into a mare so Surya won't recognize her. She flees to the forest, leaving Chhaya in her place to take care of the house and manage her domestic duties. Sometimes Chhaya is referred to in the Rigveda as Savarna, 'same kind'—identical to Sanjna because she was made from her shadow, but mortal."

The amnesiac realized he'd been leaning so far forward in his armchair that the back two legs had begun to hover a hair off the ground. Stories, yes—but he felt like Hemu was trying to get at something. The pieces seemed like they belonged to the same puzzle, even if they went at the other end of the finished picture. "What happened?" he asked.

Hemu shrugged nonchalantly. "Surya eventually figures out Chhaya is not Sanjna, and goes to the forest and finds his wife, hiding in mare form. Sanjna's father then manages to reduce Surya's brightness by one eighth, enough that Sanjna can bear the light, and she comes home."

The tone of Hemu's voice as he said the last sentence sounded as though he'd reached the end of the story. The amnesiac glanced at the tinted viewing window, confused. "But what about Chhaya?" he finally asked.

"Some versions say she leaves, but most say she stays, as another wife. The gods sometimes have multiple wives."

The amnesiac blinked. "That's it?"

"What do you mean?"

"I mean, that's the whole thing? There's nothing more?"

"You are unhappy," Hemu said uncertainly.

"No," he said. "No, I—it's just that I thought maybe there was something else. Something that might help us. I didn't know it was just going to be a story."

"I think if there was something that was going to help us, we'd already have thought of it." Hemu snorted bitterly and looked down. "I just like the ending, that's all. I just thought, wasn't it nice, that Sanjna and her shadow were able to be reunited, and then the shadow stayed?" He trailed off. "That would be nice."

The amnesiac leaned back in his seat, abashed. Hemu straightened his white tunic gently until there were no creases where the skirt bent across his lap, slightly embarrassed. The amnesiac could see how young he still was. Just barely a man, in either of their cultures. Behind the walls, the machines whirred softly, recording brain waves.

"Hemu, I'm sorry," the amnesiac finally said. The story had ultimately gone nowhere, but Hemu was right. Even if there was no lesson, it was worth more than that. The resonances with the strange things happening now, the knowledge that at least there in India, millions of others would remember the same names, the same stories. Dr. Zadeh had asked him to talk with Hemu, to try and connect with him. It was not his job to turn their conversations into scientific evidence. It was just his job to listen. "I'm honored you wanted to tell me Surya's story. To include me in this giant shared memory. I doubt I would ever have heard it otherwise. If—" He folded his hands. "I don't think I remember any stories like that to give you."

"It's all right," Hemu said. "Maybe you can remember mine for me when I forget?"

"I hope you don't forget," the amnesiac said.

"But you'll remember them anyway?" Hemu asked.

"Of course. As many as you want to tell me."

WE SUITED UP THREE OF ELK CLIFFS'S KITCHEN STAFF AND two of the wedding band—the cello and the violin—in makeshift hazmat suits created from trash bags, rubber dishwashing gloves, five sets of goggles that came from who knows where, and as much duct tape as we could gather. The rest of us dug the graves.

You and I made Marion's with a shovel and a bucket. We were on the far slope of the mountain, on the opposite side from where the resort was built. I didn't see her again after that last time—once the decision had been made, you held me so I couldn't run for her. It probably didn't matter. She wouldn't have remembered me anyway. I tried not to imagine what it would be like to open four locked doors and shoot five human beings, and then carry their silent, heavy bodies so far. I tried to concentrate on the digging instead. I wasn't sure I'd ever dug anything so deep before. Halfway through, I couldn't feel my arms. By the end, I couldn't feel anything at all.

When it was done, I wanted to lay down in the wet coolness of the earth. The hole was so low that the walls of it cast shade over me. The dank chill on my skin was colder than I had felt in months. I wondered if Marion was the last person in her family to die, or the first.

The sun was setting. You were leaning over the muddy edge, peering down at me sitting in her grave. Slowly you reached down. I took your hand, and you hoisted me out.

"They're ready to bring them," was all you said. The bodies.

The fire that night was quiet. No one wanted to ask if we'd done the right thing, because the possibility that we hadn't was unbearable.

You and I sat close together, my arm looped tightly around yours. We all watched the flames.

The next morning, we found Rabbi Levenson dead in the ballroom, propped peacefully against the bottom of the bar counter, an empty bottle of pills in his left hand. Ye-eun's name was on the label.

His shadow was still there, frozen forever beneath his still form.

Three weeks later, no one else had succumbed to the epidemic.

[II]

It rained for a couple of days, and we all moved back inside from the lawn until it stopped. The sun was so bright and clean after that. We moved right back out. That morning, you came and found Paul, Imanuel, and me working in the garden we were trying to start.

"I don't think you're supposed to bury them that deep." Paul pulled half of the dirt I'd pushed over the seeds we'd found while poking around the safe part of the mountain.

"We don't want them to wash away if it rains," I argued.

"The monsoons are almost over," he said. His hair had started to grow out of his haircut, the front now tied up with a rubber band so it didn't fall in his eyes. I wondered what my own looked like. Probably as large as a cloud over my head. "That won't happen. Don't cover them so much."

"She's right," you said, and your shadow rolled over us as you reached the garden. The arms propped themselves on the hips, and it cocked its head the way that you always do. I watched the dark shape for a moment as it lay over the ground, and wondered if I saw it wandering alone if I'd recognize that it was *your* shadow, or if I wouldn't be able to tell the difference.

"Everything okay?" I finally asked you.

Paul stood up and brushed the dirt off his hands against his jeans, and Imanuel copied him. I could tell from the look that passed between the three of you that it wasn't.

"Guys," I said.

"Come with me," you replied. You motioned with your head in the direction of the small creek that ran through the thicker part of the woods. "Just want to talk for a second." You nodded at Paul and Imanuel. "We'll be right back."

"All right," Paul said. There was something strange in the tone. As if it had been a surrender at the end of an argument, not a casual comment. You looked at each other for a long time before he squatted back down.

You led me into the trees, over to the small stream. The water smelled almost sweet. I took one shoe off and nudged a few pebbles from the edge of the bank into the softly gurgling water. You copied me.

"Blue," you said at last. Your voice was tight.

I stopped and looked at you, as you took my hand and looped your fingers tightly through mine.

I knew why you were crying then. You were crying because Paul and Imanuel had finally decided. They were going to make a break for it. They were going to leave Elk Cliffs. They wanted us to come with them, and you didn't want us to.

"Ory," I said, "we can make it if we're careful. We can—"

"We're staying here." Your voice cracked.

I looked down. "Let's at least talk about it," I began. I could feel the panic setting in. I had to convince you. We had to go with them. If we stayed here, we'd be the only ones left eventually. Then we'd never go anywhere again. We'd die or lose our shadows here. "Maybe more guests might join us, so we could make a bigger group, or a safer—"

"We're staying here," you repeated.

The words were so final, I didn't know what else I could say. Ideas raced through my mind, one after another, none good enough. "I already told them we were going with them, weeks ago," I finally stammered, throat tight. "I told them you were in."

But you didn't say anything to that. You just shook your head as the tears began to slide down your cheeks, and then looked down the mountain, over the trees below, into the setting sun.

I didn't understand at first. Why we had come so far just to talk. We all argued in front of each other now—no one cared about privacy anymore. The glow from the sun filled up your eyes, lighting the tears on fire.

Then I did.

You'd already spoken to Paul and Imanuel, long before I ever had. They'd tried to convince you to let us leave the mountain with them and travel together, to find either my family or Imanuel's. And you'd refused. You'd refused, to save our lives from whatever was out there, even though it meant never seeing them again. You'd told them not to let on if I asked to join—to lie to me. That when the day came to leave, to not say goodbye to us, so it would be too late to do anything by the time I realized.

There was no chance to convince you to let us go with them now because they were already gone.

# ORLANDO ZHANG

THE NOON SUN WAS BEARING DOWN, COOL BUT BRIGHT
enough to make Ory sweat. There was still no sign of Max.

He wiped his brow and scooted farther off to the side of the road,
to walk under the shade of the trees. McLean had become some kind
of subtropical wilderness, but warped. Along the roads, single human
limbs, twisted into strange shapes and in various states of decom-
position; entire neighborhoods charred to blackness; weird, chilling
shrines of everyday objects haphazardly placed in strange corners,
people's last attempts to try to collect and remember themselves;
tunnels, dug a few feet into the grass or asphalt, all empty.

The shrines were both the best and most worrisome sign. There
were far more of them here than in the suburbs of Arlington he
normally patrolled—more shrines meant more people to ask about
Max. But the kind of people that made shrines were shadowless
people.

The little altar just ahead of him on the shattered sidewalk looked
freshly built. A stack of salvaged objects that made no sense together,
their only connection being that they'd been found in the same place,
because they'd belonged to the same owner. An owner who didn't know
why they were important anymore, only that they were, because they
held answers to a past he or she could no longer remember. There was a
tattered teddy bear, a faded paperback book, what looked like a pair of
boxers, a hammer, a box of condoms, and a pile of dead AA batteries.

Ory touched the cover of the paperback. It was dusty, the pages
curled from having endured rain and dried countless times. He didn't
see them often anymore, books. Maybe people had used them for
kindling. Every time he did, it made him think of Paul—his own

beautiful covers decaying on bookstore shelves now. His poems that no one was ever going to read again. He hoped that however Paul and Imanuel had met their end after they left the mountain, it had been kind and quick.

The moldy spine almost fell apart as Ory edged the cover open. BOOKSTOP USED BOOKS. No name.

He heard the shadowless before he saw it. A shifting of leaves in the green ahead. Ory backed away from the sound slowly, turned to run. But instead of an empty road, there was a man standing there. A broken-off table leg in his hand.

"Trees play tricks," the shadowless said. His words were syrupy, struggling. "Willow tree, very tricky." The trees shifted again around them, tossing the sound so then it seemed to come from the left. For an instant, Ory was almost sure he'd seen a face, but made of bark, not skin. The leaves rustled even though there was no wind in them, as if laughing.

"I don't mean any harm," Ory whispered, even though his shotgun was leveled at the man.

The shadowless snickered. Nothing copied him on the asphalt. "No harm," he said, pointing at the gun. "But you have the thunderstorm."

Ory winced, but it was too late. He thought of the deer outside his and Max's shelter, his hunting knife. The Remington still looked the same in his hands, but there was no way now to be sure what would come out of the muzzle. What a memory of a "thunderstorm" might mean. "Okay," he agreed. He lowered the gun and held up one empty palm in a signal of peace.

But the man wasn't looking at Ory anymore. "Shadow," he said softly.

*It doesn't come off,* Ory almost said. *There's no way for me to give it to you.* "I just want to keep going," he smiled. "I have to keep going that way."

"Way for trade," the shadowless said.

"What?"

"Way for trade." The willow trees rustled. He pointed at the road, then held out his hand. "Way for trade."

He wanted something in exchange for letting him pass, Ory realized. "Uh—" He dug into his pockets frantically for everything he'd brought from the shelter, aside from the gun and the last of his dried jerky meat: a pouch with sewing tools, the sliver of his last bar of soap, a first-aid kit, and a few Elk Cliffs pens.

The shadowless watched him impassively as Ory held them out, unimpressed. "No. No good."

"I don't have anything else," Ory answered. His legs tingled, ready to bolt.

"But shadow does. Shadow knows things."

"No," Ory started.

"Yes," the shadowless insisted. The table leg came up, and he pointed it at both Ory and his dark twin. "Shadowless has questions, shadow has answers. Ask shadow who I am, then you pass."

"It doesn't work like that," Ory said helplessly. "It doesn't know things about others. It only knows things about me."

"Ask anyway," the shadowless hissed. He pointed at the shadow again. *"Ask it."*

Ory raised his hands, surrendering. Was there anything about the man he could glean from just looking at him? He seemed to be under thirty. Shorter than Ory, possibly Hispanic, possibly once in very good shape and not starving, when there had been stoves to cook better food on. There were scars across his forehead, and he wore a tarnished gold ring, but not on the correct finger to mean he'd been married.

The shadowless growled. Ory turned to face his shadow fully, tried to make eye contact with it on the asphalt as if he were having a real conversation with it. "Do you know anything about this man?" he asked the dark shape. He paused for a moment. Pretended to listen. He wanted to give the shadowless an answer and escape as quickly as possible, but he also wanted to ask him about Max. About where she had gone—what Ory was heading into. The woman and her crew on Broad Street had said "something bad" was growing in D.C., but no more than that. "I see."

The shadowless nearly crumpled to his knees. His eyes gleamed. "What did it say?" he begged.

"It said that it cannot be sure, but it thinks that it might know something about you." Ory held up his hand. "But first it needs to know one thing. Did you see a shadowless woman pass by here within the last few days?"

"No," the man said.

It meant nothing. She easily could have come past when he was asleep or busy, or gone another way. "All right. One more thing."

"No more," he warned.

"It has to be sure it has the right person," Ory said, gesturing to his shadow.

The shadowless raised the table leg threateningly. The message was clear.

Ory gritted his teeth and nodded. "Okay, no more." He could feel the shape of the table leg through the air as it trembled in the man's impatient grip. Every inch of his skin was attuned to it.

"What shadow say?" the shadowless asked again. He scooted closer, like a child trying to sneak his way onto Santa's lap. The trees hissed excitedly. There was a face again, for a moment, like a woman carved into wood, with leaves for hair.

"My shadow said it's certain now." Ory smiled, trying to sound confident. There was no way he could know if the shadowless would remember the real answer to what he tried to make up—his only goal was to confuse the man long enough to make a run for it while he pondered the answer. "It said that your name was Jeff, and you taught the trees how to talk to you."

They watched each other for a long second. Ory and his shadow both slid their feet an inch to the left, to bolt.

"Lie! Shadow lies!" the shadowless screamed. The trees shrieked with him, enraged.

"Wait—" Ory put his hand up.

"Lies! *Wife* taught the trees!"

"No, wait!" Ory cried as the man broke into a full sprint for him. The trees howled, branches creaking as they stretched. *The shotgun!* he thought. "Stop!" The shadowless did not stop. Ory jammed the cartridges. *Come on.* "Stop!" *Come ON!* The break action snapped shut. Shells clicked into place. The shadowless raised the table leg and lunged.

When the man landed, a few feet behind where he had originally taken off, he stayed standing for a moment. The bang echoed into silence as they both waited. Him to find out if Ory had missed, Ory to find out what the gun now did at all.

Then he fell.

Ory ran to him and stared. His chest was split open, two sides parted like clouds in the sky. Inside, it wasn't red, but dark, deep blue, and churning. There was a bang again from inside, and live white tendrils snapped, lightning snaking out from inside, electrocuting in agonizing bursts.

"Oh my God," Ory said.

"Thunderstorm," the shadowless whispered between jolts. His eyes kept track of Ory's shadow as it breathed in time with his body, trembling over the dirt. He watched it as closely as he watched Ory, as if he wasn't quite sure which one of them was in control, and which one of them had done it. His eyes were amber pools, flecked with gold in the deepest parts that glittered when the current went through them. Around them, the trees hushed, as if alive, as if afraid. Or perhaps in mourning. If the fragment of the woman who had once been the shadowless's wife still remembered anything at all.

Ory couldn't leave him like that, to suffer for who knew how long, but he was too scared to use the gun again. His hands scrambled at his belt for the knife.

I'm in Oakton now. I walked all night—by dawn, I'd made it to the Chain Bridge Road exit under the I-66 West.

It's very quiet in this neighborhood, but the townhouses are so lovely. The kind I always wished we might have one day. I imagine that before the world ended, there were kids riding their bicycles up and down the clean, smooth asphalt, and mothers standing in clusters on their front lawns with strollers, checking their ornate wrought-iron mailboxes, planting tulips along the borders of their driveways. It was that kind of place. I mean, I even saw one lone bicycle on a later street, mournfully pedaling itself in slow, lost circles, waiting for its child to come back. It looked so sad, Ory.

Just west of that was a high school. Oakton High School, judging from the part of the sign that was still upright. I know schools aren't the best places to scout alone—too many hallways and rooms, too many places for others to be hiding. But I was exhausted and wanted to get out of the damp dawn. I crossed the overgrown football field and found myself standing in the middle of the campus.

Someone had definitely lived here once. Many someones. There were the remains of their abandoned camp everywhere: discarded scraps of clothing; piles of trash, neatly pushed into corners; scuff marks on the concrete like something heavy had been dragged back and forth, maybe a table or chairs. Some classroom doors were barricaded; some were removed from their hinges to allow sun and moonlight into the small rooms. Windows had rudimentary dressings over them.

That's when I saw the drawings.

It hadn't been a shadowed survivors' camp, I realized as I walked around in the silence. It had been a camp of shadowless. Perhaps they started together, as friends or family, and then all slowly forgot, or perhaps they all gathered together once they lost their shadows and found comfort and protection in numbers. One of them had been a very gifted artist. A man, I think, because in all the drawings the same person appears, a pale shape with short light hair and two dots of blue for eyes. I think he was drawing himself.

There was no writing in most of the signs, not like the rules you and I made in our shelter. These were signs made of images, carefully rendered in a set of permanent markers or paint. Almost all the colors were there—black, blue, red, green, purple, orange, and brown. The pictures were everywhere, next to every little thing that might be confusing to someone who no longer remembered what it was. There were pictures to describe how to light a fire, how to extinguish it, never to touch it; what a sweater or scarf or jacket was for when it was cold; that people with shadows could be dangerous to those without. I stood in front of the wall where that one had been drawn for a long time, staring at each careful line of that warning. It was painted near the entrance to the school, where they would see it every time they went to the gate to investigate a sound.

Near the back of the campus, the drawings became simpler, less instructive. They seemed not to be depicting how to perform a task or how to avoid a danger, but were more a visual history of who each person in their group had been. There were twelve of them in total. Some were men, some were women. The blue-eyed man was there, next to a stern figure in the center. Their leader. On one side, another woman with long light hair embraced a brown-haired man, both of them looking at each other and smiling. The artist was trying to tell them they were a pair. That they were in love.

The last picture I found was of the same blond-haired, blue-eyed man. It looked like perhaps the first one he'd drawn. It was larger, and there were details about him not present in the others, as though he was still figuring out how to ensure that he could recognize himself, trying to make certain there were enough clues. In the drawing, the blond man was standing face forward, arms at his sides. His expression was peaceful.

Beneath his feet, there was the unmistakable black shape, stretched out at a gentle angle against an imaginary ground. It held the same calm position, arms at its sides, its hair tousled in an identical way. Where their shoes joined together, the blond man had connected them so perfectly there was not even a sliver of the white wall between their two sets of feet.

I moved closer until my face was almost pressed against the dark space on the wall where he'd drawn his penumbral twin. He had given the shadow blue eyes too, two piercing sapphire dots floating in an expressionless black sea.

# NAZ AHMADI

SIX. THAT WAS THE NUMBER OF PEOPLE NAZ HAD TO KILL ON their way.

Three shadowless, three shadowed. She remembered their faces sometimes, even the ones she saw only for an instant, if not less. Once in a while, their features were even more vivid to her than those of others she knew far better—Rojan, her mother, her coach. Memory was a strange thing.

She killed the first four as she and her sister moved south through Connecticut on their way to New York. Two shadowless, two shadowed. The two shadowless ambushed them as they passed the hideouts, biting and scratching. Crazed—starving. Naz didn't want to kill them, was afraid of killing them, and she and Rojan tried as hard as they could to just get away first, but the shadowless wouldn't give up.

The two shadowed ones were starving for something else. For those, Naz did not hesitate.

JUST PAST HARTFORD, IT STARTED TO GET A LITTLE EASIER. They moved only at night, avoiding large towns and keeping to the rural areas. Naz couldn't have said what New Haven or Springfield looked like.

The bow kept them alive. Naz was careful and managed to hunt so that Rojan could chase after and retrieve most of the precious arrows she loosed to use again. She shot little things—rats, pigeons—and they ate them raw, afraid a fire might attract attention. They ruined a lot of their spare underwear that way. They didn't die, but almost. Some nights the taste was so revolting, one of them would throw it all back up as soon as she'd finished eating it, then cry at the waste as the other one held her, at how they both were probably starving to death. When the sisters stopped for evening camp just north of Poughkeepsie, in a particularly wooded area, Naz couldn't take it anymore. Rojan had the shakes, and Naz was almost too weak to pull back the bowstring. She made a tiny fire to cook their dinner for once.

It took about twenty minutes before they were found.

Naz heard it first, to her left. A snapping twig. She threw herself against the trunk of a tree and trained her bow on the undergrowth.

"You see it? I don't see it," Rojan whispered from against another.

Branches. Darkness. Another sound, dangerously close. Naz tried to aim, but she couldn't make anything out. The glow of the flames blinded her, lighting the night so that whoever was hunting her could easily see into their camp, but she couldn't see beyond it. She kicked the ground, tossing dirt onto the fire to suffocate it.

"Oh, God, no!" someone howled. "No, no, no! Why? *Why?*"

Rojan screamed, and Naz almost lost her grip on the tail of the arrow. A man stumbled hysterically out of the darkness at her and fell to his knees. Naz screamed this time. Her arrow went wild, missing him by three lengths as she scrambled for another, still shrieking, the man still crawling.

She and Rojan had been so careful to avoid attracting attention, certain that there were predators around every corner, but there really must have been no one but the three of them for miles that night, Naz realized later. They made enough noise in that moment to alert an entire city. Rojan yelling, Naz shouting and circling her enemy, aiming the glittering slate tip of her arrow at his head, and the man moaning, hands scrabbling in agony through the dirt.

"Stay down! Stay down!" she shouted at him. "What the fuck is the matter with you? You move an inch and I'll kill you! I will *kill* you!"

"The fire," he was wailing. Finally Naz focused on him long enough to realize he had a shadow, dimly lit by the moonlight, hunched beneath him on the ground. "The fire, the fire." He looked at her like she'd murdered a child. "*Why* did you put out the fire?"

NAZ LET ROJAN LIGHT THE TINY FLAME AGAIN, EVENTUALLY. The man's last name was Wright. He refused to say his given name. "I don't want to talk about it," he said. "Please don't make me talk about it."

They didn't make him talk about it. After an hour of questions, Naz finally felt safe enough to lower her bow. Her arms were so badly cramped she couldn't move her fingers for a good while afterward. Wright didn't know how to make a fire or hunt, but he did have a lot of water, in a huge camping-type rubber bladder he'd found somewhere. Naz and Rojan offered him a third of their roasted squirrel once they cooked it, and he gave them as much of the water as they could drink. The next morning was the first time Naz's piss wasn't uranium yellow in she couldn't say how long.

"I came north through the Bronx," Wright told the sisters as they picked the tiny bones clean and then sucked on them. "Something happened in Midtown, near the Empire State Building. Something very big. That's when I knew I had to go. I doubt there's anything left now."

"We were heading for New York," Naz said. She slipped her bow over her shoulder again and pressed the palms of her hands into her eyes. Vague colors swam against the pressure. It felt nice. Now what? "I don't know where to go instead."

"I don't know where I'm going, either," he replied. "Can I come with you two?"

Naz said no, and Rojan said all right. In the end, Rojan won the argument. Wright could carry a lot of water in the rubber bladder, enough to split between three people. And he could make their endless night watches into bearable shifts.

The going got much smoother. Naz still didn't trust him, but with more sleep and better hydration, she had to admit they moved much faster. As they passed Hoboken in New Jersey, the three of them went to the edge of the Hudson River to look across at Manhattan, just to see. They stood on Sinatra Drive, just before the shore, staring out across the dark water. The moon glimmered, its reflection spliced by ripples.

"Is that . . . really?" Naz trailed off as she stared.

"Yeah," Wright said. "That must have been what everyone was screaming about as it killed them, neighborhood by neighborhood."

They stared. New York was being destroyed by its own monster. At least three times her original size, the emerald woman rose up between two skyscrapers, the huge torch in her hand blazing with real fire. With a deafening roar, she lifted the tablet in her other arm and brought it down on top of a building, flattening it to the ground. Shock waves skipped across the water as the green hands tore into the wreckage.

"I can't believe you made it out alive," Rojan said softly.

"I know," he sighed. They watched it for a little while longer. "To think at one point I thought maybe I could just wait it out if I laid low enough."

Naz couldn't understand what she was seeing. "It's almost kind of beautiful," she finally said as the giant woman tossed the hem of her long robe behind her, crushing everything in its path. Glass and metal sprayed like silver confetti as buildings collapsed. Somewhere just south of Central Park, from where the statue had been a few minutes earlier, an explosion rose up in an angry dark cloud. Her crown glinted in the orangy dusk. "Horrible, but beautiful."

They camped on the shore that night, and ate crayfish they caught along the bank. Wright still wouldn't tell them his name, but he told them a lot of other things. How he watched Boston on TV, how the Forgetting overtook New York, how he should have left with his friends when they said they were going to steal some motorcycles and head south. "Have you ever heard about the One with One Eye?" he asked them as they huddled near the small flame.

"The One with One Eye?" Naz repeated.

"Or maybe it was No Eyes. That's what my buddies were calling—it? him?—anyway. Whoever it is. Or was." Wright paused. "The One Who Gathers. That one I know I heard them say for sure." He leaned forward as Naz nodded in sudden recognition. That was the name she and Rojan had seen spray-painted on the side of a building just outside Boston. "My friends said he was in New Orleans," he added.

So they decided, why not? There was no New York now, or Boston or Tehran, so New Orleans it was. Maybe Wright's friends would still be alive there. Maybe they'd be gathered up with all of them again, by this "gathering one," whatever the fuck that meant. It wasn't much of a plan, but it was more than they'd had before. Naz caught Rojan's gaze over the top of the fire, and saw that her little sister was grinning smugly at her. *Fuck it,* Naz shrugged, and grinned back. Her sister trusted everyone too quickly, but Naz also always waited too long. They had water now, and a plan. Maybe Wright wasn't so bad after all.

They made it all the way to Wilmington, Pennsylvania, before the next shadowless found them. He was in the back of the grocery store they were trying to raid, circling the aisles. Naz had hoped he was one of the afraid ones when she spotted him. She was going to try to go around and spook him out the front door, but when he saw her, he charged, and she could tell he wasn't going to stop. He was angry—so angry—with no way to express it. No words, no writing, no hand signs. The only thing he could do was destroy something. Maybe it was the same for the monster in New York. She just didn't understand what anything was, and no one could tell her.

Wright was far across the store with Rojan, but after the first moment of shock, Naz was calm. The shadowless didn't seem to recognize the arrow as Naz pulled it quickly to the string and drew it back, and did not dodge. He just kept running straight down the aisle, straight for her. That was good. It made it so she could aim an instantaneous, painless end. Her fifth of the six kills.

"What's going on?" Wright cried as he careened around the corner of the aisle. Rojan was just behind him. "I heard the shot, I—oh, Jesus."

"I'm okay," Naz said. Rojan hugged her. All she could think about as she squeezed her back was that if it had been Rojan who found the shadowless and not Naz—Rojan could barely keep a backpack on, let alone fight someone to the death. *Thank God Wright was with her,* she realized.

"All right, no more of this spreading out to search stores and houses faster," he pronounced at the same moment. "Anytime we go somewhere new, we need to stick together. Together is safer."

For once, Naz agreed.

She killed her final sixth person in an open field under a moonless night one day south of Baltimore. It was Wright.

IT HAD BEEN NAZ'S TURN TO SLEEP. WRIGHT WAS UP TO TAKE over watch, and Rojan was already dreaming beside her. For once, Naz set the bow down beside her instead of looping it over one shoulder. It was giving her such a neck ache, to rest like that all the time. Her whole back was sore.

She woke because someone was calling her name softly. Then someone else said, "Shut up."

Naz opened her eyes.

"Fuck," Wright growled. "You made it worse."

She was still groggy. She reached down to the dirt beside her, fingers searching for that familiar shape, even though she could already see that her bow was in Wright's unsteady grip, arrow notched straight at Rojan. Finally her brain caught up.

"You know what we have," Rojan was saying. "Food we share with you, and clothes that are too small for you to use anyway."

"Bullshit," Wright spat. He gestured at Rojan and Naz's bag. "I've seen the gold. I know it's in there, under all the clothes."

"It's costume jewelry," Rojan replied. "From our mother. It's just sentimental."

"Then why not just give it to me?"

"Because our mother's dead," Naz said. Wright swiveled to point the arrow at her, and she flinched.

Wright laughed. "Not so tough now, are you?"

"You don't know how to use it," Naz answered. "Things could get really bad."

"I think they already are," he said. He pointed with his chin at the bag. "Give it to me. Now."

"No," Rojan said, but Naz slowly walked over nearer to her. She bent down to pick up the duffel. "It's our mother's," Rojan said softly.

"My mother's dead, too." Wright shrugged.

"Lower the bow," Naz said. Wright shook his head. "Lower the bow and I'll toss the bag to you."

Finally he did, and Naz tossed the bag over. He reached down with one hand and grabbed the strap, eyes still on them. The bow and arrow were in one hand. Rojan was sunken, like a hollow thing, but the tension was rolling off Naz in waves. She was wound tight like a coil, ready to lunge at the first opening. She knew it wasn't worth the fight, but she couldn't help it. The strap of their bag dropped over Wright's head. She had let her guard down, and he had betrayed them. He had pointed an arrow at Rojan. She couldn't let it go. Even if she got shot, she couldn't let it go.

His free hand started to go back toward the bow, to aim at them again so he could make a getaway.

"Naz, don't—" Rojan started to say, but it was too late.

"*Motherfucker!*" Naz howled as she threw herself at him.

They all shouted in the scuffle. Naz went straight for his eyes, to claw them out. Rojan ducked, covering her head. Wright was caught between trying to beat Naz off him and reaching back down to notch the arrow, but Naz knew he couldn't fire at such close range and hit her.

That was true. Naz was too close to be shot.

But Rojan wasn't.

"Fuck," Wright murmured. His hands went slack. "Fuck . . ."

Naz sank down next to her sister. The shot had gone wild, un-aimed, just a spasm of Wright's fingers as he'd lost grip on the tip of the arrow after pulling the string too tight during the fight, but it had somehow still found Rojan. Out of the top of one of her thighs, a long, slim shaft was sticking straight out, like a flagpole.

"Oh no," Rojan squeaked. The ground everywhere was red with thick syrup. Naz could see her going into shock. Her face was as white as the moon, bathed in a sweaty sheen.

"Pressure." Naz's hands trembled as she ripped off her belt and tried to wrap it around Rojan's leg. "We have to, pressure, to stop the bleeding. Have to stop it."

"You just should have given—you shouldn't have fought—" Wright stammered in the background.

"Naz," Rojan murmured.

"Pressure," Naz repeated.

"Naz," Rojan said again, lips trembling.

Naz turned around to follow her sister's unsteady gaze. Wright was clutching the bag, staring in horror at what he'd done. The bow and quiver were on the ground at his feet, arrows scattered all around.

Wright and Naz both realized he was unarmed at the same time. They lunged, grappling in the dirt—and Wright miscalculated again that they were still much too close to use the bow.

But Naz knew. She used just an arrow.


AFTER THAT, SHE AND ROJAN MOVED MUCH SLOWER. TO WALK carrying all the bags and propping her sister up was hard. They stopped a lot, because Naz was so delirious from trying not to sleep so she could keep watch with her bow, and because Rojan was so weak. They went back to not making fires.

They never made it to New Orleans. Washington, D.C., was as far as they got.

# ORLANDO ZHANG

ORY CROSSED ROOSEVELT BRIDGE AN HOUR AFTER WAKING. Almost to D.C. Almost to Max.

But when he reached the other side of the long, silent walk, he didn't recognize anything at all. Washington, D.C., looked nothing like Washington, D.C., anymore.

What remained was a city that had been lit on fire down to the last crevice and then doused with winter death. Black scorch marks covered everything. The roads, the earth, the sides of buildings, the roofs were all the same burnt darkness. And from the sky, a perpetual rain fell, a kind of freezing drizzle that felt heavier than water as it settled on him. The city would have glimmered, charred onyx overlaid with diamond, if not for the dark gray clouds that trapped all light.

He was a tourist at the end of the world.

JUST BEYOND THE KENNEDY CENTER, THERE WAS A GROUP OF women camped out in what once had been a luxury apartment complex's ground-level garage. The door was either gone or rolled up, and they were standing at the edge of it, chatting quietly as they adjusted the blankets draped over their shoulders for warmth. Three shadows, four pairs of feet. The shadowless one was huddled with them, describing something that caused the rest of them to nod thoughtfully. She was short and wiry, with wild hair so red it was almost orange. In another lifetime, it would have been beautiful. Now all Ory could think was that it made her a target.

One of them said something, and they all laughed. Three shadows. *This might be it,* he thought nervously. *They might have seen Max.*

*They might remember.* The fabric under his armpits was so damp he could feel it squelch.

Ory made sure the knife was pushed as far back on his belt as possible, out of view, and the barrels of the shotgun—the *thunderstorm*—were cracked open to show they were empty. *Here goes nothing,* he thought as he stood up.

"Hello," he called. "I don't mean any harm. I'm looking for my wife. Her name . . ."

That was when the small, sharp rock whizzed past his right temple.

Ory ducked. The next rock hit the ground just in front of him and splintered against the concrete.

No, no, no, this was not right at all. A searing burn erupted on his shoulder, and a tiny section of his shirt folded open to expose a sharp crimson split. The blood began to ooze. Ory snapped his arms up in front of his face for protection as he scrambled back. The two women in the front were pulling stones filed into barbs from purses strapped to their waists, flinging them with deadly aim as the other two scrambled for heavier weapons deeper in the garage. The shadowless one cupped her hands around her mouth and shouted. "Mike! Jim! Intruder at the front!" Another rock struck the ground next to Ory's boot, and then he heard what could only have been the rev of a motorcycle engine from somewhere deeper in the crumbling complex.

He turned and sprinted with all he had.

WHEN HE COULDN'T HEAR THE GASOLINE ROAR ANYMORE, Ory crawled into the first hovel he could find and poked gingerly at his shoulder. The slice was deep, but he hoped it didn't need stitches. He didn't have stitches anyway. He tried to squeeze the two sides of skin together over the meat beneath, but they peeled back open like eyelids over a red, swollen eye.

He chose another street, but it didn't matter. The few other people he found were the same.

Rocks, hammers, axes, tree branches shaved down into spears

and clubs. People were terrified Ory wanted to steal their food or kill them, and others couldn't remember whether they knew him or were afraid of him. They either ran him off or stared at him in silent terror until he gave up. One old woman with no shadow finally offered him a dried fish she'd caught in the Potomac.

"How many days?" he asked between ravenous bites.

"Nine," she said. She smiled. "I should go now, in case I forget I gave you that."

Ory finished and licked his fingers clean of the pungent oil. His stomach was already cramping from what was his first real food in days. "You haven't seen a woman, have you?" he asked her as she turned to leave. "I have her photograph."

"Honey, I can't even remember my own name anymore," she said. "I hope you find her."

"Me too," Ory said. "I think she headed east from here. We used to live near Dupont Circle before."

"Oh, no," the old woman scolded. She took hold of his face. "Don't go deeper in. Bad things, very bad things. You stay on the coast, like the rest of us. Better yet, into Arlington, or farther. That's what the young ones are doing." She shook her head. "If your dear went into the city, you won't find her. You likely won't come back either."

"What bad things?" Ory asked. But her face went blank, then twisted in fear. He left before she could attack him for the fish.

THE CLOSER TO THEIR APARTMENT ORY DREW, THE LOUDER the streets became. He started to see snatches of movement. Smoke. Dust billowing from damaged buildings. Fresh blood. Screams down long alleyways. And shadowless, running across intersections between breaks of eerie silence. Running in straight lines.

Ory had seen a lot of people run in his early scouting days, before they all vanished. There was a difference between someone who was running *next* to someone, coincidentally in the same direction, and someone who was running *with* them. He watched the streets nervously. It wasn't like in Arlington. These shadowless ran like they knew where they were going—and like they were going there together. Straight lines, sharp turns. He didn't know what to make of it. He just knew it could be nothing good.

"I'm coming, Max," Ory whispered. He was almost there. On the side of the next building, in red dye of some kind, the words *The One Who Gathers* gleamed. He turned the corner at a sprint. Home.

I FOUND ANOTHER DRAWING YESTERDAY, AT ANOTHER ABAN-
doned camp. It looks like it's by the same artist as the one who drew
the signs at the school in Oakton. I feel like I'm on the right track,
Ory. I don't know to what yet, but the right track to something. This
one—this one was the strangest of all.

The first thing I noticed were the ashes. They were from a campfire that had been put out earlier that morning, I realized as I squatted
over it. All around, bare spots on the ground, where people had slept.
Then I saw the drawing. Just behind the camp, on a section of the
sidewalk that was still mostly intact, there was a painted shadow on
the cement. A shadow, and no person. It looks even stranger than a
person with no shadow.

I stood above it, in the exact same position—one arm raised as if
talking, the other on my hip—and stared. I stood there for hours like
that. It was such an odd thing to do. I didn't even feel particularly
connected, like some part of me that was missing felt whole again. I
wanted to so badly, Ory, but I just didn't. Instead, it was eerie, like
putting on clothes that aren't yours, or going with it when someone at
a crowded party mishears your name and calls you something slightly
different for the rest of the loud, buzzing night.

Maybe I didn't feel anything because it wasn't a drawing of my
own shadow. It was of the blue-eyed man's.

# THE ONE WHO GATHERS

THE NEXT DAY, WHEN DR. ZADEH BROUGHT THE AMNESIAC back to Maharashtra Regional Hospital for another session, Dr. Avanthikar's assistants were printing reams and reams of zigzagging lines on graph paper. Brain waves, he figured when she stepped away from supervising them long enough to embrace him warmly and shake Dr. Zadeh's hand.

"So much data," she said to them. "Hopefully there's good news hiding inside it. You did a great job. Hemu hasn't had the patience to talk to someone for that length of time since before he was admitted."

"They understand each other." Dr. Zadeh smiled.

"I think he just feels comfortable," the amnesiac said. "We've both forgotten some things. We're equals. Maybe, even, friends."

"Oh, that reminds me—*one* sandwich," Dr. Avanthikar said, wagging a finger at him. She'd heard them yesterday when the amnesiac promised to bring Hemu the American snack to try, and had decided to allow it. "One."

Her tone made him happy. It wasn't the tone of a doctor assessing a patient's nutrition. It was the tone of a mother allowing her son to bend the rules because she loved him. She cared about Hemu as much as Dr. Zadeh cared about the amnesiac. "Got it," he smiled. "One sandwich."

She winked and opened the door to Hemu's room to show him in. From the couch, Hemu stared at Dr. Avanthikar for so long as she patiently reintroduced the two of them and stuck wire sensor pads on their heads again to hook them back up to their machines, the amnesiac was afraid he'd forgotten everything that happened yesterday. But when she finally left the room and the low hum told him they'd started monitoring, Hemu smiled.

"I thought you might not remember me," the amnesiac confessed.

"Oh, I remember you," he said. "I just don't know who she was, who came with you."

"She's a doctor," the amnesiac replied. "Here to help you." He tried not to think about her in there, sitting in the room behind the one where they were, listening. If she'd been hurt when she heard Hemu's words. "But how are you today? How do you feel?"

"I'm all right," he replied. "I did a lot of thinking last night. About what you said, that you'd remember for me whatever I can tell you. At first I wasn't sure I was going to talk about this with you, but I think I should. We haven't known each other long, and I know our afflictions aren't the same, but I think you'll be more likely to understand than anyone. I think you're the best person to tell."

The amnesiac put his hand up. "I'm honored to hear anything you want to share. But we have plenty of time, Hemu. I don't want you to feel pressured to share personal things with me until you feel comfortable. The Indian government granted me permission to work with your doctors for a full month, with the possibility of extension if necessary, even. We—"

"That doesn't mean we actually *have* a month," Hemu interrupted. He shrugged. "You know?"

He did know. The amnesiac looked down, unable to meet Hemu's eyes. "I hope we have more time than that."

"Me too," Hemu said. "But in case we don't, there's something very important, something I've been working on since I was brought here—ever since I realized I'd started forgetting things. I want you to help me remember it." He drew in a long breath. "Gajarajan Guruvayur Kesavan."

The amnesiac simply nodded, intimidated by the number of syllables. "Another god?" he asked at last.

Hemu shook his head, expression intensely serious. The wires hung like a headdress from him. "Guruvayur Kesavan was an elephant. Gajarajan—the king of elephants. He lived at Guruvayur Temple, in Kerala."

The amnesiac tried to keep all the terms straight. "Do they worship the sun god Surya at Guru—Guruvayur Temple?" he guessed hopefully.

"No," Hemu said. He turned around and patted the cushions of his couch. "Guruvayur Temple is dedicated to the worship of Vishnu, in the form of Krishna. His eighth and final form," he explained absently, checking beneath another cushion.

"There are a lot of names in the Rigveda," the amnesiac sighed.

"No, forget the Rigveda for now. This isn't ancient lore. Gajarajan was real—a real, living, breathing elephant. From the 1970s! I'm not talking about classical Hindu legends—I'm talking about research. Modern scientific research. *My* research."

"*Your* research?" the amnesiac repeated, but Hemu was distracted.

"Where is it?" he mumbled, picking up the pillows to see if anything was beneath them. "Hello?" he called. The amnesiac could see Hemu was working back through what he'd just explained about Dr. Avanthikar, while he still remembered it. "Doctor—with the silver hair?"

After a moment, the door opened. Dr. Avanthikar's head poked into the room, braid swinging from over her shoulder. "You left it in your sleeping room." An aide appeared behind her in the doorway, evidently having had gone to retrieve the thing Hemu had been looking for. "Here it is." She crossed the room to them, something tucked under her arm.

He felt sad to see her then. "Thank you, Dr. Avanthikar," the amnesiac said, using her name. He wanted to somehow apologize, for bringing out the fact that Hemu had forgotten her overnight.

"It's all right," she said to him gently, and smiled. She understood what he was trying to do. She handed Hemu a three-ring binder, nearly stuffed, and went back to the observation room. Tiny corners of mismatched paper stuck out from every angle, pages Hemu had torn out from elsewhere and pasted in.

When they were alone again, Hemu set the book down gently on the table between them, faceup. "Yes, my research. Everything I've been able to collect. The—" He had lost her name again. "The woman lets me; she thinks it's good for me to work on something. Are you ready?"

The amnesiac nodded. Hemu had enjoyed telling him about the god of the sun, but this was something very different from the Rigveda, he could tell. It was no mythological story. It was far more important to him.

Hemu opened the cover as if it was an antique. "This is Gajara-jan. Most holy of all elephants in India." On the first page, a cutout photograph of an elephant stared back at them, a huge, dark gray face framed by a fan of equally dark ears. It was much darker than the concept of elephants had been in the amnesiac's mind—this one looked almost black, as if carved out of charcoal. At the center, the long line of its broad forehead and muscular hanging trunk were a hundred shades lighter, like it had dipped its face and long nose into a puddle of pale satin paint.

"Oh," the amnesiac said, transfixed. There was something almost human about its expression, the expectant posture of its head. Its black eyes were gigantic. They stared not past the camera, at whoever had been taking the picture, but directly into the lens—as if the creature understood the concept of a photograph.

"Majestic, isn't he," Hemu said. He turned the book back to himself, to smile lovingly at Gajarajan's photo. "Did you know that the word that means a group of elephants together is *memory*?" he asked. "A memory of elephants."

"An elephant never forgets," the amnesiac said automatically. It was a thing people said, he realized. He wondered how he knew that. He turned and glanced at the opaque glass of the observation window for a moment, hoping Dr. Zadeh was watching them from the other side. He'd know to write that down if he saw the look—had the amnesiac ever actually seen an elephant before?

Hemu turned a few more pages. Gajarajan danced between them, dark eyes, pale curled trunk. "Not only that," he continued. "Did you know they have the same memory?"

"Like, if two elephants experience something together?" the amnesiac asked.

Hemu shook his head. "One elephant experiences something, and another remembers it."

The amnesiac lost a beat, and then decided to say what he'd heard Dr. Zadeh say, when he knew one of his Alzheimer's patients had mixed something up. "I see," he finally replied.

Hemu snorted and started flipping through his book again. "I didn't forget this," he insisted. "This is not one of those things, there's documented—" He stopped suddenly at an old article. "Here."

It was a story about Gajarajan from the 1950s, when the elephant was middle-aged. According to the clipping, he'd been born a wild elephant. But when he was a calf, hunters separated him from his family at a river crossing and kidnapped him. It was common practice at the time for nobles to gift elephants to Hindu temples, the article continued, where they would live within the grounds and be magnificently decorated to perform in rituals and parades. The royal family of Nilambur offered the young Gajarajan—named only Kesavan then—to Guruvayur Temple.

Decades after, when Gajarajan had become one of the most famous elephants in India for his almost uncanny devotion to his religious duties, several of his still-wild siblings were captured by poachers for their ivory. Before they could be killed, the locals, who kept informal watch over Gajarajan's remaining family to honor him, ran the men off with machetes. The attacks had become more and more frequent, and the locals decided the only way to keep the rest of Gajarajan's family safe would be to move them to a protected elephant sanctuary, hundreds of kilometers away. It was at this sanctuary that one of

Gajarajan's sisters, who had been born a few years *after* his capture and donation to Guruvayur Temple, met an American volunteer biologist who eventually taught her to paint after watching her scratch around in the dirt with sticks.

Gajarajan's sister painted every Friday when the biologist came to the sanctuary and brought her another canvas and more cans of paint. Almost all of his sister's creations were portraits of the biologist, who had long brown hair and wore a metal prosthetic leg from her left knee down—she had been born without her foreleg and foot.

Later that year, the Guruvayur priests began renovating their temple in preparation for an upcoming holiday. Gajarajan was put into the inner courtyard so they could repair part of his enclosure. According to the article, Gajarajan wandered around placidly as usual, gently examining the tools and tarps lying ready for use. But when he came upon a crate that contained paintbrushes, his mood suddenly changed. Gajarajan seized one with his trunk and then stepped on the paint cans until they puckered under his massive weight, bending open. By the time the priests noticed what had happened, Gajarajan was already halfway finished. On the concrete wall nearest to him, he'd used the paint meant to freshen up the pillars and the roofs to create a messy but unmistakable picture of a woman—with brown hair and one silver leg.

"Impossible," the amnesiac said, looking up from the article.

"Isn't it?" Hemu asked. "Gajarajan never left the temple after he was captured as a calf. He never met the biologist—non-Hindus aren't allowed on the temple grounds. No one showed him the—the—" He had forgotten the word for *sister,* as he had also forgotten his own brothers. "—the other elephant's art."

The amnesiac gave Hemu back the book. He didn't know what to say. Something was sparking in the back of his mind, like a tiny shock. Electrical impulses on synapses, Dr. Zadeh always said. It felt like more than that though. The Rigveda stories an entire country knew, the legend of Surya and his wife and her shadow, Gajarajan, his herd, their paintings. The shock trailed off somewhere deep when he tried to follow. Everything Hemu said—about the gods, about this elephant's urban legend—always drifted off, fragmented, incomplete. But the chatter wasn't aimless, any which way. He was talking in circles, around and around a thing he knew was important but couldn't reach.

"It's probably impossible to have amnesia, as an elephant. The other elephants would remember for you," Hemu said to himself. He touched the picture of Gajarajan. "Too bad we're human."

The amnesiac watched Hemu's face. Perhaps on the doctor's screens, their brains looked identical, blobs of color firing randomly on black backgrounds, but inside the room they were not the same at all. He had to deal only with having forgotten—he never had to live the actual forgetting.

"Hemu, are you afraid?" he asked softly.

"Yes," Hemu said.

The amnesiac tried to smile. "Don't be. I know it's not much comfort, but I—I mean, I'm doing all right. You will, too."

Hemu shook his head, eyes wide. "You don't get it, though." His voice was so quiet, almost just breath. The sensors glued to their heads could see electrical pulses but not know the exact words. The amnesiac realized Hemu didn't want the others to hear. He looked around quickly—for microphones, for cameras—as the young man leaned near. "It's not the same thing," Hemu whispered.

"Why?"

"Because you forgot everything on accident."

There was a moment when the amnesiac expected the door to crash open and the aides to run in, but nothing happened. It felt as though he had become lighter, or gravity had become infinitesimally weaker. He leaned in too, as close as he could. "What do you mean, on accident?" he asked. "You didn't?"

Hemu's eyes searched the amnesiac's desperately. "After your shadow is gone, there's a pull," he said.

"What pull?"

"To *forget*."

All the air had left the room. "The loss of your shadow makes you forget," the amnesiac said slowly, reiterating what Dr. Avanthikar had said. That was what the research group and all its consultants had posited so far—there was some correlation there, even though no one knew what.

Hemu shook his head. "No, no, I don't think so. Not really." He looked down at the couch, where nothing else sat on it with him. "It just makes it *possible*. But you don't *have* to. An elephant who has had its chains cut off doesn't *have* to leave its temple."

The amnesiac trembled as Hemu stared back at him. The look on his face was desperate. The amnesiac didn't understand at all, but he knew that what Hemu was trying to tell him was something far more important than anything else he'd shared. It was maybe the most important thing in the world now.

"There's a *feeling*," Hemu whispered. "A pull. I went toward it because I didn't know what was happening at first. Every time, it felt better and better. Once I realized what I was giving up in exchange—my memories—it was too late. Now it's just too strong. I can't stop it." He swallowed hard. "I don't know if I want to."

"But what is forgetting yourself giving you?" the amnesiac asked.

Hemu peeled off the sensors in one swift motion. Above, an alarm in the ceiling began to beep, drowning out their voices even further. "*Magic.*"

IF YOU COULD ASK ME NOW, YOU'D WANT TO KNOW WHEN I decided. That I was going to run away. That's fair, I suppose.

It was the night before I did it that I became sure.

At first I was terrified of your leaving me alone for the day. I don't know what it's going to be like once I start forgetting the big things, but it can't be good. And you didn't want to leave either. You just wanted to lie in bed with your arms wrapped around me and my hair up your nose as you spooned me. That's what we did for the first four days after it happened—just laid there. Like if we did nothing, just stayed frozen in the moment, then time really wouldn't pass, and I wouldn't forget. I'd just hang suspended forever in the first few hours after I lost my shadow.

Of course, that's not how it works. Maybe it slowed it down some, dulled the temptation to forget for a while, but it wouldn't have worked forever. Time always leaves you behind.

If I'd deteriorated any faster, I think we would have just stayed there until there was nothing left of me. But by the fourth day, when we realized that I was still pretty together, you couldn't argue anymore with me that at some point you were going to *have* to go look for food, to keep us alive. That's when we decided you'd go as soon as it was light enough to see, to scavenge ruthlessly to collect a last Hail Mary stash, one that would allow us to then live out our last few . . . days? weeks? together. You could be there for me then, when it really started to happen, you said.

After you fell asleep, into that deep, heavy unconsciousness you can put yourself into when you know you have to go scavenge the next day, I peeled back a little corner of the cardboard over the window in our bedroom—I know, I know, but I was careful not to crease it—and I watched the moon for a long time.

You don't know this, Ory, but since it happened, I've barely slept.

Maybe that's a side effect. I stay in the bed with you, limbs tangled, but while you're snoring softly, my eyes are open. I lift my hands over my head and just stare at them. Or rather, at where they should be, but I can't see them, because it's too dark. The blackness is so heavy, and it's so hard to see the outline of my fingers, that for those few hours every night, it almost feels like I still have a shadow. I never would have realized that not having one feels different from having one, but it does. And the only time I can relieve that feeling is then, when it's really dark and I can't see any of myself, let alone the subtle shape I should cast beneath me.

I sat there at the window watching the moon shift silently across the sky until I heard you stir. I crawled back in beside you, jammed my nose into your neck. Even after six days without bathing, you still smelled kind of sweet, like faint vanilla that was sharpening.

You clutched at me aimlessly, still half-unconscious, and squeezed me to you with a sleep-heavy leg that you wrapped over me. "But I have a confession about that last play," you murmured, dreamlost, face searching for my shoulder to bury itself. You don't know this, Ory, but you talk in your sleep when you're upset. We sometimes have entire conversations you don't remember at all. Your own tiny version of shadowlessness. "I have a confession to make."

"I know," I whispered, trying to calm you.

I knew where your memories were leading you. You were talking about the football game where we met.

The sky was piercing gray that day. We were huddled together on the bleachers, shivering in our windbreakers as tiny colored dots dashed back and forth across a field far below us. You leaned closer, looking like a boy, nervous and brash at the same time. A whistle shrieked. My friends had vanished into the crowd like fog burning off a lake in late morning, Marion herding them away—and yours had pulled back just far enough to watch you make a fool of yourself. I didn't know them then, but Paul and Imanuel were in that group, watching us. Plastic armor crashed.

"I actually don't know anything . . . about football." You trailed off into a soft snore. "I'm only here because my friend Paul made me . . ."

I shifted, fixing your pillow gently.

"You ready to get out of here?" you asked, the same way you had the first time. Later you told me it was the most daring, stupid way you'd ever invited a girl to dinner—that you were convinced you had to seem nonchalant to impress me, but were terrified you'd just blown it as soon as the words were out.

"Shh," I hummed into your ear, but you didn't quiet. I knew you wouldn't until I repeated what I'd said—whenever you had this dream, you never did until I answered. "I'm always ready," I finally said.

You settled, smiling faintly. I stroked your hair until I thought you'd drifted back down.

"It's so strange," you mumbled suddenly. Your voice was so clear that I looked at you in surprise in the darkness, but you were still asleep, eyes still closed. Your fingers dawdled clumsily at the collar of your shirt, where the single silver chain necklace you always wear disappeared beneath the cotton collar. "My ring is gone."

"What ring?" I asked.

"My wedding ring," you answered.

Deep inside me, something horrible bloomed. A drowning, drowning dread.

"I don't know how I could have lost it . . ." Your eyelids fluttered. "Don't know."

"Maybe you took it off and put it somewhere," I whispered. I tried to hide the horror in my voice.

"I never take it off." You smiled faintly at me from the other side of sleep. "You know that."

"Of course I know," I said. But I didn't. I didn't at all.

"Don't understand," you repeated again. "The only way is if it broke, but the chain is still here." Your next dream started to pull you deeper again. "The chain is still here." The words became less and less clear. "Do you . . . Do you think . . ." You trailed off as your leg twitched. Then you were gone, whisked away from your worry somewhere deeper, somewhere more peaceful. "Maybe . . ."

Once you began to snore, I lifted your left hand carefully off the covers in the darkness and gently felt my way down your palm toward your third finger. *Please be there,* I prayed. *Please be there.*

But it wasn't. There was no weathered silver band. Because of course you had—it made perfect sense now. Of course you had moved it from your hand to a neck chain so it wouldn't get in the way during your scavenging or attract attention if you happened to run into anyone looking for something to steal. So you didn't lose it.

Only now you had, because without it there on your finger to see every day, I had forgotten you still had your wedding band, that you hadn't misplaced it somewhere in the early days or while searching the downtown. I had forgotten you had moved it to the chain on your neck who knows how long ago, and so I had forgotten you had it at all.

I put your hand back down on the covers as softly as I could. Your bare, ringless hand. "Fifty-two," I whispered to your sleeping form.

That's when I knew I had to leave. Before it was too late.

I understood then how the Forgetting works. Why sometimes we shadowless simply don't remember anymore and why other times something changes: there's a difference between when the mind forgets and the heart does. The memory means more, the more it's worth to you—and to who you are. The heart has a harder time letting go. But what happens when you refuse to let go of a delicate thing as it's being pulled away from you? It stretches. Then it tears.

Do you know what means the most to me of all, Ory? Out of everything that's left in this world? Don't you see now why I had to leave you? That I had to do it? That I had no choice?

Do you know what could happen when I forget *you*?

# ORLANDO ZHANG

ORY SAT THERE FOR A WHILE ON THE LAST REMAINING section of curb on the street.

Of course it was more possible that Max wouldn't be there than that she would. He'd just refused to think about it, because he knew if he did, the logic to give up would have been overwhelming. He could only believe that she'd headed for their home, and then follow her. What else was he supposed to do? Just let her go? Just leave her to forget, even though it was his fault, even though she'd still be in the shelter with him if he hadn't gone to Broad Street? He was just supposed to go on living and let her die? Ory tossed the pebble in his hand and watched it skitter over the asphalt.

Their apartment was gone. The entire block had collapsed in on itself, into a pile of steel bars and sand. Ory watched the air a few feet up from the ground, where the front door should have been. Where he was supposed to have walked through and found Max.

"She's not here," he said softly to himself. Either she'd come and then gone when she saw that their home was destroyed, or she never came. Ory picked up a handful of the gray powder and let it slide through his fingers. "Where are you, Max?" He sighed. The sand hissed. "Where?"

His shoulder ached where the sharpened pebble had cut him. The streets had begun to look more menacing in the late-afternoon light—he needed somewhere safe to camp within sight of the property. He pressed down harder to stanch the cut and grimaced.

"I see you've met the four sisters," a voice said.

The shotgun was already aimed. "The what?" Ory asked.

A tall, thin man emerged from the half doorway of an abandoned business farther down the street. A shadow followed him. "The four sisters," he repeated, and gestured to the gash on Ory's shoulder. "New around here, aren't you?"

Ory slowly nodded. There was no point to try to hide it. It was obvious the man knew the answer anyway.

"Famous for their hospitality." He smiled. His eyes lingered on Ory's pockets. "You're lucky you still have your stuff."

"It wasn't like that," Ory said. "I approached them. I just wanted to ask if they'd seen my wife. She might've passed through here."

The man's eyes narrowed. "Lost shadowless?" he asked.

"About a week now. She would've—this is the building where we used to live."

"What's she look like?"

"You think you saw her?"

"What's she look like?" he repeated.

Ory scrambled for his wallet photo. "She's about five-five, dark skin, brown afro, green eyes. Her name is Max, she has a scar over her right eyebrow—" It was too much to hope for. Did the man know the faces of most of the women hiding around here?

"I very well might," the man said as if he'd read Ory's mind. "I'm a finder, you see." When he realized Ory hadn't heard the term before, he shrugged and stuck his hand out. "Give it here."

Ory passed him the photo. "Her name is Max," he said again.

The man took one look and then nodded. "Oh, I *have* seen a woman like that," he said.

Ory snatched the photo back and stared into Max's face. "Are you sure?"

"I'm sure."

"When?"

"Maybe one, two days ago." He pondered. "She was alone."

"Did you talk to her? Was she all right?"

"I don't talk to shadowless," he said. "Professional policy."

Ory felt dizzy. "Which way did she go? Can you show me?" He held the photo out again, his hand trembling. "Are you sure it was her?"

The man looked a second time and nodded. "It was her," he said. "Max." The name came slowly, as if he was trying it out.

"I'm begging you." Ory felt himself drop to his knees before he even realized he was doing it. "Show me where she went."

# MAHNAZ AHMADI

BY THE TIME THEY REACHED WASHINGTON, D.C., ROJAN WAS feverish, the color of sweating white cheese. The wound in her thigh stank like rotten meat. The most horrible part about it was that Naz was so hungry sometimes it almost smelled good to her. They hadn't eaten in weeks, and were starving; Naz's sports bra had become so loose under her shirt it was almost more like a short tank top, and Rojan's trousers would have fallen right off if she hadn't been lying down on the makeshift pallet Naz had cobbled together so she could drag her to the city, where they hoped to find better shelter than the woods. But they found when they made it to D.C. that there was no food there either. The shops had all been picked clean long ago. There were just dead bodies, empty buildings, and shadowless. Rojan's wound festered further, blooming like some horrible raw steak flower across her leg.

That was what they were doing the morning they saw their first shadowed survivors since Wright. Starving and dying.

She and Rojan were crouched in the hovel they'd made their home, listening to the sounds. All the streets downtown were close together—and there was so much activity. Screams echoed throughout the nights. Strange rain during the day that somehow soaked only every other street, and to Naz's terror and bafflement, followed movement, as if tracking her. Footsteps for which she could never pinpoint the origin. By this point, she'd lost count of how many she'd killed. It was far greater than six. But now Naz was always afraid that the next time they ran into someone—shadowed or shadowless—she'd be too weak to fight them off, even with the bow. That the next time it happened, it would be the end.

When Naz first heard the footsteps, she thought that day had come.

She dropped to the ground inside their shelter, pressing her stomach against the dusty wood floor. Rojan opened one eye weakly to look at her. As quietly as Naz could, she slid an arrow out of her quiver and nocked it. She poked her head over the half wall of their shelter to steal a glance, and almost choked. Not one or two, but an entire *horde* of shadowless was prowling outside.

"Shadowless?" Rojan whispered. Her voice was like dry leaves scraping together.

"Yeah," Naz nodded.

"How many?"

Naz looked down. Too many. Far too many. They were scrambling back and forth around the street, as if searching the perimeter of the sisters' ruins. *Can they smell us?* Naz wondered. Dust from the crumbled buildings billowed down the street, hazy in the air, swirling as bodies without shadows dashed through it, creating currents. Two of them were barely more than toddlers, she realized with a shudder. Huge heads teetering on tiny little bodies, arms and faces hairless with youth.

"It's okay," Rojan said. *It's okay if you run.*

"I'm not leaving you," Naz whispered fiercely. A shadowless darted closer, snarling.

"Please." Rojan closed her eyes again. "I want you to."

Naz looked back out at the street. She knew she should go. If she had been the one dying on the ground, she'd want Rojan to save herself, too. Naz would want Rojan to save herself so badly that she'd probably try to kill herself to free her sister. She had no doubt that if Rojan was strong enough to crawl around to find something sharp, she probably would do just that.

Instead, Naz raised her bow and let loose the first arrow.

"Naz," Rojan moaned. But it was too late. The street exploded into chaos as Naz grabbed another arrow from the quiver on her back.

She had no idea why she did it, because there was no point. She'd never kill them all. Maybe it was because she knew she'd never leave Rojan, but Rojan was going to leave her, because Rojan was going to die first. The only thing Naz had wanted to do her entire life, from the moment she became a big sister, was protect Rojan—and she had failed. There was nothing she could do to save them. Maybe she was just trying to speed it up, then, so it finally could be over. A shadowless went sailing, body jerked straight as the arrow punched into him, then fell. He didn't get up.

"How do you like that," Naz snarled. The rest of the shadowless had recovered from the initial shock, and all turned toward the sound. Their eyes locked on her. She reached back into her quiver as they began to move in, nocked another arrow, let it fly, too. Another. Another. It felt good to be doing it. The shadowless fell, but more replaced them. She kept shooting. Those familiar motions, the memory of the bow as strong in the muscles themselves as in her mind. Taking something back, before the end.

"Make a circle!" A man's voice broke her aim suddenly. Naz faltered, jolted back into the moment. The shadowless spun around, hissing. Bodies ran back and forth. There was more shouting now, and then sounds of death. Someone else was fighting the shadowless for her, she realized. Many someones. An entire group had shown up and was beating her predators into retreat. "Face out! Back to back!"

Slowly it grew quiet and still again. The dust settled back onto the broken streets. Naz stood there, dazed, holding her bow, as she stared. Across the street, six people stood amid the shadowless corpses, panting. At the front, two men wielded pipes like baseball bats—one tall and dark-skinned, and the other pale, with a barrel chest and thinning brown hair. Both with shadows. No, *all* with shadows, she realized. All of them. Every. Single. Survivor.

When the pale, balding man turned toward Naz, everything came rushing back. *What have I done? What the fuck have I done?* She ducked back down behind the wall as quickly as she could, but it was too late. *They know right where we are now.*

"Are you all right?" he called.

"Careful," his friend said.

"Malik, come on. She was in trouble."

But the other couldn't be swayed. "We don't know her."

*And I don't know you either,* Naz agreed.

"You can come out," the first finally continued, facing her direction again. "Are you injured?"

The one called Malik sighed in disgust, giving up. *So the pale, balding one is the leader of their group,* Naz observed. She knew who to aim at now, if need be.

"Gather those arrows up for her, so she can use them again," another shouted, now that it was clear they weren't about to be commanded to attack Naz, too. *At least not yet.* Naz watched them for signs of a ruse. The younger ones began to move toward the arrows and bodies shakily, still stunned from battle. "Careful when you pull them out."

"Hon?" one of the women added across the rubble. "That was brave of you. To fight them."

Naz didn't move. People said nice things all the time, then killed you for your boots. Wright had done it. These strangers had saved her, but that still meant nothing. She didn't know a thing about them.

"Really brave," the leader added. "You don't have to worry about us, though. We're friendly. We're not here to attack you."

"Prove it," Naz finally shouted over the wall.

"Prove it? Uh." He turned and glanced awkwardly at the small group behind him. A teenaged girl reached into her backpack. She looked just like the one named Malik, Naz saw as she watched her. Same nose, same eyes. Both tall. Naz swallowed hard and did not let herself think about it. "Oh," the leader said as the girl moved toward him, and then he turned back around. Naz's fingers strained on the bowstring as she peeked over. He was holding something. "Here."

It was a piece of jerky meat.

Where on this godforsaken earth had an idiot like that found meat and then managed to preserve it? There was nothing left here, anywhere, nothing at all.

Naz watched the man look around for a moment, likely for lurking shadowless who'd sniffed out the meal, and then set the tough meat down on a flat piece of rubble. "Here. A gesture of peace," he called.

That was very convincing. People tried to take your food, not give it to you. "Back up," Naz growled.

He put his arms up and walked a few steps back obligingly, and then with a flick of his hand, scooted the rest of the group even farther.

Naz didn't move. Not yet. "What was all that?" she asked Malik.

"Just shadowless," he answered. "That's how they are here. In the downtown, they're starting to roam together."

"That's different," Naz said.

"It is different," he agreed, troubled.

"How did you learn to do that?" the girl called to Naz. She wiped a wet trail on her forehead. For a moment, Naz thought it was blood, but then she realized it was just smeared with dirt.

"I was an archer," Naz answered at last. "I was training for—for the Olympics." It was such a strange thing to say in this new world.

She saw the words slowly register on all of their faces. "An archer," the girl said to her father, as if in wonder. Their shadows talked to each other as well, silent mimes. Naz watched all their dark shapes face one another and fidget on the asphalt. It was mesmerizing. "That's impossible luck."

The man in charge had moved closer while Naz was talking, close enough that he could peer into the shelter. He could see Rojan lying there, pale and near death. Naz watched his eyes study them, taking the situation in. "We could really use your help. Come back with us. Meet the General," he said gently.

"No," Malik growled softly, warning, but the leader ignored him. Naz could see the look in the pale man's eyes. It was the same look her coach had when he first met her, young and terrified, clutching her passport in the Boston airport. Naz knew if Malik had been the one in charge, the group would be gone already, and she and Rojan would be alone once more. He was a man who trusted no one, just like Naz—but the other was a man who trusted everyone, just like Rojan. He was looking at her like family.

"Join us," he said again, taking another step forward. "Both of you."

"Watch it," Naz said as she pulled the bowstring tighter against her cheek, arrow aiming this time at Malik. She looked at the girl. The other man was the leader, but this was better insurance.

It seemed less and less like a trap the more they talked, but Naz was hard to convince. There were so many of them and just one of her. But she and Rojan were also starving to death.

In the end, it took fifteen minutes for the man to lure her out from her hovel, and even then, she walked the whole way to the jerky meat offering with the bow still drawn on Malik, arms burning with acid to let the arrow fly. Later, when she thought back on that day, she couldn't imagine what his daughter, Vienna, must have been feeling in those long moments, her father trapped at the mercy of Naz's exhausted, terrified fingertips. Naz would never forgive herself for it, for aiming death so long at Malik like that as she came forward—even though later Malik said it was what convinced him she would make a great lieutenant in their army.

# THE ONE WHO GATHERS

"HE'S NEVER DONE THAT BEFORE, APPARENTLY," DR. ZADEH
said. They were in the car again, on their way to the hospital from
the hotel for their third visit. The amnesiac wasn't sure he'd slept at
all last night, but he didn't feel the least bit tired. "Confided in anyone about his elephant research or pulled the cables off his head like
that. Dr. Avanthikar hopes it's a promising sign. Did he say anything
potentially helpful when the alarms were going? The microphones
couldn't pick up anything."

*Magic.* "No," the amnesiac lied.

Dr. Zadeh frowned. "Nothing?" he asked. "What was he talking
about?"

"Just how he felt," the amnesiac said. "He's afraid of what he can't
remember, but he's also embarrassed by it. It's a strange feeling, to be
surrounded by people who you know have a better understanding of
you than you do."

"Shame is a powerful emotion." Dr. Zadeh nodded sympathetically. "It can be a huge obstacle."

It wasn't that the amnesiac didn't trust Dr. Zadeh or Dr. Avanthikar. He just didn't understand how to explain to them what Hemu
had said. Hemu needed their help if he ever hoped to stop his forgetting, but they already had him under virtual arrest, confined to two
rooms inside a hospital wing. He was more experiment than patient.
What would they do if the amnesiac told them what Hemu had
revealed and made him seem even more impossible and confusing?

"NOW THAT YOU'VE ESTABLISHED SOME RAPPORT, LET'S HAVE
you ask him specific questions about his past today," Dr. Avanthikar

said as the amnesiac took off his shoes to enter Hemu's transplanted living room. "Childhood, family, Zero Shadow Day, the moment when he first started to forget." She clicked a few screens on her computer. "Maybe you'll be able to better help him pinpoint something relevant than we can, now that you two have quite the bond."

"I'll try," he said.

Dr. Avanthikar put a hand on his shoulder to reassure him. "I know you're worried about his decline, but we still have plenty of time. Okay?"

"Okay." He tried to smile. Dr. Avanthikar opened the door.

"My American friend," Hemu nodded from inside his little wired web as the amnesiac walked in. He apparently didn't mind having the cables on again, now that he'd managed to pass his secret on. Or perhaps he was only pretending to be calm, waiting for another moment. Or perhaps he'd already forgotten what he'd said. "Any American food?"

"Oh," the amnesiac blinked. The peanut butter and jelly sandwich. "I'm sorry, Hemu. We were late leaving to get here this morning—it completely slipped my mind."

Hemu waved it off. "I shouldn't even have asked. Don't trouble yourself with it."

"I promised I would," he said. "Tomorrow."

Hemu slid his elephant research notebook carefully onto the low table so he could settle more comfortably on the couch. The amnesiac sat in the chair facing him and waited patiently for the aides to attach the cables to his own forehead again so they would match each other. "So what have they instructed us to speak about today?" Hemu asked. "More Gajarajan?"

"Unfortunately, no," the amnesiac said. "They're hoping for more of a . . . focused approach now. They want us to talk about anything about your past."

Hemu nodded, resigned. They sat for a moment.

"You know what the worst part is," he started. The amnesiac

looked up. "Is forgetting something, but remembering that you've forgotten it." He toyed with the hem of his tunic. "It's almost better to both forget a thing and also forget you've forgotten it. Maybe not better. But kinder."

The amnesiac sighed. "I'm sorry we have to do this," he said.

"It's all right. I know you're only trying to help. This just always shows me exactly what it is I've lost." He took a breath. "Did you have any family that you didn't remember you had?"

The amnesiac thought about Charlotte. "Not really," he said. "No siblings. I apparently never knew my father, and my mother died a few years before the accident."

Hemu squinted, thinking. "I have a mother," he said. "I do remember that word, what it means. Just not who she is."

"Dr. Zadeh told me that my mother's name was Anne," the amnesiac said.

"The doctors say they keep telling me what mine is named, too. But I just can't hold it."

"It's not your fault," the amnesiac said.

"So they all keep saying," Hemu sighed.

"Do you remember the last time you saw her?" the amnesiac continued. "I mean, I know you don't, I just meant—maybe we could try to work backward." He felt absurdly underqualified. Surely his own team had tried this countless times. "I see Dr. Zadeh—my doctor—do that with his other patients, sometimes," he finished lamely.

"I do remember cameras," Hemu said. "A lot of cameras. It was so bright. Every time one would finish its blinding flash, another one would be starting. All I could see was white." He peeled back his lips and made the sound of a hundred shutters clicking: *chh chh chh chh chh chh chh.* "The police were trying to help me into a van, to get me away from them. I wanted to close my eyes and just let them push me toward the back doors and into a seat."

"Oh, this is when they took you from the spice market and brought you here," the amnesiac said.

"The what?" Hemu asked, looking at the amnesiac mid-thought, face puzzled.

"The spice market."

"What market?"

"The—what was it called—the Mandai," the amnesiac tried. "The spice market. Where you were when you lost your shadow."

Hemu's dark eyes grew distant, as if he was gazing somewhere far away. He was trying to recall it, the amnesiac realized.

"I don't remember," Hemu finally said.

A few minutes later, there was a metal clang on the other side of the door, from inside of the observation room. A chair falling as someone stood up out of it too quickly, maybe. The amnesiac glanced over, but the door didn't open.

Then someone cried out *Mandai!* The wall muffled it somewhat, but the word was clear enough. *"Mandai! Mandai!"*

They both stared at the door. Suddenly everyone was screaming. "What's going on?" Hemu asked fearfully.

"I don't know," the amnesiac said. He ripped the cables off his head. "Stay here," he called over the alarms he'd triggered, and ran across the room. He shoved the door to the observation office open. Dr. Zadeh dashed forward to stop who he thought would be Hemu, but then realized it was only the amnesiac. The shadowless was still sitting where he'd been left, staring confusedly at them. Inside, the aides were shouting and pointing at a TV playing the news. Dr. Avanthikar had her silver head in her hands. There was an aerial shot of a completely empty street on the screen. No shops or buildings lining the sides, not even paint on the asphalt to denote traffic lines. A crowd had begun to swarm at its edges. "What's going on?" the amnesiac cried to her over the alarms.

The reporter's voice-over was in Hindi, but it was unmistakable that he was yelling, frantic. Dr. Avanthikar didn't look up from her hands. "The spice market is gone," she said. "It . . . it vanished into thin air."

THE NEXT MORNING, AN AIDE OPENED THE DOOR TO HEMU'S re-created living room for the last time. Both doctors nodded at the amnesiac as he stood there. *Just a few minutes,* it meant. That was all the time they had. After whatever had happened to Mandai, the rest of the night had been filled with uniforms, badges, interrogations. Interrogations of Dr. Avanthikar. Interrogations of Dr. Zadeh. Interrogations of the amnesiac, over and over. None of them could explain it. Hemu was the only one the officers didn't question. They were afraid to cause whatever had happened to happen again. They watched him through the observation window for hours in silence before they let the rest of them go home.

Dr. Zadeh and the amnesiac had woken at dawn to the hotel room phone ringing. They had no idea which official was on the line, but the message he relayed from the prime minister was unambiguous: the joint Indian-American experiment was over. They had less than twelve hours to get on a plane voluntarily before law enforcement would come and forcibly deport them. As soon as Dr. Zadeh put down the receiver, it rang again. This time it was Dr. Avanthikar. More officials were coming at noon for further assessment of her research, she told him. If they could get to the hospital before that, they could say goodbye and escape clean.

"Hemu," the amnesiac said.

"Hello," Hemu replied. He tucked his legs up beneath him on the couch.

They looked at each other for a few moments. The amnesiac wondered if he still remembered what had happened yesterday evening—not exactly what, but that it had been terrible, and it was his fault somehow, or if Hemu was simply waiting for him to speak. If he even remembered the amnesiac at all.

"I'm leaving today," he finally said. "I have to go back home."

"Oh." Hemu looked down. "That's too bad. I like—I liked talking with you. Especially about Gajarajan."

The amnesiac felt an immense relief. "You remember," he said.

Hemu shrugged. "For now. Soon I might not remember you even came."

The amnesiac walked over to where Hemu was seated. "For now is good enough for me," he said.

Hemu looked up at him and smiled. He saw it then. How tired Hemu was. How tired he must have been for a long time.

The amnesiac held up the plastic-wrapped peanut butter and jelly sandwich. "Parting gift," he said. "You asked me—"

"Oh, yes!" Hemu grinned. "I do remember that, still. Thank you. I really—this means a lot. That you did this for me." His voice was strangely thick, like he might cry.

"It was nothing," the amnesiac said, surprised at the intensity of his response. "Really. Dr. Zadeh just asked the kitchen staff at the hotel to make it."

Hemu lifted the package to look at the peanut butter smear, the purple jelly oozing out between the crust. "What's it called again?" he asked. "I mean, I remember that I asked you for it. Just not the name."

"Peanut butter and jelly sandwich," the amnesiac said.

"Peanut butter and jelly," Hemu repeated. He tucked the bag into the large pocket of his tunic. "I look forward to eating this tonight. It will be something new. A good memory—for a while at least."

"Don't give up, Hemu," the amnesiac said. He felt like he might cry, too. He knew how useless it was to say that, probably better than anyone, but he couldn't help it. "I promise I'll remember you. Whatever happens."

Hemu stood and embraced him gently. "If only we were elephants," Hemu said, "we could help each other." Then his expression changed. "Did I ever tell you about—" he began.

The amnesiac hugged him tighter.

spice market incident to Dr. Avanthikar's draft report to her prime minister. She'd stated what everyone in the observation room had seen: Persons whose shadows had disappeared began experiencing disorganized but progressive and permanent amnesia. Shadowless Hemu Joshi was asked a question about the place where he lost his shadow, the Mandai spice market, in conversation by a visiting American patient recovering from severe retrograde amnesia, "Patient RA." Mandai had been one of Joshi's favorite parts of the city, according to background information provided by his brothers. However, Joshi's reply to Patient RA made it clear he did not remember it at all. At almost the exact same time, Mandai—including all the people in it—inexplicably vanished.

"How soon until they inform the public of the connection?" the amnesiac asked.

"As soon as . . ." Dr. Zadeh paused. He reached his fingers under his glasses and massaged his eyelids. "The problem is *how* to explain it. What happened just isn't possible. There's nothing in any field—psychiatry, neurology, physics, biology . . . I mean, you were there." He set the report down. "I don't even know what I saw. Do you?"

"No," the amnesiac said. None of them knew, and all of them did.

The amnesiac took out his copy of Hemu's elephant notebook that Dr. Avanthikar had copied and printed for him before they left, as a parting gift. On the first sheet, he traced the outline of Gajarajan's towering body with his finger. His pale trunk stared back, in front of his pale face.

The amnesiac paused. The picture wasn't the same as before. He flipped through the other pages, faster and faster. Gajarajan was ivory-colored in every one of them, instead of deep gray. Not just the trunk, but all of him now. He closed the book and pretended to sleep.

"You're trembling," Dr. Zadeh said.

"I'm just cold," he lied.

A small ding echoed overhead, and then Dr. Zadeh asked the flight attendant who appeared, "Could we get another blanket?"

The spice market. Gajarajan's form. One mystery could be ignored. Two could not. *Magic,* Hemu had whispered to him, terrified, but too addicted to stop.

"We have to go back," the amnesiac said.

"Our visas have been revoked," Dr. Zadeh replied. "Pune border security would never let us off the plane."

"This is more important than that," the amnesiac said. "Hemu is on to something with the elephants."

"What?" Dr. Zadeh blinked.

He didn't know how to explain it, but he could feel the threads there: the unbinding of shadows from their people; the market Hemu had loved to spend time in; the inexplicable thing that had happened when he forgot it. How the more important the original memory had been to the shadowless, the stronger the power they had over it in the real world when they gave in to the pull. If only there was a way to reverse it, so the magic protected things instead of endangered them, the way the elephants somehow did. The amnesiac flipped through his papers until he found the right one. "Read this," he said, shoving the old article into Dr. Zadeh's bewildered face. "This is Gajarajan."

WHEN THEY TOUCHED DOWN IN NEW ORLEANS, THEY PLANNED to turn right back around and book a flight to D.C. Perhaps they could get the Indian ambassador to the United States to make an exception, if they could get him to listen.

"Let's jog," the amnesiac suggested, but there was a gate agent waiting solemnly at the end of the jetway for them. He caught Dr. Zadeh's arm gently as they passed. "Excuse me—you're Dr. Zadeh, correct?" he interjected. In his hand was a slim white envelope. "I was instructed to deliver this message to you as soon as you disembarked."

"What is it?" Dr. Zadeh asked. He slid his fingernail under the corner of the flap.

The agent shook his head. "I received it from customer service already sealed." He tipped his head as he departed.

The amnesiac watched Dr. Zadeh's eyes flick down the page, faster and faster. "What does it say?" he asked.

Dr. Zadeh said nothing for a long moment. He looked up as if lost. "There was an accident. Hemu's dead."

No.

*Magic,* the amnesiac heard Hemu whisper again. He put his hands over his face.

"He was allergic to peanuts," Dr. Zadeh continued numbly. "Dr. Avanthikar didn't know, and the sandwich—he must have forgot, or . . ." His voice trailed off. He couldn't consider the alternative.

*Magic.* The amnesiac watched the rest of the passengers drift past in silence. He knew this time, for once, Hemu hadn't forgotten at all. It was only that the amnesiac gave the sandwich to him too late.

BECAUSE HEMU JOSHI'S RESEARCH UNIT HAD BEEN SHUT down, every request to the prime minister that they put through the Indian embassy in Washington, D.C., was ignored. They couldn't find Dr. Avanthikar either—she'd been transferred to another shadowless case, either in Mumbai or Nashik, all of which were now classified.

At the assisted-living facility, Dr. Zadeh rang Charlotte, as he'd promised. The amnesiac tried not to listen and just wait. On TV, the news was reporting a shadowless incident in Brazil, the first one outside India. A child, during lunch recess.

After he hung up, Dr. Zadeh said that she told him she would come again in a little while, once she thought she could handle it. The delay made no difference to the amnesiac, as long as she would come. He wouldn't remember anything without her—one day or one month changed nothing. But then the Forgetting touched Boston, suddenly and thoroughly. Time before the accident had frozen forever, but time after it suddenly sped up. Dr. Zadeh let the amnesiac try to call her again, but cases had already started to appear nearby, in Atlanta and Baton Rouge, and it was too late. He didn't see her again.

In those early days, when Hemu's shadow magically disappearing still seemed like a miracle and not impending doom, I secretly wished it would happen to me, too, Ory. This was far before any cases appeared outside of India, back when it was only Hemu, and the Angels from, from . . . the Angels. Back when it was only Hemu and the Angels. It had just seemed magical then, and I wanted to be touched by the magic, too. I'm sure many people did, maybe even you. But the way I wanted it was different. I wanted it like a drowning man wants air. I wanted it so much that late at night, when you and the rest of Washington, D.C., were asleep, I'd creep out of our bedroom, go back downstairs, and turn on the television again, to stand in the bluish glow of the screen as ghostly images of Hemu Joshi dancing around the market played. I'd look at the dark simulacrum of myself stretched silently on the floor beside me.

"Disappear," I begged it once, barely a whisper. I waited for some kind of a cold chill or moment of recognition, but my shadow just stayed there, flickering in the changing light of the television, unhearing. "Please disappear."

When I think back about that, for however much longer I can, it makes me shiver. But none of us knew what was coming. Not for those first few days.

Of course, then we did. We saw what happened to Hemu, and I felt like a fool. Then it started to spread to Brazil and Nepal and Turkey and everywhere else. I told no one what I'd wished. I was terrified. I went to Paul and Imanuel's wedding with you, and then it happened to Boston. I thought it was coming for me. That's a stupid thing to say—it was coming for us all. But I felt like it was especially looking for me. I felt like it had *heard* me. I begged God or the universe or karma or whatever else it is that presides over the ominous phrase *Be careful what you wish for* to take pity on me for being selfish, for wanting more than my wonderful life already was. The stores and streetlights and telephone reception were all going down; people were wandering crying down the sidewalk in Arlington, completely lost and afraid because they couldn't remember where they lived anymore or the words to ask for help; you almost got killed the first time you went out alone to steal food from the locked-up Fresh Shoppe; and all I could think was, I had asked for this. I had *asked*.

Am I far enough away from you yet to keep you safe? I don't think I could ever be far enough, even if I ran until I reached the West Coast. You spent so much time after it happened to me wondering why some people lose their shadows and not others. Why it was mine instead of yours. Every time you asked, I always said that I didn't have any idea either. That I don't know if there is an answer. And that's partially right—no one knows for sure. But what I'm terrified might be true, what I'm too afraid to say out loud to you, Ory my love, is that maybe it happened to me because at one time, for one brief moment, I had *wanted* it to happen . . . And my shadow knew it, too.

# ORLANDO ZHANG

IT WAS A STRAIGHT SHOT UP NEW HAMPSHIRE AVENUE, THE finder said. But it was dangerous. There were a few shadowless there, sometimes forgetting things like streets or turns, so they'd have to run. Ory didn't care.

"Keep up" was the finder's only warning. Then they were sprinting.

They cut through crumbling concrete and skirted buildings the finder thought were inhabited. Ory saw movement in the darkness of alleys and braced for attacks each time as they darted past. *Keep up.* Their deserted mountain was one thing, but how had Max made it through a place like this, alone, and especially if she'd started to forget bigger things? It seemed impossible.

"Here!" the finder suddenly called back to Ory. The ruins of George Washington University loomed overhead. A monstrous gray skeleton. Frayed curtains flickered in one of the upper windows.

Ory slowed involuntarily. Something wasn't right. Max would never come here. The buildings were too huge, too dark, too dangerous. Even if she'd forgotten where she was going, this was not the place she'd head for.

"What's wrong?" the finder called over his shoulder, slowing but not stopping. Ory had to speed back up to stay with him. Together they swung wide around something body-shaped and still lying beneath a tarp, and kept running.

"I don't know," Ory panted.

"You want to find your wife?" the finder asked, waving an arm as he continued to jog closer to one of the cement overhangs. "I'm telling you, this is where I last saw her. We start looking here."

"Max wouldn't come here," Ory said. "It's not like her."

"Well, exactly."

It was not a surprise. Ory knew already that a man who had never even met his wife had the same or better chance of finding her than he did—because she wasn't really his wife anymore. Not entirely. He kept running. He tried not to hate the finder for saying it.

"Right here, yesterday afternoon or the day before," the finder said as he disappeared around the far corner of the outdoor mall.

"Wait!" Ory cried, and lurched forward to catch up to him. When he came around the corner, the finder was gone.

Ory stood there for a few seconds, unsure of what to do. "Max?" He called. There were overturned Dumpsters, heaps of concrete. "Hello?" A long empty plaza. And then finally he understood. "I have only the shotgun. No food," he said.

Things shifted around the corners. The finder appeared again, walking slowly out from another corner of the silent campus, still breathing hard from the run.

"How many of you?" Ory asked. He could see from the shadows of the buildings that he was surrounded. *Finder,* he thought ruefully. He wondered how many before him had also fallen for it. He wanted to be angry or embarrassed, but there wasn't any point anymore. "Five? Six?"

"Enough," the finder said.

Ory laid down the gun and took the shells out of his pockets. "I don't have any food," he said again.

Another joined the first, holding a baseball bat. And another. And another. The sky was a dead gray color. "We'll just make sure."

# PART III

THIS TENT IS NICE. IT'S WARM AND DRY, AND EACH PANEL IS A different color, so the light from the sunrise through the trees turns the inside into a beautiful, rippling kaleidoscope.

I want to stay forever. Which is probably only another few weeks or so.

⏸

There are nine of us now, in total. There were twelve before, but four forgot too much, and then I joined. When I found them, they all talked it over, debating whether it was worth the risk. In the end, they decided since they'd packed the resources for twelve survivors, they could spare the extra they now had.

That makes it sound easy. It really wasn't, Ory. It wasn't at all. At first I thought they were going to kill me.

It was late at night. I was moving through the woods just off the road, as quietly as I could in case there were any wild animals or shadowless nearby, looking for a safe place that I could stop and sleep for a few hours. Something I could put my back against so I had to watch only three sides instead of four. That's when I saw it. A soft orange glow deep in the trees. A campfire.

I know, Ory. I shouldn't have gone. But I was so curious. To be brave enough to have a fire probably meant it was a group, not a single person. And a group that still remembered to stay together as a group probably meant shadows. I haven't seen one for so long—I just wanted to see one again.

I had been right. It was a group. But not like I'd been naively hoping it might be. It was no happy camp of fellow travelers, willing to share food by the fire and reminisce about the good old days. It was more like, either you're a threat or on your way, and we'll be the ones to decide that. They saw a shadowless woman wandering alone at night, nothing more. But when I started answering their questions, I don't think they expected me to sound so . . . whole. Then things took a sharp turn when I told them that today is day sixteen without a shadow for me, and I can still remember my name.

"It's Max," I said softly, hands up to show I meant no harm. The woman holding the hunting rifle narrowed her eyes.

"Last name?"

"Webber. Maxine Webber," I answered.

A pair of young women who looked like twins edged up behind the one with the gun. They were beautiful, tall and willowy, with high cheekbones and thin noses beneath their dark skin. One trained her deer-sized eyes on me, and the other whispered something to their leader. The older woman's hair had been buzzed almost to the skin, and I could see the younger's lips move even though they were just an inch from her ear. The gun didn't waver.

"Sixteen days, you say," the twin on the left finally said, with a vaguely Arabic accent. I nodded. She looked at the woman holding the gun with an interested expression. The other five studied me from where they still sat, in a loose circle around the meager camp-fire they'd built. A man with hair so blond it seemed translucent in the dusk put a hand over his mouth, as if thinking. His fingers were stained by something, maybe mud or mashed grass, each one dark-ened to the second knuckle. The man beside him exhaled smoke, and tossed his cigarette into the flames. None of them had shadows—not a single one. Can you picture that, Ory? Nine of us standing there in the woods, and not a single shape of a hand flickered in the light of the fire, not a single profile warped across foliage or bark. Only the silhouettes of trees danced across the ground, rows and rows of gnarled black lines. There was no sign nine humans were there at all.

The woman in charge glanced at the first twin out of the corner of her eye, to avoid turning her head—and her aim—from me. The twin nodded back. She wanted her to ask me something, I realized.

"Sixteen days," I repeated, trying to sound encouraging.

The gun finally lowered slightly. I met the woman's eyes over the top of the barrel. "Can you still read?" she finally asked.

Moments later, the twins were on either side of me, one with her hands on my shoulders, the other carrying a torch made from a broken branch, guiding me through the woods at a fast walk. The woman with the gun marched beside us. I tried to keep my breathing calm, but I was panicking, Ory. I was sure I still knew how to read, but I hadn't seen any words for a few days now, since the last time I came across a road sign. What if I only *thought* I could still read, and then when they put a book or whatever it was they wanted me to decipher in front of my face, none of it made any sense? I'd never really thought about it as a thing I might lose before, but these eight must have forgotten. What if I had, too? I tried to imagine the letters of my name in my head, but the ground was so uneven and we were walking so fast in the darkness that it was all I could do to concentrate on not tripping. Suddenly, ahead of us was a giant RV beneath a draped tarp, parked in a carpet of dried leaves. They had a vehicle! I checked the ground as we approached, but the tracks looked fresh. They weren't stranded—they'd just driven it off the road to hide it here for the night.

"Here." The woman with the gun stopped abruptly and put her arm out like a barrier. The twins halted and turned to me. Behind us, I could see the faint glow of their little campfire, and the others hunched around it.

"What am I supposed to do?" I asked nervously.

The woman brushed a fly off her shorn head, and nodded at one of the twins. "Up," she said, and the one holding my arm jogged around to the back of the RV, where there was a little metal ladder attached to its side. She climbed up and struggled with a rope tied to the roof. The other twin stood beside the vehicle, torch held high.

"I don't—" I started, but then the rope unknotted and the tarp dropped away from the RV in a hissing swoosh, hitting the grass. "Oh," I murmured, transfixed. I dimly felt myself take a step forward.

Something had been painted across the side of the RV, stretched from front to back over the windows. Huge black letters in all capitals, each stroke as thick as one of my arms. I stared at the bold, curving shapes.

"Who painted this?" I finally asked the twin still on the ground, with the torch. She caught a warning glance from the leader and shook her head instead of answering me, but I could see the anticipation in her expression—they themselves had put it there. This was the only way they could test if I really could read, because even though they couldn't, they still remembered what this one thing said. "How long ago was this done?" I asked, stalling, but the women were out of patience.

"Ursula," the twin atop the RV whispered to their leader eagerly. *Ursula.* I tried to burn the name into my memory with everything I had left.

"Can you read it?" Ursula asked, her voice betraying her nervous hope for the first time. The gun came up again, trained on me. The message was clear. *Read it or you won't remember anything at all.*

I nodded vigorously. "I can, I can," I said. I turned back to the RV and looked at the paint strokes. I have no idea for how much longer, Ory, but for that moment at least, the shapes were still letters, the letters still words, and I could understand them. "It reads *New Orleans,*" I said.

# ORLANDO ZHANG

THE LIGHT BURNED WHEN HE OPENED HIS EYES. A SEARING, blinding pain that went straight into the back of his skull. Ory groaned and closed them again. Flashes came back: he was running, the singing note as a metal bat swung through the air, the deserted campus, the fine dust that covered the empty parking lot as he went down, clawing, kicking, the finder and his men slamming their weapons into his ribs.

Ory's hands went to his pocket. The wallet was still there. They hadn't gotten it before he must have driven them off, thank God. The shells, the shotgun, they barely mattered. He still had the photograph of Max.

There was enough light left in the evening sky to get his bearings again. Ory could have, but he didn't go back to see what he'd done to get away. If he'd survived, maybe so had one of them. And if they hadn't, he didn't care.

It took him the rest of the sunset to get back to the pile of sand that had once been their apartment building. Max might not be there, but if she had left any trace of herself at all to follow, he told himself that was where he'd find it.

THERE ARE SO MANY THINGS TO TELL YOU, ORY! I'M DESPER-
ate to record them all before I start to forget. I want to tell you all
about the others I'm with now, who they are, what they do, where
we're going.

I don't say this to hurt you, I hope you wouldn't take it that way—
but until I met them, until Ursula let me join their caravan, I didn't
realize how lonely I'd been. I was too busy trying to find a hidden
place to sleep each night, trying to stay off the main roads and away
from buildings that looked like they might be inhabited. Trying
not to die. But I was so lonely. And this part especially I'd never tell
you, because it would be too cruel, but I can say it now: I was lonely
out here, in this fucked-up new Virginian wilderness, but I was also
lonely in our shelter, with you. I don't mean always. I just mean that
last week.

It's not your fault. You tried as hard as you could. But you still had
your shadow and all of your memories. You always knew who you
were. But no matter how hard I try, I'll slowly start to forget myself.
I know, I know—you insist that in theory, the Forgetting can be
resisted. I don't want to hear it. You don't know, Ory. You don't *know*.
I didn't know either, until it finally happened to me. How hard it is
to resist. How much the mind wants to fill in holes instead of just
leaving them there—even when you know that every time you do it,
it'll be wrong, and you'll give up something else that will just make
another, bigger hole.

But here, with people like me, I feel light again. They understand.
I'm not sure, but I think that being with them is helping me to not
forget things—because we all want to remember. I wish you could
meet them.

When they started traveling, four of them still had shadows. Now
none of them do. It's terrible luck, but I know enough now to know it's

not worth trying to figure out why. The last one to lose her shadow, our leader, is Ursula. I think you would like her, Ory. I'd guess she's in her late forties or early fifties, with dark silvered hair she keeps buzzed as short as a man's underneath the baseball cap she often wears. And her gun. She's never without it. I think it might be the only one we have, among all nine of us. I've been with them two or three days now, and I haven't yet heard Ursula laugh once, or seen her relax for even a moment. It's like she's made out of iron. The only time I've ever seen her smile is when I read the words on the side of their RV. *Our* RV. I'm one of them now.

Then there's Dhuuxo and Intisaar, the twins—refugees from Somalia who came to D.C. as teenagers. They're the ones who went with Ursula and me to the RV on the first night. God, Ory, they're beautiful, and so identical, it's kind of chilling. When they face each other, it's like they're looking into a mirror. They could be each other's own shadow, practically. Can you imagine what it would be like to look exactly like someone else? Sometimes, when I watch them work together, scrubbing dirty laundry in a bucket of water or counting out portions from our food rations for dinner, always perfectly in sync, I feel a twinge of jealousy amid the awe. What breaks my heart about you and me is that if you lost your shadow too, eventually we could have no idea that we belonged together or that we'd meant anything to each other at all. There'd be no evidence, no physical proof. But these two, Dhuuxo and Intisaar, they would *know*. Even if all memory left them, when they looked at each other, they would *know* that they're bound together somehow. Imagine what kind of comfort that would be.

But what I'm really dying to know, what I hope I can work up the courage to ask—admit it, you'd be just as curious as me: do you think they lost their shadows at the same time? And more—do you think they forget the same memories at the same time, or different ones? Together, could they be one complete person?

The rest—Wes, very tall; Lucius, somewhat handsome; Ysabelle, with such gorgeous long, blond hair; and Victor, the one with a massive tattoo of a lion on his shoulder—I know less about, and mysterious Zachary least of all. They're quieter than Ursula and the twins, watching more than speaking. They lost their shadows earlier, so they have forgotten the most. With Ysabelle and Victor, it's a sad story, Intisaar told me. They met in high school and eloped as soon as they graduated. They'd just sent their youngest off to college a few months before the Forgetting reached the United States. Now they don't remember they were ever married. Intisaar says the only reason they know they ever loved each other at all is because Ursula tells them so, because she met them during the last year that they were still whole.

I'm rambling, but there's still so much to tell you. Thank God I could still read when they found me, is all I can say. I can't imagine what would have happened to them if we hadn't met, and they'd just continued the way they'd been going. They'd been driving straight west for days, completely off course. They never would have reached New Orleans in a hundred years that way.

"Max," Ursula called from the driver's cockpit of the RV as we bounced slowly along the pockmarked road, "come here a moment."

I edged over into a crouch beside her seat, using her armrest to steady myself. Everyone else seems to have fifteen jobs, and I have only one. Map reader is definitely an important duty, maybe the most important one after driver—that's what I keep telling myself—but it's still only one. Whenever we stop for the night, Wes follows Victor and Lucius around and gathers firewood by copying their actions; Dhuuxo and Intisaar portion food and water for dinner; Ursula checks our remaining supplies and does a head count every few minutes until we're all gathered back around the fire again, desperate not to lose another one of us; and Ysabelle helps me set up my tent after she does her own. I know. It's so embarrassing. The first night, I was too nervous and humiliated to admit it, so I struggled with the poles and fabric sheets for at least half an hour before Ysabelle finally pushed me out of the way with a tired sigh, tossed her golden hair out of her eyes, and bent the little thing into shape in less than a minute. "You'll get the hang of it," she managed to say to me as she walked back to her own. My cheeks were on fire. *I can skin a rabbit!* I wanted to say. *I can twist its neck to kill it quick without flinching!* But that would have made it even more embarrassing, I think. And besides, there's no need for that particular skill—every single person in our caravan can do it. It's nothing special.

Have I told you how nice my tent is, by the way? It's warm and dry, and so colorful when the light strikes the thin material. In the mornings it's beautiful.

The only one who seems to do less than me—almost nothing at all—is Zachary. Strange, silent Zachary.

He was in the passenger seat as I crouched down next to Ursula. I tried to make eye contact with him, but he was lost, staring unblinking out the window with his pale eyes. I wonder if he's forgotten too much to remember how to speak, but I'm afraid to ask in case it's rude. I don't know the rules yet, if there even are rules.

"You should keep this with you always now," Ursula said when she realized I was waiting beside her, and she handed me our road map from the glove compartment.

"I will," I said. When her gaze returned to the windshield, I turned the paper around as casually as I could, hoping that she wouldn't notice she had given it to me upside down.

I concentrated, looking for our location. It's not that I *can't* navigate—you know that, Ory. It's just, we were always on subways in D.C. Finding the right train line and then sticking to it isn't the same as trying to compare a road map to a broken, shifting wilderness that no longer matches it at all. And especially when getting lost and losing a few hours or days could mean the difference between reaching our destination in time or forgetting we ever wanted to go there. I know you were a Boy Scout back in Oregon, but you should try map reading when almost all the signs on the road are collapsed or overgrown with choking vines, or flapping madly, trying to fly away like birds chained to a post by one claw. You would be proud of me, I think. I focused on the page roughly where I thought we might be, somewhere just south of Fairfax Station—that was where I'd found them the first night, when Ursula demanded I read the side of their RV—and waited until we passed a sign still whole enough that I could decode it. Ursula doesn't remember anymore the way that maps work, but she knows that it has something to do with both the lines on the paper and the outside world, so she bit her tongue as patiently as she could as the seconds ticked by.

Finally I put my hand down on the swirling, colored shapes. "We're still on the right path," I said to her. "When we begin again tomorrow, we should stay on this wide road. It should take us almost all the way there if we don't lose it." We were on what was left of the I-85 South.

"You're sure," she said to confirm.

"I'm sure," I said, truly confident this time. "I can still read it."

Ursula nodded. "You should sit up here from now on," she said. "Easier to see the road."

"But what about Zachary?" I asked.

Ursula glanced at him, and he nodded. I didn't know if it was because he'd understood her words or just intuited what she wanted. He unclicked his seat belt and rose from the chair as if in a trance. "He doesn't mind," Ursula said as he edged around me, and set himself up at the foldout table in the middle of the cabin. Dhuuxo and Intisaar scooted over to give him the spot closest to the window so he could stare out it. "He can draw from anywhere."

"Draw?"

"Zachary makes all of our signs for us," Ursula said. "To help us remember important things." She held up one hand and pursed the fingers, rubbing them together, to indicate the perpetual stains on his own. "It's ink," she added. Then she pulled a paper out of the cubby in the dashboard and handed it to me. It was a picture of eight of them that were left, in excruciating detail, all without shadows. "He did that the day before we found you."

I turned around to stare at him, overcome. His pale blond hair, blue eyes. He was the one who had filled Oakton High School with drawings, Ory! The self-portrait with a shadow, the pair of lovers who must have been Ysabelle and Victor—a woman with long blond hair and a man with a lion tattoo emblazoned on his bicep. The two dark figures in identical poses that I now understood hadn't been badly faded renderings of shadows, but Dhuuxo and Intisaar. He was trying to record their memories in the only way he still could.

Our eyes met, and his gaze trailed down the string dangling from my neck. To the tape recorder suspended in the air. I looked down and touched it, to stop its slow spin. When I looked back up, he nodded to me, as if even though he didn't know how it worked, he understood what it was for. That it was the same thing as his drawings.

[II]

Ursula drove. I kept us on the path. The cabin jangled softly as we went over a pothole, but I kept my finger gently pressed against the waxy paper. I could tell it made her happy. She doesn't remember you can work a map just by looking at it, and thinks it needs to be touched. So I touch it. It's the least I can do for her while she drives us all.

When we stopped for Victor to have a smoke and the others to have a bathroom break in the weeds by the side of the road, Zachary returned to the front cabin and climbed silently into Ursula's vacant seat. He looked at the map in my hands and then out the window, where Ursula was standing in the shade of an underpass, waiting for everyone to board the RV again. He took the top paper from a stack in his pocket and sketched thoughtfully for a few minutes. When he was finished, he handed it to me and smiled. It was a perfect rendering of the weathered I-85 sign above Ursula's head. Zachary didn't remember anymore what the sign was or maybe even what a freeway is, but knew that it had something to do with my map and it was important. I stared at his picture of the little blue shield with a red border for a long time after he went back to his seat. At the little white shapes in the center of the sign. I wish I could show it to you, Ory. The difference between a *written* letter and a *drawn* one is small, but fascinating.

"He's good, isn't he?" Ursula finally said once we were moving again.

"He is." She couldn't see the subtle difference either. I lined it up with the edge of the map and folded the corner down, to clip the two papers together. "Can I ask you something?"

"Sure," she said.

"Why are we going to New Orleans? I mean, why there?"

Ursula drew in a long breath. I waited for her to speak, but she just kept her eyes on the road, grimly watching the horizon.

Eventually I looked down at the map spread across my thighs again and busied myself with glancing over its veiny roads and pale green national parks. "You don't remember, do you?" I finally asked.

"I do," she said. "It's just a little hard to explain. Have you ever heard of The One Who Gathers?"

"The what?" I asked.

"Before we started driving, we all lived together," Ursula said, tipping her head toward the rest of our passengers. "We found a good spot. We had to clear it out first, but the danger was worth it. We had good walls, good weapons, plenty of eyes to keep watch, plenty of hands to bring back whatever we found. Eventually we had so much that we started trading some of it to people who passed by—whatever they could tell us about anything, anything at all, we'd give them a little bit of food. Word got around. People started bringing us information. After a while, we noticed that the same names kept coming up."

"The One Who Does Not Dream," I said. I remembered you telling me you sometimes saw strange things written on walls when you scavenged, Ory—carved into the plaster or wood. "The Friend."

"The Friend, I've heard The Friend, too." Ursula glanced at the fuel gauge. "The one I heard the most, from survivors from as far as Montana, was The One Who Gathers."

"So all of this is in New Orleans?" I asked.

"Something like that," she said.

I nodded. She didn't have to explain more—I understood. It didn't matter that the stories were piecemeal or even sometimes contradicted one another. What mattered was that there *were* rumors at all. It meant something must be happening there. Something big. Good or bad, we couldn't know—but it was worth finding out, rather than giving up. I looked at her. I wanted to find out too, not just sit and wait for the end. Or die trying. "We'll know soon enough. We'll make it."

"Mm," Ursula agreed.

I settled back into my seat, but my heart was racing. "Maybe the last shadowed survivors are going there," I said instead of what I was really thinking, to hide how excited I'd suddenly become.

She shrugged. "Or maybe all the shadowless. Perhaps they've made it into a new city, just for us."

"Or maybe just all of our shadows."

That made her chuckle for a moment. We both knew that was silly. Shadows didn't go somewhere. They disappeared. But the joke served its purpose—it broke the tension, stopped her from saying the actual reason we were heading for this city of fragmented rumors. From saying what she really hoped, because the possibility it could be true was so tenuous that just the words might undo it. I knew because now that I'd heard her story, it was what I hoped, too. That maybe there's a cure in New Orleans, Ory. A way to stop us from forgetting. That maybe instead of running, trying to stop myself from disappearing you and then eventually just dying, I can save us both—and find you again.

# ORLANDO ZHANG

IN THE MORNING, ORY WOKE TO THE SOUND OF FOOTSTEPS, scrambling on crumbling asphalt.

"Max?" he called hoarsely. He crawled out from the rubble in the building across from their old home, where he'd hidden himself overnight. "Max?"

It wasn't Max. He caught sight of a foot as its owner rounded the corner away from him at a sprint. There had been no shadow attached, but it had been a man's foot, not a woman's. Then another shadowless ran past, at such speed he again caught almost no details—just whipping legs, a low crouch, and fading echoes.

Ory waited until it was quiet again and then crept into the street. *What was that about?* he wondered. Busy areas never meant anything good anymore. But the question was whether they were running *to* something—or *from* it. He edged around the corner and into the wreckage of the intersection to see if he could find where they'd gone.

"Don't move!" someone shouted. Ory scrambled, grabbing for a gun he no longer had. A dark man in army fatigues and a bike helmet jerked into a dodge, as if expecting him to throw a blade, and then aimed a shotgun of his own at Ory.

They both stared at each other in shock for a few seconds, then stared at each other's feet, at what trailed beneath. *He has a shadow,* Ory thought, at the same moment that the stranger realized the same about him as well.

"Brother," the man finally said. The gun dropped—a relieved smile broke out across his face. "What the hell are you doing with that?"

Ory looked down at his chest and touched his shirt, where the man was pointing. The last tatters of his maroon windbreaker hung there, wet and sooty. Only half the red letters from the giant *STAFF* word above the *Elk Cliffs Resort* logo remained. "I don't understand," Ory said, but the man wasn't listening anymore. His expression changed.

"Get down!" he cried.

They both threw themselves against the row of sand-filled garbage bins in front of them as a rock ricocheted off the top and spun into little sharp flakes. Another hit, spraying stone chips past their faces as it exploded. "What's happening?" Ory shouted.

"Deal went bad today," the dark man yelled over the pounding stones. "The Red King tried to pass off four copies of the same thing. Impossible to explain it to them—four of the same book doesn't equal *four books*. Now we're skirmishing again. The red . . ."—he touched the front of Ory's windbreaker—"that's what I mean. Enemy colors!" Another barrage scattered across the top of the garbage cans. *It's a barricade line,* Ory realized. Someone had built upright trenches along the length of his old street. "Last time this happened, they burned a whole pile in protest—that was bloody. Let's hope they're too desperate for food or medicine to try that again."

"What are you talking about?" Ory cried.

"The war!" he shouted back.

"What war?"

"The—" The man paused. "What do you mean, 'What war?' Where are you from?"

"Arlington," Ory answered.

"Arlington!" the man cried. Ory could tell by his expression he was expecting Ory to have named a neighborhood within walking distance, maybe an outer suburb. The Forgetting had changed the meaning of the word *far*. "You crossed the river?" he asked. They both ducked as a rock went sailing overhead. "You've got balls, brother."

"Li," Ory gave his middle name, just in case.

"Li," he confirmed. "Malik—James Malik." He took his bike helmet off his head. Sweat gleamed across the shaved, deep brown skin. He handed it to Ory. "You wear that. I'll get another one; we have more back in the armory. That's where the new recruits go to get kitted up."

"No, uh—" Ory tried to collect himself. "I'm here looking for my wife."

Malik studied him for a moment, conflicted over what to do with him if he wasn't a recruit for whatever this war was. "I don't know if I can help with that," he finally said. He pushed the helmet on Ory anyway. "But she's definitely not here. This is the front lines," he continued, gesturing with his chin at the path the rock had just sailed through in the air above their heads. "You know Logan Circle?"

"Yeah," Ory said. "P Street?"

"P and Thirteenth." Malik nodded. "The Iowa—old luxury condominiums. It's impossible to find anyone anymore, but if you're going to try, you should start there. The General might be able to help, in exchange for some help from you."

It wasn't much, but it was a lead. The first one Ory had. "Shadowed people are in the Iowa?"

"Almost forty. It's our headquarters."

There was a momentary break in the flying rocks. Malik jammed two fingers under his lip and whistled sharply. A few seconds later, a thud scattered concrete dust behind them, and a tan, black-haired woman in similar tattered fatigues was now crouched there. Her shadow hunkered down with her, eagle-nosed, thin. Ory stared open-mouthed. It was like a real army. An army of people who remembered.

"Ahmadi, this is Li; Li, this is Naz Ahmadi," Malik said. "Li's a newcomer from Arlington. I'm taking him to meet the General. Hold the line 'til I get back."

"Brother." Ahmadi nodded to Ory. Her grip on his hand was tight—so tight Ory knew she was as happy to see another shadowed person as he was—but she was polite enough to ignore his gaping stare at meeting not one, but two other shadowed humans until he'd shut his mouth and shook her hand back. When they let go, she rattled off a snippet of directions to Malik in a faint, musical accent. "Take Tenth back. A bunch of Reds just scrambled out on G."

"Thanks," he said, and saluted Ahmadi. She saluted back and then crouched down to spot for another break in the stone volley. Malik edged next to Ory and pointed. "When Ahmadi says go, run for that corner and turn left. Don't stop until you get there." Ory felt him rap on the shell of his helmet. "Head down. Got it?"

"Got it," Ory said. He almost saluted also, but caught himself in time.

"Go!" Ahmadi cried.

Malik bolted forward like a cannon. They ran straight for the safety of the turn onto Tenth Street as fast as they could. Every rock that cracked against the makeshift blockade caused Ory to jerk his hands to his helmet. "Make sure they can see your shadow when we walk up!" Malik shouted as they ran. Ory risked a glance behind just as they rounded the corner, to see if he could catch sight of whoever Malik and Ahmadi were fighting. It was a blur at such speed, and the details were lost. All he could make out before they were down Tenth Street and gone was a giant, hulking concrete building in the drizzle—completely painted crimson.

THE WAR. THE RED KING. THE GENERAL. ORY TRIED TO MAKE sense of any of those three names as he crept through the icy streets after Malik, but none of them sounded like things that had come from the old world at all.

Was it excitement he felt at finding shadowed humans again, or fear of them? Which was better—Arlington, with nothing left but ghosts, or Washington, D.C., with plenty of survivors, all of whom wanted to kill one another? Ghosts never wanted enough, and people always wanted too much.

But here he was, among people again, and memories and wants. These people of the Iowa wanted something. He wanted something, too. Maybe the General would agree to some kind of deal.

"So this war," Ory started, but Malik hissed.

"No talking," he ordered at a whisper. They kept moving. "Need to hear. Reds sometimes try to sneak up on you."

"Sorry," Ory whispered back. He watched each side street as they passed as well. Sometimes a dim shape would dart away, vague in the cold fog, but they looked no different than the shadowless he'd seen in Arlington that hid from every sound.

"Don't worry," Malik replied softly. "We're close now. The General will explain everything." He glanced at Ory one more time. "Do you have a different-colored shirt with you?"

THE IOWA LOOKED MORE LIKE A DERELICT FORTRESS THAN luxury condominiums now.

Ory followed Malik as he was ushered through the front doors past a skeleton guard crew. "Wait here," Malik had said, and left him just inside the entrance, under the watchful eye of two other soldiers who were mending a torn coat.

Ory glanced at the iron bars across every window, crudely welded, but solid. He couldn't have gone anywhere unless they'd wanted him to anyway. He nodded meekly at his guards as he waited, and they nodded back. One smiled. *Should I show them Max's photo?* he wondered. But then he thought it was probably best to wait for this General. If things went well, they would all see the photo then, all forty of his survivors. *Forty.* Forty shadows, Ory tried to imagine.

The heavy wooden doors that led deeper into the Iowa swept back open then. "Attention!" another guard cried, and Ory looked up to see Malik marching beside him. And farther behind, partially obscured by the tightness of their formation, was a third man. "All rise for the General!"

Ory snapped upright, careful to keep his hands in full view, even though the two soldiers had inspected him for weapons before he was admitted inside.

"Li," Malik said when he reached him. "I'm pleased to present you to the General of the Iowa, leader of all shadowed survivors in D.C., and commander of the war." And with that, he stepped aside to reveal a man in a patchwork robe, flanked by guards.

There was just a moment when Ory could not place him.

"Impossible!" he gasped suddenly.

"*Ory,*" the General replied, equally stunned.

It was Imanuel.

"WE WERE GOING TO GO BACK FOR YOU" WAS THE FIRST THING Imanuel said after they'd finished crying.

"You don't have to explain," Ory replied.

"No," Imanuel said. His expression was fierce. "I do. You have to know that we tried. We *tried.* The bridge was deserted when we first came across, but after we gave up trying to reach my family in Philly and went back for you, the shadowless had swarmed the area, and it was too dangerous to swim. We searched for another way for months. By that point, we didn't think you and Max would still be there. We just didn't think you'd have your shadows anymore. But you have to know that we tried. Paul would never forgive me if I didn't tell you that we tried."

"What happened to . . . what happened?" There was no need to say more.

"He . . ." Imanuel's eyes welled up, and he shook his head. "You know how it goes. He forgot. Then he was gone."

Ory had already known the answer, since the moment he'd realized the General was Imanuel. If Paul had still been alive, still owned his shadow, he would've been sitting with them now. His chest tightened anyway as he looked away, and they both stared at the ceiling for a long time.

After that, they didn't talk about Paul anymore. Imanuel asked about Max instead. When Ory told him about her shadow, and Broad Street, and their empty, destroyed D.C. apartment, he could tell that Imanuel knew he still believed Max was here somewhere and that he could find her. He also could tell Imanuel didn't believe it—but he didn't say anything. Ory thought it was the kindest thing anyone had done for him since the day Hemu Joshi lost his shadow.

"Also, I apologize for the fanfare," Imanuel finally said. "The entry presentation and all. I'd just walk in myself, but Malik makes the troops do it. He says ritual is good for morale."

"It *is* good for morale," Malik said.

The rain had started again. On the far side of the room, a corner of the wall had begun to shimmer lightly, as if weeping.

"Cozy," Ory said.

"It's the best option in the entire downtown. Even tops the White House," Imanuel replied.

"There's still someone in the White House?" he asked.

"No one important," Imanuel said. Thunder droned, growing more distant. "It's not really the White House anymore. They don't want to be the president."

Over the rest of the evening, Ory learned more. When Imanuel and Paul had stopped in D.C. after leaving Elk Cliffs, they'd managed to rally the remaining tenants in the Iowa to fortify the building. The top four floors were permanently closed now, all the doors and stairs sealed with concrete, and Imanuel and his soldiers existed on the first three floors—the lobby, the quarters, and the vault, where they kept valuables. The Red King's stronghold, the building Ory glimpsed as he and Malik ran that was now covered in red, was the old Martin Luther King Jr. Memorial Library.

The door opened, and Ahmadi came in with several sheets of handwritten paper. Ory noticed that she held the stack the same way Max did, each leaf fanned between the fingers for quick perusal. "Day's report," she said as she handed them to Imanuel.

"Thank you," Imanuel said. She saluted him as she left. "There are forty of us—forty-one including you," Imanuel continued. "We used to be even bigger. When we started, there were seventy of us. Including Paul." He sighed, but it turned into a hopeless laugh.

"Forty-one is still a lot," Ory said. It was. He could hardly imagine it. "D.C. might be the biggest city left in the world."

"Let's hope not." Imanuel looked at Ory. "Let's hope there's something else left, too."

*I heard a rumor once, about New Orleans,* Ory almost said, but then the door opened a second time, and Ahmadi brought one more paper, some kind of updated report, and disappeared again.

Imanuel started to skim Ahmadi's report, but then handed it to Malik. "If it's bad news, I don't want to know. There's just been too much lately."

"I'm sorry I lied about my name," Ory said to him.

"If I'd walked here from Virginia, I'd be wary, too," Malik replied, and began to read. His brow furrowed before he masked it with his usual stern expression, but Imanuel saw it before it was gone.

"The Red King is becoming more uncooperative," Imanuel said to Ory. "The bartering system was workable at first. But more and more, he just wants to use force. Why trade when you can just take?"

Malik set the papers down and shook his head.

"*Vey is mir,*" Imanuel muttered, pressing on his eyeballs with his fingers. "Sorry. That was rude." He stood up. "Ory, it's about time I show you what we're fighting for."

"WATCH YOUR STEP," IMANUEL SAID AS THEY CLEARED THE landing of the third floor, where the vault was located. Ahead of them, Malik was already opening the door at the end of the corridor. Weak torch light streamed into the hall.

Ory followed, unsure of what to expect. Opulence? A dungeon? Something inexplicable that had been created in the Forgetting? The first two levels of the Iowa had been fairly similar. Charred, boarded up, iron-reinforced. The third floor looked as it must have the day before Boston, except that every piece of furniture was gone.

"Good God," Ory gasped when he reached the door.

From floor to ceiling were stacks and stacks of books.

"Our war chest," Imanuel said.

"Good God," Ory heard himself stammer again.

"It was Paul's idea." He smiled. "I keep doing it for him."

Ory put a hand on Imanuel's shoulder, letting it sink in. Paul was no longer alive, but he wasn't completely gone either. As long as Imanuel was fighting to collect more books, some part of him was remembered. Some part of him remained. The same way that some part of Max remained as well. But the part of her left was not a book—because she was still alive, and lost. He was here because he was trying to find her. He had to get back to searching.

Ory turned to his friend, but at the same moment, Imanuel pointed inside. "Go on in. There are paths through, once you get started."

Ory stepped hesitantly between the towering stacks. It was like a geometric forest. A soldier on inventory duty briefly looked up from where she stood. "How many books do you have here?" Ory asked as he picked up a lightly weathered paperback.

"About three thousand," Imanuel said, with a touch of pride.

How many were once there? Ory wondered. A hundred thousand? A million? Three thousand books would have been perhaps a section of one genre, or maybe twenty shelves. Something a person could pass by on their way from the entrance to the elevators. But here, now, in this new D.C.—it was an entire room *full* of books. It was probably the only room left like it in the world. Wherever he looked, it seemed like there were endless numbers of them. "How many more do you hope to get?" he finally asked.

"Nothing short of all of them would ever feel like enough," Imanuel said. "But really, just one in particular."

Ory looked down. For a moment, it felt like they were standing on a mountainside again, surrounded by tables topped with fluttering white tablecloths. Ory had owned a copy, in the D.C. apartment that had crumbled to ash. And there had been another at the wedding— Paul had read his vows from it. Where had that one gone? In all the months after everyone disappeared, Ory had never seen it lying about on one of the deserted floors, gathering dust. "That's a good book," he finally said.

Imanuel smiled sadly. "It is."

"I'm glad you're doing this," Ory added.

"After Paul—I didn't know if I could keep going," Imanuel continued. "But then I remembered there was a copy of his poetry in most libraries. If there was one in this library as well, if it hadn't been burned yet or disappeared—that makes me keep getting up in the mornings."

Paul had signed Ory's copy when he bought it. Ory tried to remember exactly what Paul's note on the inside cover had said. Something about constellations—Paul's poetry was about the sun and the sky, and night. Ory should have paid more attention. He hadn't known he would need such a strong memory of it. That he wouldn't be able to just go to the shelf and take it down whenever he wanted.

"General!" Ahmadi's voice floated through the columns of paper. They scrambled out in time to see her salute Malik from the doorway. "The Reds' offensive has calmed down. They're mostly all back inside the library's gate. They're waving the big red flags."

"Trading time." Malik grinned. Ory saw him glance at Imanuel.

"No," Imanuel said.

"I want to," Ory replied, even though he had no idea what *trading* meant in this context. He didn't care. He would help Imanuel, then ask for help finding Max in return.

"I want you to not die the same day I find you again."

"Imanuel, please," he said. "Let me do this. For Paul."

He saw the muscles in Imanuel's jaw working, but Ory knew there was no response that would win over his plea to do something to honor Paul's memory.

"Good," he said at last, and nodded to Malik. He didn't look back at Imanuel. He didn't want to give him another opportunity to argue. That, and he wasn't sure of what he'd seen in Imanuel's face.

Of course Ory did want to help, even if he had ulterior motives. But the expression on Imanuel's face hadn't been guilt over not wanting to spare the resources or men to help find Max. It had been blind fear.

"IS HE NORMALLY SO WORRIED BEFORE A MISSION?" ORY ASKED Malik on the way down the stairs. Ahmadi was far ahead of them, already disappeared into the lobby on the ground floor.

Malik shrugged. "You're his late husband's best friend. The Reds aren't someone I'd send my almost-family to face."

"I volunteered," Ory corrected.

Malik nodded. "I know. And I'm not in the business of turning down a willing soldier." Ory felt Malik's hand on his arm then, to slow their descent. "When I said that you might find help here, I didn't realize that your Max wasn't in D.C., that you lost track of her pretty far from here—or that she's shadowless. If the only reason you're doing this is for the General's help, I'm sorry, but I don't think he'll give it to you. A shadowless alone, for that long . . ." He cleared his throat uncomfortably. "I don't think your wife made it across the river. I don't think the General believes she did either. He can't justify sending one of his own on such a dangerous mission."

Ory took his arm away. "She's alive," he said. "She's in D.C."

"I hope you're right. I just don't think you'll find the help you want here. If you want to stay and try anyway, that's on you. If you want to walk away now, I won't stop you."

"I said I'd do this one for Paul. We'll see about afterward."

Malik started walking again. "Welcome to the war."

Ory fell in behind him as they reached the landing. "Why does he call himself the Red King?"

"*We* call him the Red King," Malik replied. "We don't know what he calls himself."

It was still raining outside. In front of them, Ahmadi pulled her coat around herself and grumbled.

"So the Reds are . . . They're just destroying everything in the city for fun?" Ory asked as they stood under the overhang. Behind them, ten soldiers checked their makeshift armor and lined themselves up double file. One of them was carrying twice the clothes and weapons in his arms—a set for him, Ory realized.

"Not exactly." Malik shook his head. "Plenty of other shadowless do that. They're unorganized and haphazard, though. The Red King is different. He's managed to create a group and a territory. They all paint themselves red; they all live together in the old library."

"Strange," Ory said. "It's almost like . . ."

"It's almost like they remember, or he remembers for them," Malik finished for him. "At least one thing, anyway."

"What do you think that one thing is?" Ory finally asked.

Ahmadi shrugged. "Fuck if we know."

Ory sighed. He didn't know if it was encouraging or more terrifying, this idea that the Reds all might be remembering a little, or one thing, or the same thing. He glanced at the soldiers behind him. "This will sound . . . ," he started.

"Why do we risk trading instead of just killing them all?" Malik said. "We would if we could. But they outnumber us ten to one. Our only bargaining chip is to keep them thinking we have knowledge or supplies to trade in exchange for their books. But we're running out of things to offer them that they haven't already misremembered back into reality."

"How are we going to win the war, then?" Ory asked.

"We aren't," Ahmadi said. "We're going to lose. We just have to get Paul's book before we do."

I HOPE OF ALL THINGS, I FORGET YOU LAST, ORY. I HOPE I FOR-get you even after I forget where we're going. I'd rather drive forever and never reach New Orleans, but still remember you.

This morning was cold enough that when I woke up, there was a tiny bit of frost on the outside of my tent. It crackled as I unzipped the flap, a thousand tiny rolling snaps. The sound was so nice, I went to every side and bent the support poles slowly until each fabric sheet crinkled. When I came around the front side again, Dhuuxo was outside hers as well, bundled against the crisp dawn, head wrapped in a scarf so that only her eyes and the bridge of her nose showed. When our gazes met, she winked at me. "Small pleasures," she said.

I grinned and nodded back. It's only my sixth night with all of them. I still feel shy, as if this is only temporary and I won't be allowed to stay. Well, it is temporary. But for another reason.

Dhuuxo strode soundlessly across the dead grass between us. In her hand was a rose, freshly picked. I hadn't seen any flowers at all since it had grown cold, let alone a rose—but it was as beautiful as if she'd just bought it from a florist's shop.

I looked at her, trying to decide. I knew the rose could not have been from anywhere near here. What was harder to tell was whether she knew it or not.

"When I first came to America, they always had a bouquet of these on the counter at the refugee center. I used to steal them and rub the petals between my fingers until they disintegrated," Dhuuxo confided. "I couldn't help it. They felt so soft. Like this." Her cheeks wrinkled above the line of her scarf as she smiled beneath it. She stroked one of the petals on the rose's outermost layer, rolling it softly between the pad of her middle finger and thumb. It looked soothing, almost meditative. Then she handed me what was left of the bloom. "You try," she said. "I'll make the fire."

Dhuuxo was right. I couldn't stop. I carried the battered corpse of that rose around for the rest of the day, until we were inside the RV, cruising slowly along the bumpy swells in the damaged road, and Dhuuxo caught sight of it again. She laughed so hard it made Intisaar laugh, too. When they'd wiped the tears out of their dark eyes, so deep brown they almost look purple, Dhuuxo pressed another freshly picked bloom into my hands. I realized there was a pile of them next to her in the RV's little travel sink. I looked at Intisaar, who looked away from me, as if to say, *Leave it. I don't know if she found them, or* . . . Did Ursula? I want to ask her, Ory—but I don't know how, when.

"Max, come up here a moment," Ursula called to me then. I scrambled gratefully to the front seat. "How much farther?" she asked when I dropped down beside her.

I had been keeping track on the map. "We've traveled maybe a fourth of the way," I replied.

"That's more than I hoped for," she said automatically, as if she hadn't even heard the answer. She drew in a long, quiet breath. Ahead, we were coming upon a wide, open field on either side of the road. The grass had grown waist-high at least, and a few leaning weeds brushed the aluminum sides of our vehicle in a soft, hissing hum. Ursula turned to look at me as the RV began to slow. "I'm injured," she said softly. I forgot the roses. "Don't tell the others."

We pulled over so the right two wheels were in the grass and the left two wheels were still barely on the road. "Bathroom break," I announced casually to the rest of the group sitting behind us. The twins and Ysabelle were already helping Victor, Wes, Lucius, and Zachary up, guiding them in a line toward the door like mothers with children. Even though being together helps us resist the pull, the four men seem to be doing worse and worse, faster and faster. We women are forgetting things too, but not like them. I don't know if it's the same way outside our group, but it seems that men forget faster without their shadows. I don't know why.

I followed Ursula out of the RV and around the other side of it. We waded through the grass carefully, the tips of each blade flicking against our hands. The field was turning golden, and when the wind came, the grass rippled like an ocean, the shimmering, flaxen tide rolling in and out. I was starting to panic, Ory. Had she been wounded before I met them? Why hadn't she said something? Why hadn't she gotten help long before this? Did we have a first-aid kit in the RV? I patted my clothes as we walked, trying to figure out what might make the best tourniquet. When we were far enough away that Ursula could see the others but that they couldn't hear us, she turned to me and held out her hand. It was definitely blood—on the tips of her fingers was a dark, thick smear of red, as if she'd dipped them into it.

I stared, terrified. Who else would lead us if Ursula was dying? I struggled to pull off my jacket with numb, panic-clumsy hands. "Where's the wound?" I heard myself stammer.

"Here," she said, and pointed to the source. "There's no pain, but I felt the blood an hour ago."

I looked at where her hands were. She was touching the space where the insides of her thighs met. A small, deep crimson stain had started to seep through the fabric of her jeans there.

I didn't feel embarrassment or pity. I felt only relief—a release so overwhelming I sank slowly down into the grass and let the earth hold me up instead of my legs. "It's okay," I finally managed. "It's okay."

"It's not fatal?" she asked.

"No."

She sat down beside me. "I've forgotten something," she said softly.

"Yes," I said. "But it's not important." I didn't know, Ory. Was it important? Had Ursula ever had any children? Had she wanted them? Had she already forgotten their names?

We watched Dhuuxo and Intisaar gently corral two of the men close to the RV through the golden, waving stalks. They wanted to explore, it looked like. Before, that was all right. But now, whenever there was something out of the reach of the RV's wide tires that needed investigation, we did it all together, holding hands. The risk was too great now that someone could get lost, and then forget they were lost at all.

"Will it stop?" Ursula asked me.

"It will," I said. "In a few days. In the meantime, we should wash your jeans and then put some cloth there, to absorb the blood. Otherwise it'll keep soaking into your clothes."

Ursula nodded slowly. Across the field, in the shade of the RV next to Ysabelle, Zachary seemed to be sketching something on paper he had brought with him from inside. "Will it happen again?" she asked.

I didn't know what the right answer was. If it was more true to say yes or no. I tried to imagine what you would say. "No," I finally told her. By the time Ursula's next period came, it was more likely that neither of us would remember any of this.

⏸

When we got back to the RV, I gave Ursula your flannel shirt I took with me when I left, to cut into strips of fabric. I kept the collar for myself, though—it's been in my bag so long, that's the only part of it that still smells like you. I breathed it deep, trying to picture your face. Then, terrified, I snapped my eyes open.

Ory, it's so horrible. It's *horrible*. I miss you so much, because I can't see or hear you—but I can't even *think* about you, either, not in any kind of meaningful detail. Every time I slip up and do it, I almost scream. Do you know what that's like? Can you even imagine not being allowed to soothe your grief with memories, because what if I get it wrong? What would that mean? How far do I have to run before you might be safe? I looked up, trying not to start sobbing, and realized Zachary was sitting in front of me.

"Hello," he finally said.

"You remember how to speak!" I gasped.

"Yes," he said. "But . . ." He stalled. The words were slow and clumsy, as if his tongue was too cold to move. "Iron. Stony."

I studied him for a long moment. Then I realized he'd forgotten the word for *hard*.

"I understand what you mean," I said, as kindly as I could.

Zachary looked down at his fingers, at the ink stains that had soaked into the deepest layers of his skin. It was almost like he'd made his own shadow. "Hands are better," he said.

"Okay." I nodded.

In reply, he held them up, as if gripping a steering wheel.

"Ursula?"

"Ursula." There was a long pause as he sifted through the remaining words he had. "Who is Ursula?"

"The driver," I said.

"Driver." He nodded in recognition.

"Ursula," I called to her at the front of the RV. Zachary stayed sitting there, as if he was in a trance. He's almost completely gone, Ory. The look on his face . . . that's the look I never wanted you to see on mine. It was blankness. Utter blankness.

It will be terrible when we lose him. When he forgets the last thing, which is how to draw. Yesterday he drew my face for me and held it up for me to see. I didn't realize how long it had been since I looked at myself in a mirror until he handed it to me and my eyes searched every inch of his careful portrait. My freckles, the curve of my nose, the tiny scar above my right eyebrow. Do you remember, Ory? Well, of course you do. But I'd almost forgotten.

Ursula had made her way over and crouched down beside us, finished fixing her underwear. "What is it?" she asked him.

Zachary only pointed out the side window.

We looked. Green fields, the sky, and a hazy, drifting cloud just above the driver's-side door mirror.

"Is that smoke?" I asked.

Ursula grabbed her gun. "Not smoke," she said. "Dust."

It was too late to drive. They were on us before we even got back to our seats.

There was a crowd of them, at least thirty or forty. Dispersed at first, running crazily in all directions, leaving in their wake that trail of dust Zachary saw. All of them with shadows.

"My God," Ysabelle gasped. "I've never seen so many."

"Ross!" a woman suddenly shouted as she spotted our RV parked in the field. "Look, a van!" The group converged into a speeding, shadowed mass, aiming straight for us.

"What do we do?" I cried.

"Victor, Wes, Lucius, out now!" Ursula shouted.

The men snapped to attention like soldiers, grabbing whatever was there—knife, baseball bat, wrench—and shoved the door to the RV open. "Come on!" Wes bellowed at them threateningly, swinging the bat. We all spilled out behind, trying to add to the illusion that we had numbers.

"Shadowless!" a few cried. Some of the shadowed runners scattered immediately when they saw the bright ground beneath our feet. But the rest were too desperate to give up. Something small sailed by my ear as they closed in. Lucius flung a wrench. One woman was in front of the rest, eyes desperate. An axe jerked wildly in her hands as she ran.

I didn't know how to kill someone, I realized then with horror. I didn't know how to stop a person that determined, Ory. She was going to cut us down.

All I could hear was the keening note of her blade as it cut back and forth through the air. She howled and lunged right for Wes.

"*Wes!*" Intisaar screamed as the axe swung down—

But then Ursula shoved through our line in one smooth step and shot the woman straight in the chest.

The boom shook the field like a bomb. Then all sound was gone.

I could hear nothing until the echo faded. The woman jerked backward from the impact, airborne, red spray exploding out of her back as the bullet punched through—then lightning. She hit the ground hard. She didn't get up again.

"Jesus!" the man who had been running just behind her cried as the corpse collapsed to the grass. A storm of electricity swelled out of the dead woman, burning, flesh blackening, then receded. "Jesus Christ!" The man fell to his knees and cowered as Ursula leveled the gun at him. Two other women within her aim also crumpled, shaking with fear. The rest of the shadowed fled, screaming, leaving them there. "No!" he cried. "We're sorry! We aren't with them! Please don't kill us!"

"Stand up," Ursula said, with quiet rage.

The man grimaced for the blast. Then he opened his eyes. "What?"

"Stand up," she repeated.

All three climbed shakily to their feet. I struggled to look like I wasn't also about to faint. From the chest of the dead woman, tiny shocking tendrils continue to crackle, smaller each time. I tried to see Ursula's face, to see if she had done it, or even understood what had happened to her gun, but I couldn't see her expression unless I moved forward, and I didn't think my legs would hold me up if I tried.

"What's your name?" Ursula asked the man.

"Please," he begged.

"You kill every shadowless you meet?" she asked. "Hunt for them in packs?"

"No, it wasn't like that—it was an accident," he said. He curled back to the ground unconsciously. Tears were streaming down his face. *They're terrified of us,* I realized. *Of our power.*

Ursula cocked the gun. "Bullshit."

"No!"

"No?" She aimed. "You were going to steal our RV!"

"Only to run faster!" the man wailed.

"Wait," I said. Ursula stayed the gun. "Run from what?"

"Transcendence," he whispered. The two women with him shuddered at the word.

We looked at one another, trying to see if any of us recognized that name.

"Transcendence," one of the women finally repeated. "The people that dress in all white."

Ursula shook her head. "We haven't run into them."

"I don't know how," the man said. Still trembling, he climbed to his feet again. "They're everywhere here. They've been taking over all of the Carolinas, Tennessee, Alabama. We've been moving for days, trying to keep ahead. You ought to do what we're doing and get out of here now. Get north. As far north as possible."

"We're heading south," Ursula said.

"That is a very bad idea." The man shook his head. "Very, very bad idea. Go back north."

"Are they shadowed or shadowless?" I asked.

The man blinked. "What?"

"Transcendence," I clarified. "Are they shadowed or shadowless?"

The three strangers stared at me blankly for a few seconds. Then the man's shoulders started shaking. It took me a moment to realize he was laughing, almost hysterical.

"Enough," Ursula said.

The man continued to cackle until one of the women finally grabbed him and calmed him down. "I'm sorry," she whispered nervously to us as she wiped his eyes, as if afraid we might shoot them just to make him stop.

"Don't, Lauri—I've got it. I'm okay. I've *got it*." He pulled away, shrugging her off. He coughed awkwardly, and smoothed his hair and clothes. "I'm sorry."

Ursula nudged the air in front of them with her gun. "Go," she said. "Don't come back, and I won't kill you."

The man nodded grimly. "That's a good deal," he said. He looked around, trying to get his bearings. His shadow looked with him. We all tried not to stare, but we were transfixed. I hadn't seen one in so long. "Thank you. I am sorry about your van. We really didn't know you were in it."

"It's done now," Ursula said.

"You should come with us," Lauri interrupted.

"Lauri—"

"What?" she cried. "They're not like most shadowless. They could have shot us! You're not like most shadowless," she said again, a little embarrassed.

"We're trying," I said. Who are my people, Ory? The ones I'm with or the ones I want to be? "We're trying very hard not to forget."

"Come north with us," Lauri said. "Don't go that way."

Ursula shook her head. "We have to go south."

"You'll be heading right into it, then," the second woman said.

Ursula looked down. We had no choice.

The man finally nodded. "I hope you make it, wherever you're going." He gestured at the women to get a head start, and they began to jog again. "Stay away from the water." He turned back to us one last time. "I know you won't, but remember that: they're always by water. If you see a lake, run."

❙❙

We camped there. We had no choice—it would be dark before we could make any meaningful distance. Not a single one of us slept, but there was no sign of Transcendence, or any more shadowed survivors fleeing it.

The next morning, we drove until almost noon before I spotted another fossil of a sign. "There's one!" I cried as soon as its weathered, industrial-blue face glinted into shape against the horizon. We'd been between major towns for days, only trees and road, and I was in desperate need of something to help me pin us exactly to our map. I leaned down in my seat, then sideways, but the sun was too strong to see the words. "Stop us here," I said to Ursula. "I need to get out. The glare's too bright from inside here."

She coasted to a slow halt and cut the ignition. I climbed out of the RV and jogged over the gravel along the side of the road to the base of the sign, hand to my brow to cut the sun. Ursula followed with her rifle. A few feet away, the glazed surface finally gave up the blinding glow and I saw why it had been so hard to read. It was the back of the sign, an empty blue sheet, not the front.

"This side!" I said, darting around its tall metal legs. "This side, it says—"

## REST STOP, 1 MILE AHEAD

I dropped my hand. "It's not a sign for New Orleans," I said, disappointed.

"Are we going the wrong way?"

"No, no. It's just a sign for a rest stop." Ursula's waiting expression told me she'd forgotten what that was. "A small area off the main highway with a gas station, a few restaurants, and some other small stores. Travelers gather there."

"We'd probably best avoid that, then. If we can help it, I don't want to run into any more runners. Or the ones they were fleeing." Ursula replied. "But we're still going the right way?"

"I think so," I said.

She laid her rifle across her shoulder. "What's a restaurant?" she finally asked.

"It's—" I paused. I realized I didn't know what that word meant anymore either.

"Doesn't matter," Ursula said.

As we walked away, I was seized by an almost desperate feeling to turn around and look at the sign again. Not the front, but the back. The empty, sapphire space.

"Wait just a minute," I said.

Ursula stopped, but pointed toward the RV with the tip of her gun. "The others."

"It's okay," I said. "Go back in. I'll be right here."

"Max." She frowned.

"Please. I just need a minute."

I thought Ursula would refuse. Yesterday had us all spooked. She squinted at the sign for a few minutes. Finally she nodded. "Quickly then."

I went to the blank side of the tired metal plate again as she picked her way back to the vehicle through the gravel. *Quickly.* I didn't have any of Zachary's paints, but there were rocks around my feet. I picked up a pointed one and put it against the metal, dragging it slowly in a small line. The blue coating came away in tiny chips, leaving a silver scar. I pressed harder, did it again. And again. When I finished, I let the stone drop back to the ground and shaded my eyes with one hand.

You would have smiled if you could have seen it, Ory. It wasn't perfect, but it was clear enough—two thickly scratched numbers against a blue background.

I haven't said it for a long time, but I still remember. Part of me is afraid to say it, in case that time is the last time. But I still remember. I wanted to prove it to you.

Ursula was squinting out the windshield when I finally opened the side door and climbed back into the passenger seat. Through the glass, I could just barely make out the curves of the 5 and the 2 scratched there, glinting in the sun. Ursula could no longer read it, but she could tell that it was writing.

"To remember?" she asked.

"To remember," I said.

She started the RV.

⏸

The road was smoother for a while. Victor kept watch, his expression as sharp and predatory as the lion on his arm, and I fell in and out of sleep as we drove, lulled by the engine's hum. I may have dreamed about you. I'm not sure. It worries me sometimes—whether I could forget you in a dream—but there's nothing I can do about it. There's no way not to sleep. And who knows how much longer I'll have dreams anyway? After I've forgotten enough, maybe I won't dream at all.

An hour went by with only trees and more trees, worrying Ursula further, until finally another sign appeared ahead of us. She nudged me and gestured out the windshield. I sat up and rubbed my face, ready to do my job. She must have woken me up mid-slumber—I blinked several times to clear my eyes, yet the sign ahead of us remained a jumbled blur. But on the surrounding trees, I'd never seen the little green leaves withering in the late autumn air so vividly as then.

I raised the map to compare as we neared. Shapes swam in front of me, the same meandering colored lines I'd been staring at snaking back and forth across the paper through little dots. The splotches of green in places where the lines were rarer and thinner. Wide ribbons of light blue.

Very slowly, I put the map back down in my lap. A fold was wrinkled. I smoothed it out as gently as I could with my hand until it laid flat again.

"Ursula," I said, "I need to tell you something." I was surprised at how calm I sounded. Or perhaps it was shock. The RV's engine droned in the background. "I don't remember how to read anymore."

# ORLANDO ZHANG

"LAST RESORT," AHMADI SAID AS SHE HANDED ORY AN ALUMI-
num baseball bat. "Life or death. If you kill one of them, they'll burn
hundreds of books."

Ory nodded as he peeked over the barricades. They were back
on the front lines again, shivering under the freezing drizzle. A deep
hum of thunder rolled slowly overhead. On the other side of the
street, he could see tufts of crimson hair pop up, then disappear
again. Beyond, the Red King's library gleamed grotesquely under
the dim silver light. It looked freshly wet, as if the sky had bled
down onto the building.

Malik pointed at half the team. "You five with me, and you five—
including Ory—with Ahmadi. We stay together unless there's a
reason to divide. If we split up, you follow the commander I just
assigned you."

"Yes, sir." They saluted. Ory followed an instant afterward, shyly.

"You ready?" Malik asked him.

He gulped and nodded. "I just—one thing," he asked. "Before I
die. Why *is* everyone doing this?"

"Saving books?" Malik asked.

"Yeah. It's nice to read them until we all lose our shadows too,
but then what?" He glanced at the patrolling Reds. "I understand
Imanuel—the General's—reasons, but everyone else here knew Paul
only a short time. *This* kind of risk, just to have literature for a little
while longer?"

"The books aren't for reading," Malik said.

Ory blinked. "What are they for?"

"You let the General worry about that," he replied, and then his voice boomed. "On my command!" he cried. The soldiers shifted, ready.

"Survive this, and the General will explain later," Ahmadi said to Ory. "For now, you stay close to me, and you do nothing unless Malik or I tell you to do something. Then you do it immediately, whether or not you understand it. Got it?"

"Got it," Ory said.

"At least you listen." Ahmadi stifled a chuckle. "You're nothing like Paul."

"Here we go!" Malik shouted. He stood up slowly, his hands up.

Immediately, the Red side burst with color. From out of nowhere, a dozen flaming shapes erupted and dashed toward the no-man's-land between the two forces, whooping and screaming. Red-streaked hair, red scraps of fabric tied to elbows, red handprints pasted onto the fronts of chests—swirled together in an angry storm.

"Stand up," Ahmadi ordered, and then rose slowly, her hands up as well. Ory copied her actions. He tried to ignore the feeling that something sharp was going to sail through the air and puncture a hole straight through him at any moment. Ahmadi started moving forward.

"Wait," he hissed.

"Walk," Ahmadi ordered. "We have to meet them in the center."

His feet disobeyed his terror and followed her, picking their way over the rocks. His eyes darted from Red to Red frantically. "Where's the Red King?"

"He won't come out," Ahmadi answered. "He never comes out—not unless they need something very, very badly. The General is the only one who's ever seen him up close."

As they neared the center, Ory jumped as a few of the boldest Reds darted suddenly past them. "Where do they get this paint?" he asked, raising his voice over the clamor.

"We have no idea," Ahmadi said. "Look for a giant!"

"What?"

"A giant!" Malik yelled. "A huge Red negotiates the trades."

As soon as he said it, from across the no-man's-land on the Red side, a monster of a man with a shaved head began to lumber forward. He was a giant in every sense of the word: tall, wide, built like a tank. He looked like he might have been a bodybuilder or sumo wrestler before he lost his shadow. The Reds had painted him in stripes, wide red bars that started at the crown of his head and wrapped sideways around him down to his ankles. He was clothed in some kind of awkward long loincloth, likely the only thing they could devise to fit him. It was more than some others had.

"There he is!" Ahmadi yelled, and raised her arms higher to attract the big man's attention. The Reds started hooting. The soldiers pushed them back with the butts of their shotguns when they got too close, but they just kept coming.

"Over here!" Malik's shout rallied them. The big man stumbled to a halt in front of him and pointed at Malik in recognition. The other Reds around him whooped.

"How do we know what they want to trade?" Ory yelled to Ahmadi.

"We don't," she yelled back. "We just keep guessing until we get it!"

Inside the Red King's front courtyard, wounded Reds were everywhere—Reds who hours before had been running around, throwing rocks. Now they lay in various injured poses on the concrete, moaning.

The big man began grunting and waving his arms at the stricken Reds. He put his hands together in balls and then dragged them apart from each other again, over and over. It took Ory a moment to realize he was miming bandages.

"Figures," Ahmadi said, and waved over another soldier to open his backpack. "They want first aid today, since we just beat the shit out of them." She held out a roll of homemade cloth bandages, and the big man's gestures grew more frenzied—she was right.

"Book, you huge red bastard," Malik said, and withdrew the roll in his hand and put out his other empty hand. "Show us the books first."

There was much hissing and dancing. The Reds around them closed tighter. The big man snarled at the others, and some of them skittered up the steps into the Red King's library. From where they were standing, Ory could make out only a dim marble floor, the shadowy outline of several still-standing bookshelves, and yet more bodies, moving inside. The red paint on all the windows had made it too dark inside to see farther.

"Book!" Ahmadi was also chanting now. Several Reds burst back out of the half-open front doors, each one of them holding a hardcover. The hairs on Ory's skin stiffened when he saw them.

"That's it," Malik said and waved gently to them, but the Reds took them all to the big man first instead.

"Is Paul's book there?" Ahmadi yelled.

Malik was struggling to make out the titles as the big Red jostled the books around. "No!" he finally cried.

"Fuck," Ahmadi sighed. "This is going to take us a decade."

"Wait," Ory asked in disbelief. "*They* choose the books?"

"It's like goddamn Russian roulette," another soldier answered.

"What does he have this time?" Ahmadi called.

Malik was trying to get as close to the big Red as he could to read the titles without entering striking distance. The Red, not remembering that books had to be still for the titles to be read, kept jerking the pile around, afraid Malik was going to reach for it. "Hold still!" Malik snapped. The big man hissed angrily, baring his sharp yellowed teeth, but the books were still for a second as he did it. "*Encyclopedia of Insects*," Malik called. "Something about diet, a detective novel, Quran study guide, vampire stories!"

"Get the novel and the Quran study guide!" Ahmadi shouted. "Anything but insects!"

"Do it backward this time," someone else yelled. "Pretend we want the shit ones so they'll give us the good ones instead!"

"Try it," Ahmadi agreed. "See if we can trick them!"

"This better work," Malik replied, and pointed at the *Encyclopedia of Insects* and the book about vampires. The big man hissed and jerked them away, and then folded those two protectively underneath the massive bulge of his arms. The diet book, detective novel, and Quran study guide remained.

Ahmadi began arguing nonsense at him, gesturing at the books he'd hidden away as if those were the ones they truly wanted. The Reds jumped at them; someone shoved one back; a brief skirmish ensued that startled Ory into a corner of the courtyard.

"Enough!" Malik was yelling at the same time that the big man roared. Ahmadi was working to separate a soldier and a Red without getting hurt. She smacked it in the face when it went to bite her arm and sent it howling, and then thrust her hands up in the air in a gesture of peace.

"Okay, no more!" she said. "No more!" She stared them down.

"Fuck me," Ory gasped, cowering. "This is fucking insane." How had they managed to get any books at all like this?

Malik and the big man haggled with each other, Malik acting as though he wanted the two books he really didn't want and the Red trying desperately to keep them squirreled away against his chest for a more valuable trade. Eventually Malik got the Quran study guide and the diet book.

"Here." Ahmadi pressed them into Ory's hands. "Pack them up and keep them safe, and then keep out of the way until we're done. If a Red tries to touch your backpack, you run straight for the Iowa. Don't stop, even if you see one of us go down. Got it?"

"These two are that important?" Ory asked, scrambling to put them into the reinforced backpack he'd been loaned.

"Lots of memories in the Quran," she said gravely.

OVER THE NEXT WEEK, THEY BROUGHT BACK AN AMERICAN history textbook, a murder mystery, and a book on Egyptian gods.

Ory sprained an ankle, but not badly. A soldier they all called Smith Tres—because they had three Smiths in the army: Original Smith, Smith Dos, and Smith Tres—was stabbed. Imanuel checked his dressings almost every hour, even at night. He stitched him up using thread carefully pulled out of the sleeve of a coat and then lightly boiled to sterilize it.

"Hold this so it doesn't tangle," Imanuel told Ory after he'd washed his hands. The thread was still warm in his palms. "Feed it to me slowly."

Ahmadi watched from the corner, biting the end of one of her nails. It was unnerving to see her so shaken. Behind her, Malik's daughter, Vienna, hovered, trying to steal a glance. Malik came up behind her and gave her a reassuring squeeze. Ory's heart swelled for the two of them as they watched Imanuel work—that they both still had their shadows, that they were both still together.

It had been a bloody day, and a fiery one. They'd almost caused a retaliatory burning, but managed to calm the Reds at the last moment—they had just given them everything they brought in exchange for not putting any books into the flames. They came home with nothing.

"That's the other reason we don't just charge in and try to take the place by force," Imanuel said to Ory later, as they watched Smith Tres sleep. "All they have to do is just light a fire, and smile as we call off the troops." He ran his hands through his hair and sighed. It was the first moment they'd really had alone since Ory arrived—now that the shock had worn off, he could see Imanuel looked twice the age he did at Elk Cliffs. "I still think about the first one, almost every day."

"The first burned book?"

"It haunts my dreams," Imanuel said. "Because I'll never know what it was."

They watched the flames in the fireplace in front of them crackle, licking at charred wood. "Imanuel," Ory finally said, "we need to talk."

"You want to know why the books," he replied. "I mean, what they're for, once we have Paul's. Ahmadi told me."

"No. I mean, I do. But this isn't about that." He took a deep breath. "It's about Max."

Imanuel's face softened. "Ory."

"A few soldiers, some food. Just give me that." Ory took him by the shoulders, to stop him from turning away. "And when I find her, we'll come back. I'll help you get all the goddamned books you want. I don't even care about the reason. I'll get you the whole library, if you do this for me."

"Ory, she—"

Ory cut him off. "Don't say it." He didn't know if he could bear to hear it out loud. Not from Imanuel. "Don't you say it."

Imanuel sighed. "Even if she still remembers, you've seen the city. What she would have walked into. Your apartment is gone. Paul and I went to see it when we first got here. To see if there was something left to—remember you by. The whole thing was concrete powder."

"I know."

"Even if she made it here, what then? Then where would she go? The Reds aren't—"

"She's not a Red," Ory said.

"I know she's not. That's my point. The Reds don't just take any shadowless. They're not a charity. Most of the time they just kill them like they kill shadowed survivors." He stopped himself suddenly, eyes wide. "I'm not saying that's what happened to her. Christ. Sorry."

Ory put his face in his hands. "Imanuel, please. I can't give up on her."

"Ory—"

"No," Ory cut him off. There was a high, desperate pitch in his voice that scared them both. "Okay, what about after, then?" he asked frantically. Everything—reaching D.C., finding Imanuel, all the hope—was streaming through his hands like sand in a sieve. "What if I agree to help until we get Paul's book? Would you lend me soldiers then?"

They stared at each other for a moment until Ory finally looked away.

"Ory," Imanuel said. "Look at me."

Ory couldn't meet his eyes. He knew it was a pointless thing to ask for. If there was almost no chance that Max was still alive in D.C. now, there'd be even less chance she would be here once he found Paul's book days, weeks, months from now. When he finally looked up, he could see it in Imanuel's face. That Imanuel understood that somewhere deep down, Ory knew Max wasn't in D.C. That he'd never find her, no matter how long he tried. But that it wasn't so much about actually finding Max as just not stopping the search. As long as he kept looking for her, she was still real.

"Do you sometimes feel like—" Imanuel paused. "Like you don't even know who you are without her?"

Ory watched him, not moving.

"I did, when the Forgetting first happened in Boston—during the wedding," he continued. A faint smile flickered. "The wedding. Those terrible tuxedos."

Finally Ory smiled, too. He couldn't help it.

"I remember standing there with Paul, watching the broadcast. I thought, *It's going to happen to us, too.* One of us was going to lose his shadow, and it was going to be me." His eyes searched Ory's face. "I was convinced it was going to be me. Because he was so strong. So . . . larger than life, and sure of everything, always. I was always the one afraid or uncertain. Never taking risks. Standing there in front of the TV, I couldn't imagine how I'd go on without him, as just myself. I thought that meant something. A weakness." He shrugged. On the floor, his shadow did the same. "Here I am."

Ory looked down again. He didn't want to agree with it, but he knew Imanuel was right.

"I have to tell you something else," Imanuel began again at last. "I just want you to listen, that's all." He drew closer, voice dropping. "I've heard some things over the last two years. Not much, but snatches here and there. It's rumor, but so many people have the same story, there must be at least some truth to it." Imanuel was speaking faster and faster in his excitement. "They're saying—"

"New Orleans." Ory grimaced.

Imanuel blinked in surprise. The icy rain pattered against the ground into slush outside. "You know about it, too," he said at last.

"I heard the same thing back in Arlington." The group of hardened travelers standing around an empty pool played in his mind like a silent film. Their leader's leathery face and shaved head, her gun: Ursula. Had they made it after all? How many of them still had their shadows?

"Well, that's what the books are for. The One Who Gathers, the rumors say he's gathering people, but not just people—he's looking for something else. Memories. Books have memories, right?" Imanuel asked, staring hard at his hands. "In a way."

"Books also have shadows," Ory said. Imanuel looked up at him hopefully. "So do pieces of shit sitting out on the asphalt."

"Ory," he bristled.

"So do dead birds, trash cans, decrepit buildings—"

"Stop."

"I'm just saying, that's a lot of risk to collect thousands of books from a crazed warrior clan and a long, dangerous way to drag them for a rumor about a bunch of jumbled nonsense."

Imanuel refused to give up. "I don't think it's just a rumor."

Ory didn't look at him. He couldn't. They both knew what he was going to ask next.

"Ory, it's over," Imanuel said gently. Ory felt his hand on his shoulder. "It's been weeks since she forgot, and disappeared. She's gone. She was gone a long time ago. There's no reason to stay here now."

"No," Ory said.

"Ory—"

"*No.*"

Imanuel put his hands up and moved back a few steps as a gesture of peace. He took a long breath. In the dim light, Ory could see the outline of him against the wall grow and shrink as he did.

"I know how bad the odds are," Ory said. The fire hissed. "But I just *can't.*" He stared at the exhausted slope of Imanuel's shoulders. "If it was the other way around, what would you want me to do for you? What if Paul was possibly still here in D.C.? What would you want me to *do*?"

Imanuel turned away abruptly, and made a sudden sound that could have been a sob. It came from so deep inside him that Ory jerked halfway to his feet before he realized he'd even moved, arms out to catch his friend before he fell. It was the sound of pain that was too great for a mind to bear anymore. The sound of a soul dying, leaving only biological echoes behind to wander through the motions of life until the end. Ory waited for a long time, for the rest of it, for Imanuel to collapse. But nothing followed. Nothing fell into his arms.

"I would want you to tell me to give up," Imanuel finally said, but the words were hardly words. They were a moan.

Ory looked at him as he withered in the firelight. Too far. His words had gone too far. Imanuel's hands were still pressed against his face, blocking his expression from view. Their shadows twitched, weak in the firelight.

"I shouldn't have said that," Ory finally said. "I—"

Imanuel held his hand up, to cut him off. "After." His voice was hard. "After we get Paul's book, I'll lend you a few soldiers to look for Max. But I promised them all that if they helped me get what I need, all of them would make it to New Orleans with me. I can't go back on my word. Whatever you decide for yourself is up to you, but the soldiers will stay with you for two weeks and then follow after us."

"Thank you," Ory said.

Imanuel nodded. Ory thought he was going to leave, but he stayed there, head down, for a long time. "I hope you change your mind before that," he finally said. "About New Orleans."

"I can't," Ory said.

"Can't," he asked. "Or won't?"

They looked at each other for a long time. "I don't want to forget," Ory said.

The expression on Imanuel's face was the worst kind of pain. "I didn't say forget," he murmured quietly, his voice thick with sadness. "I would never say forget."

# THE ONE WHO GATHERS

THE FIRST SHADOWLESS HE FOUND WAS CALLED MICHAEL.

A teenager, about nineteen perhaps. Not that tall, and painfully skinny from weeks of starvation, with a tousle of silky dark hair and a few faint freckles on his pale, scared face. He'd been digging around in the long-emptied garbage bins in the alley behind the assisted-living facility, searching for something edible. The noise was what had drawn them to him. The amnesiac, Dr. Zadeh, and Nurse Marie stood blocking the only way out of the narrow, dead-end street with their bodies long before he heard them there.

"Easy," the amnesiac said when the shadowless finally turned around, then started, movements swift and compact like a cornered animal. The amnesiac glanced at Dr. Zadeh, who was trying to stand in a posture that both appeared as unthreatening as possible and also covered as much of the alley as possible. "Do you remember English?" he continued. "You understand what I'm saying?"

The shadowless flinched. His hands were curled into defensive claws. The amnesiac felt the weight of the kitchen knife on his belt in its crudely fashioned plastic and duct tape scabbard. He'd practiced reaching for the handle and whipping it out several times before they went outside. He didn't want to *have to* be good with a blade—but he did want to be good with a blade. Just in case.

"You look hungry," Dr. Zadeh said. The amnesiac saw recognition register in the boy's eyes. The meaning of that word, the hope. "What's your name?"

The shadowless stared at them. Slowly the hands uncurled. His eyes shimmered, tears like mirrors. "I don't remember," he moaned.

"That's all right," Dr. Zadeh smiled. "How about we give you one? Your name is Michael," he said.

"Michael," the shadowless repeated. "Michael," he said again more fiercely, in the familiar tone the amnesiac had heard so many times. A desperation not just to cling to something, but to have something to cling to in the first place.

"Michael, we're friends," Dr. Zadeh continued. "We're here to help you. I'm a doctor. You can call me Dr. Zadeh."

"What kind of doctor?"

"A neurologist," he said, not expecting the term to mean anything anymore to Michael. The amnesiac could see from his expression that it didn't. "I work on the brain." He pointed to the side of his head, at his temple. "My specialty is memories."

The word hung in the air between all of them like a physical thing. *Memories.* The amnesiac watched Michael take a step toward them, as if to move into the aura of those lingering syllables.

"You can make me remember?" he asked with terrifying desperation.

*No,* the amnesiac wanted to say. How much had Michael forgotten? he wondered. What magic had he already done? "We can try," he said instead.

MICHAEL SETTLED IN, AND THE AMNESIAC BEGAN TEACHING him the same Alzheimer's memory exercises Dr. Zadeh had taught him when he'd first arrived. It was mostly useless, but they had to start somewhere. There was a process, a scientific process, Dr. Zadeh insisted as he tried to finish his experimental treatment plan. If they were going to find the cure, they had to do it right. They needed patients, and they needed a process.

"We don't even know the cause of shadowlessness," the amnesiac had argued. "How can you develop a treatment plan if we don't even know the cause?"

"That's what will make us fail, right there," Dr. Zadeh said. He pointed at him.

The amnesiac stared back, confused. "What?" he finally asked.

"Doubt," Dr. Zadeh replied.

The amnesiac wasn't sure what he believed, but he put that aside. He didn't argue against the doctor's plan after that. He did everything he was asked, everything he could, to keep the patients safe. New Orleans had been shadowless for almost a month by then. Once the Forgetting reached the city limits, he had helped Dr. Zadeh remove all the signs on their facility—the metal address numbers on the front wall, Dr. Zadeh's name plaque by the door, the information board that was posted on the roof. Anything that would tell someone who still remembered how to read that a doctor could be inside, that there might be medicine or food as well. They added locks to doors and boarded up windows. Now the assisted-living facility looked no different from the rest of the ruined structures that surrounded it.

Once they were confident the building was secure and inconspicuous, Dr. Zadeh, the amnesiac, and Nurse Marie sneaked out a few more times to look for more shadowless to admit to the assisted-living facility, growing bolder, going farther into the city each time. Some listened, some ran. When they started taking Michael with them, always holding Nurse Marie's hand so he didn't wander off, they became much better at persuading other shadowless to trust them. The amnesiac started bringing food when they went out looking—both as a gesture of good faith and as a way to stop the shadowless from fleeing immediately, before any of them could get a full sentence out.

Even when the power went down across New Orleans and the riots broke out, Dr. Zadeh refused to give up. Even when the police finally left their posts around the city one by one, and bodies in the streets—shadowed and shadowless alike—became more and more common, he pressed on.

"How many more patients do we need?" the amnesiac asked him one night, after they'd rationed out dinner for everyone.

"As many as we can find," he said. "But I'd settle for at least eight. That's enough for two groups, including our own people—one variable, one control. Then we'll start getting somewhere."

The amnesiac looked down at the binder in his hands, the copy of the one Hemu Joshi's doctor had given him, at the list of names he had added as the very first page. Everyone inside the assisted-living facility: ten nurses, one doctor, ten Alzheimer's patients, one case of total retrograde amnesia due to vehicular trauma, and the three new-comers they'd found—including Michael. Next to the names of all three of the new people, two of the Alzheimer's patients, and one of the nurses, the amnesiac had drawn stars. Shadowless, the symbol meant. Shadowless, but still alive.

**INDIA NEWS, INC. [INI] REPORTER:** And you are—?
**ELIZABETH HERRERA:** Catholic. Born and raised.

The amnesiac scooted the list of names over farther so he could see the page beneath. It was one he knew well. An excerpt of a decades-old interview with the American biologist—the one with the prosthetic leg who had taught Gajarajan's elephant sister to paint.

**INI:** Which you offer as proof that you've never met the ele-phant, Gajarajan Guruvayur Kesavan?
**HERRERA:** Guruvayur Temple's rules are very clear: only Hindus are allowed inside the gates. I did try, though, when the story about Gajarajan first broke. I called and explained who I was—I got halfway through my speech before it clicked. Immediately they were all yelling. They called for the head priest. And still, I couldn't get in.
**INI:** What happened after that?

**HERRERA:** All bad ideas, none of which worked either. I tried to bribe them, I tried to reach someone in government to help, I even briefly considered trying to break in—I just wanted proof. To be told something like that had happened; that I'd successfully taught painting for the first time in history to a wild elephant born in 1998, some twenty years after her elder brother had been captured and permanently stationed at the temple, and then a few days before my research rotation in India was over, the elder brother spontaneously painted a picture . . . Of me?

**INI:** It is uncanny.

**HERRERA:** That's a word for it. I have another one. *Magic.*

**INI:** It's hard to disagree.

**HERRERA:** Well, what happened next was even more . . . uncanny. After I finally threw in the towel, I had only about a week left at Thiruvananthapuram before my research visa was up and I had to return to the United States. I hardly had time to finish the work I had left, but on the last day, I blocked off an hour to go see Manikam, to say goodbye. That's her name, the one I taught to paint. The much younger sister of Gajarajan.

**INI:** That must have been hard.

**HERRERA:** It was. But it's always that way. There are only so many elephants left in the world, you know? To get the data you need, the sample size you need, you're always traveling between sanctuaries. India, Thailand, Tennessee.

**INI:** Go on.

**HERRERA:** I was with her, alone in the main pasture. Well, she started making the motions she always made when she wanted to paint—it's a specific trunk movement and the ears flapping in a certain way. I had learned to recognize it. I took out her easel and canvas and paints and set them up for her. Sometimes Manikam knew what she wanted to paint, sometimes she didn't, but this was one of those times she did—it was like she'd gotten an image in her head and had just been waiting for me to get there so I could help her set up the easel and paints.

INI: Did she paint?

HERRERA: She did. Immediately. Normally, it's a slow process. She sometimes had trouble holding the brush with her trunk— she'd lose her grip on it, drop it. But this time, she jammed the bristles into the paints on her big palette almost before I'd finished preparing it. She worked . . . desperately. That's the word I'd use. When she finished, it was all at once. Usually it was hard for me to tell when she was really done, because she'd dawdle, and I'd go to remove the canvas and she'd get upset. But this time it was a fury of color, then suddenly it was over. She stepped back and stared at me, as if inviting me to look.

INI: What did you see?

HERRERA: I didn't know at first. It was so detailed. I thought it was a pattern of some kind. Sort of geometric and repeating. It was.

INI: I don't understand.

HERRERA: I didn't either. But that evening, one of the interns came into the main lab. I had the easel sitting by my desk so the canvas could continue drying. She took one look at it and asked me if Manikam had done it. "Why?" I asked. She said it was because it reminded her of the painted walls of the temple her mother used to take her to when she was growing up—one county over, in the town of Guruvayur.

INI: No.

HERRERA: I didn't believe it either. I printed a scanned copy and mailed it to them.

INI: And was it—

HERRERA: Yes. It was an exact replica of the pattern of the northern wall of Gajarajan's residential enclosure. Down to the centimeter. [Smiles.]

INI: It's not, it's not—

HERRERA: I know.

INI: *[After a long pause]* What happened then?

HERRERA: I left. I had to. My research visa was up.

INI: That . . . That must have been hard.

HERRERA: But it was okay, you know? Now I don't really care what anyone else thinks. I'm not a neurologist, but to me, that proved it. It proved that the stories about Gajarajan were true. That elephants really could remember things they hadn't experienced directly, but others had. That they could . . . I don't know.

INI: Please.

HERRERA: Like memories are something we somehow can move or share. Maybe not even all of them, but at least one. One memory. One thing that always stays, across time and space.

The amnesiac looked up from the binder, at Dr. Zadeh. "You really think we're going to find a cure?" he asked.

Dr. Zadeh was silent for so long, the amnesiac thought he might not answer, because the answer was no, and he didn't want to lie. "We have to," he finally said instead.

THEY WENT OUT EVERY OTHER DAY, LOOKING FOR FOOD AND supplies in the mornings and shadowless in the afternoons. Something was happening, but it was hard to tell what. There were signs of human life left behind—things changed places, scavenged morsels among the wreckage appeared or went missing—but the humans themselves, living ones, were becoming harder and harder to find. There was more dried blood in the corners of places than there had been before. Twice they actually did glimpse other shadowed survivors— but they weren't the sort of survivors the amnesiac wanted to meet. The first group was traveling in a set of three, and the second in a pair. All men, all wearing makeshift gear that looked as though it was for fighting, all well armed. Dr. Zadeh's little team waited inside alleys and broken buildings until the others passed both times. They didn't know what the men were looking for, but they didn't want to find out.

They managed to find four more shadowless over the next few weeks. The first two had each forgotten so much they were barely wary at all. The third was far more afraid.

She was running, clothes soaked through with sweat. She must have been going for miles. "You're safe now," Dr. Zadeh kept repeating to her, begging her to come out from the abandoned house she'd thrown herself into when she saw them coming from the other direction.

The amnesiac started tossing the food in the open window through which she'd crawled. They'd never been so deep into the downtown before.

"We just want to help. I'm a doctor," Dr. Zadeh continued.

Finally it was the shadowless Michael who convinced her.

"My name is Letty," she said softly as she walked with them back toward the assisted-living facility on the other side of town.

"What were you running from?" Nurse Marie asked her.

"Exterminators," she said.

"Exterminators?" the amnesiac asked. Beside him, he saw Michael shudder.

"You know them, too?" Dr. Zadeh had noticed the same thing.

"I thought that's what all of you were, when you first found me," Michael said. "They—" He shrugged helplessly. "Now I don't remember. I just remember that they're bad."

"Ones with shadows who kill ones without," Letty continued. It seemed like she couldn't speak above a whisper. "They go around, looking for us."

"Why?" Dr. Zadeh asked, voice stony.

Letty shook her head. "Money or food." She paused. "They also enjoy it, I think."

The amnesiac shook his head in disgust. "Who's paying them?" he asked at last.

"Whoever's inside the city hall. Someone's still trying to run things. Trying to clean up New Orleans before too many shadowless—" She stopped abruptly, mouth snapped shut, and stared in terror at them all. *Magic.* Hemu's frightened voice came back to the amnesiac, the pleading expression in the young man's exhausted, terrified eyes.

"It's all right," Dr. Zadeh said to her. "We know. About the . . . pull."

Letty's eyes darted to the amnesiac's.

"We do," he said. "It's real." The Mandai spice market in Pune flashed in his mind. Or rather the memory of it, because it didn't exist anymore. "We've seen it happen."

THE FOURTH SHADOWLESS THEY MET BECAUSE OF LETTY. They also met their first exterminators.

"She was—I don't know. But I know we were together before we forgot why, so she has to be someone important," Letty said to the amnesiac as they all crept across Lafayette Square. They were deep into the Central Business District just south of the French Quarter, looking for a street they hoped Letty would still find familiar. It was far past their usual search boundaries, but Dr. Zadeh was getting desperate. The shadowless had been disappearing like ghosts. There were so few left now, and those they did see ran well before anyone could get close enough, even Michael. If this shadowless still remembered Letty even a little, they stood a chance of convincing her to come with them.

The neighborhood clearly unnerved Letty, every sound and creak of wood pricking like a needle on a fresh new spot of skin. The amnesiac looked around nervously, her fear making him jumpy. Here he didn't know the angles to hide in, the directions to run that weren't dead ends. They wound their way deeper in.

The shadowless they sought was still alive, hiding between two empty buildings, almost exactly where Letty had said she lost her when she'd started running, so many days ago.

"You're alive," Letty gasped when she finally saw her.

The shadowless looked up from where she was crouched between a few Dumpsters. The amnesiac saw the flash of recognition in her eyes—she remembered Letty still. "Shh," she hissed.

The amnesiac and the others didn't move for a second, but Letty darted behind another of the Dumpsters immediately. "Hide," she said. She mouthed the word *exterminators.*

They all threw themselves down behind piles of concrete, burned-out furniture, any shape that would hide them as the footsteps echoed closer, but it was too late. The exterminators had already seen them.

"Look at this," the one covered in scars said to the other, probably the tallest man the amnesiac had ever seen in person. He took the gun out of his holster. "Newbies. You all know you're in Jackson's neighborhood, right?"

"Jackson's neighborhood?"

The tall one looked at the scarred one with his eyes narrowed. "I've had it with this. People crawling out of the woodwork, muscling in on our area." He pointed the gun straight at the amnesiac, and Dr. Zadeh and Nurse Marie shrieked, shouting pleading things that interrupted each other and made no sense. "You can't just come in here and take our catch. That isn't how it works."

"I'm sorry," the amnesiac said shakily. "We didn't know."

"Yeah, right," the tall one sneered. "Explain that, then." His gun moved to aim casually at Letty and the other shadowless, causing them to cower to the ground, whimpering.

"Family!" the amnesiac cried. "They lost their shadows a week ago. We're all family. We're just looking for food."

"Food here in this neighborhood also belongs to Jackson," the scarred one said. "But more importantly, so does your family now."

"No," Dr. Zadeh said.

"Once they lose their shadows, they're ours."

"What about when you lose yours?" Dr. Zadeh asked the scarred exterminator.

The tall one tipped his head at his partner. "Then I'll shoot him immediately and collect my reward for it."

"Or the other way around," the scarred one added, grinning.

"Please, we'll leave. We'll never come back," the amnesiac promised.

"No can do," the scarred exterminator said. He stepped closer. "See, even if I did believe you that these two were your family, they're still shadowless, and you're still in our hunting neighborhood." The grin dropped off his face. "But I don't believe you anyway."

"Shadowless are almost gone, or hiding," the tall one said. "Other guys have been crowding our territory for months now, taking our kills. We've heard every story there is twice. Including yours. I'm putting a stop to it."

"Please—" Dr. Zadeh started to say just as something cruised soundlessly through the air overhead. The only way any of them knew it had been there at all was the huge dark square it cast down over them as it passed.

In the same instant, Letty's shadowless friend and the two exterminators dropped into tight crouches, covering their heads. It wasn't just an instinctual flinch to some nearby movement, the amnesiac realized with a chill—it was a deliberate, *practiced* move.

"What was that?" the amnesiac gasped.

"Come on," the scarred exterminator said to the tall one, already running away.

"The shadowless," he replied angrily.

But the scarred one was already halfway down the street. "No time. I'm not dying today."

A gust of wind made everyone jump again, and the shadowless whimpered in terror, sinking even lower to the ground.

"We have to *go*, man," the scarred one yelled. "Jackson! Come *on*!"

"Your lucky day," the tall exterminator snarled at them. He pointed a finger straight at Dr. Zadeh's chest. "We catch you leaning in on our business again, it'll be the last time."

Dr. Zadeh refused to answer. "We hear," the amnesiac said.

"Don't *forget* now," he teased, sinister, nodding his chin at their still-there shadows. Then he bolted after his friend, eyes checking the sky.

As soon as the exterminators disappeared around the corner, everyone gasped, suddenly remembering to breathe again. "What was that thing?" Nurse Marie cried, and tried to grab both the amnesiac and Dr. Zadeh, but they had each moved out of her reach at the same moment, to look up. They spun around, trying to see the sky between the buildings, but the roofs were too close together, their view of the sky too narrow. Letty ran to the shadowless she knew, Michael close behind her.

"Was it a plane?" Dr. Zadeh yelled. "Was it a plane?"

Letty's friend was shaking now. She seemed to shrink down onto the asphalt of the alley. "Hey." The amnesiac crouched, so as to be on her same level. "Do you know what that was?"

The shadowless's eyes stared straight through him, unblinking. "It's coming back." She trembled.

The amnesiac turned back to look at Dr. Zadeh, who was still staring into the sky. "What is it? What's coming back?" he asked, but she was too terrified to answer.

"If it was a plane—if someone is still flying a plane—" Dr. Zadeh continued excitedly. "We have to get their attention!"

"Wait," the amnesiac said to Letty. "Keep hold of her." He ran for a utility ladder welded to the side of a building, to climb up to the roof.

"Be careful!" Nurse Marie cried, watching him ascend with a concerned expression on her face. "Keep away from the edge! You can't judge depth with one eye!" She'd been the first nurse the amnesiac had depended upon when he arrived at the assisted-living facility, when he was barely strong enough for crutches, and she still worried after him as if he was still her charge.

"Almost there!" the amnesiac yelled to her. He hauled himself onto the flat top of the building. Dusk was falling, smearing everything with an orangy-purple haze. On the horizon, so far it looked to be over the western area of Metairie, a dark thing rippled in the sky. "I can't see—" he started to say. And then he heard the screams.

Nurse Marie was at Dr. Zadeh's side by the time the amnesiac had scrambled back to the edge of the roof to peer down at them, clutching a trembling Michael to her with knuckles that had gone white. Letty cowered with her companion.

"What did you see?" Dr. Zadeh asked softly.

The dark shape passed overhead again. It was the size of a small house, with angles as sharp as blades. There were more screams from the direction in which it had gone.

"Jesus Christ," Nurse Marie said.

Dr. Zadeh took the new shadowless's face in his hands and made her look at him. "What is it?" he asked firmly, in the voice he had mastered over decades of practice, a tone of absolute authority that could cut through fear or pain, or even sometimes the terrified fog of an Alzheimer's episode, and could compel any patient to answer him. "What. Is. It."

The shadowless's eyes finally focused on Dr. Zadeh. "Deathkite," she whispered.

From his vantage point above them, the amnesiac saw the shape lean into the wind to return toward them once more.

"We have to get inside," he breathed. "Right now."

LATER, AFTER THEY'D GOTTEN LETTY AND HER FRIEND THEY had named Jo back to the facility, the amnesiac remembered that Hemu had once told him it was customary to fly celebratory kites on Zero Shadow Day. After everyone had had their fun with the moment of shadowlessness and the shadows had returned, the afternoon would turn toward food and games. Little boys loved that part most of all, the kite flying—or rather, the kite fighting. The object of the game was to be the last one still aloft. In their desperation to win, the boys often rubbed the strings with powdered glass so they could saw through one another's lines as the fabric sheets crossed, and later even cheated by adding hidden blades to the edges of the frames, to cut the bodies of other kites.

At the time, the amnesiac thought he would have liked to have seen a kite fight, if it had been possible. In a way, he'd gotten his wish. *Was it Hemu?* He often wondered, each time over the months that followed that he watched the deathkites circle overhead—wonderful things that had been twisted into something horrible and evil by accident. Was it Hemu, or had it been someone else?

"Nurse Marie?" Vivi's voice came from the dimly glowing hallway. She, the amnesiac, and Dr. Zadeh turned to see the old woman leaning nervously into the room. Candles were in each corner, but since they'd boarded up all the windows for safety against the riots, it always looked no brighter than dusk at all times. In the weak light, Vivi looked even frailer than by day. "You'd better come."

"What is it, dear?" Nurse Marie asked, rising to her feet. The knee was giving her trouble again, the amnesiac saw. "Everyone's all right?"

"We're all right," Vivi said. There was a long pause. Beside him, the amnesiac heard Dr. Zadeh sigh, exhausted. Vivi looked down. "It happened again, to Edith."

THEY WERE SHORT ONLY ONE MORE SHADOWLESS WHEN A second pair of exterminators found them. Dr. Zadeh was in the middle of handing food they'd brought to the tiny ball of rags shivering against the concrete wall, and Michael and Letty were calling quietly to it. The amnesiac never saw if it was a man or a woman, old or young. The shadowless was about to reach for the food, just one withered hand and two narrowed eyes visible from the folds of dirty fabric, but then in a swirl of layers, it was gone.

"What the—" Dr. Zadeh gasped in frustration.

" 'What the' indeed," a low voice said from behind them. "I'd ask you the same question about what the fuck you're doing here."

They all turned at once, hearts stuttering. The amnesiac's skin went cold and clammy. There were two figures there, a man and woman, dressed in old police riot gear. Exterminators.

"Looks like they were after that one that just got away," the woman replied to her partner. Her eyes landed coldly back on Dr. Zadeh.

"This isn't what it looks like," he began.

They tried to explain—their experiments, their hope to discover a cure. The amnesiac could see in their eyes that they didn't care. To them, there was no difference between Dr. Zadeh killing a shadowless in their territory or saving one. In either case, it was a body taken away for which they didn't get paid.

Dr. Zadeh shouted for Michael and Letty to run then—as far as they could, as fast as they could. He knew that no matter how it ended up, the two of them would never be allowed to live. They were worth too much to the exterminators. Shots went off as they sprinted, deafening booms. The amnesiac couldn't look, but as he cowered in front of the exterminators and their guns, hands spread protectively in front of his face, he didn't hear either of them fall.

"Please," Nurse Marie was on her knees, begging for Dr. Zadeh's life. "*Please.*" But there was nothing they could offer that the exterminators wanted.

They killed him.

# MAHNAZ AHMADI

SMITH TRES, THE SOLDIER WHO WAS STABBED DURING THE last attempt to trade, didn't develop a fever, but the General wouldn't know if he was out of the woods for at least another week. Naz was just so relieved that he hadn't died on the first night—when he'd been so pale from blood loss his lips were almost blue, teeth chattering, unable to keep warm despite all the blankets she took from her own bed and all the other beds of the soldiers under her command. They'd lost so many people recently. Both to death and to the Forgetting. A few days ago, she even saw a new Red that she'd once known the year before—he'd fought in their army before he lost his shadow and forgot he had. He'd been one of her best scouts, just like Tres was now. Both of them as brave and reckless as she'd ever seen. Both of them almost lost completing missions she'd ordered. Naz didn't know if she'd be able to bear it if another person from her team died.

But even though it seemed like Tres would survive, it still left the problem of who was going to take his place in her formation until he was healed. The army was stretched thin, but she'd been making do already missing her first scout. Now that she was missing two, there was no way around it.

"Go on, leave me behind," Ory wheezed from the dirt. "Save yourself."

Malik's daughter, Vienna, grunted, and threw his arm over her shoulder to try to lift him.

"*Save yourself!*" he wailed as dramatically as he could.

"Vienna!" Naz snapped as the girl began to laugh. "This is not a game!"

"Ahmadi, come on," Ory said, sitting up and dusting off his pants.

"You won't think it's a game when a Red bashes your head in because you joked your way through Malik's boot camp curriculum," Naz said to him. "And you . . ."—she looked hard at Vienna—"you won't think it's a game when I don't clear you for missions."

"No, I'm sorry!" Vienna cried. She snapped to attention and saluted. Naz pinched her lips tight to keep the sadness from showing in her face. It was so hard to tell anyone's true age anymore—the starvation, the scars, the strain of carrying memories alone that should have been shared among others. Sometimes she didn't remember that Vienna couldn't be more than sixteen, maybe seventeen. In some ways she seemed years older, almost the same age as Rojan. Sometimes she seemed so much like Rojan it hurt. "I'm ready to go again, ma'am!"

Naz looked away. *Vienna was not her sister,* she told herself yet again. Her sister had almost made it, but the fever from the arrow wound infection took her in the end. *Vienna was not her sister.* It never worked. "And how about you?" she asked Ory. "Finished screwing around?"

"You know," Ory said as he squared off against Vienna once more, "if I didn't know any better, I'd think you didn't like me very much."

"I think you're too sensitive," she said. "Again!"

She watched them train expressionlessly, drilling even harder. When she at last let them go, Ory gave her a wide berth and didn't speak to her for the rest of the evening. He clearly didn't believe her when she'd brushed off his remark that she didn't like him.

But it was true. It wasn't that Naz didn't like him. It was in fact the opposite. She *did* like him, because he was someone who was as close to the General and Paul as she was—but especially Paul. After all the stories Naz had heard him tell about his lost best friend Ory, and now having Ory here, looking and acting exactly like she'd imagined from Paul's descriptions, telling the same stories about Paul from his own perspective, it made her feel like she too had known Ory for a long time. Like he'd also been her friend, and she'd also left him behind on that mountain.

WHEN ORY HAD FIRST WALKED THROUGH THE FRONT DOOR with Malik, the General told him that he and Paul had tried to go back and find him and his wife, Max. That was true. But what the General never told Ory was that once they'd established the army and had the forces to spare, they had planned to go back for them *again,* a second time.

The General hadn't mentioned that second attempt because he didn't like to talk about anything that touched the memory of Paul's last days in any way. Any reminder was too painful to him. Naz was glad Ory didn't know, though. It made things simpler. Because she was the person who was supposed to have led the rescue team to travel to that deserted mountain, to find this Orlando Zhang and Maxine Webber and bring them safely to the Iowa.

THEY'D TRAINED FOR WEEKS TO PREPARE. IT WAS TO BE A small team, just a handful of soldiers and Naz, so that they could move quickly and quietly. Paul and the General had reported that when they'd attempted to cross back themselves, the bridge had been swarmed with shadowless and too dangerous to cross—but it *was* still standing, and they had greater numbers now. They could make it this time.

Paul had ordered Malik to put his best people on the job, but Malik insisted he would only accept volunteers. When Naz saw the desperation in Paul's face as he waited for someone, anyone, to raise a hand, it made her think of the first time she'd met him. She knew how easily he could have left her and Rojan there to die after the shadowless attack instead of helping them. They were total strangers, and he already had so many mouths to feed at the Iowa. For all he knew, they could have been feigning the seriousness of their injuries. The smarter, safer thing would have been to refuse to take them in. If it had been Naz who had found Paul instead of the other way around, she would have run without even so much as an apology.

But Paul didn't. He had looked at Naz and her sister and known right away—even though they were so bundled in rags one could barely see their same dark eyes, their same sharp noses. When Malik disagreed about bringing them back to the Iowa, Paul had said, "Look at them, Malik. Just look. They're *family*." And he saved Rojan—for what little time she'd had left.

Now it was all reversed—everyone gathered was staring at Paul this time, rather than at Naz, and *he* was the one who was trying and failing to save the life of someone he loved.

Naz put her hand up firmly. She was the first volunteer.

But they never went. The night before the mission was to leave, Malik had to cancel the rescue—because Paul's shadow disappeared.

"I CAN'T JUSTIFY LETTING YOU GO NOW," MALIK TOLD HER the morning after it happened. They were outside the General and Paul's room, where Malik had been standing guard since the previous evening. Inside, the sobs had grown hoarse with exhaustion. Naz could hear Paul's voice, calm and muffled through the door, but the General was inconsolable. "I'm afraid to leave them, in case Paul—" He sighed. "I need someone to lead the library trips in my place until the General comes around again."

But the General didn't come around. As Paul deteriorated, the grief overwhelmed him. Malik tried to manage him and Naz tried to manage the army. Just before he'd lost his shadow, Paul had been particularly taken with the New Orleans rumors, and then with the idea that books could be what The One Who Gathers was seeking. Malik ordered Naz to continue collecting as many as they could, as fast as they could—at that time, the Reds didn't exist yet. They would come later, but at that point, the library was completely abandoned. Just books and cobwebs. Once or twice, they ran into a shadowless or two inside, but they weren't organized. Just wanderers who had happened upon a dry, warm place. Sort of like the Iowans. With Naz in charge, they managed a few good runs before things got much worse with Paul.

The last thing he said to her was about Ory. "Find him," he begged. Naz promised tearfully that she'd do it, even though she knew that she never would now. The next day, Paul no longer remembered how to speak.

After that, the General grew afraid that Paul would run away and get lost, so they started locking him in rooms on the upper levels. They had to move him to a different one every day, because he destroyed them trying to get out.

Naz knew that the shadowless forgot, and it was terrifying, but it was the first time she really saw up close what happened when a person lost his shadow. Paul had started to become something else. She'd never believed what had happened was anything other than fantastical, inexplicable, because there was simply no other way to make it make sense—but those last days with the man she once knew proved it beyond a doubt for her. In his fear, Paul did things no human could do. He scorched walls, turned stone bricks into ice ones, weakened hallways until they were so thin they fluttered like they were made of paper in a strong wind. Other corridors branched off into insane, infinite mazes.

"That's Paul," the General would joke deliriously every morning, after they'd managed to get him out of one room and locked into the next. "Stubborn to the end!"

Naz tried to laugh out of sympathy, but nothing ever came out. It had been anything but funny, trying to move Paul each morning. Trying to put him in a new room without him hurting someone or escaping. But none of them could muster the courage to beg the General to order him put out of his misery before it was too late. Paul was going to kill them all, and they didn't know how to stop it.

In the end, they didn't have to.

Naz didn't know how the General got Paul out of his room that night, or down the stairs and through the front door without any of them hearing. Maybe Paul still remembered him, just enough. Malik and Naz found the General in his room the next morning, his clothes and hands covered in crusted streaks of blood.

They didn't ask him how he'd done it. It was too much.

It was Malik who finally spoke to the General, days later. He asked him for Paul's book—the copy from the wedding he and Paul had brought with them when they left Elk Cliffs. The army wanted to add it to the collection, with his permission. As a kind of memorial to Paul.

"I couldn't save it" was all he'd said, in almost a whisper, his eyes locked in a thousand-yard stare.

Naz never found out what that meant.

She thought of the book often after that, almost every day—but once Ory came, she realized she'd just been thinking of the concept of the book, not the actual words inside. The way it had looked when she'd seen it around the Iowa, during better times. The slim spine, the soft cream pages, the deep navy cover with a golden sun emblazoned across it. It was sort of the way she'd always felt about Ory and Max—just concepts—except suddenly Ory was right there with them. Ory, but not Max. The General, but not Paul.

A few weeks after the General had saved them from his husband, they all stopped grieving long enough to remember that there might be another copy of Paul's book in the library they had recently begun to loot. But by the time they'd pulled themselves together to go again, the Reds were there.

And that was why Naz had kept her distance from Ory. She was afraid that if he knew the story, he might blame her for Max's disappearance. Naz knew it wasn't fair, but she believed it was her fault anyway. If only she had gone to the mountain sooner, both he and Max would be at the Iowa now—the same way that if only she had gone back to the library sooner, they might have the book they now were all so desperately hoping to save.

URSULA CLIMBED DOWN FROM THE DRIVER'S SEAT AND CLOSED
the door softly behind her. It was far too early in the day to stop, and
we hadn't scouted the area to make sure we were alone, but it was a
worse idea to keep going. Now that I've forgotten how to read, we
have to figure something out fast—before we get lost.

"Dhuuxo, Intisaar, you're on watch. Ys and Lucius, take Wes and
Victor and see if there's any firewood nearby. Everyone stays within
sight of the RV at all times," she said. Her grip on her hunting rifle
was more fierce than usual, as if she was drawing strength from it.
Ory, it was the first time I've ever seen the look of weightlessness in
her that I see in the other shadowless in our caravan. Zachary touched
her shoulder. Maybe he saw it, too. "You're with us," Ursula said
to him.

Zachary collected his tools from the RV. He could tell we wanted
him to draw something—some kind of a sign we could understand
without having to read. On the grass, he laid out his paints and brushes
so we could see the colors.

"If we just stay on the huge road we've been following so far," I
tried to explain to him, using words and gestures, "we'll end up in
New Orleans." I had no idea how he could do it, but that's what I
wanted his picture—whatever wordless map he could make us—to
mean. That we had to keep going south, and we had to stay on the
widest, biggest road. And then at the end, there would be a huge city.

At least we hoped there would be. Large enough or loud enough
to catch our attention as we passed, since we wouldn't understand the
road signs. Otherwise, what would be the point of stopping anyway,
then? If there really wasn't anything in New Orleans, it wouldn't
matter if we missed it—any other place would be just as good.

Zachary nodded slowly. He, Ursula, and I took a few steps back
from the RV, to take in the big black strokes of paint covering its side

while he tried to figure out something to do. It was one thing to draw each of us, like Zachary often did. But how was he going not only to draw a city but also to convey that we were supposed to head for it and in which direction it was?

Zachary suddenly walked toward the RV, one eye closed, as if measuring something against its surface.

"Ursula," I said, "he knows what to do."

Ursula looked up from her thoughts to see Zachary touching the aluminum siding gently, examining it. When he pulled his hand away, I saw that there was a streak of color where his fingers had been, even though he had yet to touch his paints.

"Did you see—" I started to ask her.

"Yes," she said softly. "It's been happening for a long time."

[II]

Wes is taller, but Victor is bigger. We hoisted Zachary onto his shoulders. Ysabelle stood next to them, holding up his art supplies with her hands so he could reach them.

"You okay to hold him?" Ursula asked.

"Yep," Victor said. The lion tattoo on his bicep bulged. "He barely weighs anything at all."

It took Zachary the rest of the afternoon to sketch his plan onto the RV. Tomorrow he'll paint it. As soon as he finished, he laid down in the center of the floor of the cabin, exhausted, and fell deep into unconsciousness the instant his eyes closed.

I was the opposite. I don't think I slept at all once it got dark, even though it wasn't my turn to keep watch. I couldn't even lay inside the RV. Lucius gave me a surprised, amused look when I climbed out around two A.M. and went over to the place where he was standing watch for his shift, but he didn't say anything. He stared into the dark, distant trees, scanning for movement, and I looked at the RV.

*Please let this work,* I thought. It was too dark to see what Zachary's faint marks outlined once the sun went down, but I sat next to Lucius's spare coat on the grass and stared at the dim shape of the RV anyway until the sky began to brighten again.

⏸

In the morning, I tried to puzzle out what Zachary had drawn, but the pencil lines were thin, and the indentations in the aluminum siding distorted everything. Maybe not even everything had been drawn yet. They might just have been guiding lines for his paintbrush.

From around the back of the RV, Ursula, Dhuuxo, and Zachary walked slowly, carrying the cans of paint they'd brought when they left Arlington. I watched them as they approached, feeling strange—almost like I've known them as long as I've known you, Ory. How long have we been on the road now? How long has it been since I left you? It feels like just yesterday that I walked away from the shelter, but I know that can't be true. I know I've already forgotten some things—the reading proves that. How many days between now and the last time I saw you have I also lost?

"Rough night?" Ursula asked when she saw my expression.

"Can't remember," I joked.

Dhuuxo laughed, and even Ursula tried to smile, but then her face was serious again. "This will work," she said. She set the paint down and wiped her hands. "It has to."

I nodded, trying to believe her.

After Zachary mixed his paints and handed Ysabelle the right brushes to hold up to him, he turned around from atop Victor's shoulders and looked at Ursula. His hand hovered in the air, waiting.

"All right, everyone," she said. "Let's let him work in peace."

We all crept around the other side of the RV to wait. Lucius napped in the shade, catching up after his shift as lookout. He still had the rope tether on his ankle—the one that whoever is watching wears so if he forgets and begins to wander off, the tether will hopefully show him that he wants to stay, not go. I settled with my back against a tree, relaxing into the cool, rough bark, and Dhuuxo and Intisaar sat cross-legged in the grass farther away, talking softly to each other. I thought I saw another rose in Dhuuxo's hands at one point, but when I looked again, nothing was there. Ursula patrolled slowly, surveying the distance for movement.

I heard the scrape of something soft squeezing through leaves and leaned around the trunk of my tree to look. A small, skinny wolf cocked its head and peered at me. Its yellow eyes glinted, almost glowing.

We stared each other down for several seconds, perfectly still. "There are too many of us to attack me," I finally warned.

"I know," it said simply.

All right then. I settled back against the tree.

We both watched the RV. In the small space between the ground and the bottom of the vehicle, I could see Victor's and Ysabelle's feet standing on the other side. Deeper into the trees, there was another stirring—probably the rest of the wolf's pack, waiting for it to satisfy its curiosity and continue on with them.

"Are you building a den?" it asked.

"Sort of," I said. "But when we're finished building it, we'll move it."

"A moving den," the wolf mused. "That's very interesting."

"Is your den here, too?" I asked.

"No, no. But this is a fine spot. Far fewer humans around than where it is now, especially if you move yours away."

The last part caught my attention. I scooted into a crouch from my place against the tree. Where was Ursula? "You've seen other humans recently?"

"That way, where the warm breeze crosses the third colder breeze," it answered, using its ears to indicate the rough direction. They swiveled, pointing independently while its head stayed still.

I didn't know what the breezes meant, but I imagined it couldn't be more than a few miles. Within walking distance for the wolf. "Those humans, were they wearing white?" I asked.

"What is white?"

I looked around. "Uh—" Everything was green and brown. "Like snow. Did they look like they're covered in snow?"

The wolf shook its nose. "No. They looked more like you." It lifted one front paw carefully, stretching it until a dark, graceful copy of its leg jutted out from its silhouette on the grassy ground below.

Other shadowless. Were they wandering? Or also heading somewhere in particular, like us?

"There were quite a few at first," the wolf continued. "But they all split up. Headed in different directions. It's a very strange way to travel. I don't know why they don't move in a pack. It's always better to be together than alone. We wolves know that."

"But are any near here?" I asked. "It's important."

"Only one, and then two more that way." It pointed in another direction with its ears, twisting them sideways. "You want to add them to your pack?"

"No," I said. "We want to avoid them."

"If you stay here for another few hours, you won't cross their paths then."

"You're sure?"

The wolf puffed up its fur, as if to say, *I'm sure.*

I nodded. The wolf edged closer and then sat down again, to better smell me. "Thank you for telling us," I said.

The wolf shrugged. "Will you really move your den, once the others pass by?"

"Tomorrow at dawn," I said. Once Zachary had finished painting, and it dried overnight. "Are you going to build your new one here after we do?"

"I'm considering it," the wolf said, lost in thought. "I'm really considering it." Then it narrowed its liquid eyes and looked at me again. "I don't think I've ever spoken to a human," it added.

"Shit," I said.

"There isn't," it replied. "I would have smelled it."

It had happened again, Ory. The deer, the knife handle, your wedding band, now this. Damnit! I'm trying so hard. But I can't stop it all. "I've forgotten something," I tried to explain to the wolf. I'm terrified now of what else I've also forgotten, but don't know that I've forgotten it. I hope you're still okay. I hope you stay okay until we reach New Orleans. "Do you know if we're heading the right way?" I asked the wolf.

"Where are you heading?"

"New Orleans. It's a—a huge den, with thousands of people."

"I don't know," it said. It fluffed its fur again. "We don't know the names of the human dens. We mark them by the pattern of their scents. You don't know its pattern, do you?"

"No," I said.

"Sorry, then."

"It's all right." I tried to smile. The wolf looked at the RV again. On the ground, the sun had made its furry canine shadow lean toward me, so close I could almost reach out and stroke its flat, dark ears against the ground. I watched the grass move under it in the breeze, back and forth, while the shadow held perfectly still.

"I have to go," the wolf announced suddenly. "A hare."

"Oh," I stammered. "Well—good luck."

"Don't ask the sparrows the way," it said as it darted off. "They always lie."

〓

Finally, in the late afternoon, Zachary came slowly around the back of the RV, his skin dyed to his wrists. He nodded tiredly to all of us. He had finished. The new map was done. We all walked as slowly as we could, to keep from scrambling in our nervous excitement.

It was beautiful, Ory. I wish you could see it. Where they'd once written the things we could no longer read, the entire side of the RV—from roof to wheel well, covering the now-useless words—Zachary had painted a giant mural. It's a picture of all nine of us. We're in the RV, which is on a huge multilane road, heading toward a distant city. And the most genius part: Zachary figured out how to ensure we keep heading south on this road, even without signs or maps or other people to ask for directions. The moment he painted is clearly during sunset. The sky is all oranges and yellows, and dark purplish black near the top. The sun is halfway under the horizon to the right of the RV, and the RV's shadow—what a beautiful shadow he painted—stretches long to the left.

I didn't know if it was the right thing to do, but I hugged Zachary as we all looked. We're going to make it, Ory. We're going to make it to New Orleans. No matter if we can't read the signs or see the roads, or even what happens to our memories, there's no way to mistake which direction we should head now.

# ORLANDO ZHANG

THE ARMY WENT OUT AGAIN EIGHT MORE TIMES. SIX BOOKS, all useless, according to Imanuel. Not the right kind. Medical textbooks and technical manuals seemed like the most useful type to Ory—they had shadows *and* useful reference information—but Imanuel only shook his head. He wanted novels, story collections, biographies, history, memoir. And of course, Paul's book. They went for a ninth trade.

"Hold the line!" Ahmadi cried as the Reds wormed their way between the Iowa's soldiers. They were just inside the gates of the Red King's courtyard, struggling to stay bunched together to protect the items they were hoping to barter for books. Trades had gone smoothly for the last few weeks, but that day, something was off. Ory searched the chaos, but there was nothing that stood out as different from the last time. "Malik! What's going on?" he heard Ahmadi yell.

"I don't know," he called back to her. "But something's got them agitated. Keep tight!"

"Keep tight!" she confirmed again at a shout.

"I'm going to try something," Ory whispered as he came shoulder to shoulder with her.

"No, you're not," Ahmadi replied.

"Just trust me."

"You don't know what you're doing yet," she growled. "Do not fuck us up."

"I won't," Ory said.

"Don't do it, then!" she ordered again, and shoved another Red.

But Ory was already edging around the group, toward the entrance to the Red King's library, where the Reds were pouring out.

Holding only a bat, he was almost invisible in the crush. His shadow flickered up the short plaza of concrete stairs.

He could hear a strange, muffled moaning the closer he drew. Every time a Red glanced over at him, Ory pretended he was just winded or overwhelmed with fear and was crouching uselessly on the steps until he regained control of his nerves. Before they could look too long, Ahmadi would bump them harshly, to draw their attention back to the chaos. She threw him a murderous look for disobeying her, but it was too late now for her to do anything but help him succeed.

From his place just before the entrance, he could tell that inside it was musty and humid, like a swamp. Dried trails of red paint looked black against the windows, where they obscured most of the gray, overcast light. There were more bodies inside, moving back and forth as if agitated.

A massive shape blocked the light completely then as it strode past the door, backlit, and Ory realized with a tremor that he'd just glimpsed the Red King.

The moan came again. The hulking crimson shape of the Red King was moving quickly toward the sound.

If he stood up and looked inside, Ory would have only seconds. *Please don't kill me*, he prayed as he lurched forward to peer in. *Please don't kill me.*

He was still expecting to see a library, and it took his eyes a moment to adjust and understand what was there instead. The Reds had cleared out most of the room by shoving the bookcases toward the outer walls. Some places were five or six deep, others only one. A few of the heaviest were completely tipped over and had been fashioned into makeshift tables or storage, and Ory could see scattered lone pages here and there on the floor, long since lost and trampled thousands of times. But it seemed that most of the shelves were still upright and lined with books.

In the center of the room, a refugee camp sprawled, little puddles of blankets and balled-up fabric scattered across the bare floor. In the dimness, Ory could just barely make out the Red King crouched beside a woman on the ground. She writhed involuntarily, then opened her eyes and looked right at him through the doors. Her belly was so swollen it looked like it was going to consume her.

*A baby,* Ory realized, just before two Reds clamped their crimson hands down on his arms and threw him into the skirmishing crowd below.

"TOO RISKY," MALIK SAID.

"We have no choice," Imanuel replied.

"One of us could pose as you."

Imanuel laughed. "And successfully deliver a high-risk baby? How much obstetrics training did you get in the D.C. police force? The Red King will burn the whole place down for sure if it goes wrong."

"Train me, then. Teach me what to do, and I'll go in and do it," Malik said.

"We don't have four years to boot camp you through a medical degree, Malik. We have four hours, based on Ory's description of the mother. Maybe less." Imanuel shook his head. "I've delivered hundreds of babies. It has to be me." He made a fist. "This is our chance. The best chance we're ever going to get to walk in there and find Paul's book."

"Do you really think the Red King is going to let us choose which book we want, even for—whatever she is to him?" Ory asked. Ahmadi glanced up from the planning table—they made eye contact for the first time since he'd deliberately disobeyed her orders. *Stares can't kill,* Ory thought. He buckled after two seconds and studied his hands intently. The guilt he felt at having made her so angry surprised him. It was an achingly familiar sensation—it was the same way he used to feel after arguing with Max.

"For this, maybe," Imanuel finally said.

Malik shook his head. "Even so, we still can't let you go alone."

"The Red King won't let a whole unit walk in, weapons out. You know it."

"He'll have to, if he wants her and the baby to survive," Ahmadi insisted.

The Red woman's face, streaked with agony, flashed into Ory's mind. Did she even know what a baby was anymore? He tried to imagine a child in that red place, being painted crimson for the first time, having its soft downy hair dyed.

"Or he'll burn an entire wing of the library," Imanuel said.

"This is not up for discussion," Malik interrupted. "I won't allow our General to walk into the enemy stronghold with no reinforcements or weapons."

"They aren't the enemy," Imanuel said softly. "They just forgot."

Malik put his face in his hands and sighed. Ahmadi looked worn as well. They'd all been arguing for almost an hour, and were still at a stalemate.

"I'm the only one who's ever done it," Imanuel continued. "I went into all that red once before, and came back out."

"That was a year ago, at least," Ahmadi said. "The Red King had only just appeared and had half the forces he has now. You said the fever was so bad he was nearly delirious—he might not even remember you."

"He'll remember," Imanuel said.

She sighed. "General, I admire your determination, but that's just not a good enough reason to undertake a suicide mission, no matter how uniquely qualified you are. I can't work with emotional pleas. I need strategy. I need a tactical explanation for why you should do this alone."

"Well then, how about this one?" Imanuel looked at her. "New Orleans. Now."

Ory froze.

*New Orleans.*

Malik and Ahmadi were staring at each other from across the table, trying to calculate the other's reaction. He could feel the fluttering, infectious excitement radiating off them, so strong it made it hard to breathe. "You're serious?" Malik said at last.

Imanuel nodded. "If she's already in active labor, which sounds pretty likely, based on Ory's description, then we can't afford to send a unit with me. Because you'll need all the help you can get to make ready before I get back with that fucking book."

Malik and Ahmadi were almost hovering in their chairs now. Ory couldn't breathe fast or deep enough, it seemed. *New Orleans.* It was really happening. He would get his two soldiers, for two weeks. He would search again. He would—no. He wouldn't think about what would happen after. He would find Max or keep looking. There was no third way.

"Malik." Imanuel turned to him. "Give the order right now. Operations start immediately."

"Yes, sir," Malik said. He stood and saluted Imanuel fiercely.

Ahmadi put her hand on Imanuel's arm for a moment as Malik marched out of the room almost at a run. "You're sure?"

"It's time," Imanuel said. He put his hand over hers and squeezed reassuringly. "Give me a moment with Ory."

Ahmadi nodded, almost in a daze, closing the door behind her as she left.

"You . . ." Ory trailed off once they were alone. He moved around the table to Imanuel's side. He didn't want to ask, to show his friend he didn't fully trust him, but he had to be sure. "You still plan to . . ."

"On one condition," Imanuel said.

Ory nodded. "Anything."

"You actually obey Ahmadi's orders this time." Imanuel crossed his arms. "Don't follow me."

That caught him off guard. Ory figured Imanuel expected Ory to sneak off after him as soon as he left for the Red King's territory—that wasn't a surprise. But what did surprise him was that even if he could make it away without attracting the other soldiers' attention,

Imanuel *still* didn't want him to do it. "What's just *one* person to cover you?" Ory asked. "It'll make no difference to the preparations here, but you won't be alone there."

"You don't have to understand. You just have to agree." His face had the same terror in it as the first day Ory had volunteered to follow Malik and Ahmadi into his first Red trade.

"Imanuel." Ory took a step toward him, and Imanuel visibly flinched. *Was it fear of losing him too, after he'd lost Paul?* Ory wondered. What had the Red King done to him and his soldiers? What had he done that they weren't doing right back? "Imanuel. I'm not your soldier. I'm your friend."

"This isn't up for debate," Imanuel said. "If you want help finding Max, you have to agree: you report to Ahmadi, you follow her orders, or you don't get your two scouts at the end. That's my condition."

Ory stared at him for a long time. "Agreed," he finally said.

AFTER IMANUEL LEFT TO PREPARE HIS MEDICAL EQUIPMENT, Ory went to the barracks room to retrieve his armor. The rest of the soldiers were already in the main hall, assembled in front of Malik.

"Be back here in five minutes," Ahmadi said to Ory as she saw him pass. He saluted back as he ran.

In the barracks, he double-checked he still had everything he'd brought, in case he didn't come back once he'd received his two soldiers. He looked at Max's photo hidden in the flap of his wallet again. Below, he heard a chorus of cheers echo. He drew the picture closer, to make out every detail in the dim light.

He wished that she had been there in the Iowa with him. She would be thinking about it all: finding Imanuel again, Washington, D.C., the Red King. Imanuel's mission to barter a safe birth for the last memory of his husband, locked inside a paper cover. Ory knew what she'd ask him as soon as they were alone and could talk. It was the same thing he'd ask her. *"Do you think the baby will be born without a shadow?"*

TODAY WAS SO HOT, ORY. THE SUN SHONE DOWN ON US FROM a cloudless sky, relentless. Every surface inside the RV gleamed, and then stung if I set my bare elbow on it by accident.

"Just for a little bit," Ysabelle said to us when she couldn't take the temperature anymore.

I glanced at Ursula warily. She made a face that reminded me of the one you make when you're nervous or frustrated—I could tell she didn't want to stop either. "We're making good time," I replied.

"We won't make *any* time if the engine overheats," Victor added. His face was tightly drawn. I saw that Ursula also noticed before her gaze snapped back to the road.

"Don't remember how to fix it anymore if that happens?" she asked quietly.

"No," Victor admitted.

"Okay, short break," Ursula announced. "Two hours."

Ahead, there was a small dirt road off the main highway. We cruised down the shoulder, sighing with relief as our RV slipped under the cover of trees for the first time all day. At the bottom, we parked in a small clearing.

"I'll take first watch," I offered. Ursula nodded gratefully and went with Victor to open the hood, to help with cooling the engine. Steam engulfed them as she locked it upright.

"Wes," Intisaar called as he began to drift away, and shrugged her shoulders at me to mean, *I'll be right back.* They both disappeared around a tree.

I waited, but they didn't reappear. "Ursula," I warned. Her velvety head popped out from behind the hood. It was starting to feather slightly as it grew out. Then we heard Intisaar shouting.

"Inti!" Dhuuxo cried. We all sprinted for the trees, and then saw what it was that had made her yell.

"Look at it!" she cried from farther down the hill. Wes was already running.

Ory, it was a godsend. The dark, clear water, the sun shining off it, the trees surrounding us on all sides. It was our own private lake.

"Race you," Lucius said, and then took off before Victor could reply.

"So clear," Ursula murmured beside me, transfixed. "It's gorgeous."

They were all streaming past me now, making for the water. For an instant, I felt a niggling worry at the back of my mind. Something about the lake was bad. I couldn't remember. Victor jumped in and resurfaced laughing. Sun broke across the ripples.

Then the sensation was gone. I smiled and ran downhill to where they were at the shore.

⏸

They must have been tracking us for hours after that.

Ursula was driving, as usual, and I was in the front passenger seat, holding the map. I know that I don't know how to use it anymore, but I liked to keep it anyway. Knowing we still had it made me feel safer, for some reason. Like I still know how to get us to New Orleans. Even though it was afternoon, the heat of the day still hadn't broken yet, and I was bracing a hand against my brow to cut the glare, leaning back against the headrest. The keys jangled lightly in the ignition as we bounced over the potholes.

"Do you hear that?" Ursula asked me. "It's like engines."

"What?" I raised my head and squinted. The sun was so bright and everything was so flat. The light reflected right off the ground, like a mirror. At first I couldn't see a thing.

Then an open-back jeep shot past the front of our hood.

"Everyone down!" Ursula shouted. The RV surged beneath us— her foot jamming the pedal into the floor. I screamed as the tires squealed. From nowhere, suddenly we were surrounded, Ory. They'd been in our blind spot somehow, or were lying in wait and pulled onto the main road from ditches or something.

"They're everywhere!" I cried to Ursula.

"How many?" she yelled back.

"I don't know!" I tried to count. "Five cars at least!"

"Seven!" Lucius called. "No, eight!"

"Dhuuxo, get the gun!" Intisaar cried.

A dusty jeep screeched by and something hit my window, shattering the glass all over me. "God damnit!" Ursula shouted as I ducked, covering my face from the shards.

"Faster!" Intisaar wailed.

"Shadowless," the stranger driving the jeep next to us said to me through the open air of the destroyed window when I looked at him. He put his hand out as if he could reach me from his seat. Even terrified, I was transfixed by the dark image of the shadow of his arm as it hung over the sandy ground between our two vehicles, rippling from the speed. Shots erupted on the other side of the RV, from Dhuuxo, and there was screaming and cursing. She waved Ursula's gun triumphantly and pointed out her open window. "Two down!"

"Go!" the one who must have been their leader called from his motorcycle, and the bandit beside me revved his jeep closer to the RV, slamming against our right side. Victor and Ysabelle shouted behind me as they tried to keep balanced and fight back, but the jeep slammed us again and they fell backward into the cabin in a tangle of limbs. "I have one!" the bandit beside me cried, and reached out of the open window of his jeep again and into mine.

"No!" I tried to punch him, but his fingers were like iron when he finally snatched my arm just above the wrist. "Ursula!" I cried, and then, "Ory!" Between us, against the bright, sandy ground of the highway shoulder, the shadow of his arm pulled and pulled, pulling nothing.

"Stop him!" Ursula was shouting. She grabbed at the rifle that Dhuuxo had dropped when she tripped, but the RV teetered, and she had to take the wheel again. "No!"

I felt myself start to lift from my seat, to be dragged through the window. Only then did I finally realize what the man was wearing—layers against the sun and heat, every piece from head to toe a pure, ghostly white.

"It's Transcendence!" I screamed before the bandit cracked me in the head with the butt of his pistol.

⏸

I'm okay still, Ory. I'm okay. So far.

I hope the speaker's picking this up. I have your recorder hidden under my shirt, and I've pulled my collar up to hide my face while I whisper. I don't know if the guards would care, but I can't risk it. I don't know what I'd do if they took it away. If I couldn't talk to you. You're all that's keeping me going right now.

Even if the speaker actually is catching this, you'd still probably have no idea what I'm talking about—what's going on. I wouldn't blame you. I'm only beginning to understand it myself, too.

When I finally woke up, everything was quiet and dark. Something was hovering in front of me. A face, only the eyes visible, the rest veiled in a layer of white gauze. A voice I didn't recognize was speaking softly to me, trying to draw me back from unconsciousness. Something touched my head, where it ached from the blow.

"Stop," I mumbled.

"I need to keep pressure here."

"She said stop," I heard Ursula say behind me.

"Ursula," I said. I felt her hands grasp my shoulders, to say, *I'm here.*

Things began to come into focus. We were together, thank God. All alive, and not grievously wounded.

"Enough, stop," I said again, pushing the stranger's hand away. We weren't bound, I realized.

The face draped in white, gauzy fabric looked down to check the cloth that had been pressed against my scalp. The small red stain was dry. "That's very good." It was a female voice.

"What do you want with us?" Ursula asked.

The woman in white set the cloth aside and pulled her arms back through the bars. *The bars.* I realized we were in a cavernous empty hall—from the look of the walls, it had once been the main room of a church, but now all the religious fixtures were gone. Only the stone bricks and windows remained, as well as one new construction, a giant iron cage in the center of the floor, inside which we were all locked. "I'm very sorry for the rough handling. They know better than that," said the woman, as if Ursula hadn't asked the question. "They were just so excited to have found so many of you at once."

"Are we prisoners?" Lucius asked. My head spun.

"*No,* of course not," the woman said emphatically.

"Then we're free to leave," Ursula said.

The woman shifted. "We hope you won't want to."

"So then we're prisoners."

"You are honored guests." She smiled. She gestured to the bars. "I know how this looks, but these are for your protection—those out there with shadows are fearful and violent. We want to protect you from them. We want to *help* you."

I checked: the woman had a shadow. "You want to help shadowless?" I asked warily.

"Anything you want," she offered. "Name it. We will find a way."

"We want to leave," Ursula repeated.

Victor stood up, and so did Wes and Lucius. Before they could reach through the bars to the woman, the door behind her opened, and five more strangers dressed in white filed in to stand at intervals around the hall. Guards.

"Honored guests?" Ursula asked sarcastically.

"They all say that at first," the woman replied, with a smile so kind it sent a chill down my spine. "I promise you'll see."

# MAHNAZ AHMADI

NAZ WALKED SLOWLY UP TO THE FRONT OF THE IOWA, WHERE Ory and Malik were standing with the General. Above, the sky was just starting to brighten, not into warm peach, but an oppressive wintery navy streaked with gray. It was hailing lightly.

"Some day for our most important mission." The General sighed when she reached them, gesturing at the threatening sky. He stuck his foot out, a few inches over the ground. "It's so overcast, we look like a bunch of Reds."

Naz smiled, despite the grim mood. He was right. The morning had that peculiar kind of stormy light that was bright enough to illuminate the landscape, but so lifeless it sucked the shadows from everything except the deepest, most narrow corners of the world. Everything was there, but two-dimensional.

"You ready?" Ory asked.

"I'm always ready," the General said automatically, then flinched. He and Ory both smiled, surprised at the sudden memory, but it was bittersweet. It had been Paul's catchphrase, once.

Naz looked down. She hated seeing moments like this. Sad recollections. She'd heard the trademark saying in the stories Paul sometimes told, when they all used to sit around the fire at the Iowa in better times—usually when he had been trying to goad the much more cautious Ory into doing something mischievous with him as kids. Then history repeated itself when Ory met Max. She'd said it when Ory accidentally proposed far too early, when it had just slipped out at a romantic dinner; when they'd gone skydiving; the first time they'd nervously talked about children, maybe, someday. Paul said at that fateful football game, when he heard Max say it to Ory when he asked her if she wanted to get out of there, and go get dinner some-where, it was how he knew she was right for him.

Naz thought that if Max had still been here, she probably would have liked her. She seemed a lot like Paul.

"Well, you look it." Malik finally broke the awkward silence. They all turned to him gratefully. The General was lightly armored, and wearing a leather shoulder bag to carry his tools on the way there—then hopefully Paul's book on his way back. Over all of it, he'd shrugged the cleanest single piece of fabric Naz had seen in two years—a doctor's white lab coat.

"Can you believe I still have it, after all this time?" Imanuel asked. He admired the blindingly clean sleeve.

"Honestly, yes." Ory smiled. "You have a weapon?"

The General shook his head. "I don't want to aggravate them." He put a hand on Ory's shoulder. "I'm coming back." He looked at Malik and her, too. "I'm coming back."

Naz looked down sharply as her eyes grew hot. He was hugging each of them now, Malik and Ory clapping him roughly on the back and blinking just like she was. Her body moved against her will when it was her turn, arms outstretched, as if a hug would do anything at all. *You don't understand,* she wanted to tell him. *You can't go alone. I made a promise to Paul before he died. I said I would bring Ory and Max back, and I said I'd protect you. I can't fail a second time.* But before she could say it, he started walking toward the front lines.

Leaving. He was leaving. Naz could feel the panic crushing her. He was leaving, and there was nothing she could do. "Malik," she gasped.

"I know," Malik said. She felt his arm around her shoulder, hold-ing her up.

The General turned back once and waved, and then he was gone, turned onto another street. Everything was suddenly completely silent.

She turned to Malik at last. He and Ory looked as panicked as she felt, rooted to the asphalt, eyes wide as they stared into the empty street.

"What do we do?" Ory asked numbly. None of them moved for a few moments, until at last Vienna walked up.

"Dad," she said softly, "they're all waiting for you."

Malik finally snapped back to attention and turned to face the troops. "All right!" he cried. "We don't know how much time we have, so let's work fast, soldiers. When the General gets back, the whole Red horde might be right on his ass—so we had better be ready to *move*. Is that clear?"

"Yes, sir!" they cried in unison.

"My group, upstairs on packing duty. Double-check everything—we do not leave a *single* book! Ahmadi's group, the basement." He clapped once. "Let's go!"

NAZ STILL THOUGHT OF THE BASEMENT AS A GARAGE, EVEN though it wasn't a garage anymore—the luxury cars were all long gone. Parked in their places now was a row of carriages, each from a different era. And along the opposite wall, the soldiers had built low walls out of scrap to transform the parking spots into stalls—stables, to be exact.

"This?" Ory panted.

"No, the bridles." Naz gestured impatiently. "The thin brown straps with the metal bit in the middle."

She saw him pause between dragging heaps of riding tack over to her and Vienna to stare at the row of horses snorting and stamping in their stalls. She knew what he wanted to ask them—where were they getting enough grass, how had he never seen them being exercised, where had he even *found* them—but she could also tell he was thinking the same way she did: that would just waste time, and time was something they didn't have much of. There was only one question that really mattered anyway. "Why aren't we using cars?"

She smiled at being proven right.

"Would if we could," Vienna answered as she slid the reins over one horse's head and hefted a harness after it with a grunt. "Once the Reds figured out that petroleum makes a fire burn even faster, they went after it like—" she considered.

"Like flies after horse shit," Naz finished for her. She reached for another bridle, and Ory jumped to grab a harness that he guessed should go after. She grunted in approval and started on the next horse in her row, hands moving efficiently, buckling straps and fitting bands across the giant, muscled creatures. He was picking it up quickly.

"You'd be lucky if you could find enough fuel in all of D.C. now to power a motorcycle for two miles," Vienna added. She was taking the General's decision to walk into the Red's territory alone better than they were—still young enough to believe a person when he promised he would come back no matter what. She trusted almost as quickly as Rojan used to. "Carriages were the best we could do. We stole them from the Smithsonian before the Red King torched them."

"Concentrate," Naz finally admonished them, but gently. She and Vienna moved to the next horse in sync. Ory tried to scoot as quickly as he could around the stall to follow, but he accidentally bumped a huge brown bay on the nose with his shoulder. It was some kind of draft breed, with legs as thick as tree trunks. An irritated whinny screeched off the concrete ceiling.

"That's Holmes," Vienna said when Ory had finished cowering. She tipped her chin at the stall after, where a light gray horse of the same size with silvered hooves stood. "And Watson."

"Because they're clever stallions?" Ory muttered, still grimacing from the sound.

"They're both female," Vienna said. "I just named them that because they like to be near each other."

They worked in silence for a few minutes after that, which is what Naz thought she had wanted. But the longer she tightened bridles and hoisted harnesses, the more agitated she became. She had actually let the General walk in there alone. She had let him talk her out of the promise she'd made with herself about Rojan, about Paul, about Ory and Max—to protect them at all costs. She had sworn each time, and now she was about to fail *again*.

Naz put down the bridle. Damn the General's orders. She was not going to lose yet another person that she loved.

"Think you can finish the horses up alone?" she asked Vienna. "I need Ory for another job."

"I still have—" Vienna started, but when she caught the expression on Naz's face, she fell silent and saluted.

Naz nodded gratefully. "Head back upstairs," she said to Ory, and started jogging. "I need to find Malik, and then I'll meet you there."

NAZ PEEKED INTO THE QUIET BARRACKS ROOM. ORY WAS already inside, waiting for her. She ushered Malik in and closed the door behind them.

"I don't say this lightly," she started, warming up to her argument. "I know the General ordered us all to wait here, but it's wrong. We just can't—"

"Done," Ory interrupted.

Naz blinked, surprised.

"You don't have to convince me," he continued. "He did tell me to stay, but he also told me to 'actually obey Ahmadi this time.' So just order me to do it—as long as it's a direct order, I have no choice, right?"

Naz tried, but she couldn't keep the smile from her lips. Maybe Max and Paul had taught him a thing or two after all.

"Well, okay then," she finally said, relieved. "Ory, I order you to recon the situation, help the General get Paul's book, and get back here as fast as you can."

"Yes, ma'am," Ory saluted.

"Aren't you going to ask me if I'm in?" Malik asked.

"I found you in the stairwell on your way to the stables," Naz said. "You were already coming to get *me* to say the same thing."

Malik shrugged and nodded.

"The only problem is, how am I going to get close enough to actually do this without being noticed?" Ory broke in. "Imanuel's the only non-Red there, so a second one will stick out like a sore thumb."

Malik crossed his arms. "I had an idea on my way to find Ahmadi," he said. "You won't like it, but I think it's our best shot."

DO YOU REMEMBER WHEN YOU AND I WERE UP AT THAT CABIN in the Poconos, that long weekend a few years ago, Ory? We were comfortably drunk on mugs of hot buttered rum, and there was a fire in the fireplace. Infomercials rolled by on the television in the corner. We were playing What If. *"What if someone gave you a little box with a button on top, and every time you pressed the button, the box would give you a million dollars, but someone you'd crossed paths with—from the clerk at a convenience store in a town you once drove through to an old high school classmate to your own mother—would instantly die. The box would choose the person completely at random. Would you press the button? Would you press it more than once?"*

We both toasted each other and drank down our mugs, smug at how easily we could give up the imaginary money. What was money compared to a human life? Especially one you couldn't choose. I was so sure I'd never press that button, Ory. Fuck a million dollars. It wasn't worth the cost. But what if you were losing who you were minute by minute? What if chancing something that big was the only thing that would free you from this metal cage? What if it was the only thing that would get you to New Orleans? What if—

Someone's coming. I have to hide the recorder now.

⏸

I don't know what it is about this place, Ory. It's hard to hold on. Maybe it's being trapped in such an empty, unchanging room, or the questions. The endless questions.

The ones in white come to us singly or in pairs. Sometimes it's the woman from the first day, sometimes it's another woman, sometimes it's men. The guards deal with our waste bucket at regular intervals, but it's these others who bring us food, so much food, divided into small pieces so it can fit through the bars. I don't think I've been this well fed since the Forgetting began. Then while we eat to our heart's content, they ask.

"What did it feel like when you lost your shadow?"

"What were you doing at the moment it disappeared?"

"What were your feelings about Hemu Joshi and the first shadowless when the incidences in India first happened?"

It's not an interrogation, it's not like that. No matter what we do—ignore them, scream—they never shout back or hurt us or withhold meals. They just keep asking, with eternal patience. Eventually we decided that only Ursula should answer, so she began to speak for us all—but the answers she gives are always lies. That's the only power we have left.

"Do you remember the exact instant you lost your shadow?"

"I was killing a man," Ursula said. She hadn't been. She'd been driving when it happened, steering the RV carefully through northern Virginia.

"Who in your group lost their shadow first?"

"I did." She didn't. She'd told me that she had been the last, just before I'd stumbled onto their camp.

But it doesn't matter. They just ask again, on different days, with different people, as if Ursula had never responded at all.

"Did it hurt?"

"Were you afraid of losing your shadow before it happened?"

"Was there any warning it would happen before the actual moment?"

The questions are so constant that now after a few days, I can't remember what Ursula has answered before for any of them. I can barely remember how it actually happened to me now, so long ago, after all these circles.

"Are they maybe trying to cure us?" Intisaar asked one night as we reclined against the bars. Most of the candles had winked out before midnight, but the questioners wouldn't return until dawn, so the guards just left the room in semi-darkness, watching us from the dim corners as they patrolled.

"No." Ursula shook her head.

"With the exception of the bars, they really are—kind," Dhuuxo admitted. "Most shadowed survivors run or kill us on sight. These people talk to us, feed us, and bring us new clothes and blankets whenever we need them. They *want* us."

"And their questions do sound similar to what the news reported the scientists were asking Hemu Joshi, once they quarantined him for treatment," Victor added. The smoke from the cigarette the woman in white had gifted him drifted in front of his eyes, and he looked down, embarrassed.

"We already know the scientists didn't find anything useful, though," Ursula replied, her voice harsh. Zachary stirred, shivering, and she put her arm around him. She was afraid, I could tell. Afraid that Transcendence's gentle patience might be working on us. "I know they're treating us well," she said, softer this time. "But we are still in a cage."

‖

The woman we first met was one of the two who came today. We all sat silently, watching the pair of them or staring off into the empty hall as Ursula invented random lies.

It was the other one talking this time, a man wrapped in white layers. The woman was simply listening, smiling beatifically at us the entire time, as if we were her children. Ursula decided to ignore a question, just to break the pattern.

"Were you afraid when it first happened?" the man asked after the pause, continuing without frustration.

"You'd have to be stupid not to be afraid," Ursula finally said.

The man nodded noncommittally. Not agreeing or disagreeing;

simply hearing. "Did you feel the pull as soon as your shadow disappeared?"

"No," Ursula said.

The man nodded again. Then the woman did—but a few moments later than he had. I looked more closely at her eyes. She wasn't watching Ursula.

"What did it feel like when your shadow disappeared?"

Dhuuxo and Intisaar were pointedly ignoring the ones in white. Zachary stared blankly at his palms. I studied the woman as surreptitiously as I could. She was looking into the cage, but just past Ursula's shoulder. Slowly, so that no one would notice, I shifted my eyes. Lucius, Victor, Wes, and Ysabelle were leaning on the bars at the back of the cage. They were all half-dozing from boredom as Ursula answered—except Lucius.

"Did you feel it when your shadow separated from you?"

"Not even a little," Ursula drawled, lying.

But Lucius nodded. Ever so slightly.

My eyes flicked back. I saw the woman tip her head again. So minutely it was almost impossible to notice beneath all the layers.

It all made sense now. They weren't interested in what Ursula said. They knew she would lie every time. They were interested in how long she would continue to do it. How long we would all let her before one of us would start to wonder if maybe there was another way out of the cage. How long until one of us would start to answer with the truth.

[II]

I wish you were here, Ory. I need to tell Ursula, but I don't know how. The cage is big enough that I can sit in a corner and whisper to you without Lucius hearing—they all know I talk to you and ignore me anyway—but if I was to go over and say something in Ursula's ear, he'd see for sure, and know something was wrong. I've been waiting for a time when I'm sure he's asleep, but we all lay around so much, it's hard to tell. Or what if he isn't cheating the rest of us, but just trying to help in his own way, because Ursula is no closer to getting us out than the first day? Trying to win their trust so he can turn on them at the right moment? You would know what to do. You'd at least have a guess, and then we could figure it out together.

Ursula has started pacing, checking the bars again. Lucius is lying down on the other side of the cage, but his eyes just opened when she passed him, awake. No good now. Not yet.

⏸

We all woke up to Ysabelle crying this morning. "I forgot," she was saying, over and over. "I forgot what they looked like."

"Ys." Victor scooted closer. "What is it?"

"My parents," she said, and covered her face.

I felt a chill. It's getting worse, Ory. The stress, the fear. We're going to lose bigger and bigger things now, the more desperate we get. This whole time, we've had the memory of New Orleans holding us together, one thing to cling to. But now that we're trapped here, unable to keep moving toward it—we can't let ourselves unravel.

"I didn't mean to, but I tried to remember them and then I . . ." Ysabelle sobbed, voice muffled by her hands. Victor held her. He was trying as hard as he could—trying to do his job as husband to comfort a woman whom he didn't remember he loved. "But I had them, I know I did. I *know*. A mother and a father. But now I don't know what they look like. I forgot their names."

"What if we fake an emergency?" Victor asked, smoothing her pale hair. His voice was angrier than I've ever heard it. Angry that we were trapped, angry that his wife was panicking and that there was nothing he could do about it—angry that the only reason he knew she was his wife in the first place was because Ursula had reminded him. "Would they open the cage if one of us might be dying?"

"They always have the rest of us if someone does," Lucius said.

"We have to get out of here. We have to get away. We're going to run out of time," Ysabelle said.

Ursula paced along the cage, tiger-like. The guards were at attention, ready to try to stop something impossible from happening. I touched the bar beside my head tentatively as I watched them track her movement, considering. But no. It felt more solid than it had ever felt. I still remembered too well that bars do not bend. And these especially. They seemed even more impossible to escape than simply steel.

"Can you do it?" Zachary asked me softly over Ysabelle's whimpering.

I shook my head. "Can you?"

He shook his head, too. "Even all together . . . Not enough yet."

"Yet?"

He watched Ursula glare at each guard with his strange, distant eyes. "Someone giving in to the pull, for power. Little, little every day."

Did he know about Lucius, too? Or was it someone else? "Zachary," I whispered. "Do you know who it is?"

He shook his head again.

I sat down against the bars. I know you'd tell me not to try, Ory, even if I was strong enough. That whatever I'd lose wouldn't be worth it.

The only thing I wouldn't trade would be you. If I escaped but didn't remember you, that would be the same thing as dying in here anyway.

⏸

Now we know, Ory. Now we know what Transcendence really wants us for. It's not to cure us at all. You wouldn't—I barely believe myself.

I heard the sounds before I fully woke. Humming. Soft, mumbling chants. I opened my eyes.

The guards were still there, alabaster pillars around the room. But now, all around the cage, the floor had changed into a rippling, shifting sea of white. It took me a long moment to realize I was looking at bodies. Hundreds of bodies. Every one of them prostrate in front of us, foreheads to the floor, arms reaching. Every one of them with a shadow.

"Ursula," I hissed. I grabbed her shoulder. "Wake up!"

"Holy mother," Lucius murmured, drawing into a crouch. "Look at them all."

"What are they *doing*?" Ursula asked, disgust and terror in her voice. "Are they . . . are they . . ."

"They're praying," Lucius said, in a tone very different from hers. It was almost like wonder. "They're praying to *us*."

【II】

It didn't take long for him to change after that.

When the woman in white came to us in the evening, after the hundreds of others had finished their chanting and departed one by one, we all huddled as far from her as possible. She offered us a packet of crackers one by one, so fresh they even still might have had some flavor. All eight of us refused to take any. Only Lucius went forward and ate one.

"You understand," she said to him.

He chewed thoughtfully. "You want to become like us," he said.

The woman in white nodded. "Yes," she said, almost mesmerized. "We want to become like you. We want to *transcend*."

"All of you are insane," Ursula growled. "Absolutely insane."

"We're not insane," the woman replied. "Everyone else is. Your power isn't something to be afraid of. It's something to be embraced. It's the future, not the end."

"You don't understand," I said. She couldn't. She would never be able to. She still had her shadow.

The woman looked at Lucius again. He took another cracker. "Your friends have to stay here," she said. "They will not be mistreated. But they cannot come with you unless they join us."

"All right," he said.

"Lucius," Ursula whispered, horrified.

"The guns are loaded," the woman warned. There were more guards filing into the room now, barrels trained on us. Ten, twenty. The woman unlocked the door.

"Lucius," Ursula said again as he stepped free. "*Lucius.*"

"Just stop," he said. He glanced back at us. "You made your choice. No one forced you to refuse their offer to join. I made mine."

"So you're just *giving up*?"

"Ursula, we were never going to make it."

I thought she was going to yell, but Ursula just shook her head. When she spoke again, her voice was much quieter. "Whatever you think it's going to be like—being their treasured, magical idol—it won't be," she said.

The woman in white closed the cage door behind Lucius and locked it again. Lucius put his hands on the bars, this time from the outside. "I know," he said softly. He looked down. "But it'll be a better life than this cage, for a while. And when it changes, I won't remember to regret it anyway."

# ORLANDO ZHANG

"I THINK THAT DOES IT." AHMADI STEPPED BACK AND STUDIED Ory. "How do you feel?"

"Like I'm covered in ants," he said.

The paint itched horribly. They had layered it through his hair, across half his face, and all down his arms, chest, and back, covering him in crimson stripes and swirls. Ahmadi had also torn up his jeans and dragged his shoes through the mud several times to make them look like salvaged things.

"He looks good," Malik said, hope rising in his voice. He checked behind them, but they were the only ones on the front sidewalk of the Iowa. The soldiers were all still inside packing. "This could work."

Ory looked down at the red lines slathered across his chest. They were excellent fakes, the right width and pattern. And the lifeless, low-hanging clouds had costumed the most important part of all. In such light—with nothing casting shadows—he looked just like a Red. Just like Max.

A shudder of fear seized him, and Ory squatted down. He cupped his hands together just over the ground, trying to make a pocket of space between his palms and the street small enough that even without the sun, there was a contrast, and he could see.

Yes.

His shadow was still there.

When he stood up, neither Ahmadi or Malik laughed. They understood. Ahmadi grabbed the back of Ory's neck firmly in comfort—the only place that wasn't covered in lines of paint. It was the closest thing she could give him to a hug without smudging his disguise.

"Still there," he said. His chest ached. He wanted to grab her back and hold tight, but he couldn't. Because of the red paint—and because of Max.

"You make sure the General comes back," Naz said desperately. "Make sure *both* of you do."

AT THE LIBRARY, IT WAS CHAOS. FRANTIC REDS WERE POURING out of the front doors, their arms full of books, waiting desperately for Iowan troops to arrive—and panicking as to why they yet hadn't. The big man was there as usual, but so was another Red whom Ory had never seen before, a woman who looked to be in her fifties or sixties, with streaks of red braided throughout her wild, silvered hair. She'd wrapped herself in a crimson sheet not unlike a toga. One small limp breast hung carelessly out as she snatched at the other Reds. Then a pristine white shape appeared from behind the Iowa's deserted barricade line. Imanuel.

There was a momentary lull as the Reds recalibrated. Everything paused. Books froze midair. Then the woman turned to screech at him. Somehow, almost impossibly, the Reds seemed to still remember him as the Iowa's leader. They swarmed forward, dumping books at his feet, as many as he wanted, practically burying him. Imanuel scooped up copy after copy, trying to quickly choose which to stuff into the precious extra space in his medical bag. He pointed toward the building, miming his question, asking to be taken deeper into the Red King's library, to choose the book he wanted. He picked up a book, pointed at it, and pointed again toward the building as the Reds screamed.

Ory watched from his perch atop the roof of a destroyed public bathroom.

The Reds were dragging out bigger and bigger books now, misunderstanding that size didn't determine worth the way it did with food, weapons, armies. Across the distance, Ory could see Imanuel searching the growing pile to see if they'd accidentally thrown to him the one he wanted most of all. *Push them as far as you can,* Ory thought. *Bring as many back as possible.* The older woman and the big man were growing more agitated. Then an angry bellow erupted from within the darkened building, causing everyone to duck on instinct.

The Red King was finished guessing.

Everything went still as he emerged, glittering silvery-maroon in the weak hail as he came right into the center of the street. Ory was too far to make out any of his features, but even from that distance, the Red King was terrifying.

Ory didn't know what he had looked like before he lost his shadow, but what the Red King had become now was a living mountain. He had thought the big Red was huge, but now, compared to his master, he was miniscule. The Red King was the size of two men, over ten feet tall, wearing a scarlet cloak of a hundred layers and haphazard armor made from whole, bent steel doors. A human skull could fit inside each scarred, crimson hand. Red dripped off him from everywhere, leaving trails behind him.

Imanuel raised his arms. Ory couldn't tell if he was trying to smile or grimacing in terror. The Red King roared again, held out his palms. They were also covered in red, but a wetter red, red that came from inside a body. The pregnant woman was in real danger.

Imanuel took a step forward hesitantly. The Red King grabbed him with one hand and dragged him in like a rag doll.

*Do it, Ory,* Max said in Ory's mind, the same way she always imagined it before he had to kick open an abandoned Arlington door or go into a deserted shop, to give him courage. He clung to it fiercely now, the memory of the sound of her voice. *Go!*

He ran with everything he had, as fast and quietly as he could. The Reds were all still fixated on their leader as they escorted him and Imanuel in, some excited, some entranced. Ory skirted the outside of the crowd, hoping he looked like just another eager warrior. Past the rubble, into the courtyard, up the stairs—through the darkness of the doors.

He was in.

*Hide, Ory,* Max's voice urged again. He ducked behind the first set of shelves he saw, and waited for his eyes to adjust to the light. Overhead, a few books glided between the rafters of the library in slow circles, mournful birds separated from their flock, pages fluttering like wings. The Red King and Imanuel entered, flanked by crimson warriors. Across the main lobby, the pregnant woman was still there where Ory had seen her last, still swollen with child, still in pain. But now there was much more blood. Much more. She was pale with fatigue, the skin of her trembling lips almost gray.

The longer Ory watched her from behind the bookcase, the more he didn't know how much Imanuel could do for her without a hospital. In fact, it seemed like it would be almost nothing. Even if she still had the strength to push, too much could go wrong. Ory couldn't understand how Imanuel thought he was going to save her—or get the book.

*He isn't, Ory.*

He refused to believe Max's voice. He refused to believe that Imanuel had come only to see Paul's book one last time, and never hoped to make it out anyway. Surely his life was worth more than this. One pointless, unwinnable quest.

*So is staying here to look for me,* her voice said, but the Red woman's wailing drowned it out.

The procession began to lumber past Ory's hiding place then. First the Red King swept farther inward, dragging layers and layers of red cloaks, velvet curtains and afghan rugs stacked on top of one another beneath his armor. It looked so heavy Ory couldn't believe he could still stand under their weight. Then the rest of the Reds came, panicked, hopeful, ushering a trembling Imanuel deeper inside.

The woman cried again as they reached her, and Ory scooted back for more cover, deeper into the tangled maze of wood and books.

"Baby," he heard Imanuel say, to see if even though they could no longer speak, perhaps they understood.

The word seemed to do nothing. The Red King roared.

*Find the book,* Max told Ory. He turned around and peered into the nightmarish forest of shelves. *Find the book for Imanuel and then save him, while there's still time. Before the woman dies.*

He crept deeper into the library. The stacks twisted, some dead-ending, some spiraling back on themselves, some too tightly packed to squeeze through. He tried to work his way toward signs still hanging on the walls, hoping for directions to different sections and genres, but every time he heard a Red, he had to divert behind another overturned bookcase or sideways shelf to hide, getting more and more lost.

*Hurry,* Max's voice whispered to him. *Find the book before it's too late.*

Ory glanced back, and through two half-empty shelves glimpsed Imanuel, his lab coat already stained with blood, his tools emptied out all around him, trying desperately to hold the woman still so he could try something, anything. She wailed, delirious, clawing at her bare belly. Blood was smeared on the floor all around her.

Then there it was—the sign near the back, on the wall—*POETRY.*

Ory scrambled faster, heart racing, as the Red woman's scream shattered the room again—but this time it was different. There was death in the scream. *Turn back!* Max whispered suddenly. *There's no time.* He ignored her, and threw himself against the shelf, nose pressed against hundreds of musty spines, searching for the *W* names. *Paul Jeremiah West. Paul Jeremiah West. Paul Jeremiah West.*

*Ory,* Max begged in his head.

He found the *W*s all near the bottom. *Wallace, Walter, Webb, Wepford, White—*

"No," he breathed. The seconds were racing by. He checked again, but there was nothing. Nothing in the space between *Wepford* and *White.*

It wasn't there.

Ory leaned closer. On the spines of the books on either side of where Paul's should have been, there were old stains, the streaks long dried, as if someone had come to this exact place and sorted through, looking for something in particular. Someone covered in red.

"Yes!" Imanuel shouted then, from far across the library.

Ory jerked back toward the sound and peered through the fractured shelves. The Red King had pulled something small and rectangular out of the jagged angles of his armor, and held it toward Imanuel as a last, desperate offering to stop the woman's pain and save her life. A book.

*No*, Ory thought.

The cover came into view as the Red King reached down to hand it over.

*No.*

But it was. Paul's poetry.

Ory stared, transfixed, as Imanuel reached for it and the Red King roared back at him.

It was impossible. How could the Red King have known the exact book they had been looking for all this time, without being able to read it?

But he didn't have time to consider it further. The Red woman's breath shuddered weakly. *Run, Ory,* Max urged again. *Get out.*

Then the whole room collapsed into a deafening roar.

*Too late,* Max whispered. "No," he tried to argue, but he knew. *The woman is dead.*

The Reds' screams became a war call. Something bright and hot whizzed by Ory's head and smashed into the bookshelf beside him. *Fire.* They were setting everything on fire. They were going to burn it all down.

"Imanuel!" Ory yelled as he came careening around the shelves. Everywhere, Reds were running wildly. The woman was still on the floor, unmoving. He couldn't see Imanuel or the Red King through the chaos. "Imanuel!"

He spotted them through the gathering crowd. He shoved between the vicious, crazed Reds, running for the far end of the room, where the

Red King and Imanuel were sliding on the blood-soaked floor, strangling each other, both scrambling for a weapon. Ory was so close he could almost touch them when the Red King's crimson hand wrapped around a shard of broken glass. He was so close he could see the Red King in all his horrifying glory for the first time. So close he could see his face as the serrated tool sang through the air.

"No!" Imanuel screamed. Everything froze.

Ory didn't know if it was because Imanuel knew he couldn't stop the blade or because he suddenly realized that Ory was there, where Imanuel had begged him not to be.

He understood now—why his friend had been so afraid for him to join the Iowa's missions, and why all of the shadowless were so obsessed with books. Because if it was true that every shadowless got to keep one thing to cling to until the very end—one thing that would eventually be all there was left of them, until everything was gone—and that being together under a powerful leader helped them remember longer what little they still had, then only one thing made sense. Ory did not want to believe it, but he was there, and it was too late. He saw.

The Red King was Paul.

"No!" Imanuel cried again. The jagged shard plunged into him, and the sound snapped off into a horrible gasp. Blood spurted everywhere in a surging river until both he and the Red King looked the same.

Ory ran at them, his voice echoing off the walls as he lunged. "*Paul!*" he screamed.

The Red King let go of Imanuel's body and turned. It was impossible to tell if it was simply because of the sound, or if that word was the last word that could catch fire in his mind. Ory wanted to see the answer in his eyes as he descended upon him, but he searched, searched—even as he pulled the D.C. police-issue Glock 13 that Malik had given him out of the belt of his pants and aimed, he searched—and saw nothing. There was only red.

Ory had heard their soldiers tell one another legends that the Red King was unkillable, that he'd forgotten he wasn't immortal, so he was. But it wasn't true. He had forgotten his name, that he had written poetry, that he was not the size of a rhinoceros. That Imanuel was a person he once loved, not feared and hated. But he had not yet forgotten that he could die.

"Is it done?" Imanuel asked him as Ory crouched down to him. The gun smoked in his hand, emptied of the same fatal storm that had possessed his lost shotgun. Thunder moaned softly, fading in time with the last shuddering beats of the Red King's life. All around them, the shocked, disbelieving screams began.

"It's done," Ory said.

"I told you not to come," he repeated faintly. His eyes were glazed.

"I know," Ory said softly. He put a hand gently under Imanuel's head.

"I didn't want . . . ," Imanuel rasped, "you to know."

"It doesn't matter," Ory said. "You got the book." The book was Paul. Not that. That had never been.

"Book," he repeated.

Ory took it from where it lay beside Imanuel, still wrapped in a tattered plastic bag he must have brought from the Iowa to protect it. There was so much blood Ory could barely see. He pressed his hand to Imanuel's neck to try to stanch the place he thought the enraged, throbbing flood was leaving his body, but it didn't help. The wounds were too deep. He tried to pick Imanuel up, but Imanuel was too weak to help him lift. They sank back to the floor as the Reds began to crowd around them.

"Go," Imanuel said, but Ory shook his head. The Reds converged. He couldn't move. He couldn't leave Imanuel.

Suddenly Ahmadi was there, slapping his face, trying to bring him out of his shock. Ory looked up to see Malik hoisting up the other side of Imanuel's limp, pallid body. They'd broken the General's order, too. They had come.

"Retreat!" The world snapped back into focus as Malik shouted the command at him, over and over. "Retreat!" Ory's feet were somehow already obeying before he'd even understood the words, running as they carried Imanuel together toward the open doors. Behind, he could hear the blunt punch of arrow shafts through flesh as Ahmadi killed the Reds that followed, one after another.

"I can't stop the bleeding!" Ory yelled to Malik. His fingers scrambled at Imanuel's neck. He could feel Imanuel feebly trying to guide him with his own hands, to show him where to push to stop the blood from pouring out of him. *He's so calm,* Ory thought hysterically as he tried to choke the hot, syrupy liquid without cutting off Imanuel's air. *How can he be so calm?*

Most of the walls were on fire then, cracking in the sweltering heat. Rocks split against the floor around their feet as the Reds hurled them. Ory wanted to cover his head, but there was no way. He just kept running as fast as he could without dropping Imanuel, praying that nothing would land on them.

"Ory . . ." Imanuel coughed. "The book—"

"I still have it," Ory yelled, to make sure Imanuel could hear him. "I have it, don't worry!"

He did have it, just barely, pinched between his biceps and rib as he tried to keep it there and support Imanuel's slackening weight. If Ory dropped him, the Reds would be on them before they could pick him up again. If he dropped the book, they'd lose it forever. Malik would never let them stop for it.

As if he could read Ory's mind, Imanuel's hands grew tighter around his wrist. "If you can't—carry both," he managed to choke out. "Take. Book."

# THE ONE WHO GATHERS

TWO MONTHS AFTER DR. ZADEH WAS KILLED, SOMEONE IN New Orleans forgot that the electrical grid had been destroyed in the initial, panicked riots, and the power in the city suddenly came back—although the system wasn't quite the same as before. This time, instead of a generator in a factory, the wires just met and shot off in a tangle into the sky, to retrieve energy from passing storms, so no one had to service them. Inconsistent, but at least functional. Apparently far more than most cities had. According to the old man the amnesiac rescued from the abandoned bus station he'd chosen to die in, both San Diego and Oklahoma City now *hopped*—portions of the cities from single buildings, roads, neighborhoods, to entire zip codes rose between inches and several stories into the air at random times, then settled again. It was probably someone's terror of earthquakes that brought it about. The old man had left California after his son slipped during a *hop* and fell to his death. If only the shadowless could have forgotten that seismic movement existed, instead of that cities couldn't jump in defense.

"Are you the leader here?" the old man asked him, lifting his bald, leathered head from the pillow. He coughed weakly.

"Of New Orleans, or of this facility?"

"You should think about the hurricanes," the old man continued, ignoring the question. "Something should be done about the hurricanes before the season hits. Don't wait until one is already here."

The amnesiac watched him shiver through his fever as he slept in one of the many empty beds, trying to imagine all the fantastical iterations a hurricane could evolve into, all the twisted interpretations of human desire to stop a deadly storm that there were, both possible and impossible. The old man's breath was fluttering, uneven.

"Is he going to die?" Buddy asked.

The amnesiac turned and looked at the young shadowless in the doorway from his place beside the old man. "I think so," he said. "Probably before morning. He's very weak."

Buddy pushed an unruly shock of hair off his forehead. The amnesiac had found him a month ago—it was more dangerous now, but he still tried to continue Dr. Zadeh's work, when he could. "Such a shame." He sighed. "Still has his shadow and everything."

"You're doing well, though."

"Yeah," Buddy said. But it wasn't really an answer—just a noncommittal sound one would make to fill their turn in a conversation they weren't really listening to. He was still staring longingly at the thin, dark copy of the old man's bony arm where it lay, draped over the sheet.

It had been a long time since they'd had another shadow in the assisted-living facility besides the amnesiac's own. Everyone but him had either died or lost theirs. It was strange, to share all the blank space on the walls with the old man's withered silhouette.

"Such a shame," Buddy murmured again absently.

"Buddy," the amnesiac said. "Buddy."

"Yeah?"

"Where are the others?"

For a moment, the amnesiac thought he was going to say, *What others?* But Buddy finally blinked, pulling himself out of his trance. "The rain. Marie said from the clouds that she thinks a storm isn't far off. She said we can't wait any longer. We have to go into the storage basement now."

THEY STOOD IN THE SMALL CENTER COURTYARD, LOOKING UP into the roiling, sinking sky.

"See? When they look like that, a hurricane is a day out, maybe less," Marie said as she lowered the finger she'd been pointing. They no longer called her Nurse Marie—just Marie—because she was not a nurse. Not since she had forgotten she was one, when her shadow left, too. She was chewing on the corner of her lip as she pointed, because she was proud she still remembered how to read the clouds, and was trying not to smile.

The rest of the shadowless stood behind them, all twenty. "Can you tell how bad it'll be?" the amnesiac asked her.

"Bad, I think," she said. "Maybe not quite Katrina bad, but bad."

"Who's Katrina?" Buddy asked.

Marie flexed her wrist so her palm flashed at him, as if to gently scoot away the question. The shadowless at the facility had started to do that among themselves when one had forgotten something that wasn't worth explaining. A kind of gentle shorthand to mean, *Don't worry about it, it doesn't matter.*

"How much time do we have?" the amnesiac asked.

"None," Curly said. He pulled his namesake into a stumpy ponytail and bound it to keep the strands away from his face. "By the time we finish moving all the food and supplies into the storage basement to wait this out, it'll practically be here."

"Wait it out," Marie sighed. "If it's a hurricane, fine. But it might not be a hurricane, once it reaches us. It might be the memory of one."

"I know," the amnesiac said quietly. "But what else can we do?"

"Will it be . . . It?" Buddy asked. "The end?"

"We survived the riots," he replied. He put a hand on Buddy's shoulder. "And the exterminators. And starvation. A lot of things."

"Yeah, but those—" Buddy frowned, struggling for words. The amnesiac tried to judge whether it was fear or shadowlessness that was making it difficult, but he couldn't tell. He wished Dr. Zadeh was still with them. "Those things were new. No one could forget them because they hadn't existed before. A hurricane is different."

"Okay, enough. It's bad. But it's still coming. We need to take care of what we *can* do before we sit around and worry about what we *can't*," Downtown said. Not her real name, of course—only where they had found her. She thought the nickname would tell her more about herself than whatever her real name had been, and so it stuck. More and more of the shadowless had started renaming themselves like that, to remind themselves of the most important things.

"Okay," the amnesiac said. "Let's do this quickly. Food, water, blankets, clothes, medicine. I'll get our patient files. Go in groups. Everyone remind everyone what you're all doing. Like we practiced— keep reminding!"

"Keep reminding!". Buddy crowed. Everyone splintered into small groups of three or four, darting off down different hallways. "Food, main hall!" Marie called as her group scrambled toward the cafeteria—the items they needed to retrieve, and the place to take them. "Food, main hall!" the person behind her repeated.

"Blankets, main hall!" Downtown's voice echoed from another corridor. Each person repeated their team's phrase after the one in front of them said it, a circular chorus. As they all vanished into the assisted-living facility's other wings, the words blurred until it sounded more like a song being played from far away.

In Dr. Zadeh's darkened office, his research lay in neat stacks on his desk. The amnesiac took his leather bag from the hook on the back of the door and began to file the folders into it. DOWNTOWN (F), NURSE MARIE (F), CURLY (M), BUDDY (M). The handwritten labels flicked past as he slid each bundle into place. Some of the files were thicker than others; some had only one sheet. It depended on at what point they had found each shadowless—how much they had left that he or Dr. Zadeh could record as potential data. Research for a cure that would never be finished now, but at least they could use them as a record of who each of them had once been. They'd never be able to recover what Downtown's real name was, but at least her file could tell her that she hated carrots and was forty-three years old.

At the bottom, the oldest file, far thicker than the rest. The amnesiac's eyes caught on the label. It had once said one thing, then been scratched out and rewritten, then scratched out and rewritten again, until there was almost no room. He smiled and shook his head. Dr. Zadeh had tried earnestly to keep up with whatever nickname for the amnesiac had come into fashion among the Alzheimer's residents, and then later the shadowless patients, until finally he'd run out of white space on his tiny label, and given up in an exasperated sputter of tiny capital letters. The amnesiac read his cramped scrawl and smiled, but it was not a happy smile. He felt his shoulders slump. He put the file into the leather bag and sat down in the doctor's dusty chair.

GAJARAJAN (M).

For a few minutes, it felt like Dr. Zadeh might walk through the door again at any moment. Then it felt like the amnesiac had been sitting there wishing he could see him one more time for years.

Finally he stood up and went to the far corner, where a much smaller table sat by a window. A heavy binder rested atop it. The amnesiac had kept working on his own research at least, even if he couldn't complete Dr. Zadeh's. His copy of Hemu's notebook was probably four times as thick now as when Hemu's doctor had first gifted it to him.

He didn't mean to, but it was hard to resist. He found his fingers flipping through the familiar pages, articles and snippets he knew backward and forward. In the middle, he stopped on a torn-out scene from an old play. *Peter Pan,* written in 1904 by a man named J. M. Barrie.

MRS. DARLING (*making sure that MICHAEL does not hear*). The first time was a week ago. It was Nana's night out, and I had been drowsing here by the fire when suddenly I felt a draught, as if the window were open. I looked round and I saw that boy—in the room.

MR. DARLING. In the room?

**MRS. DARLING.** I screamed. Just then Nana came back and she at once sprang at him. The boy leapt for the window. She pulled down the sash quickly, but was too late to catch him.

**MR. DARLING** (*who knows he would not have been too late*). I thought so!

**MRS. DARLING.** Wait. The boy escaped, but his shadow had not time to get out; down came the window and cut it clean off.

**MR. DARLING** (*heavily*). Mary, Mary, why didn't you keep that shadow?

**MRS. DARLING** (*scoring*). I did. I rolled it up, George; and here it is.

*She produces it from a drawer. They unroll and examine the flimsy thing, which is not more material than a puff of smoke, and if let go would probably float into the ceiling without discolouring it. Yet it has human shape.*

. . .

**MR. DARLING.** It is nobody I know, but he does look a scoundrel.

**MRS. DARLING.** I think he comes back to get his shadow, George.

"A scoundrel." The amnesiac smiled. He knew why Hemu had saved this clipping among the rest of his far more serious, desperate research, as silly and unhelpful as it was—because it was so charming. If only shadows were actual objects that could be touched or rolled up in drawers like pieces of paper. The amnesiac sighed. If only it was all that simple.

He closed the binder before he read any more, lest he lose track of time. The pale, solemn face on the cover stared back at him, dark eyes hovering over the long, hanging trunk. He put it on top and zipped up the leather bag as he ducked out.

siac as he passed the main room again, on the way to the infirmary. "Water, main hall . . ." Thunder shattered outside, booming through the facility, and a few startled screams chirped down the hallways.

"Good job, everyone!" the amnesiac yelled as loudly as he could. "Do as much as you can, and get to the main hall quickly!"

"Food, main hall!" He heard Marie shout back, trying to spur herself and her teammates on.

"Infirmary, main hall," he said to himself, turning into the tiled room with a row of beds. "Old man, time to go."

"Water," the old man whispered.

"We have plenty. But we have to go downstairs to get it. Can you walk?"

The old man blinked dazedly. "I think I'm dying," he finally said. "Too much. Pushed too hard."

The amnesiac hefted the leather bag higher onto his shoulder. The old man was fairly tall, but weighed almost nothing now. "Can you sit?" he asked. "If you can sit, I think I can get you into a position where I can carry you."

The old man tried to sit. He struggled up onto his elbows, arms shivering. Bravely he grasped the side of the bed with one skeletal hand and pulled.

"Easy," the amnesiac said. He looped one arm through each of the leather bag's short straps, so it was stuck against the front of him like a backpack worn on the wrong side. "I'm going to gently lay you over my back. Ready?"

"Maybe you should just leave me here," the old man said. "I don't think it'll be long."

"Trust me, you don't want to be up here," the amnesiac said. The rain had started to thrash the roof overhead. "If you're going to die tonight, you want to go in a dry, warm place, with someone sitting next to you. I've done this a lot here. Seen people off. It's better to go in company—even if you only met them yesterday."

"You're a good man," he wheezed.

"Maybe." The amnesiac shrugged. "I don't remember."

IN THE MAIN HALLWAY, ALL THE GROUPS HAD CONVERGED, each carrying or dragging boxes. The storm hurled rain against the east wall, startling them all into a crouch for a moment. The amnesiac counted quickly. "Everyone's here. Okay, let's go. Basement!"

"Basement! Basement!" They all revised the chant. Marie held a wooden torch she'd made and lit somewhere, to help them through the dark hallways. Boxes began to scrape across the floor, out toward the central atrium garden, where the storm doors to the basement were. Just as the amnesiac turned to follow last, something banged against the front lobby door.

"Shit!" he gasped. He stumbled, recovered, barely keeping the old man on his back. "Are you all right?" he asked softly.

"Yeah," the old man gasped. "Someone's out there?"

"Don't—" Marie hissed across the room. "Don't open it."

*Shadowed scavengers? More shadowless? The storm, throwing debris?* The amnesiac watched the locks rattle, praying they would hold. Outside, the wind was howling, strong enough that he could hear the echoes of it through the concrete walls.

The door banged again. "Please!" someone cried, a woman's voice. "Please! Is someone there? Help me! The storm—" The wind swallowed whatever she said after that.

"Trappers," Downtown said. "Or kidlings. Or could be deathkites circling her. We can't be sure."

Curly was next to him. "We're out of time."

*They're right,* he thought. *Just go. Keep the others safe.* That was his job, what he had promised Dr. Zadeh he would do. To keep them together, to watch over them all, and to help them remember as long as he could. He listened to the woman outside pound her fists on the door and wail. The trees were likely bent sideways by now, everything left in the city leaning as if being devoured by a giant vacuum in the sky. The trappers used all manner of bait—children, women, puppies they'd stolen from a street dog. Kidlings didn't use bait at all. They were so terrible, they didn't have to. The amnesiac had watched the old man moan in the bus station for four hours yesterday before he was sure no one had planted him there. He couldn't give this woman the same test—she'd be ripped away by the raging wind in far less time. But he couldn't just leave her to die, either.

"I'm sorry!" he finally yelled. "We can't open the door. Go somewhere else while you still have time!"

"Hello?" she screamed. The door rattled as she hit her fists against it. "Dr. Zadeh, is that you?"

*Dr. Zadeh.*

They all took a step back. The amnesiac looked at Marie, who now was staring suspiciously at the door. Without the signs on the building any longer, there was only one explanation—whoever knew this had been Dr. Zadeh's clinic had known him personally.

"What now?" Marie whispered.

"I don't know," the amnesiac said. He shrugged the leather bag until the straps slid off his arms and it plopped to the ground, and then carefully laid the old man over Curly's back—he couldn't fight holding it all. He motioned for Marie to give him her knife.

"Are we really doing this?" she asked.

"Are you shadowless?" the amnesiac called at the door, gripping the blade as tightly as he could.

"No—I have a shadow! I have a shadow!" The woman outside scraped desperately at the wood as the wind shrieked. "Let me in!"

"Then what's your name?" he yelled. Not that the amnesiac would remember anyone from more than just a few weeks before the Forgetting, but it was all he could think of. "What's your name? If you still have your shadow, you should remember your name—"

She shouted her answer frantically. He couldn't hear the first word through the wind, but the second one he finally caught as she screamed it over and over. "Avanthikar!" she cried. "Avanthikar!"

He didn't realize what he had done until it was over. He was across the room, at the locks. He opened the door, reached out into the cold, slicing rain, grabbed the ragged thing hunched against the wind, and yanked it inside in one motion. Marie's torch snarled, angry at being whipped by the wet air. The amnesiac pressed the knife down on his captive before she could recover.

"Prove it," he said. "I'm sorry, but you have to prove it. I have people I have to protect."

"You," she stammered. The shadowless were shouting now, some excited, some terrified. It was too dark to see more than the lines on the stranger's dirty face, her bony hands, the wisp of her shadow pinned beneath her on the floor.

"Prove it," the amnesiac said again. "How did he die?" Not Dr. Zadeh, but the other. The other man they both had known and loved.

The woman looked at him for a long moment, trying to understand the words through the knife, the wind, the drowning rain. Then all of her memories caught up, from whatever distance they'd had to travel to reach her again.

"Peanut butter," she finally said.

TRANSCENDENCE DOESN'T ASK US QUESTIONS ANYMORE NOW that Lucius has joined them. They have what they want. A god, a mascot. I wonder how long it'll take them to realize that Lucius can't inflict his own curse upon them any more effectively than any of their past prisoners were able to, despite his willingness to try. I wonder how long it'll take Lucius to realize there must have been others before him, but that they aren't here now.

❙❙

The morning after he left us, I woke to the sound of metal scraping, then a loud thud. My eyes snapped open to see everyone lying in a tangled heap on the far side of the cage.

"You're up," Ursula said when she saw me. "Help us pull."

Victor's belt was wrapped around one of the bars, its leather tail now dangling limply as it waited for them to grab on again. "This is our plan to escape?" I asked as I climbed to my feet.

"The point of force just needs to be more concentrated and the power greater," Ursula said. "This is a lot better than each of us pulling on a different bar with only our hands."

"If the belt holds," Ysabelle added. As they passed our room on patrol, the soldiers watched us warily as we all took hold of the belt again. They didn't seem to think it was going to work, but they knew enough to know that when shadowless got angry, sometimes other unintended things could happen.

"Go!" Ursula cried. We all pulled, arms burning. The leather stretched. "More! . . . More! . . ."

"Mother*fucker!*" Victor cried when the belt slipped and we all collapsed on top of him at full force. "This is as pointless as everything else we've tried," he gasped.

"He's right," the woman in white said suddenly. I turned to see her floating through the main door to the abandoned church.

"Are you here to give us breakfast or to proselytize?" Ursula asked her. "Because we're only interested in one of those things."

The woman stopped just in front of the cage. "I want to spare you the wasted effort. You'll never be able to bend the bars." She bowed her head reverently. "The Great One remembered long ago that they could never be destroyed. Nothing on earth can break them."

As she said it, I suddenly knew it was true. I'd been able to feel it the moment we were locked inside—we all had, even though we'd refused to admit it to one another—but hadn't been able to describe it. The feeling that the bars were somehow more than bars. Now that she'd said it, I understood what it was. It was as if they were both the thing itself and the name for it. Perhaps simple poles of metal could be bent with enough force, but how would a person break an "unbreakable bar"?

Ursula must have known it too, but she refused to show it. "The Great One. That's what you call Lucius now?" she scoffed.

"Oh, no," the woman said. "The Great One was far more powerful. A queen among shadowless. She was the first we found. What we all aspire to be."

"Is that so?" Ursula asked. "A shame you have to refer to her in the past tense then." She grinned. Trying to provoke her. "Did she kill herself in some stupid accident because she didn't remember anything, this all-powerful queen of yours? Or did she commit suicide, to escape all of you?"

The white woman's eyes narrowed, but she didn't say anything at first. *Open the door,* I prayed. *Open the door and reach for Ursula. You'll never get it closed again.*

But she didn't. She finally looked away, and crouched down until her white layers rippled out into a small ivory lake. She looked at Zachary, who was still huddled on the ground, one sore arm from the fall tucked against his chest. "Are you all right?" she asked. She reached out and touched the back of his free hand softly. For once, he let her. He looked at her fingers, then slowly up at her face, into her eyes. "You have great power," she whispered to him, awed. "You've almost transcended."

Ursula finally took a step toward her. "Enough," she said. "He's fine."

The woman put her palms up, and stood. "He's very important to you, isn't he?" she asked. Ursula didn't say anything. "He's important to us, too."

"Hah," Ursula finally spat.

The woman in white looked at Zachary again. "You don't have to fight," she said to him, almost as if praying. "You can choose to stop struggling. You're safe here. This is your home."

"This is not our home," I said.

"And New Orleans is?" The woman's eyes wrinkled above her veil. "They are bandits there, nothing more."

"How do you know—" I started, but Ursula cut me off.

"Lucius," she said simply.

Of course they had asked him. He'd told them everything. Our journey, our hopes.

"He did it out of concern for you," the woman in white said. "You should know—whatever you think is there, you've been misled."

"Don't listen," Ursula said to all of us. "She has no idea. She's lying."

The woman rose. "Someday very soon you'll be able to see."

"You have no idea how long we can hang on," Ursula said.

"But I do." She looked down almost hesitantly, as if she didn't want to say what followed. "I've been instructed to stop feeding you."

"What?" Victor roared. The lion tattoo on his arm looked just as angry as he was. "You're just going to *starve us to death*? What kind of people are you?"

"You won't starve. We won't let that happen," the woman said. "You'll join us before you do."

Ursula glared at her in silence. Transcendence were not shadowless, but they'd captured enough of us to know how the pull worked. How much faster fear or suffering made the forgetting come. It was a foolproof plan: first be kind, offer food and protection from the outside world in the hopes that we might join them voluntarily—but if that fails, just wait until we forget they were the ones who put us in this cage in the first place. Then they would be our rescuers, not our captors.

The woman in white finally met our eyes again. "Whether now or later, we'll welcome you all the same."

Victor threw the remains of his cigarette carton after her as she turned to leave, disgusted. The rest of us watched the guards remove the belt from the bars without protest. It wasn't worth the risk of injury or of accidentally forgetting something in the struggle. It was useless anyway.

"Give me until dawn," Ursula said at last, once things had calmed down.

"To what?" Ysabelle asked. "We can't break the cage. We've tried so many times already, and it's never even creaked once." She ran her hands through her pale hair. "I don't know if I have until dawn," she whispered. "I don't know if I can hang on that long anymore. And even if we do get out, what if that woman is right? What if there is no New Orleans after all, and we've been heading for nothing all this time?"

"Stop," Ursula said. "There *is* a New Orleans. And we *are* going there."

"Really?" I snapped, before I could stop myself.

It was the first time I'd gone against her. It broke something in the rest of us. We began to fight, everyone yelling at everyone else.

Ursula turned to me in the chaos. Both of us looked on the verge of crying. "It's going to be all right," she said gently over the roar.

But it's *not* going to be all right, is it, Ory? Because if there isn't a New Orleans, or if we get there and it's not what we hope it is, then it would really be over. Everything I've done, the hope I've finally started to feel, all of it would be for nothing. I won't ever—there's no chance I—shit, Ory. Shit. I'm crying. I don't want you to hear me like this.

I thought it was for the best, my love. Leaving home. You would know that by now if you could listen. I didn't want you to see me this way. I didn't want you to have to live with whatever was left. And if the worst thing happened, if I forgot you, I didn't want to be the reason that you died or disappeared—or turned into something that wasn't you. I *couldn't* be the reason. You would've done the same thing for me, and you know it.

[ ‖ ]

When the arguing and crying had finally died away, Ursula came and sat by me in the corner of the cage.

"Ory. His name is Ory," I whispered.

"I know," she said. She nodded her chin toward where the recorder was hidden in my shirt.

"I'm afraid to forget him," I admitted, ashamed.

"You won't," Ursula insisted.

"How can you know that?"

"Because I *am* going to get us out of here," she said firmly. "And I'm going to get you to New Orleans before it's too late. I don't know how, but I will. I promise."

"But the woman is telling the truth, isn't she?" I asked. "That the cage can't be bent."

"Yes," Ursula finally said. "But it doesn't matter. We've been going about it all wrong."

"What do you mean?"

She squeezed her hands around one of the bars, almost tenderly this time. "Maybe we don't need to open it to escape."

I could see her sifting through what was left of her mind. Looking to see if she had the strength to do what she wanted—what she might give up if she succeeded. What we all might. Because even though Ursula was going to try and bear the brunt of whatever memories we might lose when she let the pull free to revolt against our captors, it was still going to take something from all of us. We wouldn't be listeners when she did it, but a chorus, because whatever she wanted to do, it would cost too much for her alone to pay the price. We would have to harmonize, because to sing all of it alone would destroy her.

Ursula looked at me again, eyes determined. "Just give me until dawn," she said.

⏸

I didn't think I'd be able to sleep. I waited to see what would happen. But Ursula only sat quietly, eyes closed, as if in deep meditation. I kept expecting her to jump up and do something crazy, but she just kept sitting there, remembering, or trying not to. We were all already so exhausted, and without any food since the evening before, it was impossible to resist the numb cold of the cage's floor. I dozed, drifting a long time before I dreamed.

It was the best dream, Ory. So warm and safe and peaceful. So real I could feel it. We were all back in the RV again, some snuggled on the soft, worn couch, some stretched out lengthwise along the floor from back to front. Ursula was in the driver's seat, like she always is, one hand on the wheel and one on the gearshift, and I was reclining in the passenger seat, nestled into the cushions. Outside, a lone road stretched beneath the stars, a gentle curve across the dark, endless plains, and our tires rolled smoothly for once, so smoothly you could barely tell we were moving at all.

"Max," Ursula said softly to me from behind the wheel as I stirred. The night sky rolled by through the windshield. "I need you to do something for me."

"Sure," I smiled drowsily.

"I need you to hold on to the back of your seat as tightly as you can so you don't crack open your skull on the dashboard."

I blinked. "What?"

"Right now, Max," Ursula said. *"Right now!"*

My hands clawed at my headrest as the nose of the RV slammed through the heavy doors of the abandoned church in a peeling scream of splitting wood and crumbling bricks. The whole wall shattered, but it didn't matter—we burst through as it collapsed behind. We dropped over a ramp, maybe a short stack of stairs, and then suddenly the world opened back up. Ory! We were actually outside now, not just in my dream—speeding beneath the dark, starlit sky, crashing frantically through a maze of white tents and tiny, twinkling torches as Ursula tried her best not to hit anyone or anything, but refusing to slow down, no matter what.

"What's happening?" I yelled, but even as I did, I knew. I turned and stared openmouthed at her. She had twisted Transcendence's power against them by giving them exactly what they wanted. She had *forgotten*. Forgotten that we'd been captive for days, that we weren't still free, in our RV, riding for New Orleans, and who knows what else. She hadn't tried to break the unbreakable bars of the cage, because the woman in white was right: The Great One had remembered that the bars could never be *broken*. But she hadn't remembered anything about whether or not they could be *changed*. Ursula had transformed the cage into our RV, with us still inside.

"Everyone to the windows!" she cried as she swung the wheel around another tent, past more torches where a mass gathering was being held before some kind of giant altar. The followers all turned in slow motion, rows and rows of tiny ghosts, their veils floating in the breeze. "I don't know who these people are, but they don't look friendly! Be ready to fight!"

"*Ilaahayow!*" Intisaar cursed as she stared out the front from between us. "There are hundreds of them!" The RV pitched through a tent as white robed figures dove out of the way, barefoot.

"Windows!" Ursula ordered her. Behind us, we could hear the roar of engines start up to begin their chase. The camp stretched out before us like a spider web, clustered and winding, some tents occupied and glowing softly with candlelight, others dark and lonely as their inhabitants milled outside. Pedestrians who had seen us racing toward them from afar had armed themselves with rocks, sticks, knives. They dashed at the sides of our RV now as it passed, trying to do some damage without being dragged underneath. "Keep them away from the wheels!"

*If we could just get outside of their lines and find a road, we might make it,* I thought. We might outrun their scouts, who would have to return to their camp eventually, wouldn't they? There was no limit to how far we would go.

Ursula jerked the gearshift, and we careened past something tall and boxy, sides smashed and corroding in the heat of a trash fire. Half a shipping container, I thought at first, but then I saw the molten, dripping tires, and the remnants of what had once been a painted mural across one of the surfaces. Only the sunset hadn't yet dehydrated and flaked into ash in the blistering heat of the flames. *That's our RV.* I watched it whisk by, too stunned to move at first. *The real one. Not our reimagined one.* I stuck my head out the window to peer down the side of our vehicle as it raced jaggedly away. Only blank tan siding.

Ursula's plan had been a success, but there was one fatal flaw—she had been the owner of the RV, or the one who found it, but not the one who painted our map. Her reimagining wasn't complete.

"The painting!" I cried. "We won't make it without the painting!"

Ursula's expression faltered for an instant as she realized I had named a thing that should have been there but couldn't remember why it wasn't. There were too many white-masked disciples streaming after us for her to consider it for more than a few seconds, though, or we'd die. "Don't worry about that now!" she shouted from the front seat. "Just keep them away from us!"

I clambered to the other side, to help Dhuuxo and Intisaar hold off our pursuers. There was a knife in my hand, a knife with a dark green handle that hadn't been there before, I realized with dim horror, but there was nothing left to do now but thrust it out the window, slash, and scream. Zachary was on the floor by our feet, his hands scrambling madly to pluck shapes out of thin air and then grasp them as solid things. He had heard me. He was trying to remember his brushes, so he could paint for us again. The soft stains on his fingers were darkening as they spread, creeping until the skin of his arms had turned into an inky swirl almost up to his elbows.

"Don't do this!" a familiar voice cried. The woman in white was there, shouting at us from the back of one of the strafing motorcycles. She didn't have a weapon, but her driver did. "There is nothing for you there! We can give you everything—power, respect, love, an army—"

Zachary lurched to the opposite windows, between Victor and Wes, covered to the chest in color now as if he'd been tarred. I didn't even know in what direction we were driving—or if Ursula did either. *Please let him remember what the painting looks like,* I pleaded. *Just one more time.* But the RV was moving too fast, and there were too many of them chasing us. I could feel it—he was running out of time somehow. There was no way for him to paint anything by reaching out the window as we sped, but if we could escape, by the time we were safe enough to stop, he wouldn't remember what the mural looked like.

"Ursula!" I yelled, but she yelled at the same moment as well, ducking as a thrown rock crashed against her window, fracturing the glass.

"No fear," Zachary said to me in a voice that was somehow not strained at all, despite the chaos. "No fear. I paint."

I looked at him, and he nodded calmly. It was hard to tell—there was just so much dark, gleaming varnish on him now, covering almost every inch of his body—but I thought I saw his navy-blue-stained lips smile at me. *I paint*, he said again, without moving them at all. I believed him, Ory.

"Left side!" Intisaar cried as an ATV screeched wildly past us, dangerously close to the front cabin. I looked away from Zachary and thrust my arm through the window to slice at anything within reach.

"No more cages!" the woman in white continued desperately, just behind us. Her motorcycle swerved around a pothole at deadly speed.

"Someone kill her, whoever she is," Ursula said. The RV shifted gears into a charging sprint.

"We were wrong! No more cages! Anything you want! We—" Her cries turned into a surprised choke as the soldier steering for them suddenly jerked like a doll. I thought I heard a storm calling from somewhere nearby. The man's head dropped back, then slowly tilted to the side at an angle that made it clear he was no longer driving the motorcycle—no one with their head at such an angle could drive a motorcycle.

"Got them!" Dhuuxo snarled triumphantly. A pistol was smoking in her grip, but then she didn't have it any longer as quickly as she had gotten it. She stared in surprise at her empty hands.

The motorcycle stayed balanced beside us for just a moment. Straight—then listing, listing, slowly toward the road's shoulder—and then it disappeared in an explosion of sand, white flags of fabric, fire. "Angela!" someone screamed, a long, horrible howl. "Angela, no!"

The word broke a kind of spell over me. She'd had no face, but now she had a name. Angela. Angela. I could imagine her as more than just someone who locked other humans into cages until they broke. As something other than a piece of Transcendence. Angela who worked in banking, Angela who went for five-mile runs around her neighborhood, when it had still existed, Angela whose husband died in the first month. Who had misinterpreted shadowlessness as some kind of religion—who had somehow fooled herself into believing that because the Forgetting was uncontrollable, inevitable, that also made it right. Angela—just another woman who didn't understand anything that had happened either. None of us did.

"Do *not* let them get away, no matter what!" another voice cried at last from somewhere near the taillights. The rest of Transcendence rallied around it, shouting. "They're coming back with us—dead or alive!"

"More speed, Ursula!" I shouted to her. The RV groaned frightfully, somehow lurching forward even faster. Another thing forgotten. "Or they're going to kill us!"

"Just keep fighting!" she called back. The motorcycles edged ever closer. Behind, gun muzzles gleamed from the off-road jeeps. There were far, far too many of them. If they managed to stop our vehicle, we'd never survive.

"Faster!" I screamed again as a white hand swiped for our rearview mirror. The RV roared.

Ursula drove so far and so fast to lose the horde, we didn't realize until we finally, finally stopped that Zachary was gone.

# ORLANDO ZHANG

THERE WAS SO MUCH BLOOD, AND ORY COULDN'T STOP IT. HE kept his hand pressed against Imanuel's neck, but the wound was too ragged, too big. Red was oozing out between his fingers, so hot it made him shudder. Bile curdled in the back of his throat.

"To the second floor," Malik was saying as he helped Ory carry Imanuel's limp frame into the lobby of the Iowa.

"No," Imanuel coughed, his voice full of liquid. "Lay me here."

"We need to get you behind secure doors," Ahmadi said from behind them.

"Doesn't matter," Imanuel replied. "Won't survive."

"Imanuel," Ory argued.

"I know" was his response. He could say only so many words in one breath now. *I'm a doctor* was what it meant. *I can tell.*

They tried to keep carrying him, but Imanuel's words had power in them. They couldn't unbelieve. Once he'd said it, things slowed—he was too heavy, the stairs too slick, their legs too exhausted. They edged forward but didn't make it very far. They hadn't meant to set him down, but then Imanuel was on the marble floor, propped in Ory's lap. Ory ran his hand over his friend's brow, to stop the blood from trickling into his eyes. He could feel Imanuel's neck strain against his hand every time he breathed. "Please don't go," he whispered. "I just found you."

"I'm sorry," Imanuel managed. His eyes were wide with fear. "I'm sorry."

"Stop trying to talk," Ory said.

"About Paul," Imanuel continued, ignoring the order. His voice was soft enough that Malik and Ahmadi couldn't hear. He tried to swallow and choked. "Sorry about Paul. Should have told you."

"Imanuel, stop."

"I tried. To kill him," he stammered. "Almost. But I couldn't." He gasped at the pain.

"I couldn't have done it either, if it had been Max," Ory replied softly. "You made it further than I ever could."

Imanuel's eyes shone with tears. "I let him go. I made. All this. I made. Him."

"No, you didn't," Ory said. He pressed his forehead against Imanuel's. He tried not to think of how it would have gone with Max. If they too had reached a point where she had forgotten too much to remember that Ory was trying to keep her safe, not imprison her—or if, unthinkably, she had begged him in her last lucid moments to end her misery, but then forgotten by the time Ory had worked up the courage to do it. The last thing she would know was fear. A corrupting, animal terror, pointed at the wrong person. Ory could see now how Paul had become what he had become: the two of them, Paul and Imanuel, standing outside in the darkness the night Imanuel knew he couldn't wait any longer, or risk the lives of the rest of the Iowa. Imanuel gently trying to take Paul's book of poetry away from him before he ended the yawning darkness of his amnesia. Trying to give love and accidentally causing exactly the opposite—which became the only thing Paul had left.

A huge bang shattered the stillness. The Reds chasing them had reached the front steps of the Iowa.

"Ory," Imanuel said, his voice thick, as though coming from underwater, "Red King won. Too many. Everything on fire." Blood was bubbling in the corner of his mouth. "Books are all we have left. Take them to New Orleans. Save the books."

"The door is breaking," Malik said behind them. "The iron bar is still locked, but if they make a hole in the wood, they can hit us through it."

They stared at each other. *I can't leave without her,* Ory wanted to say.

"Ory," Imanuel begged. Ory could see what he meant in his expression. *Max is gone.* "Save the books. Go to New Orleans." *She was never here.*

"Door is breached!" Malik warned. A loud boom shook the marble lobby. The glow of firelight danced in the corners. "We need to make a final stand or run."

"Ory—" *Be happy that you never found her. Be happy you never saw. Be happy your memory of her can't be tarnished by whatever she became before her end.*

Ory leaned down to Imanuel and put his forehead against his again. "I'll go," he said. "I'll go."

Imanuel grew heavier in his arms. "I'm sorry," he said again, breathless. "I'm sorry. You have to. Remember all of us now." His eyes brimmed with tears. "No one to help."

"It's okay," Ory wiped his face again for him. *Max. Paul. Imanuel.* "It's okay."

Imanuel took one more gasp, eyes unfocusing. Then the light went out behind them.

Ory held him for a while longer.

"We have to go now," Malik finally said. He touched Imanuel gently on the shoulder. Behind him, Ory heard Ahmadi hiccup, to stop a sob.

"Just one more second," Ory said. *Max. Paul. Imanuel.* He tried to see every line of his face. Every dark, quiet edge of his shadow, a perfect outline of him, still there flat and cold against the floor. He looked until it began to blur. *Imanuel.* "I have to remember."

THEY RAN.

"We're not going to make it," Ory panted. It felt like the Reds were going to crash into the hallway at any minute, right behind them.

"We will." Malik stumbled, recovered. "All the books are packed—just have to climb in!" Their torches lurched with every step down the corridor, throwing light over the stone walls. "You have Paul's book?"

Ory squeezed the cover until his fingers ached. "I have it," he said as they sprinted. It felt sickeningly warm, but the plastic Imanuel had wrapped it in as he took it had kept it safe from all his blood. Ory clutched it harder.

"Turn!" Malik cried as they all almost smashed into a wall. Ahmadi skidded behind them to avoid colliding. Ory could hear that she was still crying as they ran. It made it hurt more, to know that she was as torn apart as he was. That she had loved Imanuel and Paul as much as he had. He wanted to turn around and just hold her and cry with her until the Reds killed them. But he couldn't. He'd made a promise. He had to survive long enough to get their books to New Orleans. They careened down a set of marble stairs, into the garage level.

"Code Red!" Ory shouted.

A shrill whinny answered. Around the room, soldiers jumped up, scrambling for the order. "Vienna?" Malik shouted frantically in the chaos, and Vienna answered from across the room. Locks clicked, hinges squealed. The horses came out of their parking spaces already dressed in full regalia, saddles on and harnesses slung across their great shoulders. One soldier hooked one horse to each yoke, and his partner then climbed onto the second one to ride beside each carriage.

"Carriage one, ready!"

"Carriage two, ready!" Yells came down the line.

A dull boom echoed far overhead, then muffled cries. "They're in the lobby," Ahmadi cried. "Open the garage doors!"

"I'll take rear, you take front with—the General," Malik said to her. Ahmadi raised her bow and leapt into Watson's saddle.

"*General,*" Ory protested deliriously.

"Plenty of time to argue about it later," Ahmadi cut him off. Her eyes were still puffy, but murderous in their focus now. "First we get out of here alive and with all the books."

"Up here!" the soldier holding the reins of the nearest carriage said frantically.

The horse at the end of the carriage's yoke whinnied as Ory threw himself into the seat beside the young man, an ear-splitting call. "Get us out of here, Holmes," Ory said, recognizing the animal's sound.

An explosion on the floor above threatened to shatter the ceiling and crush them all to death. The horses lurched, shaking the carriages.

"We have to go!" Malik bellowed from the back of the line, his voice so deafening he could have been shouting right beside Ory. "Get those doors open *now*!" A horrible cracking sound shook the walls, and then the voices of a hundred screaming Reds rushed at them.

"They're in!" Ahmadi cried. Blinding gray light pierced the warm glow of the torches as the garage doors finally rolled open. Ory felt Holmes surge desperately beneath him at the sight, her instinct to claw out of the gloom and into the light taking over. The carriage jolted to life like a freight train, rolling faster and faster toward the blinding, freeing glow.

"Go now! Go now! Go now!" Malik shouted as each carriage took off. Ory lost sight of Ahmadi and yelled for her, over and over. His soldier lashed Holmes's straining back, the Reds roared; behind, Malik's shotgun fired, thunder boomed. Ory held on to Paul's book for dear life. "*GO NOW!*"

# THE ONE WHO GATHERS

CURLY WAS THE LAST ONE IN, SLOWED BY THE WEIGHT OF carrying the old man down the stairs. The rest of them pulled the heavy storm doors shut, and Marie clicked the padlock and slid all the boards through so the entrance was braced every few inches.

"What's your name?" the amnesiac asked the old man. He realized he didn't know it yet. They were all becoming so bad with names. He himself didn't have one, and the shadowless kept forgetting theirs.

"Harry," the old man rasped.

"Someone please get Harry some water and sit with him," the amnesiac said.

"I'll do it," Downtown offered, and followed Curly as he took Harry over to a pile of blankets.

"None of you have shadows," Harry murmured wondrously. Whatever was failing inside was getting to him—heart, lungs, exhaustion. The amnesiac could hear it in the way his words lengthened, like a song slowed down. "I wish I could give you mine, to thank you for all this. I won't need it much longer."

The amnesiac turned back to Dr. Avanthikar. "Are you sure you're all right? You're sure you're not injured?" he asked again.

"Please," Dr. Avanthikar snorted. "I'm not *that* old."

"I'm so sorry. I was just thinking of the others. I'm—"

She swatted the air. "Stop. You did well. I would have done the same thing if I had patients."

Outside, the rain was falling so heavily they couldn't hear the intervals between when each drop struck the roof anymore. It was just one endless, rolling roar.

"I was transferred to Delhi after Hemu died," she told him once they found flashlights and a spot on the floor. "They set up another research facility there. On my way home one night, some men grabbed me, threw me into a van. I thought maybe it was the family of a shadowless we were failing to cure, but it turned out they were U.S. Marines." She shook her head, as if still amazed. "They smuggled me onto the last flight out of India hidden in a body bag. It was the fastest and safest way they could think of to bypass Indian security and avoid being attacked by the angry crowds flooding the airport. Everyone thought a shadowless was inside. They stayed far back."

"Marines kidnapped you?" The amnesiac stared.

She sighed. "Well, we all wanted the same thing. To stop this. The president apologized to me when I made it to Washington, D.C. He had asked the prime minister to send me first, because he already had other doctors from Germany and Japan, and a huge classified facility in Washington, D.C.—he just wanted to fix things as fast as he could. When the prime minister wouldn't agree, your president figured it would be better to do whatever he had to do to give his international committee the best chance at succeeding and deal with a diplomatic disaster later, rather than to back off and then maybe fail."

"Failed anyway." The amnesiac sighed.

"I think he was right to do it," Dr. Avanthikar said, a little angrily. "Of course I didn't want to turn my back on India. But it was just me and one other team from Mumbai, and it was already too late. Half the country was afflicted. Your president had fifty of the most respected medical researchers in the world, and all the money, all the equipment. If I didn't go, there wasn't going to be an India anyway."

"I'm sorry," the amnesiac said. "I didn't mean any offense."

She waved his words away with a hand, calm again. "We've all done what we had to," she continued. "I'm just glad I made it here, once the classified facility—fell apart. I didn't know if anything would still be standing in New Orleans either, but I couldn't think of another place anyway. I don't know anyone else in the United States." She rubbed her hair gently, to loosen some of the mud from it. "I got lost for six months in the north of Florida." She laughed. "Did you know that now the crocodiles are the size of cruise ships? But they're lit up like them too, and you can hear the music from a mile away. They're probably in more danger of extinction now than they were before, even though they're a hundred times more terrifying. Probably the only thing they can catch is one another."

"It's good to see you again," the amnesiac said, smiling.

Dr. Avanthikar hugged him. "I'm so glad you're alive," she whispered. Her tiny arms were almost crushing. He let her hold on until his back started to cramp from leaning so far over. "And . . . Dr. Zadeh?" she finally asked when she pulled back.

Telling her was not as hard as the amnesiac thought it would be. It wasn't as hard as going into his office alone had been.

When he'd finished, Dr. Avanthikar turned back to look at the door, to see how many locks they'd managed to add to it. "Exterminators," she murmured, shuddering. "That's monstrous."

"It's all right now. There are other things, but the exterminators aren't a threat anymore, at least," the amnesiac said. She glanced at him, brow raised. "Whoever was running things from inside city hall, funding them, lost their shadow, too. The exterminators went right in and did their job. Then there was no one left to keep paying them."

Dr. Avanthikar stared blankly at the amnesiac for a few moments. Then she burst out laughing.

Finally he did, too. They laughed so hard their eyes stung with hot tears, and Dr. Avanthikar fell over. Some of the shadowless who remembered the most even joined in, chuckling in spite of how much they missed Dr. Zadeh.

"Oh, I'm sorry," Dr. Avanthikar finally said, wiping her face. She struggled into a crouch. "I'm sorry, dear. It's all right."

"Scared," Adam whimpered. He was down to just a few words now, but they were all useful ones. "Scared."

"It's okay," Marie said to him.

Adam shivered and went to sit by her. "Scared," he said. "Who?" he asked when he looked at her.

"Marie," she said, pointing at herself. "Adam." She pointed at him when his expression conveyed that he hadn't been asking about her. "Dr. Avanthikar," she tried again, to no avail.

Adam made a confused face, but stayed sitting there. "Who . . . ," he murmured, looking absently around the room.

"Poor thing," Dr. Avanthikar sighed. "He's been here some time?"

"One of Dr. Zadeh's original Alzheimer's patients. Lost his shadow first of everyone here," he answered. "Recently he's gotten much worse. I don't know what to do—Dr. Zadeh didn't tell me what we should do once they forget everything. He was so convinced we could figure something out in time. After the exterminators, I tried, but I didn't know how to continue his research."

"Might be no point anyway now," Wifejanenokids said. He pointed at the ceiling. "After this."

"That's grim," Marie scolded.

"Only because we aren't trying," Wifejanenokids replied. "At least if we tried."

Marie pointed at the same ceiling. "And how could we stop a shadowless from—" She gestured chaotically. "Once it hits?"

"All right, that's enough," Dr. Avanthikar cut in sharply. The shadowless all startled, then watched her in rapt silence. She was so new to them, and her age and title gave her an air of authority. And she still had her shadow. "We won't have a fight in this tiny space. Since we're already down here, it doesn't make sense to leave unless we have a better idea. So instead of squabbling, all of us will spend our time thinking of any possible strategies to help us survive if this hurricane . . . changes." She eyed them all, not unlike a schoolteacher. It made the amnesiac smile to see her treat them not with fear, but with the same love that she had shown Hemu—it only looked tough, on the outside. "Okay?"

They all nodded.

"That means you, too." She nodded her chin at the amnesiac.

He put his hands up in a gesture of surrender. Outside, above them and beyond the walls, there was a faint cracking sound, like wood splitting. Something was giving way in the garden, maybe a tree. He tried to imagine what might happen when the full brunt of the hurricane hit New Orleans, a city filled with thousands of shadowless still alive and waging a fifteen-way war against all the tiny factions of struggling shadowed survivors, and they all panicked as it drowned the empty parts of their memory. If the misremembering didn't kill them, the struggle between all of the magic would. The amnesiac sat down to try and think. Then he realized.

"Shit," he said. He moved all the blankets, checked every box of food. "*Shit.*" It wasn't anywhere.

"What did we forget?" Buddy asked quietly. His voice was high with fear.

"No," the amnesiac said. "You didn't forget anything. I made a mistake."

Marie edged up to where he was leaning against the stack of rations. Thunder made the ceiling of the basement shiver.

"Wait." Curly suddenly stood up. "Where are we?" He had forgotten.

Marie put a hand on Curly's shoulder, to calm him. "Too late now, whatever it is," she said softly to the amnesiac. "I doubt the building above is going to hold."

"It'll only take a minute," he said.

"Where are we?" Curly repeated. "Someone tell me."

"New Orleans," Marie whispered to him. Even as she did it, the amnesiac saw her glance at Downtown, to make sure she was actually right—not only that she thought she was, but had forgotten, too.

Dr. Avanthikar glanced at the water, then the medicine. "What did you leave behind?"

"The bag," the amnesiac said. "All the patient records—the book about Gajarajan."

Everyone was quiet. The amnesiac could see on Marie's face that she agreed with him now. That was the one thing that would be worth going back for.

"I know right where I left it," he said. The main hall, just off from the center, where he had handed Harry's nearly lifeless body to Curly in case he had to fight the stranger who had turned out to be Dr. Avanthikar. "It'll only take a minute. I'll come back. I promise."

Marie looked down, then at Curly, unable not to. "It's not that," she said.

"You just get back here, and I'll open the door," Dr. Avanthikar said.

The amnesiac nodded gratefully to her. She'd cared for Hemu. She understood. She knew what they were afraid of—not that the amnesiac wouldn't come back, but that he would, and because of the stress and the danger, there was the small but terrifying chance that they wouldn't remember to let him in. It was already affecting Curly, chipping away at what he had left. And so the doctor said it before Marie had to, to spare her the shame of having to admit it.

EVERYTHING WAS MUCH LOUDER, AS IF THE STORM WAS SOME-where inside the building instead of outside it. Every crack of lightning made him jump. The amnesiac dashed across the atrium, straight for the main hall on the other side. The bag was exactly where he had said it would be, a small lump on the floor surrounded by puddles. He jumped on it like prey and hugged it to him. The rain had found its way through the attic and was pooling menacingly in the room. *That's not good,* he thought. If it was getting in there, it would start finding its way in elsewhere. If it succeeded in too many places, it might tear the place apart, right on top of them.

As if the hurricane had read his mind, the entire building groaned. The amnesiac ducked, then uncovered his head. *It had held,* he sighed. But it hadn't.

If he'd still had both eyes, he might have noticed the roof beam being battered loose by the wind as it shuddered and finally gave way. Its wild swing as it fell might have fluttered in his peripheral vision. But on that side everything was muted, like a music system with half the speakers unplugged. He saw nothing—only heard the whine of the wood as it splintered, after the jagged edge of the beam was already halfway through its downward arc. With two eyes, he would have ducked or scrambled out of the way. Instead, he turned into it, to see what the sound had been.

For an instant, there was no pain. Only a flash of white, all encompassing, the way water hits everywhere when one slaps through its surface after a dive gone bad. The amnesiac sank into the white as it curled all the way around, sinking deeper. Then there was pain.

His face was on fire. Everything was gray, then red, then dark, a kind of dark he couldn't blink away. The fire had spread into his cheek, into his eye socket, up through the fractured cracks of his brow bone. He realized he was screaming. He tried to get up—away from the fiery pain—but he couldn't understand which way was up. He pushed harder into the floor—or was it a wall? He couldn't tell if the air his hands swiped through was beside or above him. He was on stone again, he realized dimly, not flooded grass. It meant he'd been knocked several feet backward, out of the atrium and back deeper into the main hall.

"The bag," he wailed. "Where's the bag?" The darkness deepened, boring into his brain, agony. There was nothing then, no color, no gradient of light, no registry of movement. His vision was obliterated.

More cracking threatened overhead. The roof was caving further. The amnesiac found his way to his knees and scrambled aimlessly, swinging his arms in wide circles, delirious from pain. *Where was the bag? Where was the fucking bag?* Had it stayed in the courtyard? Had it flown from his hands in the fall, even deeper into the main room? His fingers hit chunks of concrete, splintered wood, splashed into freezing puddles. "Where's the bag?" he cried again. The voice that came out terrified him. Just beside his knee, a boom shattered the stone floor as another rafter gave way. "Gajarajan!" He flung his head back and forth, even though he couldn't see anything out of whatever was left of his remaining eye. *This is how I die,* he realized. Crumbles of cement powdered the top of his head, another beam groaned. He couldn't stop. "Gajarajan! Gajarajan!"

Wet leather slammed into the ruin of his face. The amnesiac howled, but his hands moved on their own, grabbing the straps, pulling it to him even in his mindless agony. To his surprise, he felt another pair of hands on the other side of it—because someone else had found the bag and shoved it at him.

"Get up now!" the person attached to the hands was screaming. "Get up now *get up now GET UP NOW*!" And then those hands threw him in a stumbling roll as the floor where he had just been crouched exploded.

"Gajarajan—" the amnesiac cried. The hands were on him again.

"You are the last person I know in this world, and I'll be damned if you die on me, too! *Get up now!*" the voice shouted, hysterical.

"Dr. Avanthikar—" It was her, somehow she was here, she had left the basement, she had found the bag, she had grabbed it and pushed him out of the way. "Dr. Avanthikar!"

"The roof is caving in!" She shook him. "We're going to die if we don't get back downstairs *right now*!"

He couldn't pry his hands away from the bag. He felt her grab a fistful of his shirt and take off, dragging him behind her. Freezing rain stung them through the opened sky. The amnesiac stumbled after her, trying not to catch his feet on the rubble he could no longer see as they ran. Around them, he heard the walls start to moan, faltering against the wind now that the ceiling was no longer there to help them resist. Grass, mud. The murderous rain.

"Don't stop!" she cried.

Behind, he heard the walls begin to fall, inch by inch, chasing them like a rolling concrete wave.

I WOKE UP WEEPING. I CAN TELL I'VE BEEN CRYING A LONG time: my chest is sore from heaving, and my face is swollen and stings at the corners of my eyes where the tears have streaked down. The dirt beneath me where I'm sitting against the side of the RV is pockmarked with salty droplets. How long have we been parked here, in the middle of this roadless, dry valley? Everyone looks hazy in the setting sun. Ysabelle is still crying, tiny choking sounds, and Victor is sitting next to her, one hand hesitantly on her shoulder. The others are bunched together near the rear tire, comforting one another. Some are still sniffling like Ysabelle, and a few—Ursula, Wes, Intisaar—are bent under the strain of sadness, but their cheeks are already long dry. Above me, the mural painted across the side of our RV is glowing with colors more vivid than I can ever remember seeing. Urging us onward, urging us toward New Orleans.

"Max," Ursula said to me when our eyes met, "why are we all crying?" There was a horrible desperation in her voice. "It hurts so badly, but I can't remember why."

For a moment, I could feel the sharpness of a pain that had a name, and the loss of something I could still feel. Something tremendous. What have we just given up, Ory? What have we given up, and what have we gotten for it? But the more I tried to answer her, the more dull the pain became, until it ebbed away into empty exhaustion. Nothing.

I realized that I couldn't remember either.

# MAHNAZ AHMADI

IT RAINED FOR SO LONG THAT EVENING THAT EVEN UNDER cover of a patch of trees, Naz couldn't make a fire.

"Too much water is better than not enough," Malik said as he set out extra buckets to collect the downpour for drinking later. But Naz could see in his glances at each carriage that he was worried about leaking, too. The roofs seemed sturdy for now, and each cache was stacked under layers of tarp, but she didn't blame him—she checked just as often as well. The books were all they had left.

Naz didn't like that they had to stick to main roads, but they had no choice. The carriages needed flat asphalt—especially the two antique models. Trying to drag three thousand books across a wild, forested stretch of states would be no better than leaving them there for the Reds to burn. The axles would snap in the first mile.

They had pushed the horses southeast at a gallop until Clinton, Maryland, when they were sure the last of the Reds were no longer following them, and then had finally slowed down. Watson was gasping, and every step flanged droplets of froth from her bridle into the air.

"She'll be okay," Vienna said as she leaned in her own saddle toward Naz to pat Watson's neck. They both were riding even with the first carriage, where Ory was sitting. "Right?"

"She's just tired," Naz replied softly, but still felt guilty. They'd had to ride as hard as they did to survive, but she knew how much Vienna loved Watson.

"Watson is my horse," Vienna explained to Ory, as if on cue. She was talking to fill the silence, so none of them had to face it yet. The silence was where the General—now just Imanuel—was now. "Well, not *mine*—I used to take riding lessons at the Georgetown stables, before the Forgetting, and she was the horse I practiced with there. That's how we knew to go get them and bring them to live at the Iowa."

Ory tried to cooperate. "Your remembering them probably saved our lives. And the books," he replied.

Vienna blushed, caught off guard by the compliment. For a moment, she looked like the teenager she was, suddenly awkward as she remembered that Ory wasn't the grunt that she'd decimated in basic training anymore, but the new General of their small war. Naz chewed her lip. She didn't know how to approach it either. She could already feel a shift in Malik's tone, and the other soldiers barely spoke to Ory at all—just saluted and then dropped their eyes respectfully to the ground.

Naz watched a small lake to their left curl up and disappear like magic as she considered the situation, leaving behind a patch of wet mud. The creature that had been crouched drinking at the water's edge startled and darted back into the trees. Yesterday she had been giving Ory orders. Now it was the other way around. But it still seemed like he needed it the first way.

"Was that . . ." Vienna trailed off. She'd seen the lake and the animal, too. "Well, what was that?"

"I don't know," Ory said. The creature had looked like a hodgepodge—a rabbit and a pig and a frog smashed together. "It didn't seem carnivorous though, so I think we're probably fine."

"So, General," Naz said.

He made a face. "Please."

"Fine. Ory. You need to make an official address to our group once we break for camp tonight. Reintroduce yourself to the rest of the soldiers and such. It might be good to prepare something now."

"Makes sense," he said quietly.

"That's Ahmadi," Vienna sighed. She kicked her feet out of her stirrups and swung them absently. It reminded Naz so much of Rojan that she had to look away. She was always on the verge of crying now, any time she thought of any of them. *Rojan. Maman. Paul. Imanuel.* "All business."

"I am not all business," Naz finally said.

"Yes, you are. That's why my dad likes you so much."

"WE NEED AT LEAST FIFTEEN TO STAND GUARD AT NIGHT," Ory was saying to the group as the soldiers climbed exhausted from their horses. Dusk peeked at them from just over the horizon, already half gone. "Not forever, we can scale back after a few days—but we're still so close to D.C. right now, the Reds might still be on our tail. I know everyone's tired. But we're all going to have to make it with only four hours of sleep a day until we're in the clear. I'm going to take one of those posts tonight—who's with me?"

Naz tried not to smile at his surprised expression as well over half the hands in the crowd went up.

"I didn't make it through all that and then ride this far just to get ambushed my first night," Malik said. "I'll rest when we're in New Orleans."

IT SEEMED LIKE SLEEP WOULD BE IMPOSSIBLE, BUT WHEN SHE woke to the sounds of screaming in the pitch-black, Naz's first bleary thought was *Well, I'll be damned, I did drop off after all.* Then she was scrambling, ripping the zipper on her tent, bow and quiver already in hand.

"What's going on?" she shouted. The small campfire was out, no more than an angry, chugging column of smoke. Where were the Reds? She whipped the bow fiercely, searching. "General! Malik! Someone report!"

"The lake!" Vienna cried, suddenly beside her. "Leave the bow, come on!"

At the center of the camp, Ory and Malik were against the side of a carriage, trying to push it—somehow only their top halves visible in the night. A swarm of soldiers was racing to join them.

*Water*, Naz suddenly realized. *They're in water.* "Are they . . . swimming?" she asked, dumbfounded.

"Chest deep!" Ory shouted when he saw her. "Help push, before it gets inside to the books!"

She and Vienna splashed in, gasping at the icy cold. Her hands found the rough wooden side of the carriage and she kicked as hard as she could, aiming for shore.

When the wagon was safe and all the books checked, Ory came back with a blanket over his damp hair—the best they could do for a towel. "That lake that disappeared earlier opened up right beneath us," he said as he sat down next to her and Vienna. Someone had used new, dry wood to start another fire. The soldiers who'd jumped in wandered slowly in circles around the glow, some wearing their clothes to dry them, others clad only in undershorts, holding out shirts and pants like human clotheslines. "Thank goodness we parked all the carriages in such a wide circle. We'd never have pushed more than one out in time."

"Put your shoes there, so they dry," Naz said to him, pointing at the grass just beyond the flames, then shook her head. What was she, his mother? Her pants stuck to her as she shifted, slimy with lake grime. It brought all that with it too, every time it moved, it seemed. Did it also have fish?

"Hopefully we outrun it," Ory sighed as he pried his feet out of each waterlogged boot. "Hopefully it has its own territory and will stray only so far."

"Hopefully," Vienna answered.

Naz watched the water reflect the light from their camp and tried not to think. About Vienna or Rojan. Or especially Ory. Every time there was danger, she filled one girl in for the other. She didn't need a third person to worry about.

"What is it?" Ory asked.

"I just—I thought it was the Reds," she finally said.

THE LAKE WAS STILL THERE AT DAYBREAK, AND SEEMED TO stay where it was when they left.

They kept a blistering pace. Three days passed without sign of anyone. The scouts came back reporting empty fields, blank roads. Bodies—but long dead, with only skeletons remaining. Little by little, they all started to relax. It seemed that everyone had refused to leave the northern cities, turning New York and D.C. and Boston into inescapable hell prisons, but something different had happened here. For whatever reason, everyone south of that had just disappeared. Was it because the Forgetting was complete here? Or had they all heard about this mysterious new version of New Orleans, and thought they were close enough to make a break for it?

ON THE FIFTH DAY, JUST AS THEY WERE ABOUT TO LEAVE Virginia, they found a grave by the side of the road. There was a simple wooden cross jammed into the earth in front of the mound, and someone had touched a piece of charcoal to the horizontal post, as if they had meant to write something. The name of the deceased, or a prayer. But that was all there was—just a dark, hesitant smudge. Maybe whoever buried the dead had forgotten their name or never knew it. Maybe they thought there would be no point, because whoever passed by the grave on this road likely wouldn't be able to read it anyway. Ory stared at it so long, it gave Naz a chill. Then it chilled her again when she realized that she cared. That she'd gotten used to him as part of their army, because that wasn't how he thought of himself. His army was only a team of two.

"I think we should talk about succession," she said to him that night as they set up their tents. She knew it would be a hard conversation, but she'd seen his face at the grave. Tomorrow, they would leave Virginia behind and cross into North Carolina. They would leave behind the place he'd last seen Max, forever. And she knew he wasn't going to do it. So the best thing to do was just get it over with quickly, instead of dragging it out. "I think it should be Malik, then me, then Smith Tres. He's quiet, but he knows what he's doing."

"I know I was bad in boot camp, but I wasn't that bad," Ory replied.

Naz fumbled, embarrassed. "That didn't come out right. I didn't mean I think you're going to . . . die."

Ory popped the last pole of his tent into place, and stood studying his construction in grim silence as he waited for her to continue.

"I know what was promised to you, if you helped get Paul's book," she said at last. "I'd understand if you had to go back to D.C. or Arlington to search. We'd all understand. But if you're going to do it, you have to do it sooner, not later. Before we start to depend on you."

"You depend on people?" he asked, eyebrow cocked skeptically.

"Malik's getting close," Naz said. "Maybe in another ten years."

Ory chuckled. Just overhead, the strange little musical clouds— puffs of warm fog each no bigger than a deck of cards that the soldiers had taken to calling *iizingers*—scooted by in a faint chorus of flutes. "I'm staying," he finally said. "I made a promise to Imanuel."

"Imanuel's dead. He doesn't remember you."

"Neither does Max," Ory said.

It hurt to look at him, down deep. Naz tried, but it made everything tight, from the crevices of her lungs up to the top of her throat. "I'm sorry," she finally managed. "Max—"

"Don't." Ory shook his head. *Don't speak of it ever again,* he meant. He took a breath. "Who knows? I might forget someday, too."

He wouldn't ever. His shadow seemed a hundred shades darker and deeper than anyone else's. "Maybe someday," Naz said.

"I'm staying." He looked up at her. "Even though you don't believe me."

She didn't.


NAZ CANTERED A LEAN, TIRELESS GELDING NAMED HANNIBAL in circles the next day, each pass around the carriages wider and wider.

Searching for footprints, places where bodies had slept, buried shit. Anything red. Signs that they were still following.

How fast could a raiding party travel in a day, if angry enough? How long until they gave up or forgot what they were pursuing? Every morning she wanted to think that she and the army had run far enough, but every night no distance ever seemed sufficient. She wondered if as the shadowless poured after their carriages, streaming out of that broken city, they turned everything red behind them—the ground, the trees, the sky.

A WEEK LATER, WATSON STUMBLED IN A FOXHOLE AT A RUN and snapped her front leg in two. Vienna was almost crushed when the mare fell, whinnying in agony. By the time they all stopped the carriages and ran to them, there was blood everywhere, and Vienna was struggling, half-dazed, one of her own legs trapped beneath the writhing horse. Naz scrambled to help lift the animal up enough that Malik could drag her out, shuddering so hard with terror that she could barely keep her grip. The sweat that poured off her was cold as ice.

For a single instant, the face of the girl they pulled free of Watson's broken body was Rojan's, not Vienna's, and Naz almost screamed. She would have lost her hold entirely if Ory hadn't suddenly appeared behind her then and grabbed the saddle too, lifting the burden out of her hands.

Vienna's leg was fine—so was the rest of her. Just the wind knocked out of her, but not a scratch. After she pushed Malik away, she sat down by Watson's head and whispered to the mare until she calmed a little. Naz and Ory looked at each other under the shade the first carriage cast down.

"We don't have much ammo," Naz stammered, still trembling. She wrapped her arms around herself.

"Ahmadi," he said gently. "Don't. We owe it to Watson."

"I know," she replied. "I'm just saying, we've only got a handful of shells left. Malik will never order it."

"I'll do it, then."

Naz looked at him, surprised—not really believing he was going to actually be able to do it. She wasn't even sure *she'd* be able to do it, to look at Watson's big ebony eye and make it go dull—and she figured she'd already killed at least twenty more human beings than Ory ever would.

Ory either didn't realize how hard it was going to be, or was pretending not to. "Take Malik and Vienna around the other side of the carriages when she's ready," he said.

Naz helped lead Vienna away as she cried. She didn't tell her or Malik that Ory had gone to get a gun from one of the soldiers. "What are we going to do?" Vienna whimpered. "We can't just leave her there like that. We can't just *leave* her, without . . ."

"I'm sorry, honey," Malik said helplessly. "I'm sorry."

Naz put her hand on his shoulder as he bent to kiss Vienna's forehead. Through the gap between the two carriages that blocked their view, she could see Watson's long, velvet neck as it trembled against the dirt. Unexpectedly, Ory was there, grimacing. He held the gun as if it was ten times heavier than it was. The electric, stormy gleam shivered inside the barrel. He seemed to have forgotten how to use it.

"Come on," Naz said softly. "Do it for Watson. Do it for Vienna." The gun wavered as Ory wavered. He moved the cold muzzle around on the horse's temple for what felt like hours as she lay there in the dirt, whining. He was afraid it wasn't on the exact right spot, afraid he'd only miss or make it worse, torturing her with burning, searing thunder, and then need to use more and more bullets until he used too many and someone stopped him, and the horse would be in *more* agony, not less. Watson moaned. "Do it for us," Naz whispered. *Do it for me,* she realized she'd actually meant. Ory closed his eyes and turned his head away.

He was going to miss, she saw. And he was too afraid to take a second shot, so he couldn't take the first. He wasn't going to do it. Shoot the horse or come to New Orleans. He was going to run. He was going to go back to Washington, D.C., to go backward into his memories until he died.

But when he finally pulled the trigger, one bullet was enough.

"I'm staying," he said to Naz when she came out from behind the carriage.

"I believe you now," she said.

I'M SORRY I HAVEN'T—I KNOW IT'S BEEN A FEW DAYS. WE ALL lost so much the last time, I just didn't want to record for a little while. I didn't want to think about it. It's so hard to explain to you what it's like. How sometimes you don't know you've lost a thing, but sometimes you do—just not what it was. When that happens, it's easier just not to think at all. If you don't think, you won't stumble onto the fresh, cold chasm in the winding canyon of your memories. For just a little while, it's easier not to try to remember anything at all.

But then of course I miss you. And then I want to remember you. Even if it means encountering the gaps.

I hope we make it, Ory. We have to make it before I forget you so they can fix me, so I can find you once more. So I can make all of this right again, and save us both.

But it's getting worse. Much, much worse.

The roads here are winding instead of straight. They swerve lazily all around, as if a giant bent over and gently stirred the landscape with a spoon. There's an argument inside the RV every time we come to another turn, about whether we should attempt to drive through the swath of non-road in front of us or whether we should follow the curves around to save the tires, even though the hours and the miles are growing, growing, growing.

"We could just drive right over it," Dhuuxo said softly from over the top of Ursula's seat. Before us spread a large and dark puddle, too deep and too wide to plunge through without killing the engine. "Just right over, like gliding."

"No we can't," Ursula said firmly. "We can't drive over water."

"But we could," she insisted. I looked up and saw that faraway look in her eyes. A feathering around the edges. A seeing of a thing that none of the rest of us could see just yet, but soon would.

"Stop," I said.

"We *could*," she whispered.

"We're never going to make it in time if we don't do something," Wes added softly.

"We're never going to make it with enough of ourselves left if we do too much," Ursula replied.

Sometimes Dhuuxo will give up, sometimes Ursula. Sometimes neither will, and it escalates into a screaming fight until Intisaar starts to cry. I'm afraid of her now, Ory. I'm afraid of Dhuuxo. When Lucius left the group and Ursula drove us out of Transcendence's camp with an RV made from a cage and saved us, and something else, something I know I no longer remember, we all saw how much you could gain if you paid enough. I thought that because Dhuuxo came with us, she felt the same—that the price was too high. Maybe she did, I don't know. Maybe it isn't that Dhuuxo doesn't want to resist, but that she *can't*. I suppose it doesn't matter. The result is the same. She's letting go, more and more. Little things—changing the color of her clothes, changing the lengths of her intricate, tumbling braids, blooming flowers all along the sides of the road where there was nothing an instant before. The trees sing now, in a language I don't understand. Slowly, bigger and bigger things, too. The strength of the warmth in the air. The brightness of the moon, so we can continue to drive even at night. At first Ursula didn't say anything. She just looked at Intisaar every time something happened. Intisaar would nod back, to promise that she was watching Dhuuxo, that she wouldn't let her fall too in love with the magic.

But every time it happens, Dhuuxo slips further and further away. She's so far gone now that I don't know if Intisaar can bring her back. Her only choice may be to let her go—or follow her.

⏸

I think we're losing Wes, too. Now it's the two of them always trying, studying this new world they can see—not the world that's there but the world that *could be*—while Intisaar sits with her back against the back of my seat, watching them in terrified silence. Victor and Ysabelle have taken to yelling for Ursula every time they think Dhuuxo might be forgetting something, making that horrible trade. To warn her before it happens. The pull inside the little cabin is so strong now, it's not just about her and Wes—every time Dhuuxo forgets something, she's in danger of taking us with her too, even though we don't want to go. Our RV often jerks to a stop in this winding wasteland, brakes screeching, Ursula climbing out of the driver's seat like a provoked bear, roaring at them, shaking them by the shoulders, even hitting them, once.

"So help me God," she snarled in Dhuuxo's face. Dhuuxo strained to get away, and Ursula grabbed her braids at the base of her skull, pulled her face so close to her own and held it there that they could have kissed, if they hadn't wanted to kill each other instead. "I will not let you endanger the rest of us, too. If you give up one more time, I will throw you out of this caravan. I will leave you behind."

"*Please,*" Intisaar begged.

"Don't be afraid," Dhuuxo whispered. "There's nothing to be afraid of."

"Do it again and watch me keep my word," Ursula said.

I held Intisaar in terror, waiting for something horrible. An absence, a shifting, an addition to reality. The only one strong enough to stop Dhuuxo if she tried something was Ursula, because they had both forgotten so much—but she would have to use the magic right back to thwart anything Dhuuxo tried to do, and none of us know how much Ursula has left. What if what it took from her was the memory of how to drive?

"I'm sorry," Dhuuxo finally said. Her cheeks were wet then. "I don't know if I can stop it."

"You can," Ursula said. She pointed at Dhuuxo's twin sister, and they studied each other's identical features. "You have to."

She tried. Intisaar watched her, and Victor and Ysabelle watched Wes. We wound around the circular lands. Every revolution made them more and more agitated, as if each turn hurt.

"How much longer can it go on like this?" Intisaar asked Ursula softly one night as we drove under the glow of Dhuuxo's unnaturally luminous moon. Everything shone silver, almost as bright as day.

"I don't know," Ursula said. "But there has to be an end."

"Maybe it's a test," I offered. "Maybe whoever is waiting in New Orleans made the land like this so only those who really want to go will make it."

"Maybe it's a warning," Dhuuxo said then. She wiped the sweat from her tired, furrowed brow. "Maybe they made it like this because they don't want us to come."

"No," Ursula said. "The stories are about The Welcoming One, not The *Un*welcoming One."

‖

On the fourth day, the road finally uncoiled into a straight, long line. We came around the last bend and all gasped. Ursula had to stop the RV for a moment so we all could take it in. An endless stretch of green with a single gray ribbon straight through it, extending out until it faded against the horizon.

"We made it," I finally said. "We can't be far."

"I can't see anything at all," Ysabelle mused, squinting. "Just green."

Ursula nodded determinedly. "New Orleans is out there."

"What's New Orleans?" Wes asked from behind us, studying the landscape from beneath the shade of his palm.

"It's where we're going."

"No, we're not," Dhuuxo said.

⏸

Outside the RV, we stood clustered in two groups, one beside each tired taillight. The ones who wanted to remember—Ursula, me, Ysabelle, Victor, and Intisaar; and the ones who didn't—Dhuuxo and Wes. Wes was pacing listlessly in vague circles, as if trailing some sort of shifting magnetic attraction, but Dhuuxo was still, staring calmly into Intisaar's eyes. In the dirt behind us, tiny little lightbulbs the size of grapes were pushing slowly through the earth, unfurling like new crops. Farther back, a carved porcelain teacup the size of a freighter sailed silently past in the sky like a cloud, its smooth, rounded lip tilted at a graceful angle.

"Please, Dhuuxo," Intisaar said. "Don't do this."

Dhuuxo shook her head. "Trust me, *walaashaa*. Transcendence was right. Not that we should follow them, but that there's so much more out there than whatever might be in New Orleans. I can feel it."

"Let's just go there first," Intisaar begged. "If you don't like it, we can leave."

"No, it's a mistake. Trying to save what we used to have—that isn't the way. We have this power for a reason. We're supposed to use it. We're supposed to make something new."

Intisaar wiped her face fiercely, to slap off the tears before they trickled down. "What about me?" she asked. "I don't want to be new. I want to remember."

"I know you don't understand yet," Dhuuxo said. "But you will soon. I can show you."

Intisaar turned to us. "If we go faster, we can make it," she said hurriedly. "If you help me get her back inside, I can hold her. I can remember for the both of us."

Ursula sighed. If it had been possible, Dhuuxo and Intisaar would be the ones who could do it. But it wasn't possible.

"We promised," I finally said. The teakettle was passing now, following after the cup, birds clustered on its spout like dust. The porcelain gleamed in the setting sun. "We have to get everyone there, even if they don't remember that they wanted to go."

"I will not go," Dhuuxo said firmly. "I will undo the vehicle if you try and force me."

We all tensed. Ursula spread her arms protectively, as if her hands could stop anything from reaching the RV. "The RV is ours," she said. "It's going to New Orleans."

"Are you sure?" Dhuuxo asked. She looked at Wes. "Maybe it's going somewhere else."

There was a small, groaning sigh behind us then. The beginning of something. Or the end.

"Dhuuxo, no!" Intisaar screamed. I felt my breath catch, but I couldn't look at what was behind us now. It was death, emptiness. *Ory.* I couldn't move.

But Ursula could. All the air came back into the world suddenly. Everything was a few iterations lighter, like I'd taken off a hat and a coat.

I turned and looked. The RV was the same. It was still the same. It was as I remembered it.

"Go before I kill you," the silver-haired woman said quietly.

Dhuuxo nodded. She was slicked with sweat, damp from forehead to her shoes. Humid stains crept through her clothes at her armpits, her knees. "I'm sorry," she said at last. "I would have let it go. I didn't mean to—what you had to give up."

"Go before I kill you," she said again.

Dhuuxo turned slowly and strode off toward the distant hills, almost floating over the ground. Wes considered for a long moment. "I'm sorry, too," he said softly. He turned to follow his new, liminal queen.

I hugged Intisaar before she could say anything. "Stay," I said. "Stay and remember."

"She's my sister," Intisaar whispered helplessly. "I can't leave her."

"I know," I said. Her hand slipped out of mine.

Then there were only four of us, standing beneath Dhuuxo's glowing moon.

I turned around at last and touched the aluminum side of the vehicle. It felt solid, real. "The RV's okay? Everything's okay?" I asked desperately.

Our driver nodded, exhausted. But instead of going back toward the RV, she turned and walked away, into the tall grass waving in the field stretching away from the road. She walked faster and faster.

"Wait!" I cried. I chased after her. Where was she heading? None of us could drive the RV but her. "Wait!" But she just kept going until she was moving at a run. "Stop!" And then she disappeared.

But no—she'd only dropped to her knees, and the grass had appeared to swallow her.

I slowed as I came up behind the gap in the sea of weeds where her body had crumpled the stalks beneath her. She wasn't moving. Just kneeling there, staring into the distance in silence. The grass hissed softly around us.

"I'm sorry," she finally said. Her voice was thick. "I just needed—I needed."

"It's all right," I said.

"It's going to start happening much faster now."

"I know," I breathed. We had all felt it. The size of what had been lost to save the RV. It was a big thing, an anchoring thing. We had so few of those left.

"We should go. There isn't time to waste anymore."

"In a moment." I edged forward and sat down beside her, as quietly as I could. "We have a moment."

She looked down at her hands. "A moment," she conceded at last.

I waited for her to tell me what she'd just given up. Then I realized what it was.

"I don't remember it either," I said. Somehow she had forgotten it, and then forgotten it for all of us as well. "I'm sorry."

She shook her head. "It's all right." There was nothing more to do about it, except just forget more. The woman climbed to her feet. In the moonlight, she shimmered lightly. "It was just a name. There was hardly anything left to it anyway."

▐▐

We have been driving a long time, I think. I can't see where we came from—there's nothing around us for miles. Wherever it was, it's too far away to know now. The air is warm, and the road is straight.

"Where are we going?" I asked the woman driving next to me when I saw her glance over.

"It's a place called New Orleans," she said patiently.

"New Orleans," I repeated. What a wonderful-sounding place, don't you think, Ory? A place that's new. A place for starting over. I don't know what Orleans means, but it also sounds like your name. I don't think I ever believed much in signs like that, but then again maybe I did, and I just can't remember anymore. In any case, it sounds like a good sign, don't you think? "How far are we?" I added.

"I'm not sure," she said. "We're just following the painting."

"What painting?" I asked.

"The painting on the side of the RV," she replied.

There was a long silence. An unspoken understanding. That she didn't remember from where it had come either.

"We can stop so you can look at it if you want," she finally continued after a few moments.

"That's okay," I said. A strange feeling niggled at the back of my mind. I didn't know there was a painting, but the conversation was playing as if I should. I was in a big van with a painting on its side, so I must have seen it when I climbed in, right? I didn't know if I didn't want to see it because I should remember it, or because it seemed like now if we stopped the van and I looked at it, I'd just forget again in a few minutes anyway.

The driver was fiddling with the fraying leather wrap around the steering wheel. The sun was in our eyes.

"How do I know you?" I finally asked. I felt ashamed to ask it. I was comfortable sitting next to her there, in the passenger seat, as if we could've known each other for years. I searched her face for anger or pain. The expression I had been terrified to see on your face one day when I finally forgot something you couldn't bear.

But the driver only smiled. "I don't remember either," she confessed. "But we're here now."

‖

There's just so little left, Ory. You might be the only thing that's left. I wish I hadn't run. I wish I'd stayed with you in that little dark shelter, hiding in the dim, musty ballroom—was it a castle? A house?—resisting the pull as long as I could. But then I think about how much I've forgotten—I don't know what all of it was, but I know it was too much, because there are so many things I can't answer anymore—and I know I couldn't have stayed. I wouldn't be able to bear it if I'd done something to you.

"Why are you crying?" the woman driving next to me said.

I clicked the tape recorder off then, to finish talking to you later, and wiped my face.

"Is that your voice in there?" she asked. "It sounds like you."

"Yes, I think so," I said. The tires beneath us slowly lapped the cracked road under our hood, turn after turn. I could feel the steady hum of the engine. "Do you know where we're going?" I asked.

"Yes and no," she said.

Somehow it made sense to me. "Why are we going? Is it because . . . because we know people there?" I added hopefully. Maybe you're there, Ory? Waiting for me?

The driver shook her head. "I don't know anyone there. I don't think you do either. Or them."

I looked over the seat behind us and saw two other people dozing in the semi-darkness of the backseat, a man and a woman. How long had they been there? How long have I been here?

"It's all right," she said. "Once we get there, things will be better. Someone will be able to tell us why we came."

I looked down at this little machine in my hands. "Will they be able to . . ." I don't even know what exactly I need. Help, but what kind? And how? ". . . fix us?"

"I hope so," the driver said. "I think so. They'll be able to fix you."

I looked out the window. I didn't know what else to say. I didn't think it had been a mistake—that she'd said *fix you* instead of *fix us*. I wonder what she's forgotten. How she knows that it's too much. Will I know when it's suddenly too much for me? If I—if I forget you, will I know I have?

# THE ONE WHO GATHERS

IT WAS SUDDENLY QUIETER WHEN THE BASEMENT DOORS
slammed shut, but the darkness was the same. It smelled of vomit—
then the amnesiac realized it was his own. "Gajarajan," he moaned
again. He was still clutching the bag.

He was guided to the floor. One of their first-aid kits popped open,
and pills were pushed into his hands. "For the pain, swallow these,"
Dr. Avanthikar said from somewhere just above. Someone padded his
wound with cotton squares and wrapped a wide roll of fabric around
his head to keep them in place. The pressure helped, slightly.

"Never again. There always has to be a shadow in the group,"
Marie said. "If something had happened to him and then to you—"

"It had to be me," Dr. Avanthikar returned. "You know it."

The amnesiac touched the gauze band around his face softly.
It was already wet, soaked through with blood. Maybe something
else—whatever soft, liquid mirror was inside an eye. He swallowed
the pills and rocked as he tried to wait for the fiery, searing edge of the
agony to slide from murderous to simply angry. There was no point
in hoping it might get better. Not a chance. When it healed, he was
going to be blind.

"What are we going to do?" he heard Buddy whimper. "What are
we going to do? What are we going to do?"

"It's okay," the amnesiac managed. Everything felt so tight, like
whatever was left of his remaining eye had swollen to a size that was
crushing everything else in his skull. "I can still remember everything
for us. I just can't see."

Marie burst out crying at that.

"Please," he begged. "*Please*, I can feel the sound, it's pounding."

His hands clawed uselessly, unable to reach into his brain, covering his ears. "I can feel it inside my head . . ."

"We need a tranquilizer," Dr. Avanthikar said, putting her hands over his own to help drown out even more of the sound. Marie bravely strangled her sobs. Even through the doctor's soft, wrinkled hands, he heard the soft click of Marie's dreadlocks tapping one after another on each shoulder as she shook her head back and forth, taptaptaptaptaptaptap, taptaptaptaptaptap. *She doesn't remember how to read,* the amnesiac wanted to explain, but he just moaned.

"I'll do it, I can do it," Downtown said from somewhere deeper in the basement. Boxes shifted, glass vials clinked against each other.

"Are they okay?" the amnesiac begged the dark air, prying his palms away from his ears to touch the leather bag. "The book, the files?"

Dr. Avanthikar's bony hands pushed his fingers gently out of the way. The bag's zipper hissed. "Everything's okay," she said after a moment. He could feel her pulling files out one by one. "Some of the folder covers are a little wet, but all the papers inside are fine. Buddy, you lay these out in the back, on top of all the food boxes, so they dry."

"My book—" The amnesiac panicked, hearing all the files rustle up and away.

"It's here," Dr. Avanthikar said, and laid the heavy binder in his lap. He clutched it to his chest. Dr. Avanthikar touched the cover gently between his forearms. "I never thought I'd see this again," she said.

"I added—I researched as much as I could before we lost the internet here. Then I stole encyclopedias from the school nearby. I added as much as I could."

"Tell the story of Chhaya again," Buddy whispered, now back in front of the amnesiac, his voice low, as if he'd squatted down to the same height so he could see the cover of the binder where the elephant's face was.

"Buddy—" Dr. Avanthikar began.

"Please," he protested. "He always does it when I'm afraid."

"It's okay." The amnesiac grimaced. His hands scrambled weakly at the pages, turning them to the right place. He didn't need to see to know where the page he sought was. He knew them all so well he could do it by memory alone.

"Just until Downtown finds the medicine," Dr. Avanthikar said to him.

The amnesiac felt Buddy's knee press against his own as Buddy settled to listen, sitting close so that he could hover over the book as well. The amnesiac put his finger down on the page, on the hand-drawn image of Chhaya that Hemu had pasted there. He knew it was in the right place. "Sanjna—" he began. The pain washed over him, a paralyzing wave. "Sanjna wanted to run away and hide from her husband, Surya, god of the sun, for even though she loved him, his brightness was too great for her to bear. It seared her eyes and burned her skin, and she could not even look upon him without being blinded." He tried to swallow the agony. It was so overwhelming, he thought he might throw up again.

"Before she escaped, Sanjna took off her shadow and made it into a likeness of herself, and named it Chhaya, which means shadow," Dr. Avanthikar said suddenly. The amnesiac felt her hand on his shoulder and leaned gratefully into it. His finger pointed at Hemu's scrawled text, sliding from word to word by memory, and she picked up where he had left off. "She commanded Chhaya to stay by Surya's side, always in her place, and fled. Even though Chhaya was born that very moment and had not lived the childhood and youth that Sanjna had, she still remembered everything from Sanjna's life—the names of all their servants, where all the belongings were in the palace, Surya's favorite dishes—because that is the place where memories are stored. In shadows." She leaned closer. "She remembered so much, even the great Surya was fooled."

"What happened?" Buddy asked, the same way he did every time.

"For years, Surya believed Chhaya was really Sanjna. He even made a son with her—the god Shani. Perhaps if he had never found out that Sanjna had deceived him, he would have spent the rest of eternity with Chhaya, never knowing Sanjna had fled. But one night, when Surya dimmed the lanterns and pulled Chhaya into the bed-chamber, he removed Chhaya's shoes, and suddenly she began to float—because a shadow is weightless. Without her shoes, she had nothing to anchor her to the ground. Then Surya knew that she was a shadow, and not the real Sanjna."

The amnesiac suddenly heard a soft clink of glass on glass—the vials from their first-aid kit. The pain erupted again in anticipation until he felt as though he was spinning in place. The binder creaked beneath his hands as he clutched it.

"What's happening?" Buddy asked. The sound grew mercifully closer.

"Any of these?" Downtown interrupted softly. "I can read the labels but—" She gulped, unsettled. "I don't know what they mean anymore."

Fabric rustled as Buddy hugged her. The story was forgotten, as quickly as it was remembered. For once, the amnesiac didn't care at all.

"This one is fine," Dr. Avanthikar said to Downtown. "The pain is going to get worse before it gets better." He realized she was now speaking to him—a gentle, commanding tone. The same one she'd used with Hemu. "So I'm going to put you to sleep for a few hours now."

The amnesiac tried to nod. His skin prickled as it waited for a needle. Every cell in his body begged for the chemical numbness, the empty sleep that would take him away from the agony. "Please—" he managed.

"Don't worry," she said. She pressed the book more firmly into his grip. "I'll keep watch over them all."

# ORLANDO ZHANG

IT STARTED RAINING AGAIN, AND IT RAINED FOR FOUR DAYS straight, until Ory thought they were all going to go insane from the constant wet. Then it stopped as suddenly as it had begun. The ground dried up so fiercely the mud started to crack. Heat wafted off the roads in sweltering, rippling waves, burning every inch of skin that wasn't covered. Ory kept waiting to see something on the horizon he thought was real and turned out to be a mirage, but nothing that ever materialized out of that shimmering mirror was a hallucination. Just a memory, badly mangled.

There was no time to think in the day, but at night, there was plenty of time. It was so hot he couldn't sleep—he would lay shirtless on the grass, sweat beading over his upper lip, listening to everyone else snore. It reminded him of Elk Cliffs. It reminded him of Max.

He wished he could tell her about that last day in D.C. About the Red King—who he really was, and that Ory had freed him. He wished he could tell her that Imanuel had also died. He thought she'd want to know, wherever she was. If she remembered Paul and Imanuel at all anymore.

Even in the heat, Ahmadi and Malik still went out to scout each morning, with double the water and long sleeves and hoods to shade from the sun. On the worst day, before they came back, the army had stopped for the evening an hour early, the men and horses too tired to continue. Ory was in the third carriage, making sure the corners of the tarp were still tightly folded around the books. Holmes began to whinny before the soldiers could see them, and then Ahmadi and Malik appeared on the horizon, shoulders hunched and clothes crisped with streaks of salt.

"Still all clear ahead?" Ory asked.

"So far," Malik said once they'd dismounted. "The whole country is empty. Just fields. Miles and miles of fields."

"And a funny sign," Ahmadi added between gulps of water from her canteen.

"A funny sign?" Ory asked.

"Someone had defaced it. Maybe the world's last graffiti," she said.

" 'Fuck shadows,' " he guessed.

Ahmadi laughed. "No, it was just a number. Just a blank sheet of metal with a number on it."

"What number?"

"I didn't look that closely," she said as she wiped her brow with the back of her arm. "It didn't mean anything. Twenty, or fifty, maybe."

The next day it finally rained again, washing out the oppressive heat like the dirt from clothes strung through a river.

THE CLOSER THEY GOT, THE HARDER IT WAS TO SLEEP. ORY spent the hours after dinner in one carriage or another, double-checking Imanuel's inventory. It seemed important—that they be able to present an accurate account to whoever or whatever might be in New Orleans. He worked so late that Ahmadi and Malik had started coming to find him in the carriages once it reached midnight, to tell him to stop and sleep at least a few hours before they had to be up again.

"You need assistants," Vienna said once as she studied Ory from behind her father's shoulder. The soldiers who had wandered conspicuously close to catch a peek at his progress all wandered twice as quickly away.

"I'll manage." Ory smiled. "I'll count, you scout."

"Good deal," Vienna said. She saluted. "Go to bed, before your head falls off."

HIS HEAD STAYED ON, BARELY. THE SOLDIERS HAD STARTED whispering about the dark circles under his eyes, and he didn't help his case when he fell off the carriage the next day while trying to climb up the ladder. "Mondays, eh," Ory said as he dusted the ass of his pants off. They chuckled, but the concerned looks returned.

"General, you need a break," Original Smith finally said. "Not that I'm giving you orders."

"I know." Ory nodded. "Don't worry. I'll have a break once we get to New Orleans. We'll all have one."

"Amen to that," Original Smith said.

Ory made it safely onto the carriage that time, and settled in for the long ride.

That night he was in the middle of cataloging a biography stack when the knock came on the wooden door of the carriage, as usual. He opened it to see Ahmadi standing there, for once without her bow. She looked odd without it. Friendlier.

"Midnight already?" he asked.

"Eleven-thirty." Her voice was not soft, however. There was an extra layer of guardedness to her tone, as if to make up for the lack of her weapon. Of all the people in the army, she was the most frustrating. She had loved Paul and Imanuel, too. He wanted to grow close to her because of that—the way he'd become with Malik, Vienna, the Smiths—but it seemed like the more he got to know Ahmadi, the less he felt like he actually did.

Ory realized she was looking at the small stack of books beside his feet. "What's that?" she asked.

He looked down. It was a pile for Max. Every night that he spent in a carriage organizing the books, he couldn't help it—he set aside a few that he thought she would like the most. Just for a few hours, while he worked. Then he'd put them back in with the rest, scattering them so they were as unfindable as she. But for that short time he kept them for her, he felt like Max was there again. "Nothing," he said.

Ahmadi shrugged. "Well, good. Because it's lights-out."

"Okay. Almost done for the night."

"Ory." She sighed, a warning note in her voice.

He set the clipboard down and rubbed his eyes. "You know, why does everyone else around here get to go by their last name like a badass, and I have to go by my first name?"

"That's how you were introduced to us," she replied, and shrugged. "Imanuel and Paul went by their first names. Using last names was just a Malik thing for the troops—a holdover from his time as a cop before the Forgetting. He started calling the soldiers by their last names during training, and it caught on."

"Am I not one of the troops?" Ory insisted.

"You're the General."

"A general might be the head of the troops, but still a part of it," he argued.

"Vienna goes by her first name," Ahmadi said.

"Well, that's because then we'd have two Maliks. And she's just a teenager."

Ahmadi threw up her hands in surrender. "You want to be Zhang, Ory?" she asked. But he saw that the eye roll she threw him was joking, not annoyed. "Fine, you can be Zhang. Hand over the flashlight, *Zhang*. Don't make me fight you for it."

He knew she was serious about him stopping working, but she also had been smiling as she said it. The silly argument had put them both in a rare good mood—there was a hint of nervous teasing in her voice he hadn't heard before. Ory realized he was smiling, too.

*Zhang*. He considered it again as he picked up the flashlight, weighing his options. He tried not to look at the small stack of books. Ahmadi waited just outside the carriage, grin still lingering. Her dark eyes studied him intently.

*Zhang*. Yes, he liked it. He liked it very much. His hand tingled slightly as it began to withdraw, to tuck itself and the light playfully behind his back so she'd have to come closer if she wanted to take it.

He wasn't sure why the name had mattered so much. Was it more about gaining something to be one of them—or leaving something else behind?

Abruptly, he handed her the flashlight and stepped back into the new darkness of the carriage. "Good night," he said as he closed the door, to stop himself from thinking any further. He didn't want to think about anything at all anymore.

HELLO?

⏸

Hello?

⏸

This voice is mine. Did I make this for myself?

I sound different inside this small thing. So certain. Like I knew something I don't know now. I think I knew so many things. Now I don't know anything at all.

⏸

We are driving now. There are four of us. Me; a woman with very short hair, as if it was shaved off recently and then began to grow again; a man with a . . . an animal on his shoulder; and a woman with pale, wavy hair. There are things that make me think once there were more of us. Women's clothes that are too small for us, one backpack more than passengers. A huge dark mark of dried blood on the floor when none of us have wounds. Or maybe it's paint.

I think we are friends. They seem to think so, too. But were they not friends with you, Ory? Is that why you're not here? I can't find any sign of you. The backpack is not yours. There's a breast cloth inside—a cloth to hold the breasts close, for a woman. I can't remember the name. I don't want to look at the blood anymore. I don't think it's yours, but I don't want to ask any of them, because I don't want to know.

I feel . . . I'm not sure. It hurts, deep inside. When I stand, my head pounds and I grow dizzy, and my hands shake sometimes. Each day is worse. The others seem to have it, too. Sometimes the pain is so bad I just lay on the ground inside our big car, holding my middle, waiting for it to pass. I know there was something I used to do to stop this, but I don't know what.

Partway through the afternoon, the man with an animal living on his arm suddenly sat up and looked nervously at the woman with short hair, who was driving. "Where are we going?" he asked. The creature snarled and circled his biceps, dodging freckles.

The woman with short hair cocked her head, and then her eyes went wide, too. She pressed her foot down, and we all slid forward as the big car ground to a halt. "I don't know," she said.

"Should we keep going?" the golden-haired woman also in the backseat asked.

The man with an animal arm peered through the slats out the window. "Let's get out and look around," he said.

Outside, the air was sweet and warm. It smelled like honey and dust. I closed my eyes, but turned my face up so it could soak into my skin.

"We're on a road," the man observed.

"But heading for what?" the pale-haired woman asked.

"This," the driver said.

We all turned and saw her facing not the road, but the side of the big car instead.

"Oh," we all murmured at once. It was gigantic. The sun, the road, the big car, and its long, stretching shadow.

"This is you," I said, and pointed at a painted woman with a smooth head.

"And you," the man replied to me, and pointed at another woman with brown skin and a huge mass of tightly wound curls springing off her head in all directions. On another man, we could clearly see the black outline of an animal on his arm. The woman with pale hair was painted next to him. They looked at each other hesitantly. In the painting, they were holding hands.

There were others, too. But we didn't know who they were. I looked for you too, Ory, but I didn't see you there. Where are you?

"It's a message to stay on this big road until we find that," the driver finally pronounced. She pointed at a cluster of black and colored shapes at the end of the painting. "We have to go there."

"The Place," the blond woman said. She glanced at the animal-armed man, but neither of them moved closer to each other.

"Let's drive," the driver said.

⏸

Soft, floating water has started falling from the sky. Not as one great body, but in millions of tiny fragments. It acts like rain, but I know it's not—I remember that much. It glitters silver as it drops, so everything in front of us is shimmering. We're all crouched in the driver's cabin, peering out the front window to watch it.

"That's _____," the animal on the man's arm said, but I've already forgotten what the creature called it.

The driver figured out how to lower the window so that a slice of the outside sky reached into our moving home. We all stuck our hands out, mesmerized. Ory, you wouldn't believe—it was cold! So cold to the touch it burned when the little shards landed on our fingertips. It wasn't water at all. It was something else. The driver pulled her hand in at once, hissing in surprise, but I left mine out there. I cupped my palm to try to collect as many as possible. I endured it as long as I could—my hand was white fire! But then when I pulled it in, there were only a few little silver crystals there. The rest had vanished somehow, and my fingers were misted with a light, wet sheen.

"What's it called again?" I asked the creature on the man's arm again. It repeated the name, but it was gone from me once more as soon as I heard it.

❙❙

The road has been bumpy for miles now. I don't know why. I almost dropped this small plastic thing as I examined it. Beside me, a woman with very short hair is grimacing as she looks through the front window, and keeps pushing her feet against the floor.

"Wait," someone behind us said. I turned around. There was a person in the backseat—a man. He stood up and gripped the back of my chair. "Wait, where am I? Where are we going?"

"We—" the driver started to answer, but then she shook her head.

They both turned to me, but I shrugged also, feeling a tingle of fear start to rise in my chest. "I don't know either."

We slowed our house down until it stopped. The door was jammed, but the man pushed it open with the face of the beast living on his shoulder, and the three of us stepped out into the grass. So much green everywhere. It seemed like we had come from nowhere, and were going nowhere either.

"Do you think we did this?" the man asked. I turned away from the emerald forever to see him studying our moving house—the entire wall of it was one massive, breathtaking painting.

"We must have," the woman driving us said. "We must have made it to remind us."

The man brushed at his arm absently, as if the wind was tickling the skin. His fingers came away lightly tangled in a long strand of golden, silky hair.

"I keep finding them on my clothes," he shrugged, having no explanation. "I don't know why."

I climbed up the stairs after him, followed by the driving woman, who took another long look at the painting, to make sure it matched the road we were on.

"Do you think we've done this before?" I asked her over the breeze.

"Done what?"

"Forgotten where we were going, and then saw the painting and decided to follow it."

"I'm not sure. But yes, I think so," she said.

"How many times do you think it's happened?"

She licked her lips slowly as she stared off into the distance. "Maybe ten." She closed her eyes. "Maybe a thousand."

Before I ducked inside, I glanced back one more time, to make sure I hadn't missed it. But no—none of the people in the picture looked like you.

# MAHNAZ AHMADI

NAZ LEFT THE CAMP AT DAWN, LONG BEFORE MOST OF THE others were awake. She had orders from Malik to set out early with Original Smith and Dos to scout the road ahead of the army. She was to push all the way to Chattanooga, to see if the I-24 was still intact enough to allow them to cross through the ruins of the city rather than having to work five wooden-wheeled carriages through the uneven mountains.

"I want a loose triangle, twenty feet between each of us, on the ready at all times," she ordered as she secured her fiberglass bow across the back of her saddle. The black, liquid surface shimmered in the morning light.

"Yes, ma'am." The two Smiths saluted.

"Watch for mud," Malik said as he handed her a piece of jerky wrapped in a thin cloth. "Runoff from the mountains could make everything soft."

"I'll bring the horses back," Naz smiled down to him.

"Yourself too," he warned.

They set off at a canter, but soon they were trotting, then simply walking, picking their way through the firmest ground as the road narrowed, then fell off into nothing. At one point, her horse's hoof tipped something small and curved, and it rolled to the top of the grass and lay still—half a skull. Naz studied it as they passed, wondering why it looked so strange. It wasn't until she was almost past it that she realized it was because it had been child-sized. Its human no more than five. After that, she stopped looking so closely at the bones.

Dos checked the compass while Naz and Original Smith scanned the horizon with their bows. They had a few guns, but these were worth more at the caravan than with the scouts. Ory—Zhang, now—had argued with her several times to take at least one when she went out on forward duty, and wouldn't give up no matter how adamantly she refused. Other times, he seemed not to care at all. They would go days without speaking, but then suddenly every single thing she said to him would make the muscles in his jaw tighten as if he could barely manage the strain of being with them all. Other days she'd come back in from a ride covered in dust and want nothing more than to eat all the food in the camp and joke with Vienna by the fire, and he'd be beside her, practically teary-eyed with relief that she'd survived, begging her again to take a gun next time, any gun, to do it for him, please, that he could not lose another. Then the gears would abruptly shift again, and three days would go by before she realized she hadn't seen him since.

"Something at eleven o'clock," Dos whispered, her bow snapping up.

"Dinner," Original Smith said. "It's a deer."

The deer glanced up from grazing and froze, perfectly still as it stared at them. But Dos didn't let fly the arrow.

"Whoa," Naz finally said.

It was indeed a deer, but the head was wrong. From the roots of its bony antlers sprouted two small, unfurled sparrow wings, a feathered crown.

"Don't shoot it," she murmured.

"It's the same kind of thing as that weird rabbit-pig-frog animal," Original Smith said as he lowered his own bow, even though it wasn't. Those little creatures were funny, stupid; the deer, on the other hand, was not. The deer was terrifying, because it was almost beautiful.

"Fuck it, whatever it is." Dos spat, and crossed herself. "There better not be another disappearing-reappearing lake nearby."

"Enough." Naz broke her stare at the strange creature, and swatted Dos's thin arm with the tail of an arrow to draw her attention back to the path. It was newly made, the wood a lighter color. Each night when they broke for camp, she'd been teaching the soldiers how to make them. They needed all they could get. "Forget the deer. Let's keep it moving." She lowered her voice. "I don't like it here. Something's off."

The deer started when the horses began to walk again, wings disappearing, folding tight against its head as it dashed into the underbrush. Naz saw Original Smith and Dos look at each other as the disturbed foliage where it had run grew still again. She could see they felt it, too.

THE ON-RAMP TO THE FREEWAY WAS DESTROYED, SO THEY stood in the parking lot of a ruined donut shop, staring out across the wreckage of the city. Tiny pieces of ash billowed in the air in front of them, even at such a distance.

"Anyone know what we're looking at?" Naz asked.

"Downtown?" Dos offered. She shivered, even though it was much warmer there than it was in D.C. "The downtown is west of the I-24, right?"

"I've never been to Chattanooga," Original Smith murmured.

"It doesn't matter anyway," Naz said.

It didn't. It really didn't. Chattanooga was on fire. As far as they could see, north to south, a raging blaze curdled the skyline, yellow and red flames spewing black clouds that spread for miles.

"How long do you think it's been like that?" Original Smith asked.

"I have no idea," Naz said. They watched it for a little while longer. "Maybe since the first day."

She couldn't imagine what could cause a fire that size, or cause it to burn so long. Whatever it was, there was nothing to do. There was no Chattanooga anymore.

"What do we do now?" Dos asked. "We can't take the freeway through that. Can the carriages manage on terrain until we can find a smaller road around?"

"One thing at a time," Naz said.

Somehow it was hard to look away. "Pretty," Original Smith finally said. Somewhere just north of the last standing skyscrapers, an explosion sent a glittering wave of molten glass through the square maze of streets. "Is that a weird thing to say?"

Naz shook her head slowly, transfixed. She understood what he meant. "I wonder if it'll ever burn out," she said.

Just then a spear—painted red and adorned with crimson strips of fabric—punched itself through the front of Dos's throat.

# THE ONE WHO GATHERS

WHEN HE WOKE, THE PAIN WAS NOT BETTER. IT WAS SO TERRI-
ble, at first the amnesiac couldn't even cry out. When he finally could,
he bit his tongue instead, and tried to sense the state of things without
his sight. Dr. Avanthikar and the shadowless were on the other side
of the basement, where they could talk without disturbing him too
much. He sat up as gently as possible. The pain whittled itself from
acid into a spear in his skull. He squeezed the Gajarajan book in his
hands to keep from moaning until the spear dissolved into acid again.

"—the pre-storm," Marie was saying softly. "The hurricane is
likely just beginning to touch down now."

"It's too late," Downtown added. "Even if the facility upstairs has
finished collapsing, we can't cross the city. We'll be swept away in the
floods."

"Damnit," Curly growled. A hand smacked plastic, three sharp
bursts. "Fucking—fucking *things*."

"Flashlights," Downtown said, filling in the word he'd lost.

The amnesiac wondered if his shadow was blind the way he was
now. Or could it always see, even though he no longer could, and
never would again? He wondered if he'd know it now if his shadow
ever left—would he feel it immediately, or would he wander around
for some unknowable amount of time without it before someone else
noticed and told him?

The amnesiac imagined it as it would be on the wall behind him, in
the same posture, listening to the same conversation in companion-
able silence. Dr. Avanthikar was arguing with Marie now, debating
the statistical probability of leaving and dying versus staying and dying.
Downtown was calling for a vote. The amnesiac took a deep breath,

imagined his shadow doing the same. Its charcoal outline expanding and contracting. That is, if Curly had gotten the flashlight back on again—if there was any light to see it by, or if it was still pitch-dark. There was no way for him to know at all.

Whatever the hurricane morphed into would probably destroy New Orleans and kill them, but there was something else, too. He could feel it. Something else was growing—or coming. The Gajarajan book in his hands was comfortingly heavy. He slowly turned the pages, sliding his fingers in and easing each leaf over. Just like Surya and Chhaya's story, he knew what article, what picture, what scribbled notes from his old friend were beneath his palm every time he set it down. Pieces of *Peter Pan*; clippings about Hemu Joshi from *The Maharashtra Times*; mathematics; astronomy; entries from Hemu's own fractured, desperate diary; more excerpts from the Rigveda; and most of all, by far—photographs of the great elephant himself at Guruvayur temple, and stories of its incredible, inexplicable feats of memory. Hundreds of these pages, read over and over until they were memorized, compared to a handful of notecards about the amnesiac's former life that he'd lost long ago and never cared about anyway. He knew Gajarajan more intimately than he would ever know his old self. It almost felt like he was more elephant than man.

Eventually, the amnesiac realized he was barely listening to the others. He was being drawn in by something else, a subtle feeling he'd not noticed that he actually *had* noticed at first, and then all of a sudden did. It was like waking up from a dream about the ocean and realizing you were floating in water.

Something was happening.

"Dr. Avanthikar," he murmured, but she didn't hear him. She kept talking. "Dr. Avanthikar," he repeated, still sitting, facing whichever way he'd been positioned when he was helped to the floor. "Doctor."

"No, you need rest, not—" she started, but when she finally turned to face him, everything dropped. Her voice, the anger, whatever the rest of them had been arguing about.

"I don't know," the amnesiac said at last. He didn't know. There was a feeling, but without his eyes, every sensation was nonsense. But Dr. Avanthikar was still frozen in place, still completely silent. The other shadowless weren't speaking anymore either. In the whole room, almost no one breathed.

If it had been only that he had become shadowless, they would have moved by now. They would have come over to console him. They were long used to seeing shadows disappear. But something was different. The seconds crawled by. They remained paralyzed by their sight. "What should I do?" the amnesiac finally asked.

"Nothing," Dr. Avanthikar said. He heard her take a small step forward. No one else moved. The amnesiac did nothing. He waited. The air in the room felt almost solid. "It's okay," Dr. Avanthikar said softly.

"What?"

But she wasn't speaking to him, he realized. "It's okay," she said again.

"Yes," he agreed, trying to sound convincing. The wall behind him where his shadow was smoothly stretched felt as though it had expanded to contain everything in the world. "It's okay." The amnesiac tried to hold as still as he could.

"Did you see that?" Dr. Avanthikar gasped. She was beyond realizing he couldn't have. Something had gripped her, gripped them all—terror or wonder. "Did you see?" she whispered. She couldn't say anything else. They all waited, bound in place, staring.

And then it came again. The sensation that he had turned his head to look around when he had not moved at all.

"*Did you see?*" Dr. Avanthikar whispered again, close to madness.

A voice that did not come from the amnesiac's mouth, but sounded very much the same, said, "I know how we can stop the hurricane."

# ORLANDO ZHANG

THE NOON SUN WAS SWELTERING, AND THERE WASN'T A cloud in the sky. On horseback, Malik reached up to take his newly made bow off his shoulder and hook it on the saddle instead, but when his bare fingers touched the hammered metal tips that kept the string in place, he cursed and let go on instinct. The bow slid off his shoulders and smacked the dirt.

"Damnit!" he growled. "It's hotter than hell!"

From her horse beside Zhang's carriage, Vienna clicked her tongue. "Ahmadi isn't going to like that," she said. "He better clean the string well."

They had been talking about Ahmadi as the carriages ambled along. "When did she move to the United States?" Zhang asked. She'd mentioned Tehran a few times, but he'd gotten the sense that it was a thing she looked at only from the periphery, never head on, the way he now did with Max. It was just too painful.

"When she was about my age, I think," Vienna answered as her horse flicked its head.

Zhang tried to imagine what that would have been like, to move from that far so young. Now it was impossible. Without shadows, Iran seemed like a place that was so unreachable from where they were, it didn't exist anymore. Maybe it actually didn't.

"She wanted to go to the Olympics for archery," Vienna continued. "Apparently the best coach in the world was living in Boston before the Forgetting. When she joined our army, she trained everyone. She's started teaching us all how to make bows and arrows."

"You can shoot as well?" Zhang asked.

"Well, guns are easier. But I'm getting better."

"You'll have to teach me then," he said.

"Definitely!" she cried, and then grew suddenly bashful at her outburst. "Are you also from, like, China or something?" She asked.

"No—Arlington," Zhang replied. He'd almost said *we*. *We came from Arlington.* There was no *we* anymore. No Max. "Well, before that, Portland," he finally said. "I grew up in Portland, Oregon."

"With Paul," Vienna added.

He nodded, smiling.

"I grew up in D.C.," she continued. "I've never left."

"You're leaving now," he offered, but it sounded flat. It wasn't the same. There was nothing left to see.

But Vienna wasn't looking at Zhang anymore. Her eyes were trained in the distance. "Our scouts" was all she said. He looked, too.

They knew something was wrong as soon as the scouts crested the horizon. First, there were only two horses and riders, not three. And second, those two horses were running. Not in the easy, loping gait they used to cover miles at a time, but galloping—heads low, ears flat against their gleaming, sweaty necks as the earth churned beneath their hooves.

"Code red!" Malik yelled from behind. It was what they'd used to shout to warn of an impending attack on the Iowa, but it worked for the caravan, too. Chaos erupted. Soldiers on the carriages all steered their horses closer together and whipped them into a rumbling sprint, and the ones riding astride the carriages raced out to meet the two incoming survivors, bows drawn.

*Which two?* Zhang wanted to yell to Malik, even though it was wrong. *Is one of them Ahmadi?* He was supposed to care about the books, not the soldiers, and if he was supposed to care about the soldiers, he was supposed to care about them equally. Zhang craned his neck over the back of his carriage, but they were crashing along so swiftly it was impossible to get a good look. Malik was shouting for the first half of the carriages to speed up and the second half to slow down, so that he could work Zhang's into the center, for protection.

His horse screamed as it flew by. Zhang's driver whipped Holmes in terror until her flanks started to sparkle red. He yelled for Zhang to pick up his shotgun. Their carriage edged up next to the gap in the line to wedge themselves in, and Holmes snarled at the horse of the carriage beside her, who was running wild, unable to feel the reins anymore. She slammed her head into its neck and bit hard until it shrieked and gave way.

"I'm here!" Zhang shouted to Malik. "I'm here! Close the gap!"

Malik's horse thundered down the line again, from front to back, Malik waving his arm for all of them to bunch tighter. Just then, the two surviving riders reached the carriage line.

"Ahmadi!" Zhang cried. She was there. She was alive. He didn't even see who was the other. Their small cavalry surrounded them to bring them back into the caravan safely. And on their heels loomed the reason they'd been fleeing so fast.

"*Reds!*" someone screamed.

The monsters had found them. They'd grown too confident they'd outrun them, and now the shadowless had caught up—hundreds of them. The horizon gleamed crimson. They were on foot, on bicycles, on motorcycles that had been reimagined to run without fuel, some clinging to vicious living gargoyles they'd pulled off the old buildings in D.C. and spent their last precious memories to awaken. All of them probably had just one recollection left, but it was the same one. Kill.

"Fire at will!" Malik yelled.

Ahmadi was like a surgeon with her tools. She drew arrow after arrow without moving anything except for her right arm, even at a gallop, lining them up for each next unlucky Red without her eye ever leaving the center aim of that long, glittering arc. The fiberglass bent gracefully, and almost as soon as she'd notched an arrow, it would whiz out in a deadly, hissing blur. Another Red would huff like the wind had been knocked out of him. And then fall.

Horses trampled limbs, bodies were torn up as they rolled under motorcycles. Shots rang out. Behind him, Zhang heard one of their soldiers wail, and then something hit the ground and was left in their dusty wake. He struggled to aim the gun his driver had given him. Ahmadi rode by, a stream of blood coming down one side of her face, still firing. She had Malik's quiver strapped over her other shoulder now, and Malik had an axe. He raised it up, sharp edge glinting. His arm was a braid of veins and sweat. Zhang looked away as the screams erupted.

"General!" Zhang's driver grabbed his arm. "What is *that*?"

Zhang turned to look ahead, where the land sloped upward on the left in a long hill. Something covered the whole crest, row after row, fluttering in hundreds of pieces. Everything was white.

"Are those people?" Zhang asked him.

"They *are*!" he cried. They both leaned forward, straining to see across the distance. They were looking for the same thing. If they were people—were they shadowed or shadowless?

"Shadows!" Zhang yelled, to alert the others. His heart swelled. "They have shadows!" He waved desperately from the top of his carriage as they thundered closer and closer. The wind sent ripples through their strange ivory robes. "Faster!" he shouted to his driver. The Reds pursued, relentless, uncaring, but Zhang's soldiers began to cheer. There was a whole army of shadowed people, standing there as if they'd heard the Iowan army's cries and were waiting for their carriages to sweep past, to cut the Reds off and save them. Zhang just had to reach them.

But then they started to move. Long before the Iowans' first carriage was anywhere near their lines. They poured down the hillside slowly, sweeping out in front like a large white fan, simple weapons pointed outward. It was a strange position—far more difficult for the carriages to navigate through. At first Zhang didn't understand. Then he did.

"Ambush!" he screamed. A cry of horror went up all around him as everyone else realized at the same time that the strangers weren't there to help them at all. They were there to do exactly the opposite.

"What do we do?" Zhang's driver asked hysterically.

"Don't stop!" he yelled as loud as he could, so the rest could hear over the screams of the Reds. "Keep your head down and push through!"

Zhang and his driver both ducked as low as possible behind the wooden windbreak in front of their seat as the horses charged. They were close enough now to see the ones in white clearly—men and women wrapped in layers and layers of billowing, pristine fabric. Their front line dug itself in and prepared to receive Zhang's army like a wall of death.

In front, Holmes screamed like a falcon diving for a kill. "Don't stop!" Zhang ordered one more time when the first carriage was almost there. Then his own thrashed wildly as they hit too, and he heard the sound of humans howling as bones broke beneath hooves and wheels. Iowan guns boomed, lightning flashing against the bright day.

"But they have shadows!" Zhang's driver said breathlessly as they turned to make sure the rest of their line had made it through. "I don't understand—they have shadows!"

All around, the ones in white behind their front line started closing on the carriages as they crashed through the crowd. The Reds flew into a fury, attacking whatever was closest, Iowan and strange people in white. Still the robed ones came, unstoppable, like some kind of unfeeling, nightmarish hive mind.

Vienna pulled Zhang from the stupor of his terror. "Fire!" she was screaming at him from her horse. "General—the ones in white— they lit one on fire!" She pointed backward as her mare pushed to match Holmes's sprint. Zhang jerked around, clutching the top of his carriage. The ones in white were howling now, shrieking almost triumphantly.

He saw. Flames licked off the roof of the last carriage in their galloping procession. Dark smoke began to fill the air. What had these strange newcomers done? *Why?* Around them, the Reds wavered, half resolved to just kill everyone, Iowan or white ghost, the other half mesmerized by the familiar roar of the flames and the ones who had created it. "Malik, the books!" Zhang yelled at him as he rode by again. His entire right half was covered in glistening red syrup from other bodies. The axe shone. He almost looked like the Red King.

Ahmadi was there suddenly as well, eyes wild with terror. "The carriage is on fire!" she cried.

"We can't stop!" Malik said as his horse strained to keep pace with Zhang. "If we stop, we'll lose them all!"

Zhang turned around again. The soldier driving the burning cart was yelling frantically at the rest of them, calling for rescue. Zhang started waving him forward, then kicked a white-robed warrior climbing up his seat ladder. A flying knife barely missed his forehead as the man fell to his death. "How many?" Zhang shouted to Malik.

"With these—whoever the fuck they are, ten to one, at least," he said.

"Can we win?"

Malik swung his axe, flinging a sheet of blood into the wind. "The Red King and these white ghosts should have sent twice as many," he said. He raised the blade. "For Imanuel!" he roared.

"Imanuel!" the cry returned, from all around the field.

The rally spurred Zhang. He was shit in a fight, but that didn't matter. Malik protected the soldiers, the General protected the books. "You handle the battle, I'll handle the fire!"

"No, leave it!" Malik yelled, but the engulfed carriage had almost reached Zhang's own, close enough that maybe he could do the stupidest thing of his life. "Zhang!" he cried.

"Malik, go! Just keep them away!" Zhang shouted. Malik finally nodded and raised his axe again. Zhang ducked back into his carriage and rummaged around. There was some water, but not enough. Not enough to stop a blaze like that.

"I don't know how much longer I have!" the soldier driving the burning carriage shouted as he lurched into the empty space where

Malik had just been. His horse was soaked, as though it had plunged through rain, sweat streaming off it. It didn't understand why it couldn't outrun the flames. The whites of its eyes glinted in terror.

"Stay!" Zhang yelled. "I'm coming over! As long as we can last!"

"What?" the soldier cried, face pale with shock. But he didn't jump—he kept the reins and gritted his teeth.

"Keep as close as you can," Zhang said to his own driver, and then turned to the one commanding the carriage on fire. "You watch the horse," he shouted to him, and pointed at the half-wild beast galloping in front of them. "When we're out of time, you jump down onto its back, unhook the yoke, and ride off!"

"What about you?" the soldier cried.

"I—" Zhang looked at his driver, struggling to keep their own wagon within reachable distance as they flew at breakneck speed. Behind, the Reds cried out all at once, a shrill and keening scream that purged everything in Zhang's mind for an instant. It was the sound of what their color meant, if a color could speak—a dedication to a singular, absolute goal. The horses reeled, hysterical. "I'll jump back to the first carriage!"

The soldier stared at Zhang for a stunned moment, but then nodded. "Yes, sir!" he finally yelled back, and saluted with the hand not on the reins. He stuck it out to help try to grab at Zhang once he was in midair.

"On three!" Zhang cried.

WE ARE GOING TO THE PLACE. I DON'T KNOW THE NAME. BUT there is a painting of it on the side of the big moving house. I saw it just now, when we all climbed outside, because we didn't know why we were in the house or where we were going. Then we saw the painting, and the one who makes the house move said, "We should go there." So we are going there.

We are going, but I don't know why. But knowing where is enough, because it is all we have. There are some things that just can't be known.

Maybe I said this before. It is a strange way to be. To do things because something suggests you might have done them before. There is no way to know reasons this way. You can only do, not understand.

I think before, I used to understand. I don't know how this could be. But there are too many things we see to be an accident. These shapes, pictures on flat sheets of metal that stick out of the ground—someone made them once, for some reason. But they all look different, which means there must be meaning. Otherwise would they all be the same? Maybe when I looked at them, I never understood. Maybe they are not for us at all.

**❚❚**

ORY—

HOW

PLEASE, CAN YOU HEAR ME? I DON'T—

I THINK IT'S HAPPENING NOW, ORY. IT'S HAPPENING.

Ory! My Ory. I have so much to say to you, but no time left to say it. Everything hurts—it's a horrible, empty stretching. Every moment is a storm, and I'm in the center, unraveling. It's so hard to breathe now. Do you go to the same place when you forget as when you die? I wish memories were stored anywhere else, anywhere at all—my eyes, my fingertips, the soles of my feet. Everyone is so afraid of losing their body when they die, but a body is worthless. A body remembers nothing at all. Nothing at all. It's not what's terrifying to lose.

I have seconds left, I can tell. Just seconds.

I want to say something important for the very last thing I remember, something profound and eternal. But there's so little left, and I'm scared to think of any of it at all, in case I do damage to its form. Most of all, I'm afraid to think of you, even though I can't help it. Where did you go, Ory? Why aren't we together? Was it my fault, or yours? What reason could I have to ever leave you?

I'm not ready. I'm not ready, I'm not ready, I'm not ready. I refuse to forget. It took all of me, but I refuse to let it have the last thing, which is you. Ory. I remember you. I remember your name. I remember I touched your face, on your eyebrow above your scar; I remember a football; I remember night and a mountain; I remember you gave me this speaking machine, but I don't know why; I remember a dark room, and writing numbered rules by candlelight, and you cried— why did you cry?

I remember there is something we always say to each other when things are good, when things are bad, when the sun comes up in the morning, when one day it won't. When there's nothing else left. I want to tell you that I remember what we say.

I REMEMBER, ORY.

FIF—

PART IV

# ORLANDO ZHANG

IN TOTAL, THEY LOST NINE SOLDIERS IN THE AMBUSH. AND the last carriage—everything inside but what Zhang had managed to grab and throw to the other driver.

*Only one,* Zhang kept trying to tell himself, between spells of unconsciousness. *Only one carriage.* But it felt like they'd lost them all.

When he finally opened his eyes, he realized they had stopped moving. They had stopped a long time ago—the beams across the low wooden ceiling had finished creaking and settled. And there were no flames. *It wasn't the same carriage,* he realized then. He was back in his own.

"We won," Malik's voice said somewhere near when Zhang tried to focus his gaze. "Killed every last Red, and drove off the rest of the ones in white. We're safe now."

Zhang tried to nod. He meant to ask about Ahmadi, if she was all right. "Max?" His lips whispered instead. He faded again before he heard the answer.

THE NEXT TIME HE CAME TO, IT WAS ALMOST DARK. ZHANG was leaning against someone as he sat in the grass, elbows propped on his knees. *Ahmadi.* He could hear her voice beside his ear, telling him they were almost done. He couldn't hear the other, the one that had always been there to help him before. Zhang tried to understand what Ahmadi meant about the pain. Then he finally did. Oh, the *pain.*

"That's all we can do for now," Fenton said. "I'll dress them."

Zhang opened his eyes and looked at what remained of his hands. They were terrifying. Purple and black, and covered in monstrous, boiling welts. Just the air on them made his eyes sting in agony.

"Are these third degree?" Malik asked.

"I don't know," Fenton admitted sheepishly. He was the soldier with the most medical experience, three months of paramedic training before the Forgetting, but it wasn't very much. He checked the water he'd boiled to see if it was cool. Vienna was carefully opening packages of gauze from one of their first-aid kits. "I think so. Blisters mean third degree, I think."

"It'll be okay," Zhang said, mostly to convince himself. He was wide awake now. His hands looked so bad, he was already starting to panic that a few days from now, when they were infected from the dirt of the road, they'd have to amputate. Or try.

"We just have to keep them clean," Fenton said.

"You shouldn't have done it," Ahmadi murmured.

"I saved sixteen books," Zhang said helplessly. Sixteen books, two hands. Which was worth more? Sixteen books you could choose, sixteen this mysterious Gathering One might want, that was different from sixteen books chosen at random. The ones Zhang had saved he'd selected not by value, but by proximity—plunging his hands into fire, again and again, grasping for the nearest smoking page. He had no idea what he'd taken. He was just grateful that the carriage that had caught fire wasn't the one that held Paul's book. If that had been inside, Zhang probably would have died trying to reach it.

"It was noble," Malik finally said. "Even if it was stupid."

ONLY ONE CARRIAGE, ZHANG KEPT REPEATING. HE TRIED TO convince himself it was a victory.

"Only one," Ahmadi echoed later that evening. They were all trying to do the same thing, it seemed. She sat down beside him and Malik on the grass, holding both Zhang's and her small portions of dinner.

"There are still four carriages left," Zhang said to her, and tried to smile.

"Exactly. There are still four carriages left," she stammered, repeating his words. "Four." But then she gasped raggedly.

Zhang didn't understand what had happened at first. It took him a few seconds to realize she'd burst into tears.

"I'm sorry," she said. She set the plates down quickly and jammed the heels of her palms into her eyes, but failed to stop the sobs. She pressed her face into Zhang's shoulder. He wrapped his arms around her awkwardly, unable to grip her with his bandaged hands, and held her like that until she quieted. Her tears slowly warmed the sleeve of his shirt as they soaked in, until that side of him didn't feel cold at all.

"Who were they anyway?" he asked at last, after Ahmadi had settled back onto the grass beside him, hat pulled low over her eyes. "Not the Reds. The other ones, in white."

Malik sighed. "We're not sure yet. Still working on making the one we captured talk."

"We have a hostage?" Zhang asked.

"You need to take it easy," Ahmadi started, but Zhang was already up, stumbling toward the carriages.

BEHIND THEIR WAGONS, SEVERAL SOLDIERS STOOD GUARD around a small, crumpled shape beneath a tree. The man had been forced into a sit with his back pressed against the bark, and then a rope looped several times around both him and the tree at chest level, binding his arms to his sides. Two bare feet stuck out from beneath his robes, resting limply in the grass. Below them, a shadow lay.

"The hostage," Malik said when they reached him.

The captured man looked up at Zhang with exhausted, defiant eyes. He was covered in so much blood from the fight that his once-white clothes were red.

"Do you have a name?" Zhang asked.

"Truth," the man replied.

Zhang sighed. "Fine. All of you, in the white clothes—who are you with?"

"We are all truth." The man coughed, and recovered. "Truth is

Transcendence," he said grandly. A grin spread across his bloody teeth as he waited for Zhang's reaction. After a few moments, it began to fade. "A shame that you have not yet heard the news of the joy our enlightened future will bring."

Malik spat into the grass, near the man's foot.

The hostage's eyes narrowed. "Denial of the truth does not stop the truth."

"Forget truth for a moment," Zhang said. Terrible images from the fight flooded over him—the Reds, their own desperate sprint to escape, seeing an army of alabaster robes appear on the horizon, hoping for help, and then the horror of realizing they were sweeping down to attempt the exact opposite. "Why did you attack us?"

"Because you were attacking the Transcended."

Zhang blinked. He looked at Ahmadi, then Malik, then back to the hostage. "You mean the *Reds*? The crazed shadowless horde that chased us across the countryside to murder us?" He checked again, in case he had been mistaken, but he had been right—the hostage still had his shadow. "Why would you try to kill *shadowed survivors*?"

"We do not kill shadowed people," the man said. "We welcome them to journey with us toward Transcendence. We only kill enemies of the Transcended."

Malik breathed out, a long slow gust. "These guys are the *real deal*," he said.

"Insults from the ignorant mean nothing."

Zhang shook his head. "You all . . ." It sounded too crazy. "You all are *trying* to lose your shadows? You're *trying* to forget?"

"We're trying to transcend," the hostage said.

For a moment, all of them were too stunned to speak. Finally Ahmadi crossed her arms. "Well, if the Red King is what transcending looks like, count me out," she said.

"The Red King?"

"A violent, terrifying shadowless that took over D.C. and made all those others," Zhang answered. "Don't worry about it now," he added when he saw the thrill in the hostage's expression overwhelm his exhaustion. "No point to head north to swear fealty to him. He's dead."

"Sacrilege," he hissed.

"Should have told him the Red King was still alive and kicking so they'd leave their stronghold and run off to their deaths," Malik smiled at the hostage.

"This isn't our stronghold," the hostage said. "Transcendence's spread is unstoppable. But our forces are far beyond our currently settled borders. We've been traveling south for months, after an omen told us to go. A perversion of the Great One's work—shadowless that betrayed us. The false rumors have gone on long enough, and something must be done about them. We march for salvation."

"You mean war," Zhang said. *Again.*

"I mean salvation. The last showdown."

"Do all of your people so easily reveal your battle plans?" Ahmadi asked. "We didn't even have to hit you yet."

"Oh, I'm not revealing anything," the hostage said. "It's obvious we're heading to the same place. Where else could any of us be going this far south, except New Orleans?"

Hearing him say the name made Zhang shudder.

"What should also be obvious is how much more quickly we'll reach the city than your massive, slow force," Ahmadi said. "And how much forewarning that will mean for them."

The hostage shrugged as best he could with the ropes around him. Pain lined his face for a moment. "It doesn't matter. If this false prophet is even half as strong as the lies claim, they already know we're coming. There's nothing they can do to stop Transcendence. When you see what they're doing there, you'll understand. You'll beg to join us."

Zhang had no idea how many people were in New Orleans—if New Orleans was there at all—or how many of Transcendence there were, but judging by the number of troops they sent to help the Reds, and how unconcerned with their loss the hostage seemed to be, there was a greater chance that they were a credible threat to the city than not.

"Well, we'll have to agree to disagree," Zhang finally said. The phrase struck Malik and Ahmadi as funny, and they chuckled behind him. Zhang tried to ignore how utterly convinced the man in death-splattered white robes before him seemed. *We're right,* he told himself. *We are.* It was true that none of the stories he'd heard about New Orleans quite matched up, but it was also true that none of them had been warnings either. That had to mean something. It meant more than nothing, at least. "From what we've heard from other survivors, and we've heard quite a bit, this 'false prophet' doesn't sound like such a bad guy."

"That's because all you've heard are ignorant rumors. We know the truth. The Creature must fall, for the good of the world."

"The Creature," Zhang repeated. "There's one I haven't heard before."

"It's the true one. The only name that matters," the hostage replied. His eyes began to dim. That all-too-familiar faraway look. It was only then that Zhang realized some of the carnage on his clothes was the man's own, not remnants from the fight.

"He's bleeding," Zhang gasped. "Somewhere from the abdomen."

"No." The hostage coughed.

"But—"

"I refuse treatment. The sooner I'm free of you, the better."

Zhang looked at Malik, who shrugged helplessly. *Why waste medical supplies on someone we don't really want to save, and who doesn't want to be saved either?* his expression asked.

"Don't you want to live to see New Orleans?" Zhang asked the hostage as the rise and fall of his chest became more shallow.

He used his last conscious breath to answer. "I already know what's there. And I will stop the Creature as part of Transcendence or not go at all. I will not let myself be forced to ride with you as you head into your doom."

# MAHNAZ AHMADI

THE NEXT DAY, THEY KNEW THEY COULDN'T WAIT ANY LONGER.

"You've got it?" Zhang asked. The tremor in his voice betrayed his fear.

"I've got it," Malik said, clamping down even harder on his modified choke hold. "I'll keep you still until it's done."

"It'll be quick," Fenton added grimly.

Naz sat in front of Zhang, blocking his view of his hands. She had thought they might be out of the woods, but two days after the ambush, one of his fingers had started to die. The little one, on the left side. The fire had just burned too much. By the end of the next day, it was clear that they would have to amputate it after all, before it took the rest of his hand.

"If I faint after, just throw me in one of the carriages and keep moving. I'll come to soon enough," Zhang said.

"You need *rest*," Naz argued again, for what felt like the hundredth time. She hated that she'd said it. The tone of her voice made her wince. She'd tried to keep him in the same place she kept Imanuel and Malik and the rest of the soldiers—she couldn't have another Paul, another Vienna. Another Rojan. But it was a losing battle.

"It's all right," Fenton said. "As long as he stays inside a covered carriage and keeps the bandages clean, we can continue on."

It was settled then. "Just keep looking at me," Naz said to him. She slipped a hand against his cheek and clenched her teeth. She waited for him to scream.

THEY STOPPED FOR ALMOST NOTHING AFTER THAT. THEY ALL began eating just once a day, and each night, everyone slept straight on the grass, as close to the carriages as possible. One horse stayed hooked into each yoke, loose enough that the animals could doze, but tight enough that all the soldiers had to do if they had to run fast was yank the straps tight and go.

Three days out from New Orleans, they broke for camp once the scouts started fainting in their saddles. Malik made do with a skeleton night watch crew, and Naz allowed them to build a small fire, just for an hour. The men were so beaten down, some of them wept when they heard her agree.

"I can't eat," Vienna said softly beside Naz as they huddled with the rest of the soldiers to share in the glow. "Do you want mine?"

Naz looked at Vienna's handful of stale, brittle jerky. They were down to only that, the last scraps of dried meat from their stores at the Iowa—there was no time to hunt now, because there was no time to cook or cure anything fresh. "You have to," she said, even though she knew how Vienna felt. She hadn't even opened her own stash, and didn't want to. She was just too tired to even be hungry. "Just dump it all in your mouth at once and then it's over."

Vienna obeyed bravely, as if it had been an order. "Thank you," she said wearily as she tried to chew. "I'll be able to report to my father that yes, I did eat my dinner after all today." She smiled once she was done.

"Oh," Naz said. "*My* report." She climbed to her feet and dusted the back of her pants. She realized she'd forgotten to give Zhang her daily update on the distance left.

"Ahmadi, rest," Vienna said. "It's one day. The General won't care."

"*I* care," Naz replied. They were just a few days from New Orleans, but it didn't matter. If she started slacking off now, who knew what could happen. When they made it, they had to be even more ready for anything. "I'll be back in a minute," she said as she turned to make her way around the carriages. "Don't let them put the fire out before I return. I want to soak it up one more time."

It felt immediately colder as she trudged off in the dark. Or maybe it was just her. She made her way to where Zhang was set up tonight in one of the carriages—he was the only one who didn't sleep in the grass, in order to keep his injured hands clean. The back door was cracked, and there was a small flicker of light inside from a flashlight. Naz thought he'd seen her, but Zhang had been facing away as she approached. She was about to say his name, but the word died on her lips when she saw what was happening.

Zhang had unwrapped his bandages to bare his injured hand, and was holding it out in front of him. She could see his thumb and the first three fingers, and then the flat spot where his little finger should have been. There was a click, and then Zhang raised the flashlight up and aimed it against his hand so his shadow appeared low on the carriage wall beside him. Naz realized immediately what he was doing. They both held their breath as the dark shape materialized on the wooden surface.

Of course it did, but it was comforting to see—it also had four fingers.

"Well, look at you," he said to his shadow, amused. "Nice hand." He wiggled the remaining four digits as best he could without causing pain to the mutilated fifth knuckle. They were both smiling—Zhang at his shadow, Naz at Zhang—but then his face slowly grew more serious. He put his hand down and tipped the flashlight so it rested lazily against his chest. A vague dark shape in his same form trailed off into the corners of the carriage. He watched it shift as he breathed. "I haven't been very good to you, have I?" he asked his shadow quietly. "Starving you, taking you to war, cutting your fingers off. And you stay."

Naz took a silent step back, just to be sure he wouldn't see her crouching in the darkness outside and be angry.

"I'm sorry I sometimes wished it had been you instead of Max's shadow." He looked down at the flashlight. "I understand if you'd want to leave me now, after all this. But please just let me make it to the city first. Please let me make sure the books are safe. That everyone gets there. After that, I won't be angry if you leave. I'll understand. But if you still want to stay, there can be a future in New Orleans. There can be more memories. I've started to make them already. I can—I'll make even more, if you want." He stared at it. "If you're in, I'm in."

She didn't remember leaving, but Naz found herself standing by the army's dimming campfire again, watching her own shadow flicker weakly against the embers. *Still there.*

Who knew why any of them stayed or any of them left? Did hers like this new, reluctant hope she'd made for it, too? she wondered. Because she had made something, Naz realized as she thought of Zhang—even though she'd tried so hard to do the exact opposite.

# ORLANDO ZHANG

THE DAY THEY REACHED NEW ORLEANS, ZHANG HAD BEEN awake since before dawn, watching the navy sky. He'd been watching it since before sundown really, too tense to rest. Every moment they weren't galloping felt like an ambush was about to spring on them.

They were so close. *So* close. They just had to keep ahead for one more day.

"Can't sleep either?" Malik asked as he trudged through the grass to the open door of Zhang's carriage.

"Not all night," Zhang said. He glanced through the little tufts of chiming *iizinger* clouds overhead to the sky. "I know it's still pretty dark, but . . ." He didn't finish his sentence. It was almost too big of a thing to say. *But we're only a few hours away.* He could feel his heart fluttering against his ribs, like a panicked bird in its cage. *But we could make it before noon if we left now.*

Malik rubbed the stubble on his chin slowly. "Rest is important, and the troops aren't getting enough of it."

Zhang nodded. Malik was right. They'd been pulling twenty-hour days for a week at least. Their cavalry had taken to riding in pairs so one soldier could doze in the saddle while the other held her up.

Malik adjusted his grip on the rifle he was carrying. "That being said, you know the saying 'You can lead a horse to water . . .'?"

"But you can't make it drink," Zhang finished.

"I'd bet not a single one of them is in their bedroll like they ought to be."

Zhang grinned. Together they stepped around the row of carriages to look at the rest of the camp. The soldiers had been trying to act nonchalant, leaning against the wagon wheels or thoughtfully examining their weapons, but as soon as Zhang and Malik appeared against the dim sky, all of them snapped to immediate attention. Every single one on their feet, in five neat rows. Even the horses pricked their ears toward the two men.

Zhang turned to Malik and smiled. "Let's move out!" he cried, to resounding cheers.

THE ARMY CAME SOUTH INTO LOUISIANA THROUGH THE remains of Bogalusa, then Covington. The entire area had flooded from overflow off the Old Pearl River, and the roads were ankle-deep in water. The horses slogged carefully, trying to stay on the asphalt and away from the mud. At every corner, wooden buildings sagged, roofs long succumbed to moss and rot. The wind was completely still, and there was a strange fog floating over the water, making the land appear as if it was gently steaming. *Alligators,* Zhang thought, but he had no idea how rational a fear that was. Or if he'd even recognize one if he saw it—who knew what they looked like now. His carriage was in front this time, so he supposed he'd know soon enough, if they were lurking. "No one goes any deeper than the ankles," Zhang ordered softly. "And no one goes wandering into flooded houses or down any sloped streets." He hoped that as long as they stayed away from the deeper water, they'd be all right.

Malik and Ahmadi patrolled carefully alongside the procession, eyes searching for any flicker of movement, but they saw nothing. Covington was completely empty.

"This place gives me the creeps," Ahmadi said to Zhang as her horse fell into line with Holmes.

"Me too," he agreed. "Looks like it's been abandoned for months, at least."

She looked at Zhang again, and he nodded back. They didn't need to say it to know what the other was thinking. That it either meant very good news about New Orleans or very, very bad.

"As soon as we make it out of this town, we'll be officially within

New Orleans limits," Malik said on the other side of Zhang's carriage. "When we see Lake Pontchartrain, we'll have made it."

That's when they cleared the last few ramshackle buildings and suddenly could see the outline of the distant walls.

"Holy . . . ," Ahmadi said, trailing off. They stared.

After the last stretch of land and glistening water of the lake, the city rose. Walls that had not been there before the Forgetting towered like shimmering cliffs around it. They were so perfectly straight and unbroken, it was as if a smooth, sheer mountain made of crystal had erupted from the earth on the other shore. From somewhere inside, vague tendrils of smoke curled up into the warm, gray air of morning. Zhang could only guess from so far away, but the walls looked to be forty feet tall at least, and so long that they disappeared into the humid, muggy horizon before he could see the end. He guessed they probably encircled the entire city, so that the only way in or out was the long, narrow bridgeway that spanned the lake.

*New Orleans.* Zhang felt his heart start to race. *We made it.*

Without a word, they all began to move. Slowly at first, then faster and faster, until all the horses were galloping.

The Lake Pontchartrain Causeway bridge was double-wide, with a gap between the two sides of traffic. The army streamed into the right lanes on instinct, even though it didn't matter—there was no one else on the bridge, in either direction. Their half was three lanes and a shoulder, and Malik and Ahmadi stayed on either side of Zhang's carriage as they raced over the dark, rippling water. The lake was miles across—almost a marathon's length with no emergency exit, no cover at all.

"Weapons?" Ahmadi called across the front wheels as they neared, and Malik struggled for an answer. The hooves drummed like thunder.

"I don't know!" he cried back at last.

Zhang looked up at the walls again. It meant one of two things. Either the ones inside, the ones with The One Who Gathers, "The

Creature"—that possible new name their hostage had contributed—
were civilized and maintained law and defense, or they allowed no
one from the outside and would shoot on sight. Zhang tried not to
think about the second possibility as their carriages clattered past the
halfway point, toward the narrow end of the bridge.

"Weapons out?" one of the soldiers yelled nervously from behind
a few minutes later. They had all had the same thought as Ahmadi.
The army was less than a mile away now, and Zhang could see much
better. The walls jutted straight up from the first hint of shore and
overtook the exit of the bridge. Once the carriages reached the end,
there was nowhere to go—no landing, no small field before the gates.
If New Orleans decided to shoot, they'd never get the horses turned
and moving again before they were all dead.

"I don't know yet!" another answered the first.

"Should we draw?" a third called from farther back.

"Dad!" Vienna yelled, near the second carriage. "What do we do
with our weapons?"

"I don't know!" Malik cried.

"No weapons!" Zhang shouted. He stood up facing back, toward
the rest of the procession, and crossed his arms and swiped them flat
and outward, over and over. "No weapons!"

"I hope you're right!" Ahmadi said. The end of the bridge was
rushing up to meet them. Suddenly Zhang could see movement along
the top of the wall. There were platforms on the other side, littered
with lookouts, guards, torches. A thunderous clanging started then,
and Zhang realized it was a warning bell: We see you. We see you,
you are known.

As if it had been a cue, the carriages all slowed together, hooves
clattering, everything leaning forward. *Please don't kill us,* Zhang
prayed as they slowed to a nervous, twitching halt in front of a set of
tall, heavy wood-and-iron doors.

Then for a moment, Zhang forgot his fear. They had come to a
stop just a few feet away from the wall, Holmes's nose almost touch-

ing the huge metal hinge where it met the gate. He could see it up close for the first time.

*What is it?* He stared in awe. The wall was made of something he couldn't describe. It was almost like it was carved from solid, polished crystal, in a melding, swirling hue that shifted between almost diamond clear and dark, dark blue. It was the most magnificent, impenetrable thing he'd ever seen.

Just then, a dim shape soared by at eye height, inside the wall, then vanished. Zhang pointed, mouth hanging open. "Was that—" he stammered.

"Oh my God." Ahmadi jumped.

"Was that a *fish*?"

Everyone gasped in awe. It wasn't a wall of crystal, Zhang realized. It was something even more impossible than that. It was a wall made entirely of water, for miles and miles and miles—so perfectly still the surface of it shone like glass.

"What is this place?" Ahmadi whispered.

"I don't know," Zhang replied. "But we're about to find out." There were sounds from above now, from people somehow walking on top of the water wall. Every inch of his flesh became keenly aware of the fact that they'd been waiting in front of the gates for a full ten seconds and had yet to be killed. Slowly he looked up.

"State your purpose!" A shout came down from the top.

Zhang flinched. "Refuge!" he called back. "We . . ." It was almost impossible to believe that he'd come here on a hunch he had heard from a strange woman at a deserted apartment complex almost six months ago, and then been begged to believe by a dead friend. Had she and her Broad Street crew made it too, even with so many shadowless in their group? Had they perished on the way? "We heard New Orleans was still standing. We came to join your city." Was that good enough? "We can contribute! We have—" He was going to say engineers, nurses, guards, lawyers, even though he had no idea what most of the soldiers had done before the Forgetting, but the screeching sound of the sentry door in the bottom corner of the great gate cut him off. The water rippled where the hinges connected, a tiny wave traveling across the surface and disappearing. A cluster of men and women in mismatched armor trotted out, each brandishing a shotgun—and a shadow. Malik tensed, but didn't move. Zhang stared. If they had enough shadowed survivors to spare that they would send a whole group of them out to greet total strangers, he couldn't guess how many were inside the city. Hundreds? *Thousands?*

After them came another shadowed woman in simple navy clothes, holding a clipboard. She was taller than Zhang, almost as tall as Malik, with reddish brown hair and freckles. Her pale skin gleamed in the sun, as if she'd never seen daylight in her life. As she approached with her small guard, Zhang climbed quickly down from the carriage, and Malik and Ahmadi dismounted. The woman's clothes were well worn, but clean and unwrinkled. No bones jutted anywhere. Just a few feet away, she stopped and dipped her head in greeting, and said, "Hello."

Zhang tried to find his voice, but ended up only nodding dumbly. A gust off Lake Pontchartrain picked up and kicked sideways through their line, tinkling metal carriage links, ruffling his tattered coat and the papers on her clipboard.

"Do you speak for the group?" the woman finally continued. There was a faint lilt there, a trace of a French accent or something like it.

"Uh, yes," Zhang finally said. "General—uh, I mean—Zhang. Zhang, from Arlington, Virginia."

The woman's eyebrows arched slightly on her forehead as she recorded the information, but she didn't look up at Zhang until she'd finished. "Please confirm this is correct," she asked.

"Yes," he replied.

"You've come a long way," she said as she took the clipboard back. She was smiling now. "I'm glad to welcome you to New Orleans."

Zhang nodded with as much control as he could muster. Someone behind him was weeping.

"My name is Davidia. I'm captain of the wall guard here," the woman continued, in a more formal tone again. "I work for the city of New Orleans. We need to record all of your details before we can allow passage, as well as conduct an inventory of your property."

"They're all books," Zhang said. "Almost three thousand."

Davidia was very still for a moment. "You brought three thousand books from Arlington?"

"From Washington, D.C.," Malik said. "From the D.C. Public Library. We saved as many as we could."

Davidia turned and spoke softly but urgently to one of the guards next to her, to go and inform someone at once that "the newcomers brought something." The young man nodded and bolted away. *He's going to tell The One Who Gathers,* Zhang realized. He tried to follow the sentry's path, searching for proof, but the young man vanished into the crowd bustling beyond the gates, and Zhang was lost for a moment. So many people. Their shadows blended into one giant block of shade on the ground, an indiscernible mass.

"We've had reports from a few other survivors who've come from the north . . . There's no president anymore in D.C.?" the captain asked hesitantly once Zhang turned back to her.

"No," Zhang said.

The wind sharpened once more, ruffling Davidia's papers on her clipboard again. "That is sad news. But it's good that we know for certain. And what you've brought—you've all done well. It may be very useful indeed." She smiled. "We'll find out soon."

"There's one more thing." Zhang put his hand up, to stop her before he lost the chance to warn her about the ones in white. "There's a large force on its way here, to attack the city. They're moving slow, but they have huge numbers."

"Yes," Davidia said. "Thank you. We know."

Zhang didn't turn to her, but he could feel Ahmadi's eyes snap to his face, boring into his temple. *If this false prophet is even half as strong as all the lies claim, they already know we're coming.* What the hostage had claimed turned out to be true. But what did that mean about what he had said next? *There's nothing they can do.*

But Davidia was already busy with her clipboard. "Before we get any further—I need the rest of your names, please."

"Malik," Malik said.

"Ahmadi."

The captain went slowly down the line. Zhang waited, exhilarated. As each person gave their information, they all grew more and more overcome until they were almost hysterical with laughter. Ahmadi grabbed Zhang's arm in the clamor, and he saw there were tears streaming down her cheeks. When he hugged her, he realized his own face was already wet as well. He kept laughing and crying into her hair.

"And the shadowless?" Davidia asked, calling over the din.

"What?" Ahmadi looked at her, baffled. For the briefest instant, a flicker of a feeling Zhang had long forgotten shuddered through him. *Max?* he almost said.

"The shadowless," Davidia repeated, and pointed behind them.

They had all been so overwhelmed by the sight of New Orleans that they didn't realize until they turned around that in those wonderful few moments, Vienna had lost her shadow.

# THE ONE WHO GATHERS

HE WATCHED THE NEWCOMERS APPROACH FROM HIS USUAL place, atop the summit of the small slope at the center of the city. His "altar." He had heard some of the others calling the place where he sat by that name, even though it was silly. The buildings behind might be known as the sanctuary now, but his seat was no altar. It was simply a small brick square on the ground, braced from behind by a wall of average height—bare and gently curved so it provided some shelter from the back and sides.

The day was clear, the sun strong. He'd seen the carriages even before they reached the walls, when they were still on the far side of Lake Pontchartrain, barely beginning to cross the long bridge. He had summoned Davidia then, to tell her they were coming.

"They're not Transcendence in disguise, are they?" she'd asked nervously once she'd reached him at the top of the hill. She shaded her brow with her hand, but the carriages were still too far for human eyes to see.

"No, not Transcendence," he answered. "I think they're friends."

Davidia put her hand down and nodded slowly, lost in thought. "We haven't had that many come in a long time," she finally said.

"We haven't," he agreed. He knew what she wanted to ask. "A good thing," he said.

"Sorry?"

*Is that a good thing or a bad thing?* "I think it's a good thing," he repeated. "It means there are still more who wish to remember."

ONCE THE HURRICANE WAS DEFEATED, IT HAD BEEN VERY easy to remake Dr. Zadeh's former assisted-living facility into what was now the sanctuary. The storm had wiped the building clean—all the roofs had collapsed, all the rooms had crumbled back into concrete dust and wood chips, except for one of the four walls that surrounded the inner courtyard where the storm cellar lay.

Once the winds had quieted, the others helped the amnesiac's body climb over the wreckage as his shadow followed behind, trailing silently over the shattered chunks of stone and glass. When they found that last remaining wall still standing over a small patch of cobbled brick path, the amnesiac's shadow went toward it, stretching nearer even as his body stood still—two things completely independent of each other except for the point where their two pairs of feet met. The shadow rose so he was upright against the wall's smooth, blank surface, a dark and solid shape, looking at the others.

"This will do," he said.

His body went closer then, and sat down in the center of the small floor, facing out. It *would* do, the shadow felt it agree with him. The amnesiac's eyes couldn't see after the accident, not directly, but the shadow's could. In that way, he understood what was around them. They were still one, even though they were also more.

There was no ceiling where he sat, but thanks to the shadowless, with the hurricane sealed permanently around the city like the walls of a fortress, the weather inside would always be temperate. The grounds of the assisted-living facility would be a suitable place from which to watch over New Orleans. From that vantage point, he would be free to stretch and contract over any surface and shape below without obstacle, as far as he could see, and farther.

"I'll stay here," the shadow said to the rest of them. "We can rebuild and expand." Perhaps no one had realized before, because forgetting was such a terrifying thing that it sent its victims running away from one another, but the amnesiac's shadow had been proven right during the hurricane. It was like with the elephants—he'd realized that while a shadowless's magic was strong, a group of shadowless forgetting the same thing together was exponentially more powerful. There was a strength in the sharing. Strength enough to bend nature to their will to save a city—and to restore a destroyed building into a sanctuary, if they decided the price to be paid was worth it.

"Expand?" Dr. Avanthikar asked. He saw the incomprehension flicker in her expression again as they looked at each other. A shadow who could move and talk. And more—a shadow that looked more like the memories of its owner than the physical shape of him. The shadow of a *creature* instead of a man.

"Others will come. They will have felt it, what we've done." The shadow gestured out, at the rest of New Orleans, and past. "Not all the shadowless want their magic, or want it more than their memories. There are many who want help to resist the pull. To eventually be free of it, to remember again. We should be ready for them."

Dr. Avanthikar shaded her eyes from the sun that had just begun to peek free of the dissolving clouds with her hand. "I worked with Hemu since the day he was taken into custody, and never really got anywhere with teaching him how to resist the pull. Perhaps one day we'll figure it out, but right now even that's still out of our grasp—let alone how to cure them of it."

The shadow slid closer to her on the wall. He felt his body cock its head as it thought with him. "I have an idea," he said.

THE SHADOWLESS RECONSTRUCTED THE SANCTUARY ONCE they'd agreed on the plans. It was to be somewhat like a temple— the shadow and his body would watch over the grounds from where they sat at the entrance, and behind their altar, there would be two great halls in a line, connected to each other by a long hallway. In the first hall, shadowless who had come for help would rest and wait. They would take care of one another, and Dr. Avanthikar and those shadowless already in their group who were still quite strong would live there as well, to help protect them. In the second hall, shadowless that the shadow believed he could cure would be invited one at a time. He would stretch up the tall side of the building and enter to meet them through a large open space in the roof.

"It's not too high?" Downtown asked.

The shadow shook his head. "A shadow is not a body. I can travel to the other end of New Orleans from this very place, so long as there is light for contrast, and surfaces to move across."

The remembering of the two great halls was finished in a day, and a week after, the first shadowless began to appear, drawn by what they had felt happen. In trickles at first. And then once they had seen him—a strangely shaped shadow who moved and talked to them as the human to whom it was attached sat motionless and silent on the bricks before it, the trickles turned into streams. Then rivers. Then oceans. Shadowed survivors began to leave—hope buoyed by so many arriving shadowless they hadn't realized had clung to life so long—to try to find their own shadowless relatives wherever they had lived before the Forgetting began and bring them back to the amnesiac.

When the tide of newcomers began to include shadowed and shadowless from other cities, not just New Orleans, because they had heard about the shadow who had a body, not a body who had a shadow, that was when he became sure of what had to be done to save them.

A shadowless could still learn new things—and they could keep it for a while, whatever it was that they learned. An hour, if they were weak—or perhaps a day, a week, if they were strong. But much beyond that, it wouldn't stick. Nothing would stick without a shadow. That was everyone's mistake so long ago, when it was only Hemu Joshi; they were trying to make memories to give him a shadow again. It was the other way around—they needed to give him a shadow to make memories.

Stating a thing doesn't mean it becomes easy, however. Or even fathomable, according to Dr. Avanthikar. She agreed with the concept, but had no idea how to proceed—because the dark halves of the shadowless were gone forever. One could not create something from nothing.

But that wasn't the end of hope. There was more to it than that.

The shadow led both his body and Dr. Avanthikar inside the first great hall, and sat them down facing each other in the center of the smooth floor. His body's hand obediently placed a twig between them on the floor.

"Pick up its shadow," he said to Dr. Avanthikar.

But she could not do it. It was impossible—a human cannot touch a shadow. If she puts a hand on it, tries to grip it in her fingers, the shadow will simply slip away, both under and over at once. Only a shadow can touch a shadow. Only a shadow who understands what it's doing, and is not simply mimicking.

Slowly the shadow reached out to what Dr. Avanthikar had tried to touch and failed, and took hold of the little twig by its silhouette—not its crisp wooden form—and pulled. Beside him, he could feel his body shudder with the effort. It was not easy, to ask a thing to give up its shadow. He felt the world sigh as he strained. It was like ripping apart something that was never meant to be two pieces—something that didn't understand where the line it was supposed to break across lay.

"My God," Dr. Avanthikar said, transfixed. She picked up the newly shadowless stick and stared at it. Then she reached out and ran her fingers through its separated twin, perched stiffly in his own dark, untouchable palm. Her flesh slipped through both his shape and the dark copy of the twig as easily as before, a hand through smoke.

He smiled as he watched her marvel. He thought of Hemu's notebook again. Of *Peter Pan*—of when poor young Peter found his missing shadow in a chest of drawers, and thought all his problems were solved.

For the longest time, the shadow thought Hemu had included the excerpts because he was simply wishing for something that could never be—that he might be able to find his own again, somehow. The outright magic of the idea never meshed with the rest of his fevered research; even the rumors surrounding the elephant Gajarajan's almost mystical powers of memory still had grains of truth in them—there were photographs of the actual animal, interviews with people who had seen him, worked with him. *Peter Pan* was written as a children's story.

It took until his awakening for the shadow to finally understand what Hemu had also begun to grasp himself, before his death. Not that one's own shadow could be found again, because those were gone forever—but that they were far more tangible than anyone had realized, if the right hands touched them. And if that was true, then so was this: a shadow from something else might be able to be used in place of a missing one.

He set the ownerless little shadow down on the dusty brick floor. It lay still, lonely.

"Can you do it?" Dr. Avanthikar asked, no more than a whisper. "Can you bind it to something else?" She clutched the mutilated twig.

"I don't know," he said. "But I think so."

They began to try. And fail.

The problem wasn't that there weren't enough shadows to use. It was that there were too many, and all of them wrong. The shadow of a sparrow would cure a shadowless, but it drove them mad, urging them to the tops of trees or buildings while the rest chased after to save them, until they finally managed to leap into the air—and then fall, flightless. A tree's shadow would not take at all, and then could not be given back to the tree. The branches withered within weeks, mournful. A rock's shadow made a human catatonic, even though they could then learn and remember. The shadow of a house gave them great, aching pain all throughout their bones, until they begged it to be stripped off again.

That was the worst of all. The houses were how they learned the horrible danger of their experiment. If a rejoining failed midway—if the new, stolen shadow didn't take or he tried to strip it back off by force—the shadowless died.

"Maybe it can't be done after all," he said softly as they stood over their latest failure. The shadow hadn't wanted to admit it, but it was becoming harder and harder to believe. The dark outline of a salvaged car engine lay draped over the floor between him and the doctor, lifeless. It had begun to fade even as he tore it from the machine, evaporating. For the first time, he could feel himself lose hope.

"Don't give up," Dr. Avanthikar pleaded. "No matter what."

"I don't even understand what caused it in the first place. The shadowlessness."

She tried to put her hand on his shoulder as best she could. In the end, she simply placed her palm flat against the wall, over the top of his outline. "It doesn't matter," she said.

"Yes, it does," he argued.

"No, it doesn't."

He could feel the warmth of her skin as it seeped into the stone where he lay.

"Look at me," Dr. Avanthikar said. He slowly obeyed. "It doesn't matter why it happened anymore. It only matters what we do from here."

He looked down again, trying to believe her.

"You *have* to do this, Gajarajan." She called him by a name, and for the first time, it felt right. "You're the only one who can."

GAJARAJAN HAD TOLD DR. AVANTHIKAR THAT DIFFICULT DAY that he would find a way to do it, somehow, even though he had no idea how. He kept trying, and failing. It wasn't until almost two years later—just before Zhang's army arrived at the wall—that he finally made good on that promise. He only wished that she had still been alive to see it.

They had been fighting again, after damaging another shadow so badly as they tried to strip it from its solid chandelier form that it vanished the instant it came free. Gajarajan was prowling back and forth against the wall, and Dr. Avanthikar was facing away from him, looking over the rest of the sleeping city, to keep herself from falling into the argument once more.

"Look," she said suddenly. He turned from his flat surface to see her pointing across town, toward the gate. "Is that someone out there?" she asked.

He looked closer and nodded. She was right. Another shadowless had found his way to them, the first one in weeks, and was now wandering aimlessly back and forth on the narrow bridge over the water, as if lost.

"He needs help to make it the rest of the way here," she said.

"Too far gone," Gajarajan replied. "Besides, it's past dusk. The deathkites are out." Since they'd created the wall, the deathkites knew better than to fly over the city. They could feel the same magic in that thing as was in themselves. But outside its bounds, the night was still their territory.

"Gajarajan," Dr. Avanthikar said, "they come because you've called them. You can't leave them out there when they finally do. Everyone who wishes to remember again deserves the same," she said.

"I wish that were true, but the risk is too great." He sighed. He and their eight remaining shadowless patients from the former facility were still learning how to work together. They were not ready for the deathkites yet, if they could help it. "We could lose many trying to save one."

But Dr. Avanthikar never listened to him. She'd stopped listening to him ever since they began trying to fix the shadowless. Gajarajan couldn't remember the last time they'd spoken without arguing. Each failure made them more and more raw. "What about you, then? What about Marie and Downtown and Curly and Buddy? Should I have left you upstairs to die during the hurricane instead, because there were more of them to protect downstairs?"

"Yes," he said, but she was gone, marching stubbornly down to the front gate, to demand a guard contingent follow her for a rescue operation.

"Let me out," Dr. Avanthikar ordered the night sentries clustered around Davidia at the entrance. "It's an emergency."

"Stop her," the shadow said to the captain, from the wall beside her post, and she flinched in surprise at his instant appearance. His legs lay in two long dark lines across all the roofs of New Orleans.

Dr. Avanthikar ignored him. "This is a rescue!"

"Don't listen," he said. "It's not safe."

The guards didn't open the gate, but before they could grab her, Dr. Avanthikar threw herself straight into the great bound wall of storm water just beside it instead.

It enveloped her at once, sucking her in like a riptide—but the wall had been made by their shadowless, for their own protection. It released her gently on the other side into a puddle on the grass. She began to run toward the bridge.

"Open the gate!" Davidia cried. "Get her back here before the deathkites dive!" But Dr. Avanthikar had a head start, and was already over the water. Gajarajan flashed back from the wall beside the gate to the dark chamber of the first great hall at blinding speed, to rouse the shadowless for help. By the time he had woken them and gotten them outside to try to do something—*anything*—to stop the deathkites, Dr. Avanthikar was already dying.

GAJARAJAN AND DAVIDIA CONTINUED TO WATCH THE CAR- riages as they raced closer, thundering across the bridge. He could make out a new detail by then, one that caught his attention more firmly than anything had in a long time: the wooden structures rode low on their turning wheels, as if heavily burdened. The shadow leaned back against his wall and looked at his guard captain, to see if she'd also seen. They'd heard the rumors then. That he was seeking something.

"They're bringing a lot with them," Gajarajan said to her. "More than any other group before."

"Not weapons to attack us?"

"Likely not weapons." He watched, transfixed. What could all of it be, and so much of it?

Davidia nodded. "As soon as I find out what it is, I'll send someone to inform you if any of it could be what you're looking for."

"Thank you," he said as she disappeared down the hill. He returned to studying them. He had not felt hope since Dr. Avanthikar died. The strangers were coming in a dead sprint now, as if being chased for their lives, even though there was nothing behind them.

So many shadows. Every single one of them, it seemed. Inside his body, Gajarajan felt the heart beat faster. Whatever was in the carriages might prove to be very useful indeed.

# ORLANDO ZHANG

BY THE DAY'S END, ZHANG HAD BEEN PLACED INTO A ROOM on the second floor of an old wooden house named House 33. That was how things were divided in New Orleans—houses had been carved up into private rooms, with everyone sharing the kitchen and bathrooms. Ahmadi was given the room next door. Vienna, Malik, and the two remaining Smiths were assigned spots in House 32, and the rest of the soldiers placed in open rooms across Houses 34 to 45.

Living that way reminded Zhang of Elk Cliffs in a way. All of them together in a little community, sharing chores, laughing instead of jumping at every errant sound. Whenever he went into the kitchen to get a piece of bread—every House got half a loaf per tenant every other day from the city—or fill his glass with water they'd dragged up in buckets and boiled to purify, his heart thrilled to see so many other humans, doing ordinary things. Washing dishes or sweeping the floor.

Ahmadi was standing in the kitchen when Zhang walked in at dawn after the army's first night there, bent over the cutlery drawer. "Do you know where the spoons are?" she asked. They both stared at each other for a moment, and then Zhang burst into tears, startling her so badly she jumped and the drawer fell out of the counter, spilling everything. It was so fucking normal, he couldn't stop crying.

AT FIRST ZHANG HADN'T KNOWN IF VIENNA WOULD BE AL- lowed into the city, after they realized she was shadowless. Or if the rest of them would be let in either, because they had been near her when it happened. But they were allowed in—all of them. New Orleans welcomed Vienna exactly the same way they did the rest of Zhang's army, as if nothing was different at all.

"I need you to come with me for a moment," Davidia said to Zhang as soon as they'd dragged the carriages in through the gate and unhooked the horses.

"I can't leave the others," he said.

"The One Who Gathers—he'd like to meet you."

At that, everyone paused. Zhang, Malik, and Ahmadi all looked at one another. "The One Who Gathers is . . . really real?" Zhang finally asked.

"Yes," Davidia said.

It seemed impossible. But Davidia was speaking not like one who had also heard the rumors, but like one who had seen the owner of all the names with her own eyes. "The Stillmind?" Zhang stammered. "The One with a Middle but No Beginning? The One Who Does Not Dream?"

Davidia nodded, smiling. "Yes," she said again.

The stunned silence lingered for what felt like hours. All the stories, all the things he'd seen written on walls. It was really true.

"Go," Ahmadi finally managed. "We won't move until you're back."

"Watch the carriages," he said to her and Malik. He felt her hand in his own for an instant, squeezing firmly. He squeezed it back for courage and then set off after Davidia.

The walk was long, and she was always ahead. "Keep up," she said to Zhang over her shoulder, but kindly.

Zhang tried not to gawk, but he couldn't help it. New Orleans was unfathomable. Every turn was more surprising than the next. Some things still lay crumbled, but others had been rebuilt, either through magic or through labor. Zhang did a double take when he thought he even saw lights on in one of the buildings, but couldn't be sure. All around them, people talked in the streets, instead of killing or running. Some had shadows, some did not. Most amazing of all, the ones that did not didn't seem to be afraid—even when they forgot what they were doing midaction. Before they could startle, another shadowless or shadowed person would come to their aid, and they'd be laughing again within seconds.

"The One Who Gathers did all this?" Zhang asked.

She nodded. "And more."

Seeing it now, he found it hard to believe that two years ago, he was afraid to leave an abandoned hotel because someone might jump out of the hedges and chew off his arm in crazed hunger, or kill him for the contents of his pockets. Here he could walk down a street with no planning at all and feel perfectly safe. Zhang couldn't believe he almost hadn't come—but he knew why. He hadn't wanted to do it without Max.

"Zhang," Davidia said, halting suddenly at the top of the gently sloping hill they'd been climbing. "This is The One Who Gathers. Here inside New Orleans, we call him simply Gajarajan."

Zhang didn't know what kind of person he'd been expecting, but it wasn't the one that he saw. He stood beside Davidia, speechless. This was no Red King or even solemn-faced General Imanuel, and there was no fortress or palace or even modest house. It was simply a man—of vague middle age, thin, in plain, well-worn clothes. He was sitting outside on a patch of bricks, in front of a little wall nature had left undamaged purely by accident. And over his eyes he wore a thick strip of fabric tied gently behind his head.

"You're—" Zhang paused. "You're blind?"

"Yes and no," the man said. Zhang startled—his mouth hadn't moved.

Davidia nodded when he looked at her in confusion, and then she gestured behind Gajarajan, at the wall.

Zhang turned back to him, but the man didn't say anything more. Zhang thought maybe he was supposed to speak—but words failed him as he watched. On the ground, the man's shadow shifted, gliding farther back on the bricks until it broke across the line where the red stones met the wall, and began trailing up the smooth vertical face. The dark shape rose up, up, up, until it was roughly its owner's height—but the man on the ground hadn't moved at all.

"Oh my God," Zhang whispered at last.

"I wish," he said—not the man, Zhang realized now, but the shadow. Both he and Davidia laughed as Zhang stood there, dumbstruck, staring back and forth between the body sitting placidly on the ground and the shadow that moved and spoke freely behind it.

Finally Zhang stumbled, and Davidia caught him before he hit the ground. She helped him to his knees, where he scrambled into a clumsy crouch. The world was swimming in front of him. *Impossible*, Zhang kept thinking. But he looked again, and it was the same as he had seen the first time. All the rumors were real—but they weren't about a person at all. They were about a *shadow*.

And not only that. Zhang peered closer. The shadow certainly did belong to the man, because Zhang could see that the two forms were joined at the feet and hips where the body sat on the ground, but it almost seemed like the shadow on the wall wasn't his at all. They looked nothing like each other. The shadow looked more like . . . the shadow of an elephant.

"I apologize," Gajarajan finally said. It seemed to be bending down slightly on the surface of the wall, to be even with Zhang. Yes, there were definitely large, fanning ears, and a third arm that came from the center of its face—a trunk. An elephant's trunk. "I didn't realize I was going to surprise you that much. Lately, newcomers who have come trickling in have heard what I look like before they arrive."

"So you—" Zhang didn't even know where to start. "Is the man, the body, he's alive, right?"

"Of course," the shadow said. "We're one and the same."

"Are you controlling him?"

"No more than he's controlling me."

It seemed true—the shadow was currently moving along the wall and speaking, and the body hadn't been driven to mimic the actions. Perhaps if the man had wanted to move as well, he could have without snapping the shadow into following his form.

"There's time for us to talk more later," the shadow said. "You can come here anytime you like. I don't want to keep you from your people—it was probably rude of me to call for you so quickly—but I was informed that you brought with you a great many things. Things for me."

"We heard that you were . . . gathering something. Something that had to do with memories and shadows," Zhang said. "We weren't sure what."

"I'm not sure either," Gajarajan said. It shrugged its massive ears softly when it saw Zhang's expression. "But it's important that I find it. And perhaps it's what you've brought."

"What is it for?" Zhang asked.

The shadow smiled—or seemed to, somehow. "To help cure the shadowless."

Zhang stared at Gajarajan for a long time—both his body and his shadow. They were nearly expressionless, the body because he seemed almost suspended in a trance, and the shadow because he had no face in the way that humans, or even elephants, have faces. But as Zhang stared into the deep black shade spread across the half-crumbled stone, he could feel it. The shadow meant what it had said.

"You can do it?" Zhang asked fiercely.

"I have," it said. "Once." The word lingered as if solid in the air between them.

The thrill of the miracle overwhelmed him for a moment—but then Zhang realized what Gajarajan's true meaning was. "But not again," he added.

The shape of the elephant watched him evenly. "Not again," it finally agreed. "But I think I can—I just need the right tools. The right thing from which to draw a shadow. Not just any item will work. I used up all that I had."

Zhang looked back down the hill. Their carriages were no more than blurry specks from that distance. "We brought books," he said. "Thousands of books. It actually wasn't—I'm not the one who started gathering them, but Imanuel, he died, and I took over. I wanted to finish it." Zhang took a shaky breath to stop himself from rambling. "Are they what you're looking for?" he asked.

"I'm not sure," the shadow said. "But most likely not. I'm sorry."

Zhang waited for something more, because it seemed impossible that they'd come all this way, that they'd risked so much—and failed. But there was nothing more. *Most likely not.* He let it sink in. Imanuel had been wrong. They were just books after all.

"I'm sorry," Gajarajan repeated gently.

"No," Zhang said. He was twisting the hem of his coat, he realized. "Don't be sorry. It was us, we didn't understand."

The silhouette of the elephant watched Zhang calmly from the wall. After a moment, it slid closer to the outer edge so that it was nearer to him. "Don't think of it as a failure. All of you made it here. You've joined us. We'll find a use for the books, even if it isn't what you'd originally thought it might be."

"Yes," Zhang said. "Yes, we made it."

Gajarajan retreated slowly until he was centered on the wall again.

"What is it exactly that makes them not what you're looking for?" Zhang asked. "I'm sure the rumor we heard was incomplete. But as far as we knew, we were looking for things with memories and with shadows. A book seems to have those—if you take it both physically and metaphorically."

The elephant spread its humanlike hands in a slow shrug. "Shadows, yes." It nodded. "But many things have shadows. Everything, in fact, except for the humans."

"And the memories?"

"They're not real," the shadow said. "Stories about made-up characters. I don't think . . ." It trailed off. "If the point is for the shadowless to remember their past again, if I succeeded in attaching a shadow with unreal memories within it, they wouldn't recover anything from this world then. They would remember a life that no one had lived."

Zhang nodded. It seemed to make sense, if he was understanding the elephant at all.

"But don't worry about that any longer. Your journey is over. You have been gathered. We are glad to welcome you home." Gajarajan bowed.

Something pinched deep in Zhang's throat. It was suddenly very hard to speak. Home. It was a word he wasn't sure he'd ever hear again.

"Come with me," Davidia said kindly. "I'll take you back to your friends before they start to worry."

Zhang began to follow her, then stopped. "Davidia said that you already know that Transcendence is coming," he called to the shadow.

Gajarajan's form sharpened on the wall as his attention turned back to Zhang. "Yes, we do. A shadowless arrived a few months ago bearing the information. We've been preparing since then."

Zhang smiled at that. This shadow was certainly powerful in the same kind of incomprehensible way as the shadows that had disappeared and the magic they granted in their places were, but this one thing hadn't been divined mystically, at least. Gajarajan had learned of Transcendence the same way the Iowan army had learned of his existence—nothing more than a message, passed on. "Well, I know there aren't many of us compared to the people you have here, but we did fight a portion of their forces once, and lived. We'd be honored to add ourselves to your numbers, to help you defend New Orleans once they arrive."

"Thank you," Gajarajan said kindly. It rose up and unfurled its ears and trunk fully, until it had obliterated almost all of the sunlight on the wall. "That is a generous thing you offer us, and I'm deeply grateful for it. But there won't be any need."

"What do you mean?"

"The shadowless will do it," he said. "Eight of them."

AFTER HOUSES AND FOOD CAME JOBS. AHMADI WAS ASSIGNED to join the wall guard with Davidia, which was fine with her. She began to teach them all archery. New Orleans had done an excellent job of hoarding bullets, but they were still a long way off from knowing how to manufacture more of them, and Gajarajan couldn't justify the cost for them to be remembered. Arrows were a far easier option—and they didn't erupt into thunder or lightning when loosed. Most of the soldiers were assigned to construction, to repair more abandoned buildings into houses for anyone who came after Zhang's army, since they had all but filled up New Orleans's remaining rooms. It was good—it gave them something to do. Not that Zhang had been expecting a riot, but he didn't know how willing they would be to stop being soldiers. They'd been fighting for a long time and weren't used to not having to. Imanuel's ultimate goal had always been to reach a place or a time where they'd be safe, but Zhang didn't think any of them had expected it to happen so abruptly. One day, they were killing the Reds and racing south, and the next, they were all in houses, learning directions to the communal garden.

But it turned out that almost all of them were happy to stop being soldiers. They'd dedicated their lives to it before, but not because it was their calling—it had just been the only job there was to be had in D.C.

As for Malik, the city gave him caretaker leave, to enjoy what little time Vienna had left before she forgot him.

Zhang received his task last. He was cutting through the grass behind House 33 on his way to the carriages, the way he did every day, to make sure they were still secure. He was always worried about the weather or someone curious trying to sneak into one. The morning sun was glaring over the roofs, blinding white as it climbed. His shadow skipped through the weeds, jagged. It bumped into another shape and dissolved, like two streams of water meeting. He stopped short. Another pair of boots was in front of his own in the grass.

"Good morning," Yoshikawa said when Zhang looked up. The young sentry Davidia had ordered to run up to Gajarajan with news of the books when they'd first arrived.

"Sorry," Zhang said. "I wasn't looking, I didn't see you."

"It's all right. I should've called out, maybe." He grimaced into the warm glow for a moment. "I've come with good news. We've managed to find some space in one of the commercial buildings we've already renovated where you can store your books. A library again. It's not fancy, but at least it's got a roof and a door with a lock. We'd like to name it after the friend you mentioned—Paul. Gajarajan hopes you will be pleased."

Zhang was. He was so pleased all he could do was blink back tears and nod until Yoshikawa laughed.

"Follow me then. I'll show you the place." He smiled and gestured past House 33, toward the small new downtown area.

They turned off Lafayette Street into a building that looked like it had once been a pharmacy. Inside, the left half was completely bare, save several rows of empty medicine shelves, and the right half was New Orleans's only tailor, where people took turns in shifts to sew items the city badly needed: bedsheets, socks, underwear.

Zhang had never built a library before, but he had plenty of help. Volunteers poured in the way they did for the garden and the tailor. Some even brought a book or two that they'd managed to save in the early days.

The day Zhang started arranging the rebuilt bookcases into rows just like a real library, he gained two more helpers.

"Surprise!" Vienna cried as she poked her head through the door.

Zhang gasped, startled, and then started laughing. "Did you break out of jail?" he asked her.

"Nope, even better," she said. Malik followed her in. "Parole."

"I swear, you'd think she wasn't—" He gestured at the empty ground behind her. "*Teenagers.*"

Zhang smiled at him. "It's good to see you both," he said. He'd hardly spoken to Vienna since the day they'd arrived—Malik had become even more protective than he already was, trying to prevent anything from startling her, scaring her, hurting her. Anything that could force a traumatic forgetting, no matter how small. But Zhang could tell that when she must have asked to see the library, there was no way Malik could refuse.

"Over here," he said. He was more than happy to put her to work. "Can you . . ." He trailed off awkwardly.

"Yes, I can still read." Vienna snorted, as if he was being silly. "Don't give me the kid gloves, General. If you want to know something, just ask."

"It's just Zhang now." Zhang smiled. "You want to start putting the books into groups so we can see how much space each genre will take up?"

Vienna saluted happily and made her way toward the mass of stacked boxes. Malik shrugged as they watched her dig through the first pile. "She thinks it'll do more damage if I hide or avoid things," he said. "She'd rather know she's forgotten something, for as long as she can remember she's forgotten it, than not."

"SO HOW WAS SHE?" AHMADI ASKED AS SHE WENT OVER TO her small table, where a squat paper bag sat in the center. Zhang had knocked on her door next to his after dinner, to tell her Vienna had come to volunteer at the library that day.

"Just like herself." He smiled. "I think Malik was happy too, to see her like that again." He felt better than he had in a long time. "Today was a good day."

"It was," Ahmadi said. She held up the bag. Something liquid sloshed against a jar inside. "Guess what I learned New Orleans has today."

"Is that alcohol?" Zhang's mouth tingled. "Honest to God *real* alcohol?"

She nodded. "Moonshine. One of the wall guards makes it."

"Promote him immediately," Zhang said as he jumped up to retrieve a cup from the other side of the room.

"Taste it first," Ahmadi warned. She pulled the bottle out of its paper bag. "The only thing that's the same is the name."

"As long as it gets the job done." He grinned. There was only one chair in the room and then the bed, so they sat down cross-legged on the floor facing each other next to the lantern, and Ahmadi poured him half the liquor. They clinked the cup and bottle together and went for it.

"Oh, God, it's disgusting," Zhang sputtered, laughing. "It's like gasoline!"

"If only we didn't remember what the real stuff tasted like." She took another swig and coughed.

Zhang tried a second sip and coughed again, too. He drank more anyway. That warm, floating feeling he'd almost forgotten prickled at the edges of his brain. Not enough by far, but at least it was there at all. It made him remember how it was supposed to feel. He told her about his day at the library, and Ahmadi told him about her day on the wall. She was smiling more. They finished the whole bottle, still coughing with every swig.

"You're right," she finally said. She held up her empty jar and studied it. "New Orleans needs a new moonshine maker."

"Do you know how?" Zhang asked.

"No." She shrugged. "Only archery." Her eyes unfocused a little, gazing through the wall of their house, somewhere much farther. They glimmered softly in the light of the lantern. "I miss Tehran."

*I miss Arlington*, Zhang thought. Did he actually, anymore? "I miss Portland," he said instead, but it wasn't really true either. *I miss Elk Cliffs.* That was true. *Max. Paul. Imanuel.*

"It's strange to finally know you," Ahmadi said.

"What?"

"I mean, in person." She smiled to herself. "Paul used to tell all of us so many stories about the two of you as kids or teenagers. His way of remembering you. Prom. The first car you wrecked. When you both got caught toilet-papering your science teacher's house."

For a moment, the ghost of the Red King had been there, but Ahmadi's smile, her laughter, was chasing it away. She knew only the old Paul, the blustering teddy bear with a temper that was all bark and no bite. Something deep inside healed over, a little bit.

"Am I not how Paul made me seem, now that you've met me?" he asked.

"No—the opposite." Ahmadi paused. She seemed as if she'd just admitted something she'd wanted to say but hadn't meant to. She smiled again, nervously this time. "This is going to sound weird, but after all the time I had with Paul, all the stories, when you finally found us . . . It almost felt more like you'd returned again rather than just arrived for the first time." She risked a look at him. "It felt like you'd come back home."

Maybe it was the alcohol, he told himself as he watched her in the dim glow of the firelight. But it wasn't. The stuff had been so weak it was barely more than dishwater. There was no clouded, dull wonder as he leaned closer to her in the small room. Only a focusing, as if everything around them became sharper, and time slowed down. He could feel the exact contours of her through the air from two feet away, as if she cast waves of pressure in the shape of her form. Sound contracted. Ahmadi had stopped talking, staring frozen at the point of his Adam's apple.

*She's so short,* Zhang thought. His skin tingled. He had never realized how short she was. Even crouching, he had to bend gently at the shoulders to reach her.

AHMADI HAD BEEN RIGHT. IT WAS LIKE COMING HOME. SOMEthing that was familiar, something that he knew and understood. Something that remembered him back.

That night Zhang rolled over and was surprised to feel the soft warmth of another body near his own on the mattress. He opened his eyes and looked in the dark at the silhouette of Ahmadi's back above the blanket. Her back was different from Max's. Different color, different slope of the rib cage, different gentle outline of muscles. There were scars on the top of her right arm—a wide band of burns and darkened lines that circled her shoulder. For the first time in a long time, Zhang felt something like hope or happiness as he realized that later there was a chance she would tell him about them. There was a chance they would share even more things and then remember them.

He closed his eyes again, but in the darkness, without his being able to see the pale glow of her skin and the narrowness of her shoulders, it was impossible to know it was Ahmadi there, not someone else. Her warmth radiating softly beside him felt the same.

*Did you get to wherever you were trying to go before you forgot everything, Max?* he wondered. *Did you find whatever you were looking for?*

He hadn't managed to rescue her after all in the end, but as he lay there now, with Ahmadi—knowing that the night hadn't been the last of its kind with her, but maybe the first, if he wanted it—it felt like an answer, just in a different form than he'd wanted. It must have happened after all. Max must have forgotten him, or at least some of him. *Enough* of him. Because if he had become a person who could leave Washington, D.C., for New Orleans, who could give up searching—who could possibly someday have feelings for someone else—it could only mean one thing. She was gone.

Zhang wrapped his arm around Ahmadi and put his face against the back of her neck. He nuzzled her softly. To try to make it more real. She murmured, still half-dreaming, then dropped back into deeper sleep again.

"Blue," he whispered. It was the last time he'd say it, but not the last time he'd remember.

That was the cruelest part. Not that Max had left, but that she had forgotten. It wasn't her fault, but it was still cruel all the same. Zhang didn't want Max to forget him, but she had anyway. Now he wanted to forget *her,* and couldn't.

MALIK LET VIENNA COME BACK THE NEXT DAY AND THE DAY after, gradually relaxing as he saw how good it was for her. Ahmadi switched some shifts at the wall to join in. It made Zhang happy to have them all there together, completing their little family—but he couldn't relax. Whenever Vienna was in the library, he was afraid to sit down, to look away for even a second. He felt terrible for not trusting her, but he had been close to only one other shadowless, and she had disappeared once she began to forget. Just up and vanished, and never came back. He couldn't let himself believe that Vienna wasn't going to do the same. Every time she went to the tailor's side to watch them work, or walked outside to stretch her legs, or said she needed a snack from the communal garden, Zhang would make an excuse to follow her. "I just need some air," he would lie unconvincingly, scrambling for the door an instant after Vienna went through it.

When all the shelves had been fixed and the books organized on them, they painted signs for each genre, built tables and chairs, and hung up a partition to divide the tailor from the library. It took almost a week of constant work, but Zhang didn't mind. Vienna and he would've worked all the way through the nights if Malik and Ahmadi hadn't shown up each time and blown out all the lanterns just like when he'd been counting the books on the road.

The day the library was finished, they held a small ceremony. Everyone that had come from D.C. gathered to see the books as they were meant to be—not hidden in carriages, but proudly displayed on shelves. They took turns reading from Paul's poetry as huge swaths of fabric billowed on the tailor's side just above the dividing wall, the helpers swinging them up to shake out the dust. The verses were punctuated with the soft, gliding sound of shears as they cut. But every gentle intrusion only made Zhang smile. It wasn't usual, but it was more than Imanuel ever could have hoped for.

Transcendence was still coming, and they knew they'd have to face them, but for the first time in a long time, they all felt like they were finally home. *Home.* Zhang hadn't expected to truly ever feel that again.

Ahmadi took it so well that when Zhang awakened in the middle of that night and heard through their shared wall the muted, strangled sounds of her sobs, it frightened him. He had heard her cry before, like when they lost one of the carriages to fire. But he had never heard her cry like *that,* and he didn't know why she was. The next day she gamely introduced herself to Vienna and shook her hand when Malik brought her around, and then did it again every time they dropped by House 33 or the library. Every time they "met," Zhang heard Ahmadi sob again in secret later that night.

Things started to change. Vienna got confused more often. Instead of rolling their eyes at him, Ahmadi and Malik stopped saying that Zhang was being overly protective when he scrambled to follow her around. They had started trading off, in fact, so she was never alone.

"I know you're there, Zhang," Vienna said to him the next time he tried to eavesdrop on her from the hallway outside the communal kitchen.

Zhang sighed and walked into the room. "I'm just worried," he confessed. "I don't want you to feel alone or scared."

Vienna was at the sink, standing with her hands on the chipped ceramic lip, but the water bucket was untouched, the drinking glass in front of her empty. Its shadow sat lonely on the counter, without the company of the silhouette of Vienna's hands beside it.

"I'm not her," she said gently.

"Who?" Zhang asked. Vague pain hovered in his chest, an old hurt.

"Whoever it was," she replied. "Whoever it was who forgot, and then disappeared."

They didn't say anything for a time. The glass shone in the afternoon light, so bright it was almost hard to look at. Zhang wondered if Vienna had meant to get a drink and forgotten, or if she'd never intended to drink at all, and was just using the room as a way to escape the constant, crushing love they all were smothering her with. *It's not our fault,* he wished he could tell her. *You know only what you'll lose, not what we will.*

"It's a strange feeling," she finally added.

"What is?"

"To feel completely in control of your motivations, but know that at any second, absolutely nothing could make any sense," she said. "What if I'd come in here in a panic because my dad had just been shot and I needed a towel to make a tourniquet?" She glanced at the limp rectangle of fabric draped over the front of the stove. "Honestly, that actually could be the reason I came in here. How would I know I forgot something if I'd forgotten it?"

"Your dad is fine," Zhang said.

"I know," she replied. "That's not the point."

They both looked out the window, at the backs of Ahmadi's and Malik's heads on the far side of the porch. The sun slipped slowly across the sky, its white light beginning to yellow. Vienna finally moved the glass a few inches so it stopped gleaming so sharply. *We'll get you back,* Zhang wanted to say, but it wasn't true, or might not be. Gajarajan had seemed confident when they'd talked, but he hadn't figured all of it out yet—otherwise the rumors would be different. He would no longer be looking or he would know what it was he sought. The strange living shadow was the closest anyone had ever gotten to understanding the curse, but he wasn't there yet, not quite. And Zhang didn't know how he could ever get there. If Gajarajan didn't stop seeking something and go back to trying to attach new shadows, he would never understand exactly what kind of shadow was the type they needed to gather more of to help him. But if he kept trying in order to figure it out, he would kill a shadowless every time he failed.

"I'd like to go," Vienna said suddenly. Zhang turned to her. "I'd like to go to the sanctuary sooner rather than later," she continued, almost as if she'd read his mind. "I'd like to volunteer."

# MAHNAZ AHMADI

YOSHIKAWA WAS ALREADY IN THE GUARD TOWER ON THE WALL when Naz arrived for the dawn shift. "Captain Ahmadi," he said softly as she was almost to the top of the ladder.

"Oh, Yoshikawa," Naz said, surprised to see him there. "Where's Davidia?"

"With Gajarajan," he answered. "He came here just a few minutes ago and asked that she meet him at the altar."

It was finally time. "Transcendence," Naz said.

"They're only a day away. Gajarajan spotted their forces from his altar this morning at first light, about twenty miles to the north."

For a moment, she could again feel the singeing heat of the flames on her as she had ridden past Zhang's burning carriage of books, her bow glittering like molten black lava as she doubled back, urging her horse closer and closer, until she thought the tips of her hair would catch fire. Looking into the red blaze for any sign of life and not being able to see Zhang at all. "Are we ready?" she asked. "Zhang told me that he offered our soldiers as help, and Gajarajan declined. He told him the shadowless would fight. That—that only eight of them would." She didn't understand it, but that's what Zhang had said.

Yoshikawa nodded. "Yes. They are called The Eight."

So Zhang hadn't misunderstood that first day. Naz had no idea how many shadowless were inside the sanctuary, but the great hall was massive, and there were at least four hundred living in the city among the rest of them. "Eight against thousands? Why not all of them? Even the ones who can barely remember can still hold a weapon."

"The shadowless won't fight this battle with weapons," Yoshikawa said. "And it must be eight. We've been doing this a long time, since the first who heard the rumors began to trickle in. We tried many different ways. It must always be eight. Any less or more is not as powerful."

"I don't understand," Naz said helplessly.

"Most of us don't," Yoshikawa shrugged. "I think probably only Gajarajan and The Eight do. But we know it works."

She finally nodded. "So there's nothing we can do to help?"

"There is. The Eight will fight tomorrow. But Gajarajan requests that you, Zhang, and Malik go to the altar to meet with them. They're ready to face the threat—and now that Transcendence is almost here, he'd like you to tell them as much as you can about their ways. Numbers, tactics, appearance, how your own battle with them went."

Naz blinked. "Teach them everything? Now? When Transcendence is just hours away?" She threw her hands up. "I thought they must already know! Why didn't we do all this when we arrived? We could have been filling them in for weeks, instead of all on the last day!"

Yoshikawa smiled sadly as she realized her mistake. "The Eight are shadowless," he said. "If you'd told them any sooner than this, they might not remember by the time the enemy reached our gates."

NAZ WENT TO GET ZHANG FIRST AT THE LIBRARY. WHEN THEY came up the stairs of House 32, Malik's door was closed, but before she could put her knuckles against the wood, it opened.

"Saw you from the window," he said. "Transcendence?"

Naz nodded. "Gajarajan's seen them. We have a day, a day and night at best. He wants you to join Zhang and me in the final discussions with something he calls The Eight. Share our firsthand experience with them."

Malik nodded. "Come on in while I get my shoes."

She and Zhang stepped into Malik's small shared room. A half-eaten apple sat on the table. "Where's Vienna?" Zhang asked.

"In the alcove on the bed, rereading the book you let her take from the library," Malik said, coming back into the main room from where he'd just pointed with his chin. "Well, reading. She forgot she finished it before."

"If I forget again, give it back to Zhang so he can reshelve it!" Vienna called. Then, more quietly, "No point in keeping it."

Malik sighed. "Vienna, we're going to—"

"Wait, just wait for me! I can't find my gun." Her voice replied from around the corner.

They'd given them up already, weeks ago, when they'd all arrived in New Orleans. The weapons had been added to the wall guard's inventory. "You don't need a gun right now," Malik finally said.

Vienna came around the corner. "Yes, I do," she said. She nodded at Zhang, then studied Naz thoughtfully, for the hundredth first time. "Isn't she—I mean, isn't she from the precinct?" she asked her father. She turned back to Naz. "Did you come to help my dad and Zhang and me find my mom? See if she went farther downtown toward the White House?"

"We're not—" Malik grimaced. "Doing that today."

"We're going to speak to Gajarajan right now," Zhang finally said to her, more gently.

"Oh. Well, that's good, too," Vienna replied. She went over to the floor by the door, where her shoes were. Naz watched her start to tie the laces—calmly at first; then her fingers stuttered once. She'd realized she didn't know *how* she knew Gajarajan, even though she knew who he was. That she'd forgotten some things in the gap between her mother and their new lives.

"Vienna," Malik said. "You're not going. Only us."

Vienna looked up at him, one shoe dangling in her hand. "But . . ." She looked between them, confused. "Why are you going then, if not to take me to volunteer?"

Malik sat down slowly on the chair at the table. "Later. Not this time."

Naz looked down at her hands. So Vienna had told him what she'd said to Zhang in their kitchen the other day. More than once.

It seemed this wasn't the first time this argument was playing out. It made her heart break to hear it, because she knew Malik couldn't win forever. *Don't come to Boston, Rojan. Don't you dare come.* But no matter how many times she ordered her sister not to leave their home in Tehran, it made no difference. Nothing could have stopped Rojan. Nothing would stop Vienna.

"Why not now?" Vienna persisted. "You're going there yourselves anyway. Take me with you. I want to volunteer to try to receive a shadow."

"Not now."

"I want to volunteer, Dad."

"Not now!" he shouted.

Vienna didn't speak again, but she didn't put the shoe down either. She looked at Zhang, begging. But Naz was the one to help her.

"Malik," she said to him.

He finally looked up from his hands. "I just thought, if I waited a little bit . . ." He trailed off.

"I know," Naz said. She did know. She would have done the same thing if it was Rojan who was shadowless. "But if you try to wait Vienna out until she doesn't remember, that won't mean that you can decide for her. It'll just make it wrong."

Malik buried his head in his arms.

Naz reached out and put her hand on his big, slouching shoulder. "You have to let her do this. Before she forgets she wanted to. Don't take away the last bit of freedom she still has from her."

DAVIDIA WAS ALREADY BESIDE THE SILENT, SEATED BODY AT the altar, talking quietly with the surface of the wall. As they crested the hill, Naz saw Gajarajan's ears ripple slightly, like an animal catching a sound on the breeze.

"Vienna," he said warmly. "It's an honor to meet you at last. I'm glad you came."

It was the first time Vienna had seen the leader of their city. She stared openmouthed at him. At the blindfolded man—unmoving, almost unaware, almost nonliving. And at its shadow behind on the wall, man*like*—the same rough size, with the same motions—but not shaped like a man at all.

"Hello," she finally whispered.

Malik was overcome with the urge to protect her and thought what was in her face was fear. But Naz could see what she was thinking. It wasn't fear. It was hope. That was the reason she had wanted to volunteer—to give Gajarajan permission to work his dangerous magic, and possibly fail, without fear, because she'd asked him to try knowing the chances. Naz's hands twitched, wanting to hold Vienna and cry, but she wouldn't want it. Not from a person she no longer remembered she knew. More than that, it wasn't Naz's place. Malik was here, and the grief belonged to him, not her. *Vienna was not her little sister.*

"I know it's been a difficult time for you, but I'm very pleased you've come to share what you remember about Transcendence with The Eight," the elephant said.

"That's not why I came," Vienna blurted out. Malik stepped protectively in front of her, but she leaned out from behind him again. "I mean, I'll tell you everything I remember, of course. Anything that will help," she stammered, moving around her father completely to face Gajarajan. "But that wasn't the reason I came."

The elephant shifted on the wall. "What is the reason, then?"

Naz could feel Malik about to speak again. She reached out and grabbed his arm firmly to stop him—not a shake, but a hug. His other hand appeared on top of hers unconsciously. Naz squeezed as hard as she could.

"I want to volunteer," Vienna said. "To be the next shadowless who tries to rejoin with a shadow. I know you're close, but you're afraid to hurt anyone else until you're sure you can do it. But you're never going to be sure unless you keep trying. I want you to try with me."

Naz waited, trembling. Before them, the wall darkened as Gajarajan slowly grew. His ears unfurled, trunk lifted in a muscular, graceful *S*. Naz didn't know if he was happy or insulted. He was just terrifying.

At last his trunk curled to his chin. "You're very brave," he said.

"Does that mean you'll do it?"

"Yes," the elephant said. Malik started, as if he'd been hit with something. But before he could argue, Gajarajan spoke again. "But I need something from you in return."

Davidia glanced at the wall from where she stood. "She's a child," she said softly to him.

"She's a shadowless," Gajarajan replied. "And the only shadowless that's seen Transcendence with her own eyes."

Naz wanted to look at Malik's face, but she couldn't move. All she could do was keep watching the huge shadow spread before them. "Vienna," Malik began.

"Tell me the price," Vienna said to the wall.

"Vienna." Malik took her by the shoulders. "Honey," he pleaded, voice breaking.

"I accept," she said fearlessly, staring into the dark shape of the elephant.

"Hear the price first," Gajarajan said.

Vienna nodded. "Name it, then."

"Become one of The Eight."

They all cried out in disbelief. "You're joking," Naz said, incredulous.

"I'm afraid not. In fact, we may not succeed without her."

"But you have eight already!"

"We do. But perhaps not the right eight. Transcendence is strong— and Vienna knows them better than any of the current members." Gajarajan looked down from the wall. "It will cost her memories to take one of the eight's places for the fight, yes. But it could also be the difference between winning and losing this last battle."

Beside Naz, Zhang shook his head. "Is that what you tell The

Eight every time you need them to do something for you?" he asked. "Everything you tell them to voluntarily forget?"

"I would never force anyone to do something they didn't want to do," Gajarajan said. "Each of The Eight is here willingly. They want to help the city." His ears waved, big gentle fans. "You've seen what's out there. Without their help, New Orleans would be the same as every other place—or worse. How do you think the wall that keeps us safe was built? Where the first food came from before what we had planted grew? How do you think all of the dangerous little mis-rememberings are all fixed so quickly?"

"Even if it means slowly dying for it?" Naz countered. "That's a high price to pay."

"Is it, though?" Gajarajan asked. "Any one of you also could have died fighting the Reds to save your home in the Iowa. What The Eight do here is the same thing. Except once I figure out how to give them shadows again and make the shadows stay . . ." He seemed to smile. "In fact, the price you might have paid for the same goal was far greater, then."

Vienna touched her father's arm. "Gajarajan's right, Dad," she said. "I might lose something, but if we don't win against Transcendence, I'm going to lose everything anyway. All of us are."

"If the situation was so dire, why didn't you say anything before?" Malik asked, barely controlled.

Gajarajan shrugged softly with his ears. "I told you. I would never have sought her out, because to join the sanctuary must be a free choice, not a forced one."

Naz didn't want to agree with him, but she could feel the defeat already beginning to set in. It didn't matter that it was Vienna, their Vienna. It wouldn't even have mattered if it was Rojan. Vienna knew the shadow was right—without Vienna's help, they might not win. She had to do it, even if it meant that she would have to sacrifice who knew how many of her precious last memories to save them all.

# ORLANDO ZHANG

DAWN SEEMED TO COME EARLIER THAN USUAL THE NEXT morning. As the sky slowly brightened, Zhang stood in the guard tower with Ahmadi, Malik, and Gajarajan—both the shadow and its body, which was seated behind them in the corner of the small enclosed platform. Far below, the world was very different than it had been when the sun set. Outside the city, and stretching to cover most of the long bridge over Lake Pontchartrain, the ground was blanketed in white, as if they had woken up to snow. Transcendence had arrived.

"I wonder what they did to the deathkites overnight," Ahmadi mused quietly.

None of them replied. Whatever they had done, it had been effective. There was no sign of even one of them now. No vast, colorful shapes catching the light, no silent angular shadows drifting over the water and fragrant grass, waiting for prey.

"We should tell The Eight," Malik said tensely, glancing across the city toward the first great hall, where the shadowless waited inside. "They should know. Every bit of tactical information . . ." He trailed off, as if realizing how far it was. Zhang hadn't thought of phones for a long time, until he realized he'd put his hand into his pocket as if to retrieve one.

Gajarajan glanced at them for a moment, considering. The wall of the tower was suddenly brighter, containing only pale morning light, and then just as suddenly, the familiar gray pattern was cut back into it. The elephant ruffled his ears.

"I've informed them," he said.

"Thank you," Malik said, surprised. "That was—I appreciate it."

Gajarajan shrugged. "To move using light doesn't require a similar effort to walking. It made more sense for me to go than any of you."

"Or him," Ahmadi said, indicating the blindfolded body sitting quietly in the corner. The man made no move to acknowledge he'd heard her. "Why *did* you bring him?" she asked.

"I'm not sure," Gajarajan said. "It isn't very useful, is it? Better dexterity, as it's a solid form, but that's about it."

Zhang couldn't help but shake his head. To be talking about a human body in such a way—especially his own. It was hard not to be entertained sometimes at how strangely Gajarajan understood people. More often than not, he seemed to Zhang more like a robot than an elephant, or the shadow of one—a disembodied intelligence that regarded their flesh like cars: interchangeable models. Zhang had always thought of the great gray animals as sort of like humans, really—with families, personalities, identities. Just bigger, and with tusks. But he supposed that was simply his attempt to understand them. Maybe that wasn't how they were at all.

Ahmadi was leaning cautiously over the edge of the tower, staring into the vast white. "What are they . . . doing?" she whispered.

"Praying," Gajarajan said.

Zhang looked at him sharply. "Praying to what?"

"Their leader." The shadow edged forward slightly, as if to also get a better look. "A shadowless at their center."

*Madness,* Zhang thought. An army of shadowed people, led by a shadowless who wanted to remove all human shade from the world— against a council of shadowless, led by a living shadow, who wanted to give everyone back their dark twin.

"Well, eight to one is good odds," Malik said as hopefully as he could. Zhang knew he was wondering the same thing the rest of them were. Why Transcendence needed only one.

"Don't fear," Gajarajan said, as if answering his thoughts. "The Eight are powerful, too."

"Why eight?" Ahmadi asked. "Yoshikawa said it's the strongest number. But why?"

"Eight is the number of verses about Surya in the Rigveda," the shadow answered.

"Surya?"

"The god of the sun," he replied, as if it meant something to them.

Just then there was a small ripple across the alabaster army below. Something was about to begin.

"The Eight are ready?" Zhang asked, resisting the urge to run, to hide anywhere he could find.

Gajarajan nodded. "Vienna will lead memories related to Transcendence, knowing most what they look like and how they act, and Downtown and Curly will lead any memories related to defending New Orleans. The rest shall harmonize, to help shoulder the burden of forgetting and intensify the strength of each act."

*Downtown and Curly.* Zhang had heard their names from the other New Orleanians from time to time, along with a few others who were no longer there—Marie, Buddy, and a shadowed doctor named Dr. Avanthikar. Of the original Eight, Downtown and Curly were the only two left who still served. The others had entered their endless wait long ago, and now remained in body only. No mind. Everything had been spent, down to the last recollection.

To know that two of the original Eight were with Vienna gave Zhang hope their plan might just work. She didn't really know what she was doing yet, but The Eight did, and they were intensely powerful. After all, they had been part of The Eight that had remembered the very first and still the most massive work of magic: the reimagining of the deadly hurricane that almost destroyed New Orleans into the gigantic water wall beneath them. Zhang watched the crystalline surface shimmer as the sun struck it. He understood it now—if unguided, how hard it would be to resist the urge to want to forget again thereafter. To do things even more incredible.

"Easy," Gajarajan said to Malik as the white shifted further.

"This is crazy," he replied, fists clenched. "Look at how many there are."

"Easy," the shadow repeated. "This isn't your battle."

Gajarajan had gathered everyone in New Orleans last night and reiterated that they were not to fight. That The Eight would do it for them. All the rest of them had to do was run to the center of the city on Vienna's command, and stay there, no matter what. Whether Transcendence was inside or outside the gates, whether they were attacking or not. *Simple enough,* Zhang thought. *Simple and terrifying.* But where were The Eight? They still hadn't arrived, and the army below was beginning to shift in waves, like a great ivory tide.

"They're moving," Ahmadi warned. Her fingers spasmed, wishing there was a bow to grab for. She was struggling as much as Zhang was to place all their safety in someone else's hands. Zhang turned around again, but the far hill in front of the sanctuary was still empty. *Where were The Eight?*

"There she is," Malik gasped. They all looked to where he was pointing. Across the city, Zhang could see eight small figures moving out from the first great hall into the sun. From this distance, and with no shadows, they almost looked like they were floating.

"Vienna, Downtown, Curly, Fromthelandoflakes, Skinny, Old-Timer, Chef, Survivedthestorm," Zhang said to himself. He tried to picture each one of them as they headed toward the city gates beneath him, to make himself believe that they could do it. That whatever their plan was, it was going to work. *Vienna, Downtown, Curly, Fromthelandoflakes, Skinny, Old-Timer, Chef, Survivedthestorm . . .*

"Gajarajan," Vienna said when they had reached the ground below the watchtower's ladder. They stood facing the gate in a pyramid formation, Vienna in front, Downtown and Curly behind her, and then the remaining five behind them.

"It's time," Downtown called up to them. "Something is stirring."

A chill went through Zhang as he looked backward, at the rest of New Orleans. Everything was empty and still. He knew that all the shadowed and shadowless were hiding just inside doors and windows and behind walls, ready to do what seemingly suicidal thing Vienna was about to ask for—but the sight of the city so utterly dead was frightening.

"His name will be Lucius," Gajarajan said to Vienna. "Their leader."

Zhang had no idea how Gajarajan knew it. Vienna nodded gently, as if from far away.

They watched the white waves begin to split from one endless alabaster surface into hundreds, thousands of small fluttering shapes, men and women covered from head to toe in their strange white robes. Maybe they were all hoping they would forget because they couldn't even see who they each were anymore.

"False prophet!" someone finally called from deep within Transcendence's lines. "Show yourself!"

Zhang nearly cried out when their gate trembled in response. Ahmadi clutched his arm with fingernails like razor blades as Malik forced himself to obey Gajarajan's nod to crank the wheel to open the huge doors. "Why are we doing this?" Zhang hissed. "Why open it for them?" But the shadow beside them said nothing. Zhang clutched the railing of the tower's low wall until his knuckles turned white.

Transcendence seemed equally surprised that they were opening the city to them. The first row lowered their weapons uncertainly. From inside, The Eight stared them down.

At last, one white shape pushed through the many to the front. "Transcended ones, we greet you." The man bowed, and his shadow copied. "If you join us now, we can offer you protection during the battle, and then mercy afterward. You will be accepted into Transcendence as honored guests."

"We wish to speak to Lucius," Vienna said.

The man in white paused. He was close enough that Zhang could just make out his eyes from the tower as they narrowed suspiciously. "Your own leader doesn't show himself. What makes you think you have the right to demand to speak to ours?"

"The One Who Gathers has a shadow," Vienna said coldly. She gestured to the towering, shimmering height of the living storm bound to stillness on either side of the gate. Something one still bound to his dark twin could never make. "Who do you think is really in charge here?"

The man in white finally bowed again. It was impossible to tell, but Zhang thought he might have been smiling beneath all the veils and layers. "Our leader asked to meet you before we even arrived. I am happy to have found you worthy of his audience."

Zhang braced as their crowd parted around another shifting section of itself. A group emerged, tightly clustered. At least ten disciples surrounded their great shadowless messiah, a tall and almost handsome man of indeterminate age. The front two on either side held on to him as they walked by linking their arms with his at the elbows, like human chains. *Trying to keep him from utterly destroying the city until they're ready,* Zhang thought grimly. He was also draped in the same robes, but more layers of them, and longer, and was the only one with his head completely uncovered.

Lucius.

It was the look on the shadowless's face that caught Zhang: it was nothing like how the ones in Gajarajan's sanctuary seemed. Their gazes were absent, but not angry, not afraid—as if their memories had simply gone off somewhere else for a time and might return. It was even different from what he'd seen on the faces of the Red King and the Reds. That had been greed and rage, twisted out of control without memory. Lucius was something far worse—he was nothing at all. Emptiness that could never be filled. His eyes were not simply dimmed or distant—they were dead.

The escort of disciples came to a stop in front of the first man that had been speaking for them all. Lucius stared at The Eight for several seconds, studying them in silence. From above, Zhang studied him back intensely. There was something almost familiar about him— almost like a face he'd met in another time, another world—but he could not place him. The disciples clung to him, practically melding onto his body. Their shadows twisted behind them into a grotesque mass.

"You lead the people of New Orleans?" Lucius finally asked. The voice was disarmingly quiet and smooth. "A city of shadowed people?"

"We have many shadowless as well," Vienna said. "New Orleans welcomes all who want to remember instead of forget."

"Once a man transcends, he cannot return," Lucius replied.

Vienna grinned. "You're wrong."

The disciples around Lucius pulled tighter, and Zhang flinched—but nothing happened. Lucius only nodded. "You haven't been shadowless for very long," he finally said. "You'll see."

"I *have* seen," Vienna replied. "When I heard the rumors, I didn't believe most of them either. But then I arrived in New Orleans and—"

"You *came* to New Orleans?" Lucius asked. "You didn't already live here?"

"From Washington, D.C.," Vienna answered.

Lucius's eyes narrowed as he searched the incomplete archives of his mind for information that was attached to any of those words. "On your way, you didn't see a very large thing to ride in—a large vehicle—did you?"

"A large vehicle?" Vienna frowned. "No. There's no fuel anymore."

"Oh." Lucius glanced down for a moment, at the grass that tickled the billowing hems of his robe. Zhang waited for something more, or the reason he'd asked, but Lucius said nothing. He simply waited. But for what?

The longer Zhang watched, the stranger the scene in front of him seemed. Lucius was there, as Gajarajan had said he would be, and he was shadowless, and Transcendence clearly worshipped him—but everything felt as if it was tilted one degree off center. As if Zhang was the one who wasn't remembering something that he should have understood, instead of all the shadowless.

"We came in horse carriages," Vienna offered, as if that might have been what he meant.

But Lucius only shook his head and waved a hand to dispel the words. "Never mind," he said. Then, even more quietly: "I can't remember why I asked."

"Enough talk," the first Transcendence disciple, the one who had been appointed to speak, growled to The Eight. He pointed at Vienna. "Join us now, or after we destroy your false prophet and free you."

From the corner of his eye, Zhang saw the shadow of the elephant shift on the wall beside him. "Remember, don't fight them," he whispered. "Not a single one."

And then he stretched out of the tower in a flash and spread himself across the earth just to the left of The Eight, his shape burned starkly against the grass like black fire—a shadow with no body.

A cry of horror went up from the fluttering, alabaster army as the closest ones saw it. "The blasphemer!" the man in white shrieked. "The monstrous one!" The city echoed with their screams. The disciples around Lucius cowered, howling, and even Lucius looked momentarily stunned at the unnatural, impossible sight. In the tower with Zhang, Malik, and Ahmadi, The One Who Gathers's body continued to sit placidly, out of sight.

"Destroy them!" one of the disciples cried. White surged toward the gates, toward the city, a deafening avalanche.

Vienna raised her hand straight above her head. The signal. "*Now!*"

Zhang slid down the ladder and ran, before he could think better of it. Ahmadi and Malik thudded onto the grass after him. "Now!" Zhang cried again, to help relay her call, but he didn't need to. She had forgotten something—something that made her voice audible everywhere in the city at once. All around them, every New Orleanian not sequestered in the first great hall was pouring onto the deserted streets, running as fast as they could for the open plaza of the city where The Eight waited, moments from being surrounded by Transcendence. Zhang, Ahmadi, and Malik crashed into another waterfall of people exploding out of a joining street, and were sucked into the current. He looked for Ahmadi, but all he could see were arms, the backs of heads, hair whipping in the wind. *Don't fight,* he tried to remind himself as he felt the panic rise. They all sprinted straight for the swarming white and crashed into their lines.

"Zhang!" Ahmadi screamed. Zhang turned around frantically, but he couldn't see her. Not see—tell apart. Because everyone suddenly had the same face.

"What the . . . ," the person next to him said then, as a shocked silence suddenly fell across both armies.

Vienna had changed all of them—thousands of New Orleanians—so that they all looked just like Transcendence. Everyone was now wearing the exact same pale, swirling robes, veiled to the tops of their noses. Zhang looked at the man standing next to him, and to both his horror and exhilaration, couldn't tell who he was at all. He had no idea if he was New Orleanian or Transcendence.

He was almost too awestruck to wonder what it had cost Vienna.

"Mix with them!" someone from the New Orleans side cried out then. "Mix with them so we're too intertwined for them to attack!"

"Retreat!" a Transcendence general yelled back. "Retreat!" People began pushing and yelling, trying to move but afraid to injure anyone in case they were facing an ally instead of an enemy. The crowd surged in multiple directions, but it was too late—all of Transcendence's army had thrust itself through the city gate in its rage at having seen Gajarajan's monstrous form. The iron doors clanged shut behind them as they struggled to peel away from the disguised New Orleanians.

*He was useful after all,* Zhang realized as he looked up at the tower, where Gajarajan was no doubt back inside—and where his body had just finished spinning the wheel to close the gate. Everyone stood frozen at the realization that both groups were now trapped together inside the city.

"Zhang?" someone called in the momentary pause.

"Ahmadi," Zhang hissed. "Ahmadi!" He squeezed around confused shapes. Everyone was still coming out of shock. "Ahmadi!" But the white-robed figure he bumped into next in the jostling crowd wasn't her.

Lucius.

Zhang pulled back in terror—but the shadowless simply stared impassively at him as the disciples clutching his arms floundered, trying and failing to swat away anyone who got too close. It was equally plausible that Zhang was shocked because he was a New Orleanian as because he was one of Transcendence's own who had accidentally just touched the hand of his god—but the fact that the not knowing didn't seem to trouble Lucius was unnerving. Was he really so powerful that even the instinct to flinch against the possibility of a knife in his gut was gone?

But then the disciple on Lucius's left tugged on his elbow until the shadowless turned toward him, the one on the right following, to move deeper into the crowd. Zhang watched, transfixed. He understood suddenly then why everything had seemed so strange before. Lucius's dead expression, the way the disciples had clung to him as they walked up to speak with The Eight. They hadn't so much been holding Lucius *back* as holding him *there*.

Zhang looked at the shadowless again just as Lucius's pale, resigned eyes met his own. He had never been their leader, or at least if he had been, he wasn't anymore—he was their hostage.

"Lucius," Zhang started to say to him. He reached out as the disciples turned, their knives emerging swiftly from their robes. "Wait—"

"*Marie!*" Downtown and Curly shouted at that same moment over the din.

From above, everywhere, there was a deafening, groaning whine, like a great beast awakening to the sound of its name. *Who was Marie?* Zhang thought frantically, and remembered that she was one of the original Eight at the same moment that he realized from where the sound had come.

She was the one who had known the most about hurricanes.

The water hit the city in a deafening boom.

Everything happened on instinct—Zhang closed his eyes and squeezed his nose and mouth shut to hold his breath before the wave pummeled him. The freed flooding storm enveloped everything, surging with the starving rage of a tsunami. *They did it!* Zhang reeled. *Downtown and Curly! The hurricane!* The Eight had lured the entire Transcendence army into a trap, and then freed the storm from its imprisoned shape, unleashing it directly inward onto New Orleans.

His lungs began to burn. Everywhere, the sounds of bodies being thrown against the ground, of air being strangled out of lungs and cold liquid glugging in, assaulted him. Zhang fought desperately to keep his last gasp inside his lungs. But he was still . . .

He opened his eyes.

Over and over, the waves crashed, towering, inescapable, as they filled the city. Zhang waited to be consumed by the deafening roar— but every droplet curved sharply around him. He looked down at his false white robes, the grass beneath his feet, amazed. There wasn't a single inch of him that was wet.

Through the spiraling flood, he caught sight of others crouching, bewildered like himself, each encased in a narrow tunnel of air. New Orleanians. All of them safe. He stared in disbelief. The hurricane knew the difference between the ones it had protected as the wall and their enemies.

Above, around, the war was being decided. Zhang watched in stunned, horrified wonder as other white shapes thrashed in slow motion, suspended in a current of bubbles and clear, sparkling death. No matter how hard they kicked for any twisting, curved surface, the hurricane simply pulled them back in, like fish on a line. Even though the New Orleanians were all veiled, Zhang stumbled between the swirling columns to the cowering shape he thought was Ahmadi, and was right. He held her as the other white shapes each wrung themselves a final, agonized time, and then at last all floated still, veils spread like graceful fins.

Gajarajan nodded slowly. "Perhaps. The Eight will know the right thing to use for a new wall when it comes."

Zhang rubbed his face. The hurricane had finally spent the rest of the destruction it had meant to wreak before it had been bound, and what was left of it was draining slowly around the closed gate—around either open side of it, since there were no longer any walls—and into Lake Pontchartrain. Everywhere, New Orleanians wandered, bewildered but alive. Downtown and Curly's magic had managed to spare not just their people, but even the buildings of the city as well. The only lingering sign there had been a storm at all was the faint drizzle that now hung in the air, coating everything in a misty sheen. And all of the drowned bodies. The ground looked covered in snow again. Only this time Transcendence wouldn't ever move—until New Orleans burned or buried them.

*It was over.* Zhang could hardly believe it, even as he saw the destruction with his own eyes. *It was finally over. Transcendence was gone.*

"Well, I hope the right thing comes quickly," Ahmadi said. "It's going to be much harder to defend the city until then."

"I think the worst is over," Gajarajan replied. He turned back to the quiet battlefield. "We'll be all right until The Eight can devise something new."

Zhang looked at the elephant. "Do you think . . ." He trailed off.

"I don't know either," Gajarajan said.

Zhang nodded. And they would probably never know, he guessed—whether Lucius didn't have enough power to stop, or at least dampen, the drowning wall as it choked the life out of his disciples, or if he'd been able, but didn't try. If he had wanted to be free so badly that he let Downtown and Curly plunge Transcendence's army into a watery grave—and himself.

"Vienna!" Malik cried. Zhang turned around to see him take off running, white robes flapping damply in the warm, humid air. Another white shape put its arms out as he swept it up in a crushing hug.

"Dad," she said softly.

"Oh, thank God," Malik whispered. Zhang felt his throat tighten as he watched. He had known that feeling all too well once. *Thank God it wasn't me, whatever was taken from you. Thank God you still remember me.* He felt Ahmadi's hand on his arm, a tentative, nervous touch. He leaned into it.

"Did you see?" Vienna asked softly as Malik brought her over by the hand. The other seven of The Eight trailed slowly behind, as if dazed. Gajarajan moved gently between each of them, his dark form propped up directly against their bodies instead of against something facing them. Perhaps that was the way he embraced? Zhang wondered. "Did you see—what I did?"

Zhang held out the front of his white robe. "I did see," he said. It was too incredible to believe. To try to comprehend that Vienna, *Vienna*—who on some days was still so innocent it seemed as if she was more child than young adult—had worked magic across an entire city, and saved thousands of lives in an instant. "I think it's safe to say that you are, without doubt, the *best* soldier the Iowa has ever or will ever have."

Malik and Ahmadi laughed, Malik almost hysterically. Vienna started at the outburst and put out a hand on instinct, as if to bat away the sound. Malik saw it as he wiped his eyes. His smile was gone—he hugged her again. *Oh, no,* Zhang realized. "It's okay," he said to her. "The Iowa isn't important. Don't worry. It doesn't matter. You can forget that."

"It seems like it was important," she said, brow furrowed. "That place."

"You're here now," Zhang said. "That's more important."

She looked up at him. "And you—I know that I know you, but not from where. Are you from the Iowa, too?"

"Yes. I was Imanuel's friend."

"That's it." She nodded, having finally found something to grasp on to. "Ory."

Zhang chuckled for a moment. He hadn't heard it in such a long time, his first name sounded almost wrong now. But something strange had happened to Gajarajan. He'd snapped from where he was against the grass beside the rest of The Eight to the picket fence in front of Zhang and Vienna in a blinding instant, as if someone had flicked on a light.

"His name is Zhang," the elephant said. There was something odd in the tone—suspicion, or a question.

"Zhang?" Vienna asked, confused.

"Yes. Zhang," Gajarajan repeated. "Not Ory."

"It *is* Ory," Zhang said to him. "My first name is Orlando. Zhang is my surname. At the Iowa, it was just something we did for morale— like real soldiers. Going by our surnames." He nodded encouragingly at Vienna. "She forgot the one, but she still remembers the other. You still know who I am."

Vienna nodded. "I remember."

Gajarajan was silent against the fence for a long time, lost in thought. Why this had struck the shadow so intensely baffled Zhang—but almost never did he understand why the things that mattered to Gajarajan mattered and why others didn't. He turned to Ahmadi, planning to leave the elephant to his strange, brooding thoughts.

The great dark ears were folded, perfectly still for the first time ever, Zhang noticed then. The sight was even more unsettling than when he warped into impossible shapes and heights.

"I didn't know that," Gajarajan finally murmured, almost as if in awe.

# THE ONE WHO GATHERS

GAJARAJAN RETURNED TO THE SANCTUARY LATE THAT NIGHT.
There had been the New Orleanians to tend to, and then the dead.
Then finally, the shadowless who had won the battle for them all. They
were not as bad as Gajarajan feared, but for Survivedthestorm, it was
time to let him retire from The Eight, to begin his wait in the first great
hall while Gajarajan looked for a suitable shadow. He had done as much
as he could, and it was wrong to ask him to forget more. There would
be others to take his and Vienna's place.

Tomorrow Gajarajan would go and bring Malik's brave daughter
there, to the second great hall, as they had agreed. But there was
something else to do first.

The moon was almost full, casting silver light down onto the sanctuary, every corner of it reachable without having to move his body
from the altar. Gajarajan draped across the open roof, looking down
into the second hall, where a small shape rested on a simple bed. He
shifted forward and was inside then, against the floor, silent. The rhyth-
mic, shallow sounds of slumber continued from under the blankets,
undisturbed. The shadow rose up against the far wall, where a table
sat. He studied the things on top. A change of fresh clothes, instruc-
tional objects he'd brought in: a leaf, a dried flower, a spoon—and
the patient's personal effects at the time of admission to the great hall.
Some had many, in the earlier days. This one had brought hardly any at
all. Just one thing, in fact. The thing from which he'd been able to take
the first shadow that had ever fit back onto a shadowless.

THE NIGHT DR. AVANTHIKAR HAD DIED, THE SECOND GREAT
hall was empty. It had been that way for weeks—because Gajarajan

had failed so many times and was afraid to try again. To torture another shadowless with the hope of recovery, only to have it fail or drive them insane. Or kill them. It was what they'd been arguing about in the first place that drove her to such a risky move, to go outside the gate, into the dark with the deathkites.

Davidia's guards brought both Dr. Avanthikar and her shadowless rescue in without dying themselves, somehow. The deathkites' screeches faded as they slammed the doors shut behind them.

"We tried, we tried," one of the guards was saying, over and over, terrorized by the sight of the doctor as she was—all the blood, the almost surgical openings in the flesh. Everyone loved her as much as Gajarajan did. "We tried," he stammered.

"Why?" Gajarajan asked her softly as he slid from the side of the gate onto the grass beside where they had set her, so they were both lying down.

She turned her head to look at him. "That's just always the way, in medicine, I've learned," she said. "The one who discovers something great always did so only because some complete *gandoo* they worked with refused to let them give up on an idea that seemed useless." A tremor of pain ran through her. "Look at me. My team and I tried everything, *every* idea, and Hemu just refused to shut up about that stupid elephant. And then you awakened."

Gajarajan smiled at her. The outline where his form met the torchlight ached, in a great, sinking pain.

Dr. Avanthikar tried to swallow. He could see her eyes going glassy. "This is the first time you've believed less in your power than I have since we began trying to rejoin shadows. Maybe this patient is the one, and I'm the infuriating colleague who refuses to let you quit."

Gajarajan didn't tell her that the shadowless man had already succumbed to his wounds. The body flayed by the deathkites until it had unfurled layer by layer, like red rose petals blooming out from a center spine. Dr. Avanthikar wheezed, and he reached out and touched the shadow of her hand where it rested on the grass beneath her shredded palm. Far up on the hill, he felt his body double over and shudder in agony as the lines in her face suddenly softened, released.

"Keep trying," she said. "Do it for me."

"I will."

Gajarajan let the faraway body writhe. It could bear the pain for her. The time it would have to was very short anyway.

THE MAN DR. AVANTHIKAR HAD WANTED TO SAVE HADN'T survived, but Gajarajan had vowed to listen to what she'd said anyway. After she died, everyone who followed the rumors to New Orleans was brought safely inside—no matter what. The first shadowless to come after they'd buried Dr. Avanthikar was the patient who now lay in the bed behind Gajarajan. This one he would not give up on, he'd promised the old doctor's headstone.

Gajarajan would never know if it was because of Dr. Avanthikar, or if it was just pure dumb luck that this patient turned out to be the first and only one he figured out how to cure, but it didn't matter. It didn't matter, because he'd done it. It was possible.

The second great hall creaked softly as the roof settled overhead. Gajarajan shifted forward until he was draped across the table. It was slightly more difficult at night, with only the moonlight and no sun or torches to help with contrast, but he reached across the surface of the wood until he felt what he was looking for. The thing from which he'd taken the cured patient's shadow.

A tape recorder.

IN THE OLD WORLD, THERE WOULD HAVE BEEN PHOTOGRAPHS and documents to compare. Persons would have had wallets whose driver's licenses could be entered into databases and matched instantly, as they had once done for his own body, after the car accident that led to his birth. There was none of that now. All Gajarajan had was a woman who had arrived on foot, alone, who remembered nothing, and a tape recorder with fragmented thoughts locked inside.

Zhang never spoke about his life before the Forgetting, or even before arriving in New Orleans, really. The shadow thought of him only as Zhang, or the General, or the one who brought all the books. In the tape recordings, he was always called by his first name, and there was no mention of the others in his group, or Washington, D.C., or what he'd been doing there. When the shadowless woman had shown up at the gate, she hadn't been able to speak at all anymore. There was almost nothing left. Gajarajan spent weeks painstakingly analyzing the recordings to draw out what was needed, to make the recorder's own little square shadow much, much more detailed and complete than he had ever been able to do before—the most human-shaped shadow he'd ever been able to craft from something else—before he tried to take it from the thing and place it on her. It was nearly finished by the time Zhang and his army eventually arrived at the gates.

Perhaps he should have asked Zhang more about himself sooner. But Gajarajan had always been bad with names anyway—he hadn't even noticed that almost every one of the Iowan soldiers had given only a surname at all until Vienna forgot Zhang's and called him something else.

"Ory," he murmured softly. He reflected off the wall back to the roof. The sleeper did not stir. There would be plenty of time to tell them both the good news tomorrow. "I've found your wife, Ory," Gajarajan said to the moon. "Max is here."

# MAHNAZ AHMADI

THAT WAS A SURPRISE. NEITHER ONE OF THEM SAW THAT COM-ing. Not in a million years.

The day after Vienna and The Eight had saved the city from Transcendence felt like a day out of time. They all wandered around, staring at everything that still existed, still was theirs. Shopkeepers neglected to open shops. Sentries didn't show up for duty. Zhang failed to unlock the library—but no one wanted to read anyway. They were all too busy just living. Looking at lampposts, sprigs of grass, a smudge along the bottom of a wall from someone's boot, and marveling they were all still alive.

The only thing that reminded Naz to do anything at all was her stomach. By evening, she and Zhang both were in House 33's kitchen, chopping potatoes from the community garden while they waited for their turn at the cooking pot outside. The stove was free, but there hadn't been any thunderstorms for a few days, so the wires that trailed off into the sky weren't able to catch a current—they were back to the pot and front-yard fire pit for now. But Naz didn't mind. She hadn't had even a moment of electricity for two years. Having it for a few hours every few days now was like magic.

Some of their housemates from the other rooms were laughing about something at the kitchen table. Zhang was dicing expertly, even one finger short. His hand had healed so well.

The soup was Max's recipe. Naz thought maybe it was progress, that he had suggested it. Max apparently hadn't been the best cook, but Naz was. She was still trying to decide if she was supposed to make it well—would that impress him or seem cruel?—or not so well—would that comfort him, or make him even more depressed?

"I'm starving," she said just as a knock rattled the front door.

"Think it's Malik?" Zhang asked as the knife paused. "Maybe he came for dinner?"

She didn't think it was—Malik hadn't been up for visiting since Vienna had left for the sanctuary so Gajarajan could begin trying to make her a new shadow, or whatever it was that he did. Then they heard their housemates' surprised voices.

"Oh! Why—"

"Gajarajan! What an honor!"

Naz looked at Zhang. Surprise was etched across his forehead.

"I didn't know he went anywhere," Naz heard one of them say to the other as they came back through the kitchen and disappeared to their rooms. "The human part, I mean."

"Zhang," Gajarajan's voice reached them then. His body smiled as soon as it stepped into the kitchen. Behind it, on the wall, Gajarajan looked at Naz, and the grin lessened slightly. It was almost as if he hadn't expected her to be there.

"Hi," she said.

Gajarajan bowed slightly, spread across both the wall and the counter.

They waited, but Gajarajan just kept looking at Zhang, as if unsure of how to proceed. Between the two of them, the shadow's human body waited patiently, vaguely facing her, but not quite. Naz tried not to stare.

"It's nothing to be embarrassed about," Gajarajan finally said to her. "It's a strange thing to see a blindfolded man walk as if he could see."

"I'm sorry." Naz managed to look away, to the shadow, and smile. "Other than when Transcendence came, I don't think I've seen you do it." She didn't say that it wasn't so much the walking as that he never bothered to point the body in the right direction once he set it somewhere—in their kitchen or upon the altar.

"Don't be. I use it so infrequently, I've made it into something strange. There's just so rarely any need."

"Is everything all right?" Zhang asked then.

On the wall, the shadow nodded—the man did not. "Yes, everything is all right. It's better than all right."

Zhang relaxed a little. "Would you like some soup? It'll be finished soon."

"No, thank you. The body has already eaten." Gajarajan shook his head. "I'm actually here because, well—I've discovered something very unexpected."

Zhang set the knife down beside the cutting board and turned back to the shadow. Naz watched, waiting for one of them to say something. The starchy water slicked from the potatoes began to collect at the blade's serrated edge as it rested on the counter.

"If it would be possible to meet in your room, that would be best," Gajarajan continued.

Naz put her hand on Zhang's shoulder.

"I think it might be best if Zhang and I met alone at first, Ahmadi. It's a . . . sensitive subject."

That made Zhang edge closer to her, in a way that made her heart thrill. "All three of us go," he said firmly.

THE MEETING LASTED ONLY A FEW MINUTES. IT SEEMED AT the time as if it had gone on forever, but the sliced potatoes were still sweating when Naz finally went back downstairs, even though neither one of them wanted dinner anymore.

Gajarajan still needed a few days, to make sure everything was perfect, he'd said. On Ceresday—New Orleans's eighth weekday, thanks to Wifejanenokids's old mistake—Zhang could come by anytime. He would be waiting.

Afterward, Naz and Zhang sat outside on the porch, bowls of soup untouched beside them, staring out at the empty street. Everyone else was inside their houses, eating. The rest of their own housemates hovered momentarily in the kitchen one at a time, then escaped back to their rooms, sensing the danger.

"What time will you go, on Ceresday?" Naz finally asked. "I think you should do it in the morning. Just go first thing."

"Ahmadi," Zhang pleaded. He looked more tired than she'd ever seen him in his life. "I know we have to talk about it, but not yet. Just not yet."

Naz nodded and turned back to what was left of the sunset. They sat that way in the quiet for a few more hours, just feeling how it felt to be the two of them together, side by side. She tried not to think about how it very well could be the last time.

They didn't fight until they got up to the room, well after midnight.

# THE ONE WHO GATHERS

IN THE COURTYARD OF THE SANCTUARY, SWORDS CLANGED. The volunteers leapt backward into their ready stances again.

"Watch your blind spots," Malik instructed. "Faster!"

"You trained them well," Gajarajan said against the wall beside him as the volunteers sprang for each other once more, some striking, the others parrying. Farther away, he could feel the sensations in his body's flesh—the twitch of long-unused muscles, microscopic imitations in response to the sparring matches the shadow's eyes were seeing.

"They're tough," Malik said. "They had to be. There was no room for mistakes in D.C.—or on the road here."

"And you want to go back out there."

Malik studied the volunteers grimly as they continued to train, arms crossed. "You agreed my idea was a good one."

Gajarajan nodded. He thought of Dr. Zadeh. "It is. I just meant—I was taught once by a wise man that sometimes people do drastic things in the face of difficult circumstances. A sort of coping mechanism. I worry this mission may be such a thing."

"Of course it is," Malik said.

Gajarajan said nothing—waited for Malik to continue if he liked. He respected that. That Malik was a man who didn't shy away from understanding his grief, even if it made the pain sharper than if he left it as a dark, vague thing. It was a sign of true strength.

Malik looked down. "I just—I don't know what else to do with myself for the next few months. Not being able to see her. And maybe—never again."

"Vienna—" Gajarajan began, but Malik waved his hand as if to dispel what the shadow was about to say next.

"I understand there are rules," he said. "That what you do in the sanctuary is dangerous."

"Those rules are as much for your and the rest of the city's safety as hers," Gajarajan replied.

"I know." He nodded tiredly. "It drives me mad. But I agreed when I let her walk in." He leaned forward and stared hard into the wall where Gajarajan was darkly cast. "But I can't keep sitting here in New Orleans waiting indefinitely. I need to do something. *Anything.*"

What Malik had proposed to him seemed like a death wish, but if anyone could succeed at this task, it would be him and his soldiers. He had come to Gajarajan the day after Vienna entered the sanctuary, shouting the elephant's name as if possessed, until the shadow flashed up onto the curved wall of the altar to receive him. The body was perched ready to stop him in case he lunged; Gajarajan had thought he'd come to try and take his daughter back by force now that the reality of her absence had finally sunk in. But it wasn't that at all. He'd come to ask for the exact opposite: to be allowed to leave the city. He wanted to take a small team and search the strange new wilderness for more people—shadowed or shadowless—and help them reach New Orleans, too.

Gajarajan slid to the left along the wall, closer to Malik. "I'm worried about the danger," the shadow finally said. "About sending you and your volunteers back out there again. To where the shadowless are succumbing to the pull, and there's no one to stop them."

"I know. But we can do it." Malik brushed away a fly as the soldiers training took a break, panting from exertion. For a brief moment, his face darkened. Gajarajan imagined he was remembering the ghost of the first Iowan General again. Of the terrifying shadowless he'd called the Red King, and of the monsters in white who came out of the wilderness after their carriages with fire. "We've survived much worse."

"Are you afraid at all that something might happen to you out there? Something that might prevent you from returning to Vienna?" Gajarajan asked.

"Yes," he admitted. "But I think it would be worse if I stayed."

The shadow studied Malik's face. There would be no deterring the man, he could see. The strain was there beneath the fierce expression. The knowledge that the only thing he could do to help his daughter was not to do anything at all for her. Something had to fill that hole before it consumed him. But more than that, he was also right: there were shadowless out there in need of help, who might not find the city or hear the stories on their own.

Gajarajan nodded. "All right. But for this to be worth anything, you need to be able to show those you find indisputable proof of this place and my power. Otherwise, you're no more convincing than the rumors."

"If I can get you that indisputable proof, you agree that we can go?" Malik asked.

"If you can, then—" Gajarajan started.

"I will," he interrupted, certain. "In D.C., I listened to the legends about you for more than a year before I made it here. Hoping, but not fully believing, since I had nothing to go on but gossip. Because it wasn't just my life on the line if that gossip was wrong—it was Vienna's, too. I was desperate for one of those someones speaking the rumors to not just talk but to *show me*—something I could see with my own eyes and touch with my own hands, to prove you were real. If anyone here can find something like that, it'll be me."

"What would that sort of something be, though?" Gajarajan asked.

"I'm not sure yet," Malik said. "But I'll know it when I see it."

# MAHNAZ AHMADI

After her shift at the wall, she went upstairs and piled everything into a bedsheet like it was a folding rucksack. There wasn't that much anyway. Just her bow, some clothes, and the remains of what family trinkets she and Rojan had started out with in their duffel bag.

There was a room left on the top floor of House 47, the most recently finished house—and the farthest open spot away from House 33—so she went there. Zhang said he didn't want her to go, but she couldn't stay. Not after she knew that the shadowless who had been successfully rehabilitated was *his* Max, and that she'd be ready to rejoin the world in a day. What was Naz supposed to do? Just sit at the communal kitchen table while Zhang brought her through the door and they talked upstairs? While he—moved her into his room right beside hers? It was better this way. She needed time to think.

In her braver moments, she wanted to be happy for him. To find anyone again after what had happened was nothing short of a miracle. What would she give if Rojan could come back? But this was different. Zhang had added to Naz's life, but she had taken Max's place in his.

House 47 was full of a group of university students from Memphis who had walked to New Orleans because some of them used to have parents who lived in Metairie. They all knew one another pretty well and let Naz keep to herself. That was good. She signed on for a few extra shifts on the wall, and decided to spend some time with Malik before he left, which he was convinced would be soon, despite the fact that nothing he'd brought to Gajarajan had been anywhere near the "indisputable proof" he needed to be able to go. She almost went to him after she put her clothes in House 47 and signed up for his crazy mission, too, but she stopped herself on the walk over. It would have been for the wrong reasons. She would have been doing it to punish Zhang, to force his hand in choosing.

In truth, she knew she probably should have done it. She should have forced it. Max was his wife. If Naz was on the road for five, six months, it would make everything a lot easier. She'd come back, and it would be over. Maybe then she'd go out again, and just keep going out every time another mission was ready. But it turned out she didn't have the guts. Or maybe she had too much hope. Impossible hope. But she also was watching the impossible happen right in front of her.

It should have been the most romantic story in the world: wife loses her memory and disappears, husband traverses the country, braving wilderness and war to find her, against million-to-one odds. Naz was sure that Zhang prayed every night that Max wasn't dead, that he'd really be with her once more, never actually believing any of it was possible. Otherwise, none of this between he and Naz would have happened. He was the one who leaned forward to kiss her that night in her room, not she. He thought he finally had to forget Max, because she was never coming back.

Except here she was. And she remembered.

# ORLANDO ZHANG

ORY WAS SURPRISED TO SEE THAT THE ENTRANCE TO THE sanctuary had no door.

"I guess I'd just assumed," he said to Gajarajan. They were standing inside the first great hall, all of Ory and half of him. Gajarajan's body remained outside, on the other side of the altar. Over the top of the wall, draped like thin black tulle and then trailing across the ground to where it sat upright against the entrance beside Ory, was his shadow. "Usually places where humans live have doors."

Gajarajan considered. "I suppose the places where elephants live don't," he said, and ruffled his ears. "There are only two doors in the entire sanctuary." For a moment, he continued to ponder the idea in silence. Then the shape of his massive head angled slightly more toward Ory, the curved tusks disappearing as they turned from semi-profile into straight on. "Are you feeling all right?" he asked gently. "Yes," Ory lied, and tried to smile, but he just felt ill. It seemed clammy inside the great hall, nothing like the sweltering heat outside. *Keep it together,* he reminded himself, and forced his teeth to stop chattering. His fingers found and squeezed the square outline of his wallet through his trouser pocket for strength, where the fossil of Max's photograph lay tucked inside. He still had it, even after so many months and miles—although it had long faded beyond anything recognizable. He'd crossed states, fought in wars, fallen into moving lakes, and now it was no more than a gray slip of paper with a vague, human-shaped smudge at the center. Almost as if it had slowly become a portrait of Max's shadow rather than of her.

"I can imagine this is . . . an intense moment," Gajarajan finally said. "To be able to meet your wife again."

Ory managed to nod. "Were you married before?"

"No," the shadow said. "Not really."

Ory looked down. It had seemed like a strange choice of words, but then he realized it wasn't at all. *Not really* had in fact meant *yes*. "I'm sorry," he replied.

"Don't be. I don't remember." Gajarajan shrugged softly, such a subtle and human gesture.

Ory didn't know if he'd ever get used to seeing it. It had taken him forever to be able to look at a person with no shadow. Now there was a shadow that moved all on its own.

"I'm going to get you settled first, and make sure you're comfortable and prepared," Ory realized Gajarajan was saying. "Then we'll bring Max in."

"How is she doing?" he blurted out.

"Very well," Gajarajan replied. "The body was in bad shape when it arrived. Dehydrated, exhausted. It was very difficult, the rejoining— you know how dangerous it can be. I didn't know if it was going to take. But it did. Now she's healthy, happy—and ready to meet you again. She remembers you."

Ory did his best to nod. It seemed beyond believable—that the single shadowless Gajarajan had been able to save out of all of them so far was Max—*his* Max. He was still too afraid to fully believe it.

"Please, after you," Gajarajan said, and gestured to the other end of the first hall, his dark arm sweeping across the wall. "I'm coming too, don't worry."

As they walked, the shadowless sitting on mats in little clusters looked up at Gajarajan, then Ory. Some seemed to have no idea who he was, or had known and forgotten, but a few must have heard the news. "Congratulations," they said softly, with a happiness that was almost more like awe. *They found each other, after all this, in the end.* He could see what it meant to them, what they were watching happen. *She remembers again. It worked. It's possible after all.*

At the end of the first great hall was a corridor, and then a door.

"One," Gajarajan said, meaning *the first of the only two doors.*

Ory nodded as he looked at it. What would it be like to live in a place where you had to walk this far before you hit a barrier? He had imagined that when you became shadowless, there were hundreds more doors, not fewer.

Gajarajan's shadowy arm slithered across the face of the wood. "The second door is just inside. It leads into the second great hall."

"What's this, then?" Ory asked as the first door started to move, the shadow's dark, two-dimensional outline impossibly pushing the three-dimensional thing open.

"The visiting room," Gajarajan said.

In the small space, there were four chairs around a simple wooden table. Max's tape recorder was in the center of its bare surface.

"Oh, God," Ory said.

"It's the same one," Gajarajan confirmed.

"The same one," he repeated, entranced. He clenched his fists to stop himself from leaping at it. "Can I hold it?"

"Of course," Gajarajan said. "It belongs to you and Max."

For a moment, Ory didn't move. Then he did. He sat down first, and gently touched the cool plastic. Then he realized it had no shadow beneath it. "Does it—?"

"Unfortunately, no," Gajarajan said softly. "It doesn't play. I had to use them—the recordings. To form her shadow into the right shape. Otherwise it would have been just a rectangle, hardly the form of a woman at all." He paused. "At the time she arrived, I didn't know what had happened. Who you were, if you were still out there . . . My first obligation was to Max. To restore her memories, as completely as I was able."

"No, that . . ." Ory nodded. "That was the right thing to do."

Gajarajan shifted on the wall, edging closer. "It might be best to leave it on the table during the reintroduction," he added kindly. "As an object you both share."

Ory nodded again and pulled his hands back into his lap. "Yes, that's a good idea," he heard himself say. He looked up at the second door, the one on the other side of the room. It was far, far heavier. It almost seemed as if it wasn't made of wood, but another material entirely.

"That one can be opened only from this side, the outside," Gaja-rajan said when he saw Ory studying it. "A good friend remembered that a long time ago." He draped himself across the chair next to Ory, sitting without needing to pull it out first. He had left the one directly across empty, Ory noticed. For Max. "I didn't want it that way, but it's for the best, for everyone's protection. Taking and rejoining a shadow can be . . . complicated. If something goes wrong, it would be very bad if a shadow or shadowless could let themselves out."

"How do you get in and out then?" Ory asked.

Gajarajan pointed up, at the ceiling. "There's an opening in the roof in the room. I stretch up the outside wall and then reflect down through there."

Ory nodded numbly. It occurred to him again just how far away from his physical body they were.

"I . . ." Gajarajan paused. His chest was on the back of the chair and his head on the wall behind it. "I just want to apologize for how long it took me to realize that you were the Ory in the recordings." He lifted his great ears against the surface of the wall, in a gesture of helplessness. "I really had no idea. I'm so sorry."

"It's all right," Ory stammered. It was too late to be angry. "She's here now."

"She is," Gajarajan nodded.

The shadow stood, and Ory braced himself when it vanished. Gajarajan had to check on Max one more time, to make sure she was also ready for him to open the door that was separating them. Ory waited in agonizing silence, trying to decide if it had been fifteen seconds or fifteen hours. She was just feet away from him. He couldn't stop straining to catch any hint of sound in the silence. He tried to figure out what he would say. Would he introduce himself again, or greet her as he always had? Should he shake her hand? Hug her? Could he kiss her—if she wanted? Would he have the courage? The time passed by in a garbled blur.

Then suddenly Gajarajan was back, in one instant darkly reflected against the far wall, ears ruffled with excitement. *Max was ready.* Ory trembled. It was really happening. He was already crying.

He watched the elephant reach for the second door that only opened from this side. Across the front, Ory realized there were letters burned into it, in all capitals. SHADOWS INSIDE, it said. A stamp in the shape of an elephant's face—wide ears, twin tusks, long, drooping trunk—was seared after.

"Are you ready to meet Max again?" Gajarajan asked.

"BREATHE, MAX," GAJARAJAN SAID. THAT WAS ALSO THE FIRST thing I understood once I began to remember English again, as soon as I recognized my name. I tried to breathe, and nodded at him as he hovered beside me on the wall. He had come in through the roof to make sure I was ready first, and then would go back the other way around to open the door that could be opened only from the other side. To unite me with you again, Ory.

"I'm breathing," I said. Gajarajan draped his trunk over my shoulder to reassure me and seemed to smile.

The sanctuary is a good place. I like it here. I've learned about how it is outside in the city, gardens and horses and bicycles and people, and I want to see it. But I also want to be able to come back here, to the second hall. Once you leave, you can never come back here, though. You can lose your shadow only once. That's what Gajarajan says.

He started telling me about you as soon as I'd remembered enough words to have a true conversation. He played me the tape. My tape. The recorder was so old and beaten up that the sound came out faint and tinny, so I had to strain to hear it. Gajarajan and I would wait until it was night, after all the other shadowless in the first great hall had gone to sleep and the city was quiet again, and listen. It was so damaged it almost didn't sound like me, but just enough. I could make out a woman speaking, a soft high voice, and understand most of her words.

"All my memories were in here?" I had asked in the beginning.

"Yes," he nodded. "You made this before you forgot everything. When we found you, you were carrying it in one hand, holding tight. You kept your memories."

That's what all the other shadowless like to say, he told me. That I "kept my memories" even though I lost my shadow. You, the shelter in Arlington, leaving home, the caravan, the terrible kidnapping by Transcendence, the last lucid moments of my journey south. How badly I wanted to make it here, to see if all the rumors were true. It's a strange thing to think about—my memories. That I still had them even though I didn't know I had them.

I shouldn't complain. Most shadowless come here with absolutely nothing, or lose what little they do have left soon after. And so few of us arrive bringing with us something that means more than the shade from an empty bottle, a piece of trash. To find a shadow that will match a person is much more difficult than it seems. Another thing from nature might be too strong or different, and a useless object might be too weak. And even if it does match approximately, nothing comes with it. No recollection. That was the only trouble with the books you brought, Gajarajan told me. The shape and size were just about right, but the memories are of invented characters, not real humans. They aren't like my recorder. The shadowless would be made into *new* people—not old ones.

That's why my shadow was the one that finally worked. Gajarajan has been able to separate many shadows, and even reattach some of them to the shadowless, but they never stuck, or not all the way. They didn't *fit*. So far I'm the only patient whose shadow has.

And then, just yesterday, he told me that you had come to New Orleans, too. Against all odds, you didn't disappear when I forgot you, and you found me again. Maybe it was because of this tape recorder after all. Because you were inside the whole time.

"Gajarajan really made that for you?" the young shadowless girl beside me asked. She was staring at my shadow as it lay flat across the floor behind me, the same way she had been since Gajarajan brought her here early this morning. At its long arms, its slender waist, the floating cloud of tightly wound curls springing in all directions from its head.

"He really did," I said.

She continued to stare, transfixed. She had dusky skin, and the same soft, buoyant afro that matched the shape of my own shadow's, when I looked at them both in front of me. "Did it hurt?"

"I don't remember." I smiled. I crouched down next to where she was sitting on the edge of what would become her bed now, since I would leave the sanctuary, and my shadow copied. Perfectly bound, perfectly in sync. "But I don't think so."

"Vienna fought together with your husband against a great danger—more than once. She's a good friend of his," Gajarajan said, sliding across the wall to where we were.

"I am?" she asked.

"You are," Gajarajan said. "I hope to be able to help you remember soon."

I smiled again as I looked at her. *Vienna.* I don't know how many other shadowless you know, Ory, but here was at least one then. At least you were friends with one other like me. I hoped that would help make it less strange, if you *did* think it was strange. "I look forward to seeing you again, Vienna," I said.

Vienna shook my hand. My shadow shook hands with nothing. "Me too. Remind me—if it works, if I meet you again, remind me how we met so I can know."

I memorized her face. It was easy, burned into my brain in an instant. Gajarajan had taught me techniques to boost memory, once my new shadow took. Letter games, patterns, rhymes. He learned them himself a long time ago from a wise old man he called Dr. Zadeh. His own teacher, he'd said. Now that I can make memories again, Gajarajan thinks that I actually remember new things better than someone who never lost their shadow in the first place.

"It's time for me to take Max outside now, to meet her husband," Gajarajan said then to Vienna. My heart began to thunder. "I'll be back soon, and we'll talk more about how we'll find you a new shadow." His ears ruffled, and I had the impression he'd winked at her. "It shouldn't hurt," he added, answering her previous question. "I promise. I'm getting better at this. I learned a lot from Max."

"It'll be over before you know it," I added to reassure her, although it was a lie.

Most of the rejoining was just fragments to me. Moments out of place and time that played like damaged film, stuttering and without sound. But enough to know that it had not been easy for Gajarajan. Not easy at all. It had been harder to join the tape recorder's shadow to me than any other shadow he'd ever tried on another shadowless before, including even the alligator's. He'd had to fight it onto me, as if it hadn't wanted to be joined to something new. Later, Gajarajan told me he'd never had something resist that hard before. But the shadows he tried before had been made of birds and mice and trees and rocks—never something that was partly made from a human. And never something that contained so many memories.

It didn't matter. It had worked. I remembered. And I hoped it would be smooth for Vienna, but even if it went as roughly for her as it had for me, she would say the same as I would—that it was still worth it in the end. To remember who I was. I gladly would have suffered far worse to have my name back once more. To have you again.

"In the meantime, why don't you think about anything you might still have with you that has great meaning to you?" Gajarajan said to her. "It's all right if you don't remember. But if you do have anything, that might be a good place to start."

Vienna worked something out of her collar and held it up. A locket on a tarnished chain. "Maybe this?" she asked. Inside were two badly weathered faces, a woman with short hair and a gentle smile and a man with a serious face. They both looked just like her. "My mother and father." She pointed to the photographs. "When we lost her, he gave it to me. I don't remember her name. But I remember that this was hers."

Gajarajan drew closer, flickering from the wall to the floor so he could glide right up to her to see. "That might do very well," he mused. "Let's look closer at it when I return." He was back on the wall, beside me, trunk curving into a smooth arc. Waiting for me.

*Breathe, Max,* I thought. I made my way across the hall, hand trailing along the familiar walls that had once felt like the extent of the entire world to me. Before I had remembered there were other things out there.

Then we were in front of the door that could be opened only from the other side. Gajarajan hovered, facing me at the same height. Through the dark shape of his ears and head, I could make out the marks that had been written or carved or burned on its surface since he had began trying to replace our shadows more than two years ago. There were signs of fear and rage, grooves from claws or teeth, places where fire or some other corrosive thing had touched, but there were also beautiful things, too. Simple shapes, words, drawings of houses or people or flowers, as memories had come back to the others, bit by bit. I wondered what it must have been like to forget everything twice, once the shadows could no longer be made to cooperate. Or remember, but the wrong things. That you once could fly rather than that you once were someone's wife.

I suddenly felt afraid. I jammed my hand into my pocket, but the tape recorder wasn't there.

"Ory has it, Max," Gajarajan said. "He'll give it back to you."

"I know," I replied. I remembered. I was only nervous.

"We don't have to open the door until you're ready."

I nodded. "Is he also nervous?"

Gajarajan laughed. "Yes, he's very nervous. He loves you very much."

It seems strange to me, that I can love you too when in a way I've never met you. But I do. I feel it as surely as I know myself. I tried to imagine both of us together again, doing a thing I can now remember that we had done, but something was off. I could see you there in my mind, dressed in a tuxedo at Paul and Imanuel's wedding, but not myself.

"Max?" Gajarajan said softly.

I smiled as calmly as I could. "I'm ready."

Gajarajan disappeared. *Breathe, Max,* I said to myself. *Max, Max, Max.*

Then from the other side, the door opened.

A MAN WITH BEAUTIFUL DARK EYES AND BLACK HAIR WAS seated at the only table in the room, staring at the tape recorder in the center. As the door swung open, he jerked upright. Our gazes met, and he gasped, the upward movement of his body out of the chair stopped short.

"Ory," I said. It was you. I knew it beyond doubt. I could finally see you again, all of you, instead of simply remembering. Everything was happening so fast. You were the man from the tapes. My husband. The man I had loved, and loved now. The man who knew all my memories, too. Ory.

But you did not say Max in return.

"*You,*" you whispered in shock, and I realized then that something was wrong. There was no joy in the tone of that word. Only horror.

Then you called me by another name.

Ursula.

PART V

# M

THE MOST IMPORTANT THING I'VE LEARNED SINCE LEAVING the sanctuary is that people's original shadows look just like them.

I didn't know it was strange that mine didn't resemble me perfectly. The only other shadow I'd ever seen before I left the second great hall was Gajarajan's, and it didn't look human at all, even though he said that his body was. I didn't even know to notice whether your own matched you or not, Ory, in the moment that I met you again.

At first it was hard for me to understand why you had flinched so violently when you finally saw mine, after all the shouting and confusion passed—why out of the whole terrible accident, *that* had finally been the thing that made you fall to your knees and wail.

Now I understand, though. Mine doesn't look like me because it looks like Max. Because it's made of her memories.

"How is it?" Malik asked from above.

I stepped back and surveyed his handiwork. In front of me, the gigantic face of an elephant painted all in black loomed. The ears and tusks were wide, the trunk held up, like an inviting hand. The eyes were two pristine white diamonds, narrowed in thoughtful consideration. "It looks good," I said at last, nodding. "It looks very good."

"Now I just have to do it to the other side, and then again on the other two carriages." He sighed.

"Be glad Gajarajan's an elephant, and not a porcupine. You'd be painting for a week," I said as lightly as I could, but I was still looking at the huge dark shape glistening on the side of the old Iowan wagon. At Malik, holding a wide bristle brush in his hand, painting the side of a vehicle. It was like watching echoes.

"Hey," he said. I looked up. His concern that the similarity might have dredged up painful memories was clear across his face.

I smiled to allay his fear before he could ask. It was all right. It really was. It wasn't an unfortunate coincidence—I had been the one who had given Malik the idea to paint the carriage. "You finish this one, and I'll start on the second," I offered, picking up his spare brush. He handed me the jar of paint, and I dipped the thick bristles into the dark liquid and stirred slowly, watching it swirl like tar. I had no memories of painting—there was nothing on the recorder that said I'd done it myself—but I'd watched Malik closely as he'd worked. It seemed easy enough.

Wherever we had finally lost the RV, I hoped it was still in one piece. Zachary wouldn't know the difference, because a painting didn't know if it was whole or damaged the way a human did, but I hoped anyway that he was still untouched, immortalized perfectly across the side of the vehicle, as vibrant and ornate as the moment he became it. I hoped other shadowless would see it as they passed, and he would point the way for them, too.

As Malik and I waited for both carriages to dry, we sat on the grass, splitting an apple between us that the head volunteer at the communal garden had given him earlier. He finished his half in two bites, but I ate much more slowly, savoring the crisp sweetness. Partway through, I realized he was watching me.

"Is there anything you need help with?" he asked. "I mean, I know there's nothing I can do that will ever—help with the big thing."

*There's nothing I can do that will ever help Ory see you as Max* is what he meant. *Sometimes it almost feels like you're the one who lost your memory, not me.*

I tried to shrug nonchalantly. There was nothing *I* could do either that would ever help you see me as Max. No one can help you— except you.

"But maybe something else," Malik continued. "You're doing so much for me. I want to repay you, if I can."

I dropped the apple core on the grass beside me and nudged some dirt over it with my boot. "Actually, there's one thing," I said. It was a small thing, a little silly. I had meant to do it alone the day before, but my nerve had failed. I want someone to be with me all the time now, I've realized. Everything had seemed so clear at first, that I was me and understood the world, but after what happened in the sanctuary's visitation room, I don't trust myself anymore. I want another human to explain the new things, to reassure me I'm right about the old ones—or even to just prove to me by their presence that I really do exist.

I wanted someone to be there for this, too. Someone who could tell me if I was doing it correctly, reassure me that what I can recall myself knowing how to do is real. Someone who is not you. Because even though you're always the person I think of automatically in every situation, I'm not the one who you do.

"Anything," Malik said.

I smiled. "Could you show me how to read a map? I want to make sure I really do remember how, before tomorrow."

IT'S STRANGE NOT TO HAVE THE RECORDER ANYMORE.

I let you keep it, even though there's nothing left on the empty, shadowless tapes. What remains of the little machine is yours. It was the least I could give you, Ory. I can't imagine what it must have felt like for you to sit across a table from a person who accompanied your wife on a journey for the last few months of her life and not be able to ask that woman a single question about what she was like toward the end, or how it finally happened, because she thought she *was* her.

You did tell me how you had known my name, though. Once the screaming had stopped.

*Your hair has grown out* was the first thing you'd said.

You said that when you first met me in Arlington, Virginia—when I was Ursula, not Max—it was short. Buzzed almost to the skull. Over the journey it must have grown longer and longer, and I had either not cared or not had time to cut it, and then forgot entirely. By the time I showed up in New Orleans, it was probably a soft downy mess, almost to my chin. Just different enough that Gajarajan might not have realized as he listened to Max's garbled, faded audio logs that I was the woman with a shaved head who appeared in almost all of the entries—not the woman speaking.

The shadow had flickered then, on the wall beside us. He said he hadn't realized I was not Max, but also confessed something else— that even if he had, he wouldn't have cared. He would have tried to give me her shadow anyway.

That was the end of the meeting. I didn't see you again for days. And even then when I did, from across Carondelet Street just as dusk was falling, we didn't speak. We didn't speak for a long time.

AFTER GAJARAJAN LET ME LEAVE, I WENT AWAY FROM THE sanctuary, straight into the city. I got as lost as I could. I wanted to be far away from you and him. Somehow Davidia found me, and convinced me to let her get me a room to live in, and assign a shadowed survivor who could watch over me until I understood how life outside the second great hall worked. I didn't want Gajarajan's help, but I knew what he'd told the captain to do was right. I didn't even know where to find food. I let her enlist a neighbor or two to help so it didn't have to be the elephant, flashing up onto walls beside me to check in, reminding me what he'd done.

Weeks passed. I was free but purposeless. I had no job, knew no one, understood nothing about this new place. I spent every other afternoon in the neighborhood just beneath Gajarajan's hill, among the half-finished houses that the retired soldiers from your army were busy renovating. We were always needing more and more room, they said.

It was clear that you still didn't want to speak to me. I respected that. I understood, as painful and lonely as it was. I would never corner you on the street and beg to finish whatever we'd started in the visitor's room of the sanctuary. But I also couldn't just leave it completely. Each time I went to that neighborhood facing the bottom of Gajarajan's hill, I waited behind the houses and watched. All I wanted was just to see you again.

I finally did. And I also saw someone else. A woman with golden skin and long black hair—standing in the middle of the road, as if also waiting for you to come down from Gajarajan's altar. You'd been having so many meetings with him lately. About me? About something else? I didn't know. You and she both stiffened when your eyes met, and I saw your body slow, but you continued to walk until you were just in front of her. You spoke in a way that was both fierce and gentle. You didn't touch her or smile. But there was a familiarity there, in the way you mirrored each other, one shifting closer by just microns when the other exhaled, then repeating in the other direction. Like magnets—constant.

*That must be Ahmadi,* I realized.

You were on speaking terms again, at least. Beyond that, it wasn't clear. And I didn't want to know.

"Are you . . . her?" a man leaning against a ladder, hammer in hand, asked. *Are you Max?*

"Who are you?" I replied.

He cleared his throat, chastened. "I'm sorry. Always too curious, Malik used to say. I came with them, from the Iowa. My name's Original Smith," he said. "Well, that's less important now—Smith Dos passed away a while ago. But there are still two of us, I guess. The other's Smith Tres."

I looked at the ground. His shadow appeared the same as he did, an outline of his form as perfect as your own was to you. I didn't understand. "There are multiple versions of you, too?" I asked.

"Oh, no," Original Smith said. "We're all different people. We just happen to share the same name. That's all."

I WENT HOME TO MY ROOM IN HOUSE 55 AND DIDN'T GO BACK to the district near the base of the sanctuary's hill for a long time.

As much as I could, I wanted to avoid seeing you and Ahmadi again. Not so much for your sake, but more for hers and mine. I felt a sort of kinship with her, even though we'd never met. She was just as innocent as I was in all of this. And I was sure she was afraid there would be a terrible, inescapable triangle among us, regardless of who you chose. So I stayed away, even though it didn't really matter. There still was a triangle—her, you, and Max. Not me, but the other Max. The first one.

During the days I wandered, speaking only to other shadowless, afraid of the looks the shadowed ones gave me. They all knew. Horror, revulsion, pity at what had happened to me shone in their eyes. I wanted to blame the elephant. It was his doing. But the more days I spent outside, watching New Orleans, I realized that although what had happened was his fault, it also wasn't. It might have crossed Gajarajan's mind to consider the likelihood that the tapes belonged to me versus the chance that I might have taken or been given them from someone else, but when he ultimately chose to try and save my life, there was no scheming in the decision. It was just a terrible condition of his nature, that Gajarajan doesn't understand why it would matter to whom the tapes had truly belonged. Elephants don't see it the same way people do, and especially neither do shadows. He didn't realize that it makes a difference to humans if the body is the same or not—not just the mind.

What happened was a mistake, but it was also a success. It *had* worked, despite the unintentional pain. The reason Gajarajan had failed to do it again after me was because he only understood the *what*—not the *why*.

Some time later, I heard that you had also realized the same thing.

Gajarajan had discovered that he had to use something that already contained human memories inside of it to create a shadow of sufficient depth and strength that would agree to be attached to a person. That was why everything else he'd ever tried had failed—a sparrow, a car engine, a chandelier, a brick. Only the tape recorder had succeeded. But the reason for its success was also the reason for its failure.

Gajarajan didn't understand what memories mean to humans—only how to restore them. You understand what they mean, but not how to make them. Together, you both can be wise enough.

You and your army turned out to be the key Gajarajan had been seeking after all. In all of New Orleans, there is only one thing that both contains human memories and also carried no danger of re-creating my accident. Your books.

It's not as good as bringing back a body's original memories, but that's impossible now—Gajarajan has proven that the result could be far worse than simply losing someone forever. The next best thing is to give a shadowless *some* memories, so they can have some concept of self to start from. But because the shadow will now be made from a past that never existed, because the source of the shadow has never been alive in the real world, there will be no chance of discovering later that the memories are an accidental perversion of nature—a re-cycling of a person already in existence.

It made me happy to hear that Gajarajan had accepted human help. That no one else would ever have to accidentally suffer. New Orleans would still be New Orleans, a house would still be a house, the sun would still be the sun. No one would ever become someone else by mistake. No one else would ever lose someone twice.

Once the library was moved into the sanctuary, Vienna would be the first shadowless to receive this new kind of shadow. You saved her just in time, I heard from Gajarajan later, when I finally visited again. He was planning to use the locket that she had offered—an innocent move on his part that might have turned her into a remnant of her own mother instead of herself. It made me shudder to think of what that would have done to Malik. She will never be Vienna again now, but she also will never be something far, far worse.

THE DAY I HEARD FROM THE SHADOWLESS AT THE COMMUNAL garden that a shadow from a book had taken to her and had stayed, I was both exhilarated and in despair. I wanted for no one else to ever suffer what I'd suffered, least of all Vienna—but now that you and Gajarajan had found the key, now that the books worked, I would be the only one. The only one who was a copy of someone else instead of something original.

That night, alone in my room, I caught myself holding a block of handmade soap given to me in my rations, talking to myself. Holding it as if one of my fingers was on a button, angling the end slightly toward my face as though it had been a speaker.

*Oh, Ory,* I sighed. *I wish you'd never given me the recorder.*

I knew only what I couldn't do: have you again, be Max, or forget. But I didn't know what I *could* do.

On the worn rug beneath me, a dark silhouette also stood, in the same posture, holding a shadow of the same object, lips moving around the same longing words. But the rest was slightly different. I was taller and not so young—it was slim, with narrow hips and small breasts, and a loose, soft afro that made its delicate shape seem like a dandelion when we both stood at certain angles. *That's what Max really looked like when she did this,* I thought. I remember clicking the machine on, whispering into the little metal speaker, so vividly that I would never have believed it had been someone else who had done it, and not me. It was all so, so real. But the proof was right there on the floor. That was Max. Not me.

Suddenly I realized there was one thing that I *could* do.

THE NEXT MORNING AT DAWN, I FOUND MY WAY TO THE RIGHT house and knocked nervously at the last room on the upper floor. Willed myself not to run.

"Oh," Malik said when he opened the door, surprised. He was silent for a moment. "Max," he said.

My throat tightened. He was the first person kind enough to acknowledge me by that name since I'd left the sanctuary.

"Are you all right?" he asked.

I nodded stiffly. "Call me M," I finally said.

I changed it last night, Ory. You'll always think that the tape re-corder is the real Max, and that I'm someone else. So I'll be someone else. M is a small difference, but enough, I hope. Enough to make me something more than a bad copy, an incomplete translation. Both to you and to me.

Malik smiled sadly, and his whole face changed. The terrifying hard lines became kind. "M," he said, "what can I do for you?"

"I heard about your mission," I replied. "That you plan to spread the word about New Orleans, to give more people the courage to come."

Malik nodded. "Not just spread the word—I want to be able to *show* them. To give them indisputable proof that Gajarajan is real, and so is his power. Otherwise I'm no better than the rumors."

"That's why I'm here," I said.

"I don't understand."

I pointed at the ground, where the shadow that was attached to me, but did not reflect the form of my body at all, lay. "I'm your in-disputable proof."

THE SYMBOL OF OUR MISSION MUST HAVE A TITLE BEFITTING its importance, the elephant said when he agreed. I became The Hand of Gajarajan. The first former shadowless person in the world. He also agreed that we should paint the carriages. He recognized that I knew what I was talking about—that a giant painting emblazoned across the side of a traveling vehicle was far easier to recognize and under-stand to shadowless than words would be.

I couldn't be next to you, but it turned out that we could still be together, in a different way. I would be The Hand of Gajarajan, and you would be his librarian. Two halves of the same purpose. You'd had the right idea about how to save your wife, but the wrong rescuer turned up in the end. Max had managed to build a shadow inside an object, but had no way of making sure the one who stripped it from the machine would then place it on the right body. What Gajarajan did was an accident borne of love and hope—but we lost many things. We lost Max, but we also lost Ursula.

My hope is that in time, now that we have the key to make new shadows safely, more shadowless will come, and more books. I hope that we can find enough of both that everyone who wants a new shadow can be given one from our carefully managed library, so that no one who's ever born hereafter will be a substitute for someone real, instead of an original.

The night before the mission left, I met you one last time. Malik is an experienced, strong captain—if anyone can get us out and back, it will be him. But there's no guarantee that we'll return, and this really could be the last chance you'll have to learn what happened to your wife—truly the last. If I die, there will be no other version of her left, no matter how pale a substitute. You knew it, too.

I shared as many memories—of mine, of Max's—as I could with you. Not the things you experienced with her, because you already know those, but all the things that happened in the tape that you never got to hear. The RV, the others who traveled with us, the dangers we overcame. What we lost and gained. What magic we did. Everything you asked, I answered, with as much detail as if each memory had been the key to a riddle whose answer would mean life or death. Each was, I suppose, for both of us—just in different ways. For you, it was death. For me, it was life.

I'm not sure if you were there when we rode off, two full carriages, seven mares, and six volunteers, amid the resounding cheers. There were so many gathered, and the horses moved so fast, it was hard to see. The crowd whooped so loudly that the new Eight—the six that had defended us against Transcendence, now with Ramirez and Playedviolin to replace Vienna and Survivedthestorm—rushed out of the first great hall to make sure something terrible wasn't happening. From the driver's bench of the first carriage, I watched the city slowly vanish into the distance as the bridge grew longer and longer behind us. Away from everything I loved. It was strange to think that when I first arrived, I hadn't known who I was. But now, as we left, it could not have been more opposite. I felt it so deeply that I couldn't believe I had ever been anyone else but myself. The wind stung my eyes as they teared.

"You going to be all right?" Malik asked me gently.

I nodded. "I will," I said. "I'm just remembering."

We rode in silence after that, until sundown. According to the gate records over the last eight months, New Orleans received thirteen survivors—twelve shadowless and one shadowed—from Baton Rouge. The greatest number of people all from the same place, aside from your group from Washington, D.C. There was a good chance there were probably more there. As the horses surged, carrying us on, I looked at Malik for a long time and tried to pretend he was you. To pretend the man I loved had been placed inside this other new one. I studied the dark, weathered skin, the tired eyes and thin lips. The unfamiliar lines across his hard face. I tried to imagine you speaking not with your own voice but with Malik's rough, gravelly murmur. Would I still love you like I love you now? Or would I fail to see you just as you'd failed to see me?

Beneath my feet, my new shadow shuddered as the carriage rumbled over the worn road, keeping perfect time with me. Where all the recordings I now have are contained. The ones about the shelter, about Paul and Imanuel's wedding, about things before even that—and about the caravan, about friends who are no longer here, and about the long, mysterious road south. All the memories I had finally shared with you the night before, and the one single one I hadn't.

I told you everything you had wanted to know when we'd met. But there was one thing I didn't say to you and will never say, because I can't. It's not something that can be said—only something that can come as an answer. And you would never ask me the question. But even if I never say it, it's still real, because a thing does not have to be said to be real. It just has to be remembered.

I will remember it. For myself, for you, and for Max.

Fifty-two.

# ACKNOWLEDGMENTS

THANK YOU FIRST TO KATY DARBY AND EMILY PEDDER, WHO were the first writers to make me believe I could also be one. Without you both, I never would have made it this far, because I never would have started at all.

Thank you to Sathyaseelan Subramaniam, in whose eyes I have never been anything but a writer, which gave me the courage to continue. Thank you to Jillian Keenan, who has watched me scribble stories for over twenty years and always known that I'd make it to print. And thank you to Rahul Kanakia, who made me think more deeply about this story than anyone else, and Marsha Sasmor, who magnanimously read more drafts than should have been humanly possible. I'm also grateful to David Lipsky, Darin Strauss, Emily Barton, and Jonathan Safran Foer for their guidance throughout my time at NYU and after, as well as to the Elizabeth George Foundation, whose generous support made it possible to finish the manuscript.

To my agent, Alexandra Machinist, thank you for believing in *The Book of M* even more than I did. At William Morrow and Harper Fiction, I'm eternally indebted to my incredible editors, Emily Krump and Natasha Bardon, for helping me make this novel the best that it could be, and to the entire amazing team at HarperCollins. I feel fortunate that this house is where my book calls home.